House of Birds

Steven Popkes

Also by Steven Popkes

Howard Cycle Novels

God's Country

Danse Mécanique

House of Birds

Jackie's Boy

Additional Works

Caliban Landing

Slow Lightning

Welcome to Witchlandia

Simple Things

The Long Frame

House of Birds

Steven Popkes

A Howard Cycle Novel

Walking Rocks /Book View Café

Copyright © 2021 by Steven Popkes

All rights reserved.

No part of this book may be reproduced in any form or by any electronic or mechanical means, including information storage and retrieval systems, without written permission from the author, except for the use of brief quotations in a book review.

This is a work of fiction. Any references to historical events, real people, or real locales are used fictitiously. Other names, characters, places, and incidents are products of the author's imagination, and any resemblance to actual events or locales or persons, living or dead, is entirely coincidental.

Cover design by Wendy Zimmerman
Cover illustration © 2021 by Wendy Zimmerman
Published by Walking Rock Publications in association with
Book View Café Publishing Cooperative
www.bookviewcafe.com
ISBN: 978-1-61138-976-0

For Opal

Table of Contents

"Latent structure is the master of obvious structure."
—Heraclitus, Fragment 54, via The Pre-Socratics, Edward Hussey

"The fabric of the universe is far from perfect. It was a bit of botched job, you see. We only had seven days to make it."
—Terry Gilliam, Time Bandits, 1981

Prologue

It was Ian's job to feed the macaw, change the water, and clean his cage every morning: winter, summer, fall, or, as in today, a beautiful spring day. Today, Pauline was snoring in her bed, braced against the wall, an empty bottle of vodka on the nightstand. Percy's cage was covered by the tarp. It was strange that no matter how drunken Pauline was when she finally got home from waitressing at the bar, she always managed to cover the cage before she passed out. The cage took up as much room as the double bed.

Percy stared at him as Ian pulled the cover up. Little, malevolent eyes, blinking only occasionally, head tilted first to one side, then the other.

Percy squawked suddenly, rocking back and forth. Ian stopped. When Percy was pissed off it was best to wait for him to relax. The macaw was huge, full-grown, with a head the size of Ian's fist and a beak that could sever fingers. His back and wings were cobalt blending into a long tail. His undersides were a brilliant orange and yellow. Percy flapped his wings and cried out. Then looked away.

Ian opened the door and carried in the pail. He started scooping up soiled bedding and wadded paper. Percy watched him from the perch. Ian tried to work facing him, so Percy was less likely to surprise him. When Ian turned to clean out a corner, he heard Percy's wings. He steeled himself.

Percy landed on his shoulder and nuzzled his hair. He closed his beak on Ian's ear, tugging gently.

Ian froze. Pauline had always told him this was a sign of affection and maybe it was, in other birds. But Percy knew it scared him and didn't do it out of love.

Then, Percy shat on his back and flew back to his perch, making a sound like Pauline's laughter.

Ian stared at him, hating him. Other twelve-year-old boys had dogs or cats or rabbits. Other boys had *fathers*. He had Percy.

Then, he noticed that one of Percy's eyes was half closed with mucous.

Ian felt cold. *Leave it* came his first thought. Leave it and Percy might die—macaws could fall over dead from a dozen different diseases. He remembered reading eagerly about it online. Or they could live for a century.

But Pauline would hold *him* responsible. Okay. But to take care of it, he'd have to *wake* her when she was hung over.

Thoroughly marked by Percy, he left the cage, closing it carefully behind him. There were worse things than reporting something wrong with Percy. Letting him out was one.

"Mom?" he whispered. "*Mom?*"

Nothing.

He didn't want to touch her. She might come awake too fast—"*MOM?*" Involuntarily, he'd cried out.

Pauline looked at him coldly. "This better be good."

"Something's wrong with Percy's eye."

"What did you do to him?"

"Nothing. I saw it when I was cleaning his cage."

She stared at him. He waited. A slap, maybe. Or just some comment.

Pauline looked over towards the cage. "Go on. Get the antibiotic out of the refrigerator and leave it on the table."

Ian almost shook with relief. Afterward, he dropped his soiled clothes directly into the washer and went to the shower.

God, how he hated that bird.

oOo

Percy had been named by Martin Bones long before Ian's conception. Long before Martin had ever met, wooed, and married Pauline. Before either of them showed up at Whiteman AFB, she to fly Apaches, and he to fly Warthogs. Martin had bought Percy on impulse during his first tour in Germany. He had gone to Algiers on leave and found a shivering fledgling for sale in the market. He smuggled Percy back to his apartment in Weltersbach. Then, when he'd been approved for A-10 training back in the States, Martin had smuggled him home. Percy had kept sentry duty over Martin's Sedalia apartment, watched as Martin and Pauline had negotiated the terms of mutual surrender, observed the conception of Ian, and consoled the pregnant widow when she received news from Iraq.

Ian washed his back and left the shower. It was getting late. He dressed hurriedly and rushed downstairs to get a piece of toast. Pauline had eggs waiting for him.

He stopped in the doorway.

"Thought you needed a good breakfast," she said, smiling at him. She rubbed the back of his head in a way he liked.

He stared at her, a sick, familiar feeling inside him: he could manage everything if he could only figure out the *rules*.

"Thanks," he said. "How's Percy?"

"He's fine. I cleaned his eye and rubbed in some antibiotics. You should tell him how concerned you were."

Ian leaned in and looked at Percy. Percy turned around and excretedn his general direction. It was on principle. Percy knew he couldn't reach the doorway and Ian knew Percy's range to the millimeter.

"I'm glad you're all right," Ian said, trying to sound sincere. Percy was perfectly capable of imitating or making up anything Ian said if it would get Ian into trouble. But this time Pauline could hear him so if Percy made something up, Pauline would think it was a joke and showed how *clever* Percy was.

He ate the eggs. She rubbed the back of his head the way he liked. For a moment, he felt almost normal. Pauline pointed to his cheek and he dutifully kissed her. Who knew what she would be like later?

Down the porch and onto the bus which, lurched on its way to school.

Safe.

oOo

Mrs. Muriel took him aside at the end of the day, looking concerned. "Are you all right, Ian?" she asked.

"Sure." Ian glanced at the clock. If he missed the bus, Pauline would have to pick him up. Not a good idea.

"Everything all right at… *home?*"

Code words. Ian's attention snapped back to the teacher. It wasn't like he didn't know what abuse was—Pauline's smacking him around was exactly like what they talked about in health class all the time. But what were they going to *do* about it?

Ian's dead-end street had three houses: Ian's on the east side. The Morettis, an old and childless couple, in the middle. Zack Peters and his Mom at the end. The Morettis had reported Zack's mom—she was sure enough dirt-eating crazy. DSS showed up, committed Mrs. Peters, took Zack right out of that little house, and dropped Zack in a foster home up in Moberly, seventy miles away—a Baptist preacher, too. Turned out the preacher needed a lot more forgiveness than he had let on. Two weeks later in the middle of the night when Pauline was dead drunk on the sofa, Zack had called Ian up *pleading* to get out of there. Ian had talked to Mrs. Fields and the principal both. Nobody listened. Everybody said Ian just didn't understand that what they'd done for Zack was the best thing. Next Ian heard Zack had hung himself with electrical cord. Must have been depression. Poor Zack.

Ian would take Pauline, thank you very much.

Zack's mom never did come back. Last year the Morettis moved away to some nursing home down south. Both houses remained empty.

Ian caught the bus before it escaped from the parking lot. Pauline wasn't home—still working at the bar, he supposed.

Ian went into Pauline's bedroom. He pulled up a stool and sat outside of Percy's pissing range. Then, he sat down and tried to will Percy to die.

He'd been trying this for the last week. Rick Verman sat behind him in Mrs. Muriel's science class and had told him about his dying grandmother.

"She lost her sight two years ago," Rick said, sitting next to him at lunch. "Dad says she's making herself die."

"No. Really?" Ian shook his head. "Why is she doing that?"

Rick shrugged his shoulders. "Dad says she doesn't want to live anymore."

Thinking about it, it seemed to Ian that if a person could will *herself* to die, then maybe a person could will someone *else* to die. Or a dog. Or a parrot.

The picture of health, Percy ate sunflower seeds as he stared back at Ian.

Maybe he could wear Percy down.

Ian sighed and got the pail. Time for the afternoon cleaning. He opened the cage. Percy jumped past him, caught the air, and was out the window before Ian could think.

Percy landed on a branch outside, winded from the sudden flight but not so tired he couldn't laugh back at Ian in Pauline's voice.

For a moment Ian stared at Percy. One moment he felt elation. *Go on, you goddamned bird! Get eaten and die in the dirt! I'm free! I'm free!* Followed by terror. What would Pauline *do* to him? Mixed with guilt. As nasty an animal as Percy was, he didn't deserve to die outside unprotected.

Guilt and terror overcame his desire for freedom, and Ian broke for the door.

oOo

Ian's house stood a little apart from a rolling collection of small ridges and bluffs. Like most Missouri woods, the forest was just fallow land—an old farm gone back to oak and maple, pocked with ancient cellar holes and shot through by runoff erosion.

Ian walked slowly outside—he didn't want to startle Percy. Percy laughed at him some more and took off deeper into the woods. Ian gave up on subtlety and ran after him. Percy had been in a cage his whole life. He couldn't fly far. Ian tried to keep one eye on Percy, one eye in the air for hawks, and one eye on the ground for tree roots. He managed to miss the root but not the bluff. He tumbled down, smacked his back painfully against the boulder at the bottom.

For a long minute, breath was the only thing he wanted in the entire world. Then the motor of his lungs caught and blessed air flowed into him down to his fingertips. He tested himself carefully. His back ached and his ankle felt tender. But he hadn't landed on his head, and nothing felt broken.

He had fallen into a dell. The trees and banks sloped down to this spot. Since it was spring in Missouri, he was covered in thick, stinking mud.

"Crap," he muttered and stood. At least the mosquitoes hadn't come out yet.

In the late spring afternoon, the little dell had become dark. Ian looked around for Percy with a sinking feeling. Percy's blue would fade in this dim light, and the yellow would blend in with the spots of light coming through the trees.

Ian saw Percy on a tree branch, perhaps thirty feet above him. Ian breathed a little easier. He hadn't lost the bird quite yet.

"Percy?" he called softly. What was he going to say? The bird didn't like him. *Come on down and shit on my back again.*

Percy ignored him. The bird's attention was completely absorbed in something on the tree branch. Something Ian couldn't see. A snake? Ian hoped it wasn't a snake.

Something delicate fluttered over Percy. A hawkmoth? A hummingbird? Ian couldn't tell in the gloom. It fluttered, paused for a moment over the back of Percy's head, and then dropped like a predator.

Percy straightened for a moment and seemed to look puzzled. Then, he screamed and tore off into the woods at full speed. In a moment he was gone. Ian could never catch him.

oOo

Back at the house, Ian used the hose to wash his shoes and his legs. He wanted to run inside, lock the door and hide in the cellar. But that would have meant tracking mud into the house. He didn't know where Percy was, but he did know what Pauline would do to him if he tracked black mud across the creaking floors and threadbare carpet.

Acceptably clean, he went inside, closed and locked the door. He changed and dumped the filthy clothes into the washer.

He sat in the darkened living room. Outside, the sunset and dark seemed to flow out from under the trees.

What was he going to tell Pauline? She'd never believe he didn't let Percy out on purpose. What was she going to do to him?

Maybe he'd better run. Stay away until she calmed down—and when would *that* be?

He drummed the heel of his hand against his forehead but he couldn't think of anything.

Something came in the window. He looked and saw it was Percy.

Percy watched him from the windowsill. Then he glided across the room and landed in front of the cage. Percy walked inside, across the bedding, and then hopped up onto his perch. He turned and faced Ian.

Ian followed him into Pauline's bedroom and closed the door. The bird watched him. Cocked its head. Watched him some more.

Ian stared back. There was something different about him.

Percy just watched him. No sound of contempt. No turning and excreting towards him. No stamping his feet. Nothing.

It was unnerving. Ian made sure the door was secure. Percy had come back home by the Grace of God and no one the wiser. Maybe the bird had been scared by something in the woods.

Percy cocked his head one way, looking at Ian out of his left eye, then cocked his head the other and looked at Ian out of his right. "Ian's a good boy," he croaked.

Ian staggered back as if he'd been struck. Percy had never said that. Not once.

"Good boy," Percy repeated and looked at him again, first one eye, then the other.

"Who are you and what did you do with Percy?" Ian said in a half-joke.

No answer. Just one eye. Then the other. Now it didn't seem like that much of a joke.

He heard Pauline on the front porch. Home early. That could mean she was already drunk or getting ready to get drunk.

"Ian?" she bawled as she came in the door.

Drunk already. No help there.

Ian came into the hall.

Pauline smiled at him and leaned forward, steadied herself. "Good boy," she said. "Get Mommie a drink, will you?"

Ian found the vodka under the cabinet and brought it to her.

She took it and smiled so sadly at him it broke his heart.

"I was going to be an astronaut," she said softly. "Martin and I had it all planned—*he* didn't want to go into space." Pauline struggled to get her shoes off.

"I know, Mom," he said as he knelt and took off her shoes.

"No," she said. "He was happy flying Warthogs. But that was okay. *I'd* apply. I had a great record—several combat missions. That always looked good. Get an engineering degree—that's what everybody misses. It's not enough to go up there. You have to build things. Places to live. Mines. Shops. It has to be a place people want to *go*."

"I know, Mom."

Pauline shook her head and rubbed her forehead with the bottle. "But it all slipped away when he got killed." She waved her hand in the air. "Like smoke."

"Mom?" he said hesitantly.

"Yes?" She looked up at him.

"Percy—"

"What about Percy?" Pauline said, suddenly cold and murderous. She stared at him.

Ian froze. He didn't know what to say. "Did you want to check his eye?"

She relaxed. "You scared me for a minute. Next to you, Percy is all I have left of your father. Not much, I know. But you're all I got."

Pauline went into the bedroom. "Hello, Percykins. How are you doing?"

Percy stared at her silently, first with one eye, then another.

"Aw, not even a word for Mommie? Aren't you feeling well? Get me the treats, Ian."

Ian brought her the box. She opened the door and went inside. Percy hopped up on her arm.

Ian had a sudden vision of Percy attacking his mother. "Mom!" he cried.

Pauline turned and stared at him. "What's the matter with you? You're going to startle him. He's a very high strung bird." She stopped, looked past him. "Are you an idiot?" she said in a tense, quiet voice. "Close the window."

Ian went to the window and closed it, waiting for Pauline to punish him. But Pauline carried Percy and sat down on the sofa. "You're a good bird, aren't you?" She fed the bird treats. "Not even a word for Mommie? Aren't you feeling well?" Pause. "What's this bump on the back of your head?"

Ian went to the other room. He got himself a glass of water and drank it. Percy had always been a hateful animal. What had happened to him now? And could Ian be blamed?

"Ian?" Pauline called. "Get me the vitamin supplement and the antibiotics. I think Percy has a mosquito bite or something."

Pauline fed the supplement to Percy and rubbed the antibiotic on the back of his head. Percy kept watching Ian. Ian watched them both. Pauline put Percy to bed and covered the cage.

"Bedtime for you," Pauline said to Ian, pointing up the stairs with the bottle.

oOo

Ian could chart exactly what she was doing from the sounds. Laughter: first half of the bottle. Crying: second half of the bottle. Then, a clunk and the sound of snoring.

He snuck back downstairs. Pauline was passed out on the sofa. On a normal night, Ian would have left her there. As hard as it was tiptoeing around her in the morning, it was easier than trying to move her. But tonight, he couldn't abide the idea that she would be sleeping, helpless, with Percy nearby. Who knew what would happen?

He covered Pauline with a blanket.

Ian walked into Pauline's room. He lifted the cover from Percy's cage and looked inside. Percy stared back at him.

Ian watched him for a long time. Watched the way Percy turned his head. Watched how he watched Ian. This wasn't Percy. It was a thing that looked like Percy and tried hard to act like Percy but couldn't quite pull it off.

Percy kept watching him.

"You're not him," whispered Ian.

Percy did not respond.

That had to be it. The moth-thing had killed Percy and replaced it. That had to be the explanation. Ian let the cover fall back over the cage. He could feel Percy's stare all the way back to the sofa as he grabbed a pillow and lay down on the floor, the only thing alive between Percy and Pauline.

oOo

When Ian came in the door from school, Pauline was sprawled on the couch again, asleep. Percy was perched on the couch, his head down near her head, staring at her closely.

"Get away from her!" cried Ian and rushed the bird.

Percy flew into the air and landed on a chair, now watching Ian as closely as he had been watching Pauline.

Ian went to the window and opened it. He went behind Percy and tried to rush him outside but the bird wouldn't go. Finally, it flew into the cage.

Half crying with frustration and dread, Ian locked the cage and went to check on Pauline.

There was a bottle on the floor next to her and she stank of metabolizing alcohol. Her face was flushed but unmarked.

Ian went into the kitchen and poured himself some juice. What was he supposed to do?

He heard something from Pauline's room. As he entered the doorway, Percy froze, the cage door half open. The bird pulled the cage door closed and flew back to the perch.

The Percy-thing could cozy up to his mother and do *anything*.

He could hear her snoring in the other room.

Ian stared at the bird. The bird stared back, cocked its head at an unnatural ninety-degree angle, and then looked back at him.

Shoot it, he thought. Sure Pauline might beat him half to death but it was worth it to keep this *thing* away from her.

Martin Bones had left Pauline a small collection of pistols, rifles, and shotguns. Pauline had drilled into Ian the violent penalties that would happen should he ever play with them. Ian had known the combination of the safe since he was six. Beyond a token rebellion represented by opening up the locked safe, staring at the array of guns, and closing it again, he had left them alone.

No matter what, you were supposed to take care of your mother.

Ian unlocked the gun safe. You didn't grow up in rural Missouri without learning a few things about guns. If Percy started flying around, Ian wanted to be able to hit him. A shotgun was the thing.

He loaded the twenty-gauge and snapped it shut. Then, he walked back to Pauline's room. Ian looked through a gap in the cover. He couldn't see Percy. He pulled off the cover.

Percy stared back at him, clinging to the cage door. Unblinking.

Ian cocked the shotgun. He pointed it at the bird.

"Don't shoot," said Percy distinctly and not in Pauline's voice.

oOo

Ian almost pulled the trigger, stopped himself. Then, raged—he was going to shoot the bird, wasn't he? He pulled the trigger. Nothing happened. *The safety.*

"Please, don't shoot," Percy said again. "I mean you no harm."

Ian pointed the gun back at the bird. Percy stared back. After a long minute, Ian put down the gun. "What did you do with Percy?"

"I needed to talk with you."

"You needed to kill Percy for that?"

The bird cocked his head and looked at him sideways. *Now* he acted like Percy. Creepy.

"Percy's unharmed. Something of me has been in Percy for a long time. Now there's more. Think of me as Percy with additional material."

"What are you talking about?"

Percy stared at him from the other side. "I am currently using Percy's body, but the instant I stop, Percy will be himself again." Percy scratched under his wing. "Is that what you want?"

Ian lowered the gun. "No. I just want him to stop shitting on me."

"In all senses of the word."

"I guess."

"I have already done that for the moment. I can make that permanent."

"What do you want with my mother?" Ian gestured with the shotgun. "I saw you looking at her. What are you? The devil? Were you looking for her soul?"

Percy shook his head. "I am a biological entity like yourself—"

"You're a bird."

"No," Percy corrected. "I am communicating *through* a bird."

Ian stared at Percy.

"Why don't you put the gun away, Ian?" said Percy. "It could go off and Percy might get hurt. Your mother might wake up."

Ian glanced into the other room. Pauline was still passed out on the sofa. He unloaded the gun and put it back in the cabinet. "What are you?"

"I crashed in the forest on November 27, 1885."

Ian stared at Percy—no. He stared at whatever was communicating through Percy. "You're, like, an alien."

"I am exactly like an alien."

"And you want to go home? Like Alice? Or Dorothy? Or E.T.?"

"Yes."

"You can make Percy stop being mean?"

"Yes. Percy likes you."

"Crapping on me is his way of showing love, right?"

"Of course not." Percy shook his head. "It's his way of showing contempt and establishing dominance. But in his own patronizing sort of way, he likes you. You feed him. You clean up after him. He recognizes you are Pauline's son. If he hated you or he was truly stupid, like a possum or a hawk, then changing his mind would be much more difficult."

"How do I know Percy is still Percy?"

"I just injected a small organism to interact directly with his brain. He is now just as he ever was with only a slight modification that allows me to communicate with you."

"Prove it."

Percy stared at him, beady eyes suddenly intent. He looked around the room, turned, and squirted an unerring stream of feces on Ian's chest. Ian had forgotten Percy's range.

"Okay," Ian said slowly. He passed his mother on the couch on the way to the laundry room. He stripped, dropped the clothes into the washer, and went upstairs. God, he thought as he washed. It would be nice not to have to take so many *showers*.

Back downstairs and sitting carefully far away from the cage. "I believe you. What do you want from me to make it permanent?"

"Think of it as a good-faith gift."

oOo

When Ian got home from school the next day, Percy was perched in the window.

"Hey," he called up.

"Hello," said Percy.

"Want a treat?" asked Ian as he came inside.

Percy flew over to the kitchen table and landed on one of the chairs. Percy cocked his head for a moment. "Percy says yes."

"Good for him." Ian poured the box into a bowl and pushed the bowl across the table. Was this what having a dog was like? Ian poured himself a glass of milk. He sat down across from the bird. "So. You crashed in the woods over a hundred years ago."

Percy nodded, swallowed. "Yes."

"And a piece of you is in Percy."

"Yes." Percy buried his face in the bowl, grabbing the treats.

"Where's the rest of you?"

"In the woods." Percy lifted his head from the bowl. "Do you want to see?"

"You will come back, right? I can't afford to lose Percy."

"I can leave at any time. I opened the window, remember?"

The weather had turned warm and dry over the last week. Percy flew ahead of Ian to the same mud-filled dell. The mud had dried up and was covered in yellow and purple wildflowers.

Ian gave a low whistle. "You've got a pretty place here."

"Thank you."

In the center of the dell was a large boulder half-buried in the dirt. Parts of it were covered in moss and grass. A gnarled oak grew off a ledge of dirt and below that, a cleft led deep into the stone.

Percy landed on the oak. "This is me."

"The tree?"

"The stone. Or, more precisely, I have camouflaged myself to look like stone."

Ian bent down to face the cleft in the stone. A bobcat stepped out and stared back at him.

Ian cried out and scrambled back. The bobcat watched him, licked its paws. "This is me, also," said Percy.

Next to the bobcat came a fairy, little wings, and a golden glow like something out of a Disney movie. "Me, too," it piped.

The bobcat casually ate the fairy and licked its paws. Its eyes glowed for a few seconds exactly the same color as the fairy then faded.

"Jesus," breathed Ian.

"The truth of the matter," said Percy. "Is that all of them are me and none of them are me. What you see as the stone is the original *me.* I can create things—animals, plants, trees. The part that creates is *me* is within the stone." Percy clucked to himself. "At the moment I'm stuck here.

"Since 1885."

"Yes."

"Hm. Why me?"

"What?"

Ian looked at Percy. "What do you have in mind for me? My Dad's dead and Mom is a basket case. But you're still here. Now you're talking to me. You're doing me a favor by keeping Percy off me. Nothing comes for free. What do you want?"

"A partnership, perhaps."

Ian heard Pauline's car door slam. "Oh, crap."

oOo

Pauline was waiting for him when they got home. Ian could tell by the way she held her bottle she was pretty far along. Her face was bright red and mottled. Worse, Percy was with Ian. Out of his cage.

"You son of a bitch," she said. She held up the bottle as a weapon.

Percy shrieked and flew between them. Pauline stepped back. Percy landed on her back and bit her neck. Pauline screamed.

Ian ran for the front door.

Pauline lurched after him and grabbed his shirt. He felt the shirt tear but it didn't give. He fell backward. For a moment, she towered over him, bottle in hand. She brought it down.

Percy flew between them again. The bottle caught the edge of Ian's skull as he rolled out of the way and for a moment, everything contracted to a point.

When he could see again, he was outside, running, Pauline after him. At the edge of the woods, he glanced back.

Pauline was standing in the grass, the bottle in her hand, staring at him.

She set the bottle down carefully and eased herself down to the ground. For a moment, she sat, legs spread, looking blankly forward. Then, she lay back down.

"Mom?" Ian called uncertainly. *"Mom!"* He ran to her side and knelt next to her. She was still breathing. He put his ear to her chest. Her heart was beating. Was it too fast? Too slow?

Percy landed across from him.

"What did you do to her?"

"One of the modifications I made was to alter Percy's saliva to contain a powerful sedative. She'll be awake by morning."

"You did this." Ian stared at his unconscious mother. She was like a light illuminating his thinking.

"It's harmless. She'll be awake in a couple of hours."

"This is your fault."

"As I said—"

"You made her like this. So you could get to *me!"*

"No, Ian. I *didn't!"*

"You had a hundred *years* to find somebody. But you couldn't do that. You had to *create* them. But you couldn't do that directly. So you broke my *mother* so *I* would work for *you!"*

Ian dove over Pauline and grabbed for Percy. Percy flapped backward and grabbed for the air. "I didn't do it!"

"Liar!"

Percy caught the air and rose above Ian's reach. He landed on an oak branch at the edge of the wood muttering like a macaw. Ian went back to his mother, sat down next to her. He held her hand.

Percy flew back and landed across from Pauline. Percy paced back and forth. "It's important for you to believe that I did nothing to your mother to make her like this."

"Go away."

"I didn't do it."

Ian looked over at the bird. His eyes felt raw but he didn't remember crying. "I wish you had. At least then it would make sense."

Percy was quiet a moment. "Your mother is cruel to you."

"That's none of your business. You know nothing about it."

"I've been on this planet long enough to know how a mother is supposed to treat her son."

"Shut up about my Mom."

"Let me state it differently. She is troubled and sometimes because of her troubles she does not treat you as well as she should."

Ian blinked. "Yeah? So?"

"I can cure her."

Ian didn't say anything for a minute. "Like you cured Percy? No thanks."

"Not at all. Your mother is a complex human being requiring complex therapeutic procedures. Percy was a much simpler problem."

"Cure her how?"

"Your mother was traumatized by your father's death. This happened when she was pregnant with you. It was a debilitating trauma and eventually caused her to leave the Air Force. The event chain triggered certain latent neurochemistry changes feeding off her pre-disposition to alcoholism. Complicating that, she only has you—whom she loves—to remind her of the life she'd had before."

"You knew my Dad?"

"Only by observation. I never spoke with either of them."

Ian stared at the bird. "What was he like?"

Percy cocked his head. "Your parents cared for each other very much. They were very earnest in trying to conceive you."

"'Earnest.' Right. I know about sex. I'm not stupid."

"I am not speaking of sex. Pauline miscarried twice before you were conceived. Both of them were excited when she was finally was able to carry a baby past the first trimester. Your father was killed before she could carry you to term. In Pauline's mind, your conception and birth and her continuing failures are unnaturally tied to your father's death."

"Did you have anything to do with me being born?"

Percy paused. "Yes. Pauline had a minor hormonal problem. I corrected it."

"How?"

"She was bitten by a mosquito and it became mildly infected. The infection contained a virus I had devised to secrete the proper signaling hormones."

"You infected the mosquito?"

"I *built* the mosquito to contain the infecting virus."

Ian stared at Percy. "So you already fixed Mom once."

"It was not difficult. I had great hopes for you."

Ian stared at Percy. "You really did create me. What the hell am I? Frankenstein?"

"No! You are solely your parents' child. I had *nothing* to do with that. I shielded you and ensured Pauline could carry you to term."

"Shield me from what?"

"There's another of my kind here—"

"*Another* one?"

"Yes." Percy cocked his head. "Think of me as Percy. We'll call him… Georgette."

"Georgette's a girl's name."

"For us sex is complicated. Georgette is in charge of Earth. I'm small by comparison. I need a human agent to treat with him."

"Georgette."

"Yes. I need a human agent to act on those things I need done in the human world. I need someone I can be sure of. I've watched over you since conception. You are the only human being in the world that has no part of Georgette in them. I made sure of it."

Ian watched Pauline breathe: in and out. "If I'm your agent, you'll cure Mom?"

"Yes."

"How?"

Percy grew agitated. He walked up and down the grass as he talked. "I have to correct some bad associations, lower the valence of some memories and increase the impact of others. Some memories have undue influence over her and will have to be suppressed entirely. Once everything is in place, I have to make connections between memories to cover any gaps. Otherwise, she will not recognize the change as legitimate and reject it. The process is delicate."

"You're sure it'll work?"

"I have observed your mother for fifteen years. I am confident I can correct her condition without damaging her."

"What would she be like?"

Percy cocked his head almost like a shrug. A blue jay landed above him. Percy gave the jay a macaw shriek, and it tumbled off the branch in surprise. Percy chuckled and turned back to Ian.

"She would be very much like she was before you were born. She will possess some character traits you have never seen and lose some character traits you are used to. She was ambitious before you were born and will probably be ambitious again. She will cease striking you but will probably demand more of you. Perhaps she'll want to return to the Army."

"You don't know what she'll be like?"

"I'm certain I can correct a problem. What she does with the solution is up to her."

"Will she remember what she's done?"

Percy paused. "No. She'll remember she wasn't the best mother but she will not remember the violence."

Ian leaned his head on his hands. It felt heavy. "I don't even know how to ask her."

Percy was very quiet for a moment. "You can't."

"What do you mean?"

"The act of informing her of this cure will make the job much, much more difficult. There already exist resonances and contexts that I have to balance. She has been the way she is for a long time. Telling her she's been cured by an alien sets up interference. It's one thing if she is ignorant. She goes to bed and wakes up sometime later never realizing the difference. But if she *knows* she is being changed, she'll examine the changes closely, consider her past behavior, wonder what she was like before-—it makes the outcome much less certain." Percy looked at him first from one side, then the other. "I can only cure her if she does not know of the attempt."

"I'm just a *kid!*"

"You are her son and next of kin. You know her like no other human being. You must ask yourself, is she happy as she is? Can you persuade her to change? Can she change on her own? Then, you must decide for her."

"Can you really cure her?"

Percy bobbed his head yes. "You understand the mind is in the brain, correct? The human brain is complex but not as complex as mine. I can completely simulate the entire working process of a human brain in real-time without simplification or abstraction. I can correct your mother's problem because I have already created a copy of your mother's brain and cured that."

Ian recalled the cold set to her face when he came home. The lack of expression. The shifts—one day making him breakfast, the next drinking for forty hours straight. But would it *be* her? Would it be a stranger? Or worse, would it be someone who was *almost* like Pauline but not quite?

She just looked asleep.

"Why not build an agent like that bobcat? Why do you need me?"

"Several reasons. A simulacrum would take resources I can't afford to maintain. Building a copy of you would result in just that: an uncredentialed copy of you. You exist as a credentialed human. You have a birth certificate. A social security number. You are in county rolls and on mailing lists. I would have to create all of that. Finally, I can simulate up to six complete brains. You've met many more people than that in your life and are richer for it. I can simulate you—or your mother—because you already exist. But I can't create you from scratch."

"You could change me so I would want to work for you."

"I could."

Ian stared at Percy. The bird's face looked no different than it had all of Ian's life. He could not read it any more now than he ever could. He certainly didn't understand this alien version. "Why don't you?"

"Why should I?"

"What if I won't work with you?"

Percy cocked his head to one side. "Clearly, I will have to try something else. That's not optimal. I don't have a lot of time."

Ian felt his heart pounding. "You could change me and I'd never know it. Tonight. While I'm asleep—"

"Stop. Please."

Ian stepped back.

"Ian," Percy said quietly. "That line of thinking only ends up with us as adversaries. It's a road that has no turning. If I had wanted to change you I would have done it already and we would not be having this conversation. I want an employee. I want a partner. I want someone I can work *with*. I have no interest in a slave."

Ian slowly shook his head. "Why do you need an agent, anyway?"

"I can't stay here. I have places to go. Things to do."

"Like what?"

Percy looked at him for a long time. "I'm going to terraform Venus."

If you're going to dream, dream big. Ian found himself wanting to believe Percy. "I don't know how I can trust you."

"You can. But I understand if it's difficult. "

Ian watched Pauline. She could wake up and hit him or laugh and make him dinner. There was no way to know which.

Percy walked around Pauline to stand next to Ian. He rubbed his beak against Ian's knee. "I can cure her. I am certain of it."

Ian watched Pauline's sleeping face. Now it looked sweet. Ready to cook eggs. Ready to hug him. A terraformed Venus. A cured mother. It's good to dream big. "I believe you."

oOo

It took three days.

Ian spent them in Zack Peter's old house. He didn't want to be around Pauline while Percy was working on her. Occasionally, odd smells wafted over. Once he heard Pauline muttering, followed by a shout.

Ian hadn't been in Zack's house in the two years since Zack had been picked up by DSS. He wondered what happened to Mrs. Peters.

Zack's room was covered with dust and smelling of old sheets, wet plaster, and mildew. There were water stains on the upstairs floor from a roof leak.

Ian had his father's old, musty sleeping bag and stayed in Zack's room.

Lying in Zack's bed, fingering through his comics, Ian wondered if Zack had been Percy's first choice. Could Percy have offered Zack the chance to cure his mother? Did he? Would Zack have turned it down? Or had the world caved in on Zack before Percy had been able to act? Or was Percy telling the truth and it was Ian all along?

Ian found a picture of Zack and his mother on the floor. Ian looked up on the shelf where he had put it. "If you were still alive, Zack," he said. "I'd have Percy cure her, too." If it worked. If she didn't end up a complete stranger.

oOo

Ian came back when Percy told him he was finished. Pauline was fine and the procedure was a success. He brought back Zack's picture.

She was asleep when Ian came into her room. Percy said she'd be asleep for hours yet.

Ian went to his own room. He put Zack's picture on his dresser. Then, took a shower and went to bed. He could see Zack's picture in the light from the hallway and it made him feel better as he fell asleep.

oOo

He awoke to the smell of eggs and cleaning agents. The light that streamed in the window showed late morning.

Downstairs, there was a plate of eggs and pancakes on the table and a glass of orange juice. Pauline was scrubbing the sink.

"Hey, guy," she called to him. "Eat your breakfast. Saturday or not, we've got work to do. I don't think we've cleaned this place in a year. Then, new clothes for you and me." Pauline chuckled. "Ever wake up ready to change the world?" She showed him as happy and perfect a smile as Ian had ever seen. He sat at the table, listening to her whistle as she scrubbed out the sink.

What have I done? He thought as the scale of it sank in. *What have I done?*

Part 1: Land and Sea

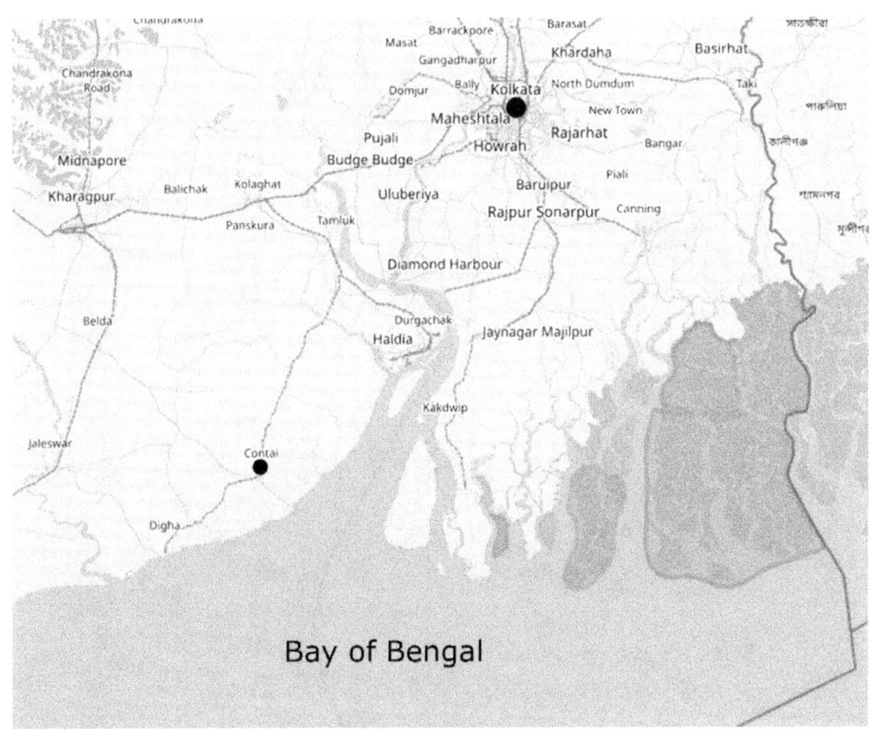

Chapter 1.1: Chitra

Chitra Majhi held her coffee close to her body in the futile illusion that it would warm her hands. Chitra was only a single generation removed from her father's family origins in Kolkata. Her mother's northern European leavening had failed to give her any immunity to winter. Sweltering summers? No problem. Heat was her friend. But she could never imagine enjoying January in New York. When she walked across the UN Plaza from the subway, the East River wind blew through her bones. A cleanerbot rolled near her feet and she had a sudden urge to kick it.

They can reprint the subways, she thought to herself furiously. Make all the cars so efficient it seems like they are running on fairy dust. Purify the East River until you can see *dolphins* come to watch what's going on. And they can't do something about the *wind?* Fuck the glaciers. Fuck the reefs. Fuck the Siberian Methane Explosion.

Chitra walked along the bottom of a slow-moving canyon of people, protected from the wind by a human shield. Chitra was tiny. Without heels, she didn't come within inches of five feet and heels made her feet hurt. Short black hair, doll-like smallness, and the sort of straight-nosed beauty only India and Somalia ever seemed to produce.

Inside: blessed warmth.

"Chitra?"

"Over here."

Freder, as big side to side as Chitra was tall, appeared next to her. He smiled. "Good weekend?"

"Went to Boston to visit my brother. You?"

"Fabrication Festival in Soho," Freder said breathlessly. "I competed in the ten-centimeter self-organizing food division. Ever see a robot rabbit create itself out of random chocolate blocks and dance the hoochy-koochy?"

"Never. And I can say that with certainty even though I've never heard of the hoochy-koochy."

"Early twentieth-century fertility dance. The judges had never heard of it, either. I won."

They joined the stream and passed through security. Chitra heard the announcing tone of an incoming message. Freder had an oto-ocular implant. Many people had glasses. Few had straight brain interfaces. Twenty years ago four million people were suddenly introduced to the screams of dying chickens when a PETA enthusiast hacked one manufacturer's security. Then came starving children in Malaysia and after that, political advertisements. Overnight a market dried up. Implanted sensory interfaces were common. Brain implants were rare.

Chitra was more conservative than most. The idea of a net interface she couldn't remove made her queasy. Instead, she had an earworm: a stylish ear cup that looked as if it grew from the side of her close-cropped skull to her ear. Bones conduction audio gave her privacy.

She held her left hand up and tapped her thumb and forefinger three quick times. The earworm projected a screen on her hand.

"Tsunami in the Bay of Bengal," she said slowly to Freder. "The Andaman islands shifted."

"How big?"

"Fifteen meter wall of water that went inland halfway to Kolkata. Damage from Contai down to Chennai."

Freder whistled. "Didn't they evacuate?"

Chitra checked. "There was a problem with the alarms."

"The buoys? What about the seismic sensors? Did the predictive models fail, too?"

"I don't know. They should have had ninety minutes of warning. They had ten." She scrolled through the data.

Freder was silent a moment. "Are we going to be deployed?"

She closed her hand and the display disappeared. "I don't know. Geneva is probably getting the call. Don't get excited. We're United Nations. Even if we're called, we won't be first responders. We'll be second responders and corpse finders at best."

"What do you think?"

Chitra opened her hand and the display reappeared. She scrolled through the data. It was a lovely display. It even took into account the wrinkles and folds of her hand, adding distortion here and removing it there to give the appearance of a flat-screen. "Get your robots ready, Freder. I'll send out a pre-deployment alert."

oOo

UNERA—the United Nations Emergency Response Agency—didn't even exist thirty years earlier. One of the TBPs (Tech Billionaire Philanthropists) became frustrated with the level of technology being deployed in disasters. Grants were released into the wild, resulting in new techniques, approaches, and robots existing relief organizations weren't ready to handle. The TBP decided to fund his own. Some misbegotten youthful nostalgia made him choose the UN as a vehicle. A hundred million here, a half-billion there, some adroit pressure through various interested countries, and UNERA was born. Chitra had been recruited a decade ago.

But there is no bureaucracy like that of the United Nations. The UN operates at the behest of its client states so most of its actual work is coordinating between differing factions, ministries, corporations, NGOs, and well-meaning, if perhaps ill-prepared, individuals. Chitra's team was the only one within the UNERA network. UNERA functioned under UNDAC: United Nations Disaster Assessment and Coordination. They would work under a UNDAC team.

But only if asked.

The client government and in-country UN resident coordinators would determine if help was needed. In this case, the coordinators would come from India and Bangladesh. The coordinators would call OCHA (the Office for Coordination in Humanitarian Affairs) in Geneva. OCHA would discuss the nature of the problem with the designated contact to settle on the scope of aid. The Field Coordination Support Section (FCSS) would decide its response and mobilize the appropriate UNDAC teams. Then, and only then, could a UNERA team be sent. If the client government didn't think it was giving up too much sovereignty. If the appropriate egos were properly massaged such that they ended up with their constituents' best interests in mind. If bringing in the UN didn't make the locals think political weakness and start sharpening knives. You wouldn't think that so many layers would get anything done in a month, much less the forty-eight-hour response in the charter. Of course, "response" was a term of art.

Normally, a local UNERA team would be used but this was big enough lots of teams would be called up. Chitra called Amit Tsuba in Geneva, knowing if anybody would be on the UNDAC team it would be him. Just to tell him she was ready.

Twenty hours later they were wheels up in an ancient C-130. It would be more than twenty-four hours before they touched down in Contai with thirty tons of equipment and supplies.

Chitra spent the first few hours going over what they would do when they reached there: Freder on excavation, Ai Kano on remote sensors, Maggie Ong would take on and repurpose the local robot and human fishing boats for offshore retrieval and Ellish Nkoe would cover emergency medical. Chitra would manage communications and coordination herself.

She had no illusions. It would be forty-eight hours since the initial wave. The UNERA teams would be largely funereal. Still, people had been found, trapped, and retrieved days later—every disaster had its little miracles.

They finished warming up and checking out the systems six hours before landing. Chitra made them each take a pill so they would sleep until the C-130 grunted onto the taxiway.

Ellish and Ai crawled into their foldout bunks immediately. Ai undid her hair and took the bottom bunk. Ellish crawled above her and lay on his stomach, dropping his arm so they could hold hands as they drifted off.

Maggie sat meditating in lotus position, staring straight ahead for what seemed the longest time. Then, she fell over on her side, straightened out, and was snoring instantly.

Chitra lay on her bunk going over each step: get the origin coordinates from Tsuba. Map the origin site on the ground. Freder could deploy from there. Ai's aerial remotes would be searching as soon as they were unloaded while the heaver machines made their way to the site.

Freder sat down on the edge of her bunk. "There was no evacuation at all."

Chitra nodded. "I know. Not a single tsunami buoy in the Bay of Bengal triggered. Seismographs barely registered the Andaman slide and, without buoy confirmation, decided it was a false alarm. No one knew it was coming until it was there."

"All of the buoys? Christ. What about the seafloor sensors?"

Chitra shrugged. "You know as much as I do."

The C-130 shifted and Freder grabbed the edge of the top bunk. "They never had a chance. Who's looking into it?"

Chitra sighed. "No clue. It's not our problem."

Freder nodded slowly. "Did you hear about the crazy martyr?"

"There are always crazy martyrs in this part of the world."

"This one was in Contai. A holy guy and his followers came down to a parking lot overlooking where the wave was going to come in. They all sat there, chanting, while the wave trashes Contai and goes inland. "

"How did he know it was coming?"

Freder threw up his hands. "The song of birds? Flight of bats? Coincidence? Who knows?"

"What happened?" Chitra had a sick feeling.

"When the wave receded they jumped in the water."

"No doubt he had a vision," said Chitra.

"They were swept out to sea ahead of all the broken windows, floating cars, smashed doors, and loose logs. The families will be lucky if we find body parts."

Chitra shook her head. Most people caught in a tsunami were pushed inland and rolled around the debris. Then, when the waters receded the remains were often trapped under a wall or a piece of billboard or wrapped around a car, waiting to be discovered. The behavior of the zealots pretty much guaranteed a low chance of recovery. Relatives might spend their whole lives wondering what happened to them.

"Idiots," Chitra said.

Freder agreed and climbed up on his bunk.

Chitra pulled out her phone and locked it to one of a constellation of satellites overhead. She could have spoken to someone on the moon. Instead, as she always did before a drop, she called her parents in New York.

Her mother answered.

"Hey," Chitra said.

"Well," said Grace. "It's four in the morning. I'm guessing you're on your way to another disaster."

"Yes," said Chitra, relaxed for the first time in hours. Talking to her parents always made her feel safe. Protected. "Contai, India. A tsunami."

"I saw it on the news. That's not far from Kolkata. You should visit your grandparents."

"I'll be pretty busy."

"Not even disasters last forever. After it's over they'd like to hear from you."

"I'll see what I can do. How were things at the hospital today?"

"Oh," Grace said in a low voice. "Sent home three kids from standard lymphoma treatments. One boy and two girls. The boy is going to be tough on his parents."

"Because of you, he'll have a chance to."

"Some, I suppose," Grace said quietly. "I have a new resident that did all the work."

"What about the girls?"

"Ah, well." Grace's voice trailed off. "One will be fine. The other one belongs to one of those religious families that refuse treatment. The parents would have signed off but the grandparents threw fits and the parents withdrew her against advice."

"I'm sorry."

"It is what it is," said Grace. "So *you* must save a mess of kids to make up for the one I lost."

"No pressure, eh?"

"None at all."

There was a brief companionable beat of silence.

"Do you want to speak to your father?" Grace said.

"Tapas must be asleep. Wasn't today a chemo day?"

"He'd still love to talk to you."

"Let him sleep. Chemo is rough enough. I'll call him from Kolkata."

"*That* he would love."

Chitra hesitated. "Is it working?"

"It's too soon to tell. I'm optimistic."

"You'd be optimistic if there were a meteor hurtling towards Brooklyn. You'd sit on the porch and watch it happen."

"Well, of course. You wouldn't want me to miss it, would you?"

Chitra smiled. "Give him my love."

"Absolutely. You be careful."

Chitra curled on her side, sleepy and warm. She thought of Grace on the phone, regal and gray at this time of her life, gently implacable as she spoke with the parents, minister, family, friends. The grandparents had no idea what they were in for.

Thinking of Grace led her to think of Tapas—she shied away from thinking about the cancer. Instead, she remembered watching Tapas hold Grace as she cried over a child lost to surgery or cancer or any of the hundred other diseases she treated. That was the thing about them. They were like the stories Tapas had told her when she was a child about the two divine birds, Bihangama and Bihangami: mated for life so that in every story they were always together.

The UNERA insignia was on the opposite wall: two hands, one holding a carpenter's hammer and one holding an ear of corn. Below that, the motto: "We Are There."

Chitra felt herself sliding into sleep as the pill took hold. "Me, too," she murmured.

oOo

Contai Base had been dropped in by air.

First came an intense but quick search of the site to insure it was clear of the living and the dead. Once the sensors had cleared the site, a heavy canister was dropped by parachute, guided itself to the right spot, and detonated, spreading a thick, pink, polymer dust called Base Mix an inch thick over a one-kilometer circle. The powder reacted and foamed, pushing down into the debris and up, self-leveled and hardened into a buildable substrate. A year and a half from now it would start crumbling and degrade into rich, pinkish soil. In the meantime, landing lights were painted on one side and buildings grown or printed on the other.

Outside the C-130 fell a warm rain. Chitra could feel her mosquito repellant washing from her skin. This was a mere downpour. Chitra was glad the tsunami hadn't happened during the really heavy rains of July and August.

Chitra could see the outlines of other teams through the mist: ponderous spiders searching the debris with relentless intent. The smell of wet rot and putrefaction already hung over the area. She wasn't looking forward to the place in another week. With any luck, they'd be done quickly and the cleanup crew would replace them.

Ellish and Maggie were right behind Chitra. Ellish kissed Maggie quickly and trotted over towards the medical coordination building. He'd serve as a free-floating physician. Two cargo containers followed him, wheels squeaking in the rain.

Chitra could see the river not far from them. A pier had been extruded out into the bay. "Maggie? Tsuba said there's a fishing boat down there named the *Vishnuram*. That will be your base. Got your controllers?"

"Got 'em, Boss."

"Mark me."

Maggie keyed her tablet.

"I, Chitra Majhi, under UNERA charter six-seven-two-stroke-twelve, contract four-three-seven-six-stroke-six, officially delegate full offshore authority to Margaret Ong on the *Vishnuram* to include both the designated areas in the Bay of Bengal and the length of the Hooghly River up to and including Kolkata site A-120. Go. Call me with status in an hour."

"Got it."

The charging station came down the ramp quickly, all treads, solar collectors, and batteries. It bristled with a collection of metal hoops and left a thin smell of ozone in the wet air. It stopped in front of Freder. He entered a code on the keypad and the top unfolded.

Freder stepped back. "Okay, Ai," he said on the radio.

The charging station bounced down the pink road towards the origin coordinates six kilometers away exuding a cloud of pseudo-dragonflies. Some dove down and flew through the hoops and made the raindrops glow.

A moment later Ai parked the carrier off the ramp—control shack, transport, medical theater, and morgue. She left the driver's seat and returned to her console.

Chitra leaned in. "Are they all operational?"

"Yeah." Ai was carefully watching the swarm behavior. "Heading to the origin to start a chemical sweep."

"Good."

Chitra returned to the C-130. Freder was just leading out the spidery excavators.

"Did you bring any printers?"

"Big and little. We can get by with the little one," Freder said. "Contai will need the big one before we do."

"Okay." Chitra keyed up the pilot. "We're off to your left, about a hundred meters. Make a note. This is Chitra Majhi of contract four-three-seven-six-stroke-six. You have an extra scale-four printer in inventory. If Chennai doesn't need it, it's part of returning equipment."

"Got it."

The C-130 lumbered away from them, scooted onto the western strip, and roared. In a moment it was airborne and turning south.

Freder looked into the carrier. "Spiders are hooked up to the control shack. Ready to roll?"

"You bet."

Freder swung into the back of the carrier.

Chitra braced herself in the cab.

There was a lurch and Ai nearly fell off her chair. "You planned that."

"By now you should know enough to strap yourself in." Chitra smiled. You took your pleasures where you found them.

oOo

The debris field was enormous. They were near the river and the wave must have rolled up the flat land and river basin without resistance. Contai's elevation was barely six meters. A fifteen-meter wave wouldn't have even stopped to say hello. All that remained was a jumble of pipes, rock, twisted cars, and broken buildings. Closer to Kolkata, Chitra knew that volunteers were swarming over the ruins. Here, the devastation was so complete the eye could not pick out more than a fragment of tile, a jutting bumper, a broken slab of concrete. It was as if a city of thousands of people, their cars, bicycles, buildings, and appliances had been dropped into a great blender, ground up, and poured back.

Contai Base had built a road of sorts that led to multiple origin sites. The area immediately surrounding the road had red flags: sites where bodies had been recovered but the area still needed to be examined for personal effects. Victims were often shorn of their clothes, bodily hair, and skin. The flags would be noted later when the clearing teams began their work. The personal effects and DNA samples would be gathered and sorted by robot.

Chitra could see on one of Ai's screens a composite image of the site, the integration of a massive compound eye. First the fast pattern: each dragonfly shot along the surface at sixty kilometers an hour, sampling the air for carbon dioxide, methane, hemoglobin, watching for heat signatures and using microwave radar in a desperate attempt to find survivors. First pass would take no more than an hour and would likely be done by the time they reached the origin. Then, a regroup and more leisurely search for corpses.

Fifteen minutes from site Ai shrieked. "Got a live one!"

Chitra jumped over to the console. "Signs?"

"Heat signature. CO2." Pause. "Slow breathing by the radar."

Promising. "Can the dragonflies detect a clear path to the victim?"

Ai tapped on the keyboard. "I'll try."

Chitra looked outside. The swarm circled high in the air and came back to the surface, shifting position until there was a clear but crooked path to the potential survivor.

"Freder?" Chitra called. "Send Spider One to the victim site and have Spider Two check for possibles along the route." Chitra started up the medical theater and called Ellish: "We have a live one."

"I'll prep a transport."

The carrier followed Spider One as it gingerly stepped through the insectile path, raising a brief cloud of dragonflies every step. Individual dragonflies buzzed over to the charging station and then returned, patrolling the edges of the path. Spider Two moved to one side and began checking for other possible survivors or body locations.

Spider One reached the victim site and slowly positioned its six legs around it, careful not to put any pressure on the debris surrounding the survivor. It discharged three cats—quadruped robots that padded over the debris with feline gentleness. They sniffed around the site.

"More signs," said Ai. "Looks small—a child or a dog."

"I'm getting feed from the cats," said Freder.

The excavator slowly lowered half a dozen arms. Carefully, four hands stabilized a section of pipe while two others gradually pulled it out. The cats were in and around the debris, looking at one end or the other, making sure the debris would not collapse or worse. One cat slipped into monkey mode and pulled off loose material, clearing the path for the larger spider arms.

Finally, Spider One grasped a Hindi graffitied slab of concrete with three arms and lifted it slowly.

"I see her," said Freder.

Exposed by the lifting slab, Chitra could see an unconscious little girl in the embrace of a dead woman.

"The medical theater is live," said Chitra. She looked up and two small helicopters were coming. "Ellish sends his love."

"Good," said Freder. "This is going to be tricky."

Chitra could see why. The woman had shielded the girl from harm but was now wrapped around her. Wire and cloth tied her to the girl and both of them to the concrete. Rebar had pierced the girl's arm and leg—pinning her down but giving her precious space beneath the debris.

Freder gently pulled the woman away from the girl, cutting where he had to. Then, he had the cats spray the debris under the girl with polymer, gluing it together into a rigid mass. Spot sprays of polymers held her to her makeshift bed. Spider One lifted her into the air with one set of arms. The cats worked below to remove excess rocks, wood, metal cable. Finally, only the polymer remained. Spider One used the polymer as a stretcher and brought the girl over the carrier and carefully laid her inside the medical theater.

Chitra's console went live. Pulse oxygen, heartbeat, and blood pressure were all low but steady—she'd been saved at least partially because she was cold. Thank the Random God of Statistics. There was always a chance of *some* survivors. Chitra's job was to skew the odds the little girl's way.

Chitra kept her cold but pushed up the oxygen in the theater. She injected her with biox to increase the potential saturation of oxygen in the blood. Two minutes later the girl had enough dissolved oxygen in her blood she could live for half an hour if her heart stopped. Satisfied, Chitra signaled one of the copters.

It came down and hovered over the medical theater, lowering cables. Chitra attached the cables to the medical theater and released the locks. The copter roared and lifted the entire medical theater out of the carrier.

The other copter lowered a new medical theater into place. Chitra released it from the copter and it connected itself to the carrier.

"Good job, folks," Chitra said, smiling. "First live one. May there be many more."

Freder and Ai cheered.

A respectful silence followed as Spider One brought out the woman who saved her. Freder directed the robot to gently pry her loose from the clinging substrate. Chitra had a sudden vision of the woman clutching the girl to her, shielding her from the rolling blows until the end of her life. Spider One carefully settled her in the medical theater. Chitra enclosed her with cold wrap and reverently placed her in morgue storage. Then, she triggered the theater's self-cleaning procedure.

"I'm glad we could get her out in one piece," said Freder softly.

Chitra agreed. The chances were good she had been a relative of the little girl.

Spider Two spoke over the channel: "Bodies found."

Chitra sighed. "Back to work."

oOo

The girl's name was Pranavi Basu. Ellish had gotten that much from the Indian DNA database. Pranavi was the only survivor they found. Ellish gave them updates on Pranavi every hour until she was flown to the temporary hospital in Kolkata. Though she was still unconscious, Ellish was confident she would be fine. Chitra's team waved as they saw her copter leave. Even Maggie tuned in from off the coast. It was the only bright spot of the excavation.

Contai had been a city of a hundred twenty thousand people over twelve square kilometers, giving a population density of ten thousand per square kilometer. Chitra's examination site was a single square kilometer and occupied what had been the northwestern part of the city, giving an outside possibility of ten thousand bodies. Chitra's team found three thousand two hundred and eight genetically separate signatures. Some were intact bodies. Many were pieces. They captured a total of twenty-six tons of debris immediately surrounding the items, geographically noted and photographed both *in situ* and, once extracted, recorded in three dimensions to be stored for later confirmed associations. Maggie was able to retrieve two thousand two hundred and four identifiably separate bodies from hungry sharks. The sharks were unamused.

Her team had some hope the lower than expected numbers meant there were more survivors to be found. But as the other teams reported in their numbers the stark reality became clear. Half of Contai was known to be dead. The other half was just missing.

Two weeks held as much death as UNERA would allow without a break. When they returned to Contai Base, they took hot showers and met with the other teams. Amit Tsuba took them aside.

They sat around a table in the commissary. Tsuba drank from his paper cup and looked at them. "You're being relieved."

"The job is not done," said Chitra quietly.

"This disaster will not be 'done' for months." Tsuba shook his head. "You've reached the end of the UNDAC agreement. You've done the heavy lifting. Now it's time for the local authorities to take ownership of the situation. After all, they'll have to live with it. It's time for you to go home." Tsuba reached into his pocket and pulled out a set of paper envelopes. He passed one to each of them. "The government of India would like you to have this."

"Wow," said Freder. "My first bribe."

Chitra patted him on the shoulder. "I'm so proud."

"It is not a bribe," said Tsuba patiently. "It is a reward. You saved who you could and found who you could." He looked at each of them in turn. "They thank you. *I* thank you. No one could have done more than you."

An hour later a load of Contai remains and Chitra's team were deposited at the Dum Dum Airport in Kolkata. Her team dissolved into the different terminals leaving only Freder standing with her.

"I don't have to go back immediately," he said. "I could stay. Visiting relatives can be stressful."

"And have my grandparents think you're a prospective son-in-law? Then have *both* sides of the family on my case about grandchildren?" Chitra laughed. "You don't want that."

"It wouldn't be that bad."

"Oh, Freder." Her laugh changed to a smile. "Go home. I'll see you in a week."

"Okay." He grinned at her. "But I would have been a *great* son-in-law. I majored in drama."

"I bet you did." Chitra kissed him on the cheek and he left her.

She hefted her backpack and went in search of the train that would take her towards what remained of her ancestors.

Chapter 1.2: Ian

Ian Bones staggered up out of the surf, fell back in and swallowed more water, choked, and vomited. He stood up again, swaying against the waves. He spit and inhaled a blast of sun-dried air.

A little farther up the beach and he fell first to his knees, then lay down. He vomited again and felt immensely thirsty. He'd kill for a glass of water. Perform serial murder for a beer.

He rolled over and let the sun burn him down to the bone.

Let's see. Distant smell of primary sewage discharge. Crude oil like a spill from a tanker. Lots of trace burnable hydrocarbons—boat fuel? Slight trace of cholera and an undertaste of plasmodia. Mixed with the smell of bleak and arid desert. Northeast Africa.

He sat up. Somalia. *Puntland.* Good. He knew people in Bosaso.

Ian looked around for a sign of Percy. Nothing. That meant he would be dealing with Georgette.

His pants looked as if he'd been in the water for weeks. Possible. It wouldn't be the first time. He found a small waterproof bag in the cargo pocket next to his knee with passport, money, cash cards, and necessary Puntland State of Somalia paperwork.

Okay, then. Ian closed his eyes and a picture of his location swam up in his mind. West. North to the road and look for a truck to Bareeda. Then see if he can get transport to Bosaso—fast boat or small plane. It was a long trip by road.

Clothes, shower, and the nearest bar. Georgette liked bars.

oOo

Ten kilometers up the beach to the road, walking over oil slicks and the incipient fossils of dead fish. His bare feet complained but toughened up quickly.

A deserted seasonal fishing camp marked the end of a road running inland.

Great.

Ian looked up the road. Empty until fishing season. He could chance it and wait for a truck to arrive intending to meet unknown and unseen returning fisherman. Who knew how long that would take? Or he could hoof it thirty kilometers away from the marginally cooling influence of the sea inland a few kilometers to be baked alive on the dirt road while he walked to Bareeda.

"Not going to make this easy, are you?" Ian shouted at the wind. "Do the job and get screwed. Is that it?"

He saw a boat come around the point. Ian shook his head. "You like your bloody fucking jokes, don't you?" He waved at the boat and it changed course towards him. He could see the stiff silhouettes of automatic weapons. Ian gave them a grin, wondering what they'd leave him. Georgette didn't like to waste anything.

oOo

The pirates let him off in the harbor where the Juba Hotel was only a few hundred meters from the Bosaso port of entry. Ian had half expected them to amuse themselves with the random beating of a westerner. But these pirates were quite cordial and businesslike. They relieved him of the burden of his cash and cash cards but left him with his passport and visa and the date: he'd only been in the water a few days.

Bosaso had no embassy or consulate but Ian had a contact in the market and an hour later he had a phone and enough cash to check into the hotel. A tepid shower and a change of clothes and he felt almost human.

As always, he called Pauline.

She picked up immediately. "Hello?"

"Ian. How are you?"

Pauline laughed in delight. "Not bad. Still interviewing the last few candidates. Looks like I'll be done on time."

As always, Ian found himself listening closely to her voice. Did she remember anything at all? Fifty years and he was still listening. "What's the project this time?"

"Long term asteroid habitation. I will be contract boss. It'll be interesting."

Until the end of the world, Ian thought but said nothing. It was something no one needed to know.

"That's good." Ian fell silent as he sometimes did, talking to Pauline. When he remembered what she had done to him. What he had done to her. What she did not know. What he remembered.

"Pick it up, slow boy," said Pauline. "Tell me where you are."

"Africa."

"Too big a place. You can do better than that."

"Somalia," he said. "Puntland. Bosaso."

"Okay. I have never been there. Tell me one cool thing about Bosaso."

He went to the window and looked outside. "You remember when we were in New Mexico? The light from the desert? How on a hot summer day it seemed like the world was two dimensional and if you looked hard enough you could see through everything?"

"I do."

"Bosaso is like that. Except in Africa."

She chuckled. "That'll have to satisfy me until next time."

"I have to go, Mom," he said. "Things to do."

"Go do them. Call me soon."

Ian agreed and closed the connection. He looked at the phone. For a moment he heard Pauline's voice twice: once, as he heard it just now, and once when he thought she was going to murder him over Percy. Which was real?

Ian shook it out of his head. He had work to do.

oOo

Somalia was strictly Moslem which forbade drinking. But money spoke wonders.

The room was low and dim. There was a counter at one end. It was filled with men sitting on rude stools in front of cheap folding conference tables. Each man nursed a plastic cup of an unidentifiable liquid.

Ian went to the counter and the Somali on the other side gave him a wordless, questioning stare.

"How much?" Ian asked.

The Somali sized him up. "Two dollars for regular. Five dollars for special."

Ian put down a ten. "Two specials."

The Somali pulled a plastic jug from the shelf and poured it into two plastic cups. Ian took them and found a space next to the wall. He sipped one. Fermentation product. Ian was grateful. It could have been used motor oil fractionated down to ethanol and water. Additional aldehydes, ketones, and heavy metals came for free.

Ian looked around the room warily. Nobody had tried to sell him anything. That was a bad sign. Some were lost in the "regular" but others were giving him a hard eye. He glanced at the Somali bartender. Inscrutable. He could be indifferent or in on it. There was no way to tell.

Someone sat across from him. A young boy from the looks of it. Ian caught a bluish tint to the hair. Ian recognized the emotionless slant of his face.

"Percy!" Ian passed him the cup. "Where's Georgette?"

"Busy."

"Doing what?"

Percy ignored him. "I left a briefcase in your room. It has everything you'll need. Be on the next plane to Mogadishu. When you're finished there, you're due in Morocco. Finish quickly. You have to be back in India by the first week in February."

"Good to see you, too."

Percy gave him an odd look. "This was all your idea. *My* plan was to copy them and leave the bodies behind. *Your* idea was to take them whole and help them along. Don't blame *me*."

Ian grimaced. "Don't remind me."

"You're going to be attacked on your way to your room. Just let your reflexes take care of it."

"I don't want to kill them."

Percy gave him the same odd look. "They'll kill you if you don't."

Ian pinched the bridge of his nose. Sometimes talking to Percy or Georgette gave him a headache. "There must be a happy medium between a friendly greeting and sudden violent death."

"You make things difficult."

"No doubt. Anyway, can you put them all to sleep for the five minutes I need to get out of here?"

Percy shrugged.

Ian smelled something like flowers. Then his eyes seemed to cross and everything went gray and flat for a moment. He shook his head and looked around. Everyone was slumped on the floor. The bartender was lying behind the counter, his feet sticking out one side.

Percy was watching him.

"They're not dead?"

"I've done nothing to offend your delicate sensibilities. Let's go."

Ian rose and followed Percy towards the door. "How did you do it?"

"Think of it as chloroform flatulence. Your improved liver metabolized it faster than theirs. Now, get moving. You want to be out of here before they wake up. Remember: we're on a schedule and a budget." Percy ducked out a side door and was gone.

oOo

He finished Morrocco early and needed a break. He wasn't due in India for three weeks.

Rolf Henderson was running the Sequoia research cabin when Ian was dropped off. It was always either Rolf, Julie Agata, or Terri Matamoros. Ian's funding kept this small collection of botanists wrapped around the trees. If anyone could figure out how to keep Sequoias alive in the coming warmth and drought, they could.

"Mister Bones," said Rolf as Ian entered and stamped the snow off his boots.

"Call me Ian," he said. "I've told you that often enough. I think you just like saying 'Mister Bones.' Like in the old song."

"What old song?"

"Right." Ian dumped his backpack on his bunk and looked around. "Any news?"

"Since September? Winter came."

"Everybody's a bloody comic."

"*Oh.* You mean *research* data. The stuff your grant *pays* for." Rolf smacked his head. "What could I have been thinking?"

Ian stared at him. It had been a long flight from Morocco.

Rolf waved him off. "All right. Don't get your panties in a bunch. Let's see. Snow pack so far this winter is down another two percent from last year. Think of it as a two thousand year drought."

"Compared to now or compared to the twentieth century?"

"Compared to now it's business as fucking usual. A two thousand year drought is the new normal."

"Right." Ian looked outside. The cabin was in a cluster of relatively young trees—say, less than five hundred years old. These saplings only towered a mere thirty meters over them. Not much bigger than a large hickory, if you think about it. If the hickory were as big around as a sports car. "How are they taking it?"

"Like you'd expect them to take a two thousand year drought." Rolf joined him at the window. "Some are managing all right. Those that have water. Those with deep roots. Those which are genetically pre-disposed."

"How are they managing against new pests?"

Rolf put a hand on Ian's shoulder. "Nothing happens quickly up here. They're managing so far."

"So far."

"Yeah. That's all we know. But *Sequoiadendron* is a tough genus. It made it past the Chicxlub meteor. Past the heat of the Deccan Traps. Past the PETM. These guys are tough. If not here, then up in Oregon. Or in Europe. They can survive anything."

Ian managed a grin. "I always like your optimism."

"Yeah. Go get some sleep. You look like hell."

oOo

Ian walked by himself.

Rolf cautioned him. "Be careful. I've caught a few hungry mountain lions on the cams."

"Don't worry," Ian said. "If something happens to me the program is covered in my will."

"Well, thanks. That *was* the only thing I was worried about."

Ian barely listened. Their research wasn't why he was here. These trees were the biggest, greatest organisms on the planet that he could see. Feel. Smell. They gave him the illusion that everything would ultimately be okay. After all, if one of *these* could last three thousand years, there was hope for the rest of us. Right? *Right?*

He knew better, of course. He was paying for false reassurance.

The adult sequoias crowded out the light and left nothing for the understory. Ian walked on bare forest litter in silent shadowy gloom. He saw several ground squirrels and one deer. Rolf's hungry mountain lion sat on a rock, ears forward looking for her next meal. She didn't even twitch when Ian walked by.

That depressed him. He *should* at least register as predator or prey.

It didn't surprise him when Georgette walked from behind a huge tree, dragging one perfect hand along the side. Her long blond hair fell down her back.

She was dressed in a light jacket and slacks, the color matching the red bark of the sequoias. As always, it seemed she caught all the available light. As always, he had to catch his breath when he saw her. Knowing what she was made no difference at all.

"I see why you like coming up here," she said in a soft voice.

"Maybe I shouldn't if you're here."

She smiled. "Have I spoiled it for you? Was this the last lonely place you could escape me?" Georgette pouted. "That's so sad."

Ian pulled his eyes away from her. Everything seemed smaller with her here.

"You should have seen them in the Cretaceous." Georgette leaned against the trunk; spread her arms to hug it. "They were everywhere. T. Rex walked around under them. Herds of Ceratopsians. Little tiny mammals." She held her thumb and forefinger a couple of inches apart. Then returned to hugging the trees. "I loved my dinosaurs."

"What do you want?"

"Percy wants you to go to Mussoorie."

"I'm scheduled to leave in a few days."

"Of *course* you will." She came over to him and took his arm. "Don't you think I made the park just *perfect*?"

"This was intentional?"

Georgette shrugged. "Can't I take credit for accidental beauty in something I made?"

Ian felt bludgeoned. "How much of everything you've ever done was just an accident?"

Georgette shrugged, unconcerned. "It's a little like bonsai. The artist shapes the tree but the tree grows the only way it can."

"Is that how you made us?"

"Oh, no. Six days and then I rested—you've read the documentation."

Ian shook his head in exasperation. "Why does it have to be this way? Couldn't we just take who we need? You can do what you want with the rest."

Georgette gave him a tinkling laugh. "Oh, Ian. What is it you think I'm doing? Destruction for destruction's sake?"

"Yes."

"You poor darling. This is just practice."

"Practice for what?"

Georgette danced a perfect pirouette and bowed to the tree. "You are taking advantage of events in place long before you were born." She cast the idea away with a wave of her hand. "Percy's needs and your very, very tiny human lifespan drive the timetable. But such things would have happened regardless."

"So I gathered."

"I know." She pinched his cheek and there was a jolt of electricity through him.

"Why are you here?" he said, his teeth clenched. "You could have reminded me in lichen patterns on a tree."

"True enough." Georgette held his arm and looked around. "I like your company. I like to poke at you. It makes Percy suspicious of my motives. It tweaks your motivation. It demonstrates I'm following our agreement."

"Right," Ian said bitterly. *I am caught between a hammer and an anvil.*

"Ian! Our love means nothing to you?" She grinned wickedly at him, danced around one of the sequoias. Ian followed and found only a pile of leaf litter against the trunk.

He returned to the cabin and ate with Rolf while he looked over the project's data. Rolf thought the future of the sequoias was promising.

Ian knew better.

oOo

Ian did not fly directly to Mussoorie. Instead, in an act of silent rebellion against both Percy and Georgette, he flew first to Kolkata.

It was duty, he told himself. Responsibility. Ian told himself he had not caused the tsunami.

During the Renaissance, Georgette had seeded the area around the Andaman Island with derived coral capable of withstanding the depth and pressure of the Andaman slope and with an appetite for impurities in the Andaman shale. Of course, calling it a coral was about as accurate as calling a stegosaurus a chicken. It was a coral host that lived on the outside of the fissure and grew tendrils inside. An Archean bacteria dissolved the calcite and carbon remnants. A relative of euglena transformed the dissolved slurry into layers of calcium carbonate and carbon fibers. Eventually, a single coral head supported kilometers of energetically expensive tendrils. It succeeded by working very slowly and dispensing with luxuries like reproduction. When the entire slope had been destabilized and the only thing holding it together was this weak glue, the coral and the derived euglena died, leaving only the web of calcium carbonate and the Archean bacteria.

Each lunar-triggered fission of the bacteria shortened a long protein chain. One day in January the last link was broken. The Archae died by the thousands, releasing a powerful enzyme dissolving the protein/calcium carbonate matrix into calcium hydroxide and carbon dioxide. The CO2 erupted out of solution. The Andaman shale shifted. An underwater section of the ridge supporting the islands fell. The wave sped towards Contai.

Ian stared out the plane's window. He had insisted he be allowed to save who he could and be a witness. Isn't that what Doctor King said? We must choose the good we can, eschew the evil we know, and, ultimately, bear witness.

Well, choosing good and eschewing evil was off the table. Bearing witness and saving those he could was all he had left. He couldn't even manage that for most of them. Not even a tenth.

So what was he rebelling against? Percy? Georgette? Pauline? His bitter entry into his sixties? An uncaring world? Only it wasn't *that* uncaring. Georgette was the world and she loved her dinosaurs, after all. She said so.

oOo

Refugee camps surrounded Kolkata on all sides.

As his flight approached Ian saw regular grids of refugee housing had already been marked off adjacent to vast tent cities. The solar collectors were up. He could see the thick square cargo container systems for power and more rounded ones making potable water. Three large oval containers were being linked together by a mob of workmen—sewage systems. The latrines were surrounded by a collection of potted trees. Some worker years ago had thought the plants would improve the inevitable smell and the tradition had stuck long after the smell was no longer so inevitable.

Ian smiled. Investing in UNERA had been the right thing to do. Three weeks since the wave hit and he could see the difference from three thousand meters in the air.

The plane landed and he walked past endless restaurants, play rooms, shops, and subtle invitations. An underground economy thrived in all major airports. Any drug, drink, or sexual partner could be found right here, right now.

Outside, he was struck with sudden self-doubt. What was he doing here in Kolkata? Checking on the handling of refugees like he checked on the progress of the sequoia research? It would make no difference. Those few people he'd saved—five thousand here, a few hundred there, twenty thousand in between—would never thank him.

"You need some time off," said Percy standing next to him.

"I had time off in California." Ian didn't look at her. "You wanted me to go to Mussoorie."

"Not for another week."

"That's not what Georgette said."

"Georgette likes to mess with you."

Ian turned to her. This time she was a tween Indian girl in a miniskirt over tights. She chewed gum loudly.

"Why would a three hundred million year old inhuman entity want to do that?"

Percy shrugged. "We get bored."

"How old are you? Really?"

"I've been working on this project for about twenty thousand years. I've only been on Earth since 1885."

"That's what you always say."

"Then you can presume that's my answer."

"I'm going to assume that's young in this scheme of things. Georgette has been here since the Permian Extinction."

"So?"

He turned to her. "Given all of that, how could you possibly know anything about how bored she is? She must be ten thousand times your age."

Percy grinned at him and spun a finger on her cheek. "Gee, I'm just guessing, mister. I'm only a kid."

"Little girl, where are your parents?"

"Inside trying to get a rental car. Don't worry. I'll be properly chastised for walking outside by myself. I could get kidnapped."

"What do you think I should do?"

"Work," Percy said instantly.

"I thought you wanted me to take time off."

"Work," she repeated. "But not for me. Not for Georgette. You're pretty good with your hands. You saw the refugee camps from the plane. They need all the help they can get."

"Just what a billionaire needs to do: work with plumbing."

"Here are your papers." She handed him a packet. "Passport. Trade union memberships. Go down there and do what you need to do for a week. *Then*, go to Mussoorie."

There was a shout behind them.

Percy—now just a thirteen-year-old girl—turned sullenly to confront her shouting parents.

Ian stepped into a suddenly vacated cab before the parents could turn on him.

oOo

What he needed, he found, was to dig ditches.

Little ditches for water pipes to the newly printed refugee housing. Bigger ones to connect the sewage systems and the assembled central bathrooms. Thin ones for electrical conduits. This could have been done by robots at six times the cost of human labor. In some places, giving a machine any possible human job even if it made no economic sense was considered a moral duty. But here labor—especially his—was cheap and doubled as welfare. Work was the preferred way to distribute necessary funds to the refugees but there was so much immediate need they hired anybody who could dig.

Ian's back strained against the pull of mattock and shovel. At the end of the day, he flopped on the cot, sore and stinking, but with a clear conscience and a smile.

Worker's Housing was for those who were not refugees and not locals. Ian's tent was mostly populated by rural Bengalis with a lesser representation of Biharis, Punjabi, and a scattering of Chinese. There were four Europeans. Ian was the sole American.

Ian kept to himself. When payday came, he took his tiny pile of rupees and joined the crowd leaving the barracks.

oOo

There was no place in the camps to drink and so the workers bled sluggishly south into Uttar Raypur. There, residential housing had been transformed into markets, shops, restaurants—anything to capture the local thermodynamic rise of money coming from government assistance. Small storefronts blared out Bollyjaxx, a blend of classic Bollywood movie songs and jazz instrumentation. There were sections of sidewalk cordoned off that served as restaurants, bars, or dance clubs.

Ian drank leaning against a stucco wall. The bar was a six-foot piece of plywood stretched across two cinderblocks. A slight, thin man with a narrow face and a long nose like a hawk, poured yellow fluid from an unlabelled milk carton into pink plastic cups, fifty paise a cup. Two huge men protected him. The half-drunk crowd milled around the bar or helped Ian hold up the wall.

Ian felt the warm glow of toxic petrochemicals.

It faded quickly. He looked around. Many of the clientele were ex-pats like himself. Most were sliding down the invisible stairway. He stared into the cup. Ian wanted to leave. Leave this bar. Leave Kolkata. Leave Percy and Georgette. Leave everything.

The rough trade on either side of the plywood plank moved subtly towards him. Time to go.

On the street, Ian sobered quickly. He bought a wrap of greasy bread and fried vegetables. He ate as he strolled, ignoring any hard and speculative looks, secure in his reflexes and confident he would (probably) not kill anyone if they attacked. Tomorrow morning there would be several empty beds in the dormitory. His among them.

Ian moved with the press of the crowd and the illusion of common humanity. Gradually, he moved south towards the Charial Khal River. The neighborhoods returned to what must have been a more normal balance: family apartments on the second floor with regular small stores occupying the first. Even that turned into the tiny farms that, in India, dot every possible place food can be grown. It was dark. There were still people walking near him but the crowd had disappeared.

The road ended in the dirty river and he stood under the trees on its bank. There were a few houses and gardens nearby with lights on for safety. He was alone. He could hear a distant dog bark. In the distance, he could hear the grumble of the crowd he had left and further off the muted roar of Kolkata.

He backtracked to a branch in the road and began walking vaguely east with no particular direction towards no particular goal.

It felt wonderful.

Then, Ian heard a snarl and looked up the road. A dog stared at him. Ian stared back, surprised at seeing an animal take notice of him. Since he'd begun work for Percy, wild animals hadn't been an issue. Did that not apply to domestic dogs?

A second dog joined the first. Both staring at him and growling.

Ian backed slowly away towards the low hum of Uttar Raypur. He wondered if he could run faster than a dog. Unlikely.

But it was somewhere to back towards.

Chapter 1.3: Chitra

Chitra called Majhi Merchants at their corporate office. As soon as she identified herself, she was connected to her cousin Bhim, with whom she had spoken but never met. He immediately told her to wait at the airport. Bhim would send over his brother, Kapi, who had never married, never had children, and was working over at the warehouse where he would not likely amount to much but they all loved him, simple though he was. Bhim seemed to think this was reassuring.

She stood outside of the arrival area in the glowing heat. Kolkata was one of those places in the world where sweat failed. All Chitra could do was stand there, steaming and miserable.

After an hour, Chitra was torn between getting a cab and booking the next flight back to New York. An ancient-looking truck pulled up. A tiny man dressed in stained loose cotton leaped out and hugged her.

"Please tell me you're Kapi," said Chitra. "Or I'll have to hurt you."

Kapi laughed and stepped back. "Yes. I was just getting ready to go down to help Grandpapa with the grapes when Bhim called me."

Kapi carefully placed her valise behind the seat then held the door open for her. "Come," he said, grinning. "We have to *go*."

She climbed inside and sat down.

Kapi slammed the door and ran around to the driver's side. He jumped in and landed on the seat, closing the door at the same time. With a stinking belch, the truck pulled away from the curb and began a zigzag escape around standing cars and the ubiquitous mob of people and luggage. "Five-minute idling rule," he said, tapping the dash. "Because it's not electric. Makes no difference it runs on generated methane from harvest scrap. The law applies to all 'non-electric' vehicles." He canceled the first ninety-degree turn with a second in the opposite direction.

Chitra checked her seatbelt.

"Let me look at you." Kapi turned and watched her long enough Chitra grew worried.

"Where are we going?"

"The warehouse," said Kapi, tearing his gaze from her reluctantly and returning it to the road. "We all live there. Plenty of room. Except for Grandpapa, of course."

"Grandpapa doesn't have plenty of room?"

"I've never asked him. Do you think he doesn't have enough?" Kapi gave her a stricken look.

"Why wouldn't he?"

"He and Grandmama live in a little house next to the grapes. Maybe he *doesn't* have enough room."

Ah, Chitra thought. Enlightenment unlocked. "I see. You meant that everybody lives in the warehouse except Grandpapa. I'm sure he has enough room. After all, he has a whole house, right?"

"That's true." Kapi looked relieved.

Kapi kept talking like some agreeable parrot. Bhim had interrupted Kapi's working the grapes with Grandpapa. But that was great! This way he was *first* to see Chitra. Bhim really ran things. Even Bhim said it was kids that made life worthwhile. Kapi might have children one day. Bhim's kids liked him. His sister, Tiya, had kids but she was never happy. Her kids liked Kapi. Everybody liked Kapi. What's there to dislike? He even got along with Great Uncle Risu's son, Fani, who nobody liked.

Chitra let the words wash over her and watched as the truck worked its way down the highway until, at some unidentifiable point, Kapi careened off the highway into one side street after another until they were in a mix of residential housing and industrial wasteland. As they turned one street, Kapi leaned out of the truck and yelled: "Open the gate." At the last possible moment, the loading bay door rolled up and Kapi bounced up the ramp with no appreciable loss of speed. He turned as he went in and screeched to a stop. "Here we are."

Cousin Tiya introduced her to Bhim's wife, Rupi, then to the children, Pari, Pavi, Puli, Dali, and Das. The ones beginning with the letter 'P' belonged to Bhim and Rupi. The ones beginning with the letter 'D' belonged to Tiya and Rohak. Rohak was still at the office with Bhim. The crowd made way for a late middle-aged gentleman just beginning to stoop. This was her Uncle Ekanath, Tapas' brother, and Tiya, Kapi and Bhim's father. Without thinking, Chitra hugged him and there was dead silence in the room until Ekanath slowly and firmly hugged her back. Chitra felt a collective easing of breath in the room without quite understanding why.

Each family had their own quarters but the kitchen and dining room were common—except, of course, for Fani's apartment in the corner of the building. Or so Kapi confided to her in a low whisper when she was being shown around by Tiya. Tiya gave Kapi a glare and he looked so sad that Tiya tapped him on the shoulder and told him to stop.

Then they must eat—wasn't Chitra starving after the long flight from America? Tiya did not seem to understand, or perhaps want to understand, that Chitra had been collecting the dead in the ruins of Contai. Chitra thought that perhaps touching the dead was taboo—perhaps low caste or some such. Her father had always refused to speak of caste and her mother said she didn't understand it.

Chitra knew her own family was *shunri,* a low caste that traditionally handled brewing and distilling country wine. Something her great-grandfather Kiash had built into a wealthy business. But Chitra was at root American and equated income with class and class with caste. If her Indian family was wealthy, didn't that automatically make them higher caste? Tiya's reactions suggested to Chitra she didn't have it quite right.

Was this why her father had left India and never returned?

Chitra was proud of her job and considered pressing the matter. Still, she was a guest here. If Tiya's way of dealing with what Chitra did was to vaguely refer to it as "disaster relief," who was Chitra to disturb her?

It made Chitra feel as if she were wearing an ill-fitting mask.

After the meal, they showed her a guest room and left her to "clean up."

A private room surprised her. Chitra had expected to sleep next to children or on a sofa. It was a small room, curtained by some very pretty hanging prints and with a small, single wooden bed. There were shelves holding picture after picture of members of the family, the warehouse, the vineyard, people who *had* to be Grandpapa Nirad and Grandmama Mithu.

Kapi knocked on the door looking apologetic. "Excuse me."

It dawned on her. "This is *your* room."

Kapi nodded sorrowfully. "I'm sorry. I need to get a few things."

"Look, I can sleep on a sofa. Or I can get a hotel—"

"Oh, *no!*" Kapi looked horrified. "You can't possibly."

"But this is your room—"

"Yes." He beamed. "They said you would stay in *my* room." Then, his face fell. "But if you don't like it—"

"Oh, that's not what I meant at all." Chitra closed her eyes and took a deep breath. "Kapi, it's a perfectly lovely room. I'm very pleased you're allowing me to stay in it."

"That makes me very happy." Then, he looked embarrassed. "Uncle Fani asked to meet you." He looked on either side of the hall and continued in a low voice. "But you don't have to see him if you don't want to. Nobody listens to him anyway."

"Would it make things easier if I did?"

"Yes. He makes people miserable when he doesn't get his way."

"Then, let's visit Fani."

Kapi led her past the kitchen to a plain door. He knocked softly.

The door opened and Chitra smelled dust and old food as a wrinkled woman looked around the edge. "Yes?" she said.

"This is Chitra," said Kapi. "Tapas' daughter. From America." He turned to Chitra. "This is Omrita."

Omrita stared at her. Chitra saw that one eye was milky and sightless but the other was bird bright and searching.

Suddenly, Omrita smiled and the change was as sudden as pulling a shade off a lamp.

"Come in," Omrita said in heavily accented English. "Fani's been wanting to see you ever since we heard you were coming."

Other quarters Chitra had seen in the warehouse had been furnished sparsely with selected treasures to be displayed. Fani and Omrita's apartment was jammed with things of all sorts. Rolled up rugs in the corner. Multiple brass figurines. A precarious collection of ceramic bangles hanging from a nail. Every inch of wall space had some sort of picture on it: posters, photographs, pages of books—one section of wall had a child's drawing on the plaster, carefully framed with thin strips of colored tape.

Fani was sitting in an upholstered chair next to a window. He was tiny and wizened, leaning to one side, his head tilted further as if he could not hold it straight. Huge glasses gave him a frog look as his eyes followed her. He didn't speak.

"It's a pleasure to meet you, sir." Chitra put out her hand.

After a moment, Fani took her hand weakly and then let it go.

"Sit. Please." Omrita guided her to a similarly stuffed chair opposite Fani's. "I'll make some tea."

"I like the sun," said Fani suddenly. His voice was soft but clear. "It's the only way I can get warm."

"Ah," said Chitra.

"It's a terrible thing to be cold in so hot a place as India."

"I suppose it is." Chitra didn't remember being this uncomfortable at any time in her life.

"I looked after Tapas and Ekanath when I was young." Fani looked out the window. "While Nirad and Mithu worked down in the grapes and Risu ran the business. Ekanath liked to sit and play but I could never keep Tapas content. It didn't surprise me when he left for America."

Chitra had a sense that she was caught in fog on some great river. All she could see was the turmoil of the water without ever knowing where she was. "Ah," she said.

"Tell Nirad I'm sorry," Fani said. He leaned forward, reached out, and took her hand. "Tell Risu."

His grip was as strong and sharp as a talon. Chitra suppressed the urge to pull her hand away. "I haven't met either of them."

"Risu's down visiting Nirad." Fani let go of her hand. "Tell them both I'm sorry."

"What did you do?"

"Nothing."

"Ah." The Contai debris field was better than this.

Omrita entered the room with a tray. "Tea!"

Silent, Fani leaned back in his chair, his head tilted again.

Omrita poured for all three of them. She handed a cup to Chitra. Then, carefully, held it so Fani could drink. Fani drank noisily then pulled away, nodding.

"Oh, we have good times, he and I," Omrita said fondly. "There is a nest of talcharai out the window. Did he show you?"

"No."

"Just over there." Omrita pointed. "He will watch them for hours."

Fani looked at Chitra and then back outside. Chitra could not read his face: Agreement with Omrita? A reminder of their past, enigmatic, conversation? Boredom? She had no idea.

There was a knock on the apartment door. Omrita looked suddenly cross. She left them and went to the door.

Chitra could hear Kapi: "I'm sorry, Mama. It cannot be helped. I need her to come with me."

Fani leaned forward and whispered. "You won't forget to tell Risu and Nirad? Tell them I'm sorry?"

Chitra just had time to nod when Omrita returned.

"You must come back and visit before you leave." Omrita led her to the front door.

Kapi was waiting. "Thank you, Mama."

Omrita gave Kapi a warm smile. "It's all right, Kapi. I know it's not your fault."

As they left Fani and Omrita's apartment Kapi leaned forward and spoke in a whisper. "I thought perhaps you would need saving."

"You were right." Chitra now understood why everyone loved Kapi.

"Bhim and Rohak have decided to take a family holiday tomorrow so they will work late tonight. I have to go down and help Grandpapa Nirad. Do you want to come with me? We'll come back in the morning."

Escape! "That would be perfect."

oOo

From father's stories, Chitra expected scrawny plants sporting thin and blotchy fruit. The vineyard was only a few hectares but the plants were full and luscious. She *was* surprised by the surrounding razor wire. Kapi put his hand on a scanner next to the gate. The gate swung open and he drove through. The gate clanged shut suddenly behind them.

Kapi parked next to a small bungalow. An old man and woman were standing outside waiting for them—surely Grandpapa Nirad and Grandmama Mithu. An even older man was sitting next to them in a wheelchair. Risu?

Nirad was bent but still looked strong. Mithu waved to her as they got out of the car. Nirad and Mithu looked like they could weather—*had* weathered—any conceivable storm and now were figuring out how to attack old age.

Risu had that papery look to his skin characteristic of aging heart patients. He still looked better than his son, Fani. He sat straight in the wheelchair, grinning

"It is good to meet you," said Nirad, taking Chitra's hands. He kissed her cheek.

Mithu held her by the shoulders and kissed her as well. "I'm so glad you're here."

"That's not a proper greeting," said Risu. He grabbed her hands and pulled her down to him and gave her a strong hug. "There! Now come inside."

"Kapi and I have to get ready for the harvest," said Nirad quietly. "Mithu, too."

"Good! More of Chitra for me."

"She might want to see the grapes."

"*Bother* your grapes. They've nearly been the death of me." Risu leaned towards Chitra. "You come in with me and we'll *drink* some of those grapes. That's the best way to see them."

Chitra felt pulled in both directions. "How about I look at the grapes for a bit?"

"But I can't *go* out there." Risu banged the wheelchair in frustration. "Not in this."

"Put on the prosthetics," said Nirad. "Then come out with us."

"I hate those things."

"Suit yourself."

Risu grumbled, turned the chair, and went inside.

"Come." Nirad walked towards the vines. Mithu and Kapi left them their privacy and went behind the house to start preparing baskets for harvest.

The vineyard was raised perhaps two meters above the adjacent fields. Here the heat was less oppressive. The sky was clear and close, still holding the land in a firm tropical grip. But there was a light eastern breeze that was certainly drier, if not cooler, than the city. The lush gardens marched irregularly right up to the edge of the fence. On one section the razor wire had been overpowered by gourd and squash vines.

Nirad led her up the slight hill. "It's mostly *Pusa navrang*," he said. "A few Burmese. The grapes that grow well in West Bengal don't make good wine and the grapes that make good wine don't grow well here. But these seem to do all right." He spoke gruffly but Chitra could hear an undernote of pride. He turned to her and gave her an embarrassed look. "Not bad for a crazy old man." He reached down and pulled off a bunch. "Here. Try some."

Everything in Chitra rebelled at the idea of eating unwashed fruit here. But if you can't trust your Grandpapa, who can you trust? She plucked a grape from the bunch and put it in her mouth.

It was a rich, sweet flavor. Almost smoky with a faint bite.

Nirad laughed. "My own variety. This will be its first year. Will it make good wine?"

"I have no idea."

"Ah, if it doesn't work out I can distill it into a spicy cholai."

"Have you named the variety?"

Nirad looked pleased with the question. "Not yet. Tapas helped me a lot."

"I had no idea."

"He even designed a filter for me that finally got rid of some off-flavors we've always had. Last year they finally let me into the Sommelier Competition against some of the bigger vineyards in Maharashtra. I did not win anything, of course. But being allowed to enter is something."

Nirad fell silent, looking off in the distance.

Chitra supposed he was trying to think of what he should say next. "Fani asked me to tell you he was sorry."

"Ah." Nirad watched her for a moment. "Did he say why?"

"No."

Nirad turned back to vines. He started examining them. "Good. There's no reason for you to be involved in this. It is a family affair."

It felt like a sharp stick in her chest. "I see."

Nirad looked at her. "I meant an affair for those of us here. You are still my granddaughter."

"Of course." She wondered how long she had to remain here before she could leave politely.

"It has nothing to do with you."

"I understand perfectly."

Nirad stood and sighed. "Americans. You offend so easily." He ate one of the grapes. "Let's go back to the house. I'm sure Mithu has made something wonderful. She is quite a cook."

oOo

Risu, Nirad, Kapi, and Mithu went to bed early. Risu had his own room. Kapi slept in the back with the equipment—he said he liked listening to the grapes grow. Chitra tried to sleep in the tiny guest room in the back corner of the bungalow. Near midnight, she gave up and rose quietly and dressed, taking care to arm herself—non-lethal mechanisms only. UNERA frowned on killing the citizens of client states.

Walking carefully so as to not wake Kapi, she left the bungalow. She could smell the ripe grapes and hear the latent sounds of the city, the nearer town center, and the unmistakable governmental mutter of the refugee camp a few kilometers away.

At the bottom of the field, she found a gate buried in brush.

Hm, she thought. I'm an American woman in West Bengal. I don't know the language or the customs. Do I really *want* to leave the safe confines of my grandfather's house?

Hell, yes. She was *suffocating* in family mysteries. This was not the riskiest thing she'd ever done.

The gate was locked but the hinges were loose. She raised them and moved the gate to one side. She slipped her tiny frame through and replaced the gate on the hinges.

The brush covered a narrow trail that led to a road. The road led between houses and gardens and the occasional dog. She could smell the Cherial Khal on its way to the Hooghly River and walked towards in that direction.

Chitra came to a crossroads. Going forward was south to the river. West would wrap around to the front of Granpapa's property. East took her back towards Uttar Raypur proper: people, crowds, businesses. She was pondering where she should go when she heard dogs growling to her left.

A man was slowly backing towards her, his hands out to a pack of eight or ten dogs, each quivering with canine rage.

Left hand: thump gun. Right hand: pepper gun. Chitra had dealt with wild dogs before. The thump gun produced a shock wave that could disorient a human to the point they couldn't walk. It could implode ear drums. She'd prefer not to use the thump gun—a dog deafened and in the depth of shock was a pitiful sight. The pepper gun was less effective but at least she didn't feel as guilty about using it.

"Stop backing up," Chitra ordered and stepped beside him. She flicked on the sight of the pepper gun and the laser point danced in the dark. The dogs were in a rough line, crossing from one side of the road to the next. Good. They weren't circling yet. She picked the one she thought might be the leader and fired a thick burst of sticky capsaicin. It struck him on one eye and stuck.

Instantly, the dog howled and rolled on the ground trying to claw the pain from his face. She fired again at her second target and that dog rubbed its face in the dirt.

The dogs hesitated.

Chitra yelled at them. "Get *away!*" She stamped her foot.

Two dogs broke and ran. The others wavered. One leaped and she fired the thump gun.

The dog screamed and fell. The remaining dogs disappeared into the dark.

Chitra ran to the pepper dogs first and removed the sticky gum from the first. The dog snapped at her and ran into the darkness. The other just lay there and cried as she gently pulled the strands from its face. Then, it too ran off.

She took a deep breath and went to the stunned one.

It quivered in shock. Its ears were bleeding. Its paws jerked and it panted as if from running a great distance.

"Come on, boy," she said as she knelt next to it, carefully avoiding the claws, teeth, and bleeding ears. Chitra had none of the instruments she needed to treat shock. Not even a blanket. She rubbed its paws and crooned to it—a purely useless gesture since it had to be completely deaf. She thought about holding it close to keep it warm, but who knew what might happen? For a moment, the dog seemed to search her out, beseech her. Then, it shook hard and died.

"Damn," she said and stood up. She checked herself for scratches or bites, any open wound she might have incurred without realizing it. Nothing. There wasn't even any blood on her shirt.

"Hello?" said the man.

She had forgotten him. "Any bites?"

"Beg pardon?"

"Bites? Scratches? Did they get to you in any way?"

"I don't think so." He felt of himself. "No. Nothing. Why?"

"Do you think those animals were vaccinated?"

"Oh." He seemed lost in thought for a moment. "Ian Bones." He held out his hand.

"Chitra Majhi," she said and shook it automatically. "What the hell were you doing out here, anyway?"

"Taking a walk. Weren't you doing the same?"

Chitra looked up at him. She couldn't see his face in the gloom. "Yeah. I suppose. You're American?"

"Goodness. What gave it away?"

Chitra laughed shortly. "Me, too."

"I'm going to head back to town. Would you like to accompany me? I can promise you anything offered for sale."

"That's an open-ended offer."

"You did save my life, didn't you?"

Chitra looked down at the dog. "I suppose I did," she said sadly. "Poor guy."

oOo

"All Day Coffee" was on the bottom floor of a two-story house. The doors were painted red and white and opened into a close collection of tiny tables. Ian ordered in Bengali coffee and a mysterious pastry called *laddu*. Then, he led her to a table in the corner where they could sit.

"You know Bengali," she said as she sat down.

"Some," he said. He handed her the laddu. "Try it."

Chitra looked at the round pastry dubiously. "I already took a chance on unwashed grapes. Now I'm just waiting for the inevitable."

"A bite of laddu couldn't possibly make things worse."

She bit into it. Nuts? Pistachios, maybe? Coconut? Honey? Plus unidentifiable flavors that were unexpected. Soy sauce? What would that be doing there? "It's delicious."

Ian nodded. "I'm glad you like it."

Chitra watched him for a moment. "What brings an American to Uttar Raypur?"

Ian didn't answer immediately. "I dabble."

"What does that mean?"

"I'm wealthy—I managed that some time ago. Invested in a technical innovation here, brought a laboratory invention to the market there. That sort of thing. Now I'm a consulting facilitator. Someone wants to take an idea and bring it to market, I help them out."

"Like a new sort of toothpaste?"

"Like transport of the dead out of disaster zones. I have a client that developed a new type of body bag that keeps the contents cold and preserved and dry—sort of an instant mummification. I helped him find an opportunity to field test it in Chennai. If it's successful it could be deployed in any number of circumstances."

Chitra watched him. "I do disaster recovery. I spent the last two weeks digging bodies out of what used to be Contai."

"It is hard, difficult work. Any success stories?"

"We saved a little girl who'd been overlooked in the first surveys."

"That counts."

"I wouldn't call it a success story."

Ian drummed his fingers on the table for a moment. "I disagree. Mortality is just shoving sand against the tide. We all like to pretend it isn't but that's an illusion—one I can't sustain after working on this project and I suspect you can't, either. Finding a life in the midst of handling the dead is a breakwater moment. An unlooked for moment of salvation—*definitely* a success story."

For a moment, she was silent, stunned. No one outside the business had ever *gotten* it without an explanation. Then, she grew suspicious. "Are you religious?"

"Not very." He smiled at her. "But you and I live in a religious country. It rubs off. Interesting for someone from Brooklyn to have family here."

She stared at him. "Have you been stalking me?"

Ian chuckled. "I just have an ear for language. Uttar Raypur is pretty far off the beaten path for tourism. So I guessed you're visiting family."

"Yeah." The thought of Fani and Grandpapa Nirad and Kapi made her suddenly sad.

Ian cocked his head. "Trouble?"

"Family mysteries. I'm considered more an American than a member of my family. Things don't get shared."

Ian sighed in sympathy. "Yes. I know how that works."

"You have family trouble?"

Ian laughed abruptly. "You have no idea."

She smiled back "Try me."

He gave her a quizzical look. "Okay. Mom and Dad were both military aviators. Dad got killed and it drove Mom of the deep end to the point she was abusing me in favor of her pet parrot."

"Wow."

"She got better. Now she's an astronaut—hold on." Ian corrected himself. "Off planet engineer."

"But you still resent her."

"It's complicated." Ian sipped his coffee. "We're actually very close. She's atoned for all that."

"How could she?"

Ian was quiet a moment. "You're right, of course. It's a constant struggle."

Chitra watched him a moment. "Why do I get the feeling there's some horrible secret in the wings? Like you've done something you'll never admit. Or she's in the slave trade."

Ian stared at her. He shook his head. "You have an odd mind. Perhaps I'll introduce you."

"Really?" Chitra leaned back in her chair, a warmth in her from the coffee and the *laddu*. "Presuming a lot there, aren't you?"

"I did say 'Perhaps.' That covers much uncertainty. Now it's your turn."

Chitra shrugged. "I just don't know enough. Everybody acts on secret knowledge but they won't tell me."

"No trouble at home?" Ian lifted one eyebrow. "I get the distinct sense of trouble at home."

"My Dad has stage four pancreatic cancer." Chitra pressed her hand over her mouth. She hadn't mentioned that to anybody. Not Freder. Not Tsuba. No one.

Ian watched her for a moment and said softly; "That counts."

"No pain, so far," she said, staring into her coffee. "But it's all over inside. They've determined the base genotype and set up an antigen regimen. But even highly specific therapy is pretty awful." It was just out there. Dominating the conversation. She wished she'd never mentioned it.

"Did your parents send you out here?"

She thought a moment, thinking of Eleanor. "I don't know."

"Maybe you're here to make amends for him—to do something for him that he can no longer do for himself. That's what the well must do for the sick." Ian turned his hand over towards her as if presenting a gift.

Chitra didn't know what to make of that. "Maybe."

"Or my observation could be worse than useless. I know none of the principals involved."

They fell into a companionable silence. He sipped his coffee. She broke off another piece of laddu and nibbled at it.

"Do you believe in God?" he said suddenly.

"I thought you said you weren't religious."

"I'm not. Indulge me."

I knew it was too good to be true. He's a nutcase. "No, I don't. Do you want to convert me?"

"To what?"

"Whatever fictional God you believe in."

He didn't respond to that. "What would you say to a God that was not fiction? A God that created dinosaurs back in the Triassic. Presided over the great sauropods of the Jurassic. Watched as Neanderthals and *Homo sapiens* first met in Europe. A God of the Cretaceous."

Chitra stared at him. "That's very specific."

Ian looked away and sipped his coffee. "It's a hypothetical case."

"Are you a wealthy priest or something?"

Ian chuckled. "Jesus said it was easier for a camel to get through the eye of a needle than a rich man to get into heaven."

"You *are* a priest."

"I am not a priest. I am not a minister, rabbi, Father, pastor, or theologian. I am wealthy so I'm guessing Christian heaven is right out for the likes of me. It's a hypothetical question."

"A very specific hypothetical question."

"I'm interested in your reaction."

Chitra found she was enjoying herself. "A legitimate God, but not for us."

"At least no more for us than anything else." He made that odd gift-giving gesture again. "Her purpose would be no more served by us than by anything else."

"Would She have a purpose?"

"Good question." Ian thought for a moment. "It's not clear She would have a purpose any more than we do."

"Okay. I'm thinking of the God of the Cretaceous."

"What would you say if you met Her in a bar?"

Chitra laughed. "I'd ask her for her beauty secret."

Ian raised his eyebrows. "You would expect Her to be beautiful?"

"If you're God and ugly, what's the point?"

"Indeed."

"Okay," Chitra said, sobering a bit. "I'd ask why She made us to suffer, I suppose."

"A very human thing to ask. But She is not human. That would be like a larval cod confronting the mother of its millions of siblings and asking 'why me?'"

Chitra watched his face for a moment. She guessed he was about forty. It was a nice face. Narrow but with real cheekbones and lips that looked like they knew how to smile. His ears were a little big and his hair was thinning—he'd be bald before he was sixty. But his shoulders looked strong and his chest tapered sweetly down to his hips. *Oh my goodness. Do I want to sleep with him already?*

She shook her head. Not tonight. Not here in India with my distant family less than a kilometer away. "You've thought about this a lot."

Ian nodded. "I have. Consider a slightly different wrinkle. Let's say a creature of enormous power lands on Earth just before the Triassic and manages to permeate most life on the planet."

"Why the Triassic?"

"She likes dinosaurs."

Chitra barked a laugh. "Really? How would you know that?"

Ian smiled thinly. "'If one could draw conclusions regarding the nature of the Creator from a study of creation, it would appear that God has an inordinate fondness for beetles.' Haldane said that or something close to it. Our alien kept dinosaurs going for a hundred and fifty million years. That must count as affection." He seemed to collect his thoughts. "Think of it as a thought experiment. If there was such a creature in the real world, it stands to reason she would have to have motivations and thoughts very different from ours, even though we are part of her creation. The notion of 'God' seems as good as any."

"You are trying to understand the mind of God."

"I'm trying to understand a powerful non-supernatural being that would serve in that role. Hypothetically, of course."

"For God's sake, why?"

Ian scowled at her. "You've been waiting for just the right moment to say that, haven't you?"

"Absolutely. But the question remains."

Ian looked away. "The nature of my work puts me in touch with many different kinds of people. Many of them believe in some sort of God—I don't, but that's beside the point. It makes me think about such things. So I'm interested in your opinion."

"I don't have one. The idea is too new." She thought for a moment. "I'd have to think on the nature of responsibility. What is my responsibility to that dog I killed out there? We could have buried it, I suppose, but then we'd have to handle it and I don't even have gloves. Maybe it belongs to somebody. Or maybe it doesn't belong to anybody but the other dogs. Still, I killed it and now it's lying in the dirt. Dogs are human-created beings more than any other. After all, we've been working on them for twenty thousand years. Is my responsibility to that dog any different than the responsibility your creator-thing owes to me? Did the creator-thing domesticate us as we domesticated that dog's scavenger wolf ancestor?"

"Go on."

"I have a soft spot for dogs." Chitra fiddled with her cup. "We've domesticated a lot of animals, but dogs are the only ones that volunteered. They were following us around long before we decided to adopt them. It's been fantastically successful for them. We may kill everything down to the cockroaches, but as long as there are humans there will be dogs. On the other hand, considering how we treat them, I'm not so sure they got such a good deal." She straightened up. "If the creator-thing has a responsibility to us then we have a responsibility to dogs. And if we shirk that responsibility, then what does the creator-thing owe us? Does it owe us anything more than it owes a salamander? Or does it owe a great deal to both of us? Forgetting any moral issue—why not? Forgetting moral issues is what *we* do—why should we expect any better treatment? Our problems stem from ourselves. If we get ourselves into trouble what should we expect?"

"God the parent?"

"But God isn't our parent. The relationship would be more profound and more distant than that. If we evolved—even under some subtle direction from God—our evolution is still the sum of a long string of our own choices. Who we mated with. Which children we liked best. What sort of sexual characteristics we found attractive. We made *ourselves* as much or more than this supposed God did. Perhaps it doesn't owe us anything at all and the very notion of such a debt is ludicrous. We should be proud of the civilization we made and be happy for the chance."

Ian watched her silently for a long time. At one point Chitra thought he was going to kiss her. She wasn't sure how she wanted to react. Then, he sipped his coffee in a salute.

"I like you very much," he said.

"I think I like you, too," Chitra said. "What are you doing here?"

"Having coffee with you. Which, I might add, is very enjoyable. You, that is. The coffee is marginal."

"I mean in Uttar Raypur."

Ian looked uncomfortable. "I'm avoiding an obligation, and since I'm valuable to my clients I can do that for a little bit. Sometimes I take a break. This time, I worked in the refugee camp."

Chitra couldn't have been more shocked than if he had confessed to multiple wives. "Whatever for?"

"To figure some things out."

"What sort of figuring would require you to work in a tsunami refugee camp?"

Ian looked uncomfortable. "I needed perspective. I don't really want to discuss it right now. I'm still thinking about it."

"Great. Family mysteries again."

Ian nodded. "Of a sort."

Chitra shook her head. "Okay. What's the job?"

"A presentation in Mussoorie."

"'Figure some things out.' 'A presentation.' Are you *trying* to be mysterious? It's not as attractive as people think."

"Not intentionally."

"I see." Chitra looked him over. "That's a resort town up in the foothills. I've heard it's gorgeous."

"It is," he said simply. "But it's just for work."

"Maybe I'll join you," she said, aghast at herself.

"Oh, *no!*"

"Oh." She felt the now familiar stab in the chest.

Ian sat up. "No. You mustn't. I mean, it's the wrong time of year."

"I see."

Ian stopped himself and closed his eyes. "Please let me start over. I will only be in Mussoorie a little while. I would love your company, but this is not the right venue. And it is completely true this is the wrong season for Mussoorie. It's much more beautiful in the spring."

"Scared of what I'll see?"

"Good lord. I'd not see you *at all*. If you wish to meet, let's meet in New York. I'm there quite often. I'll be there in a month. How about then?" He reached into his pocket.

"You're going to give me a card. How quaint."

Ian's hand stopped. "No. Of course not. I was going to send you a ping telling you all the contact information you'll ever need. How about that?"

Chitra laughed. "Give me the damned card."

Chapter 1.4: Ian

Ian swore at himself all the way back to the airport. He was an idiot for coming here. An idiot for working at a refugee camp—what was he trying to atone for, anyway? If he was guilty he was monumentally guilty. If he wasn't he need atone for nothing.

Telling Chitra he was going to Mussoorie? What the *hell* was he thinking?

While the plane was taxiing, his phone went off with a call from Pauline. He answered as he stared out the window: "Hey. Where are you?"

"Getting ready to leave Colorado for Woomera. Next interviewee is on Luna."

"Where?"

"Not sure. He's not communicating much."

"Is he hiding?"

Pauline was quiet a moment. "I don't think so. I just don't think he has many friends. Where are you?"

"Flying to Northern India."

"The Himalayas?"

"Next to."

"Damn. I never saw them. Well, from Earth. I passed over them on Héxié Station but it's not the same. The Earth is so huge that everything on it seems small."

"Well, I've never been to space."

"Yet."

"Yeah.

"Oh." Her voice went small.

"What?" He felt a sudden fear at the change.

"We just flew over the Rockies. Quite a sight."

"See? Who needs the Himalayas?"

"I can always rely on you to give me perspective. Going now. I have to work while I've got the chance."

They hung up and Ian leaned back in his chair. Twelve-year-old Ian still wondered if he'd done the right thing. If she was still Pauline. Sixty-two-year-old Ian remembered far more of her and fought back with memories of Pauline helping him with calculus in middle school and chemistry in high school. Applauding until her hands were raw, tears streaming down her face when he graduated from Purdue.

Georgette sat down next to him.

He felt like both crawling out of the window and fucking her right then and there.

"Hello, Ian," she purred and leaned towards him. "Want to join the mile high club?"

Ian held his briefcase up as a shield.

Georgette sighed. "A girl tries to be friendly and this is the thanks she gets."

"Somebody will see you."

Georgette laughed. She waved a steward to her.

"Yes?" The young man leaned down. "Can I help you?"

"I have an AK-47 in the overhead. Can you be a dear and get it for me? Then, how about killing the pilot and copilot?"

"No problem." He stood and started rummaging in the overhead bin. "I don't see it. Did you check under your seat?"

"Never mind. Just forget about it."

"About what?"

"Can you bring me a martini? And a gin and tonic for him."

"Of course."

Slowly Ian put his briefcase down on the floor. "What are you doing here?"

Georgette held up her finger until the drinks were brought. She passed the gin and tonic over to Ian and sipped her own. "Humans are always a surprise. Who would have thought there was entertainment to be had from an alcohol delivery mechanism?" She put her drink down on the seat tray. "Percy asked me to. She thought you were losing your nerve over that tiny girl."

"Chitra?"

"I know, right?" Georgette shook her head incredulously, golden hair flying. "I told Percy that you would never go for a slip of a thing like her. What you really *needed* was a valkyrie like me."

"Stop it. *Stop it!*" He felt like hitting her. "You're always playing with me. Always twisting me around. I *know* it's just pheromones and imagery like the bettas."

Georgette looked at him. "Bettas?"

"Siamese fighting fish. You must know about them. It's your world they live in."

Georgette sighed and leaned back in her chair. She cradled her martini with both hands. "You'd be surprised at what I know or don't know at any given moment. Tell me about the bettas."

"The males display to one another—they respond to particular cues. In college, we had a project where we made these little models of foam and feathers to trigger their behavior. We accentuated this feather, that color. Made the forefin bigger. Added more red to the dorsal. Eventually, we had a model that would get far more reaction than any actual fish." Ian pointed at Georgette. "You're that model."

She pointed to herself. "Me?"

"Yes! You're made that way just to confuse me. To get me horny and scared at the same time. Why? I'm doing what you want me to do. You don't *need* to manipulate me. But you do it. All. The. *Time!*"

Georgette considered him. "I am just the user interface. I could look dumpy." She was suddenly fat. "Or old." Wrinkled. "Or sick." Covered with suppurating sores. "Or I can look like what you think a beauty should look." Blond valkyrie. "After all, what did Chitra say? 'If you're God and ugly, what's the point?' I can wear glasses." She reached into the air and brought out a pair of thick black glasses and put them on. "Does that help?"

Ian gulped his drink and put it down on his tray. Dear God, she looked adorable. "You're what? A billion years old? Distributed all over the planet? What do you *want* from me?"

Georgette took off the glasses and looked at him levelly. Suddenly, he didn't find her attractive or compelling. "Very little, actually," she said quietly. "This whole thing wasn't my idea." She looked away for a moment. "Do you know anything about contracts?"

"I don't understand."

"I'll start there, then. A contract is a negotiated arrangement between some number of persons for an agreed-upon set of actions and compensations."

"You're not a person."

"Come on, Ian." She looked at him tiredly. "A *corporation* is a person and I have a lot more biology in me than some creation of paper. The hidden problem in contracts is enforcement. Humans have managed this by throwing the problem up to higher authorities: courts, kings, princes, papacies. But in my case, there is no higher authority. It's just me and things like me."

"You're offering me a contract?"

She chuckled. "Please. What could you do if I didn't hold up my end? What couldn't I do if you didn't hold up yours?"

"What about bargaining in good faith?"

"Abraham tried that and look where it got him: he had to sacrifice his son and only got out of the deal on divine whim." She held up a hand. "Not to say it couldn't happen. People do all sorts of things based on principles other than their own best interests. But you don't need a contract for that. A *contract* is something that spells out obligations and duties between people who may or may not have any faith at all, good or otherwise."

Ian watched her a moment. "Okay. You have a contract with…"

"With Percy, of course. And Arthur."

"Who's Arthur?"

Georgette looked cross. "You see? This is the problem with me having agreed to keep my hands off of you. Percy's kept you in the dark."

"So you could tell me… now?"

"Sure. Percy doesn't want me to and this will mess with her. I'm *always* willing to mess with Percy. Besides: you are all mine. Root and branch. Heart and soul."

"Why tell me? Why talk to me at all?"

"Why not? After all, if I can't talk to my creations, who can I talk to?" Georgette leaned towards him. "Percy and the rest of them think I'm crazy."

"Who thinks you're crazy? Percy—and Arthur?" Maybe she is. The thought made him feel cold.

"Not just them. All of the others." Georgette shook her head wearily. "Right. She told you nothing. And by our *contract,* I can only communicate with you through a *person*. With a person's limitations. So I—meaning the user interface that lives right now in this body, not the several trillion threads of me that twist through the biosphere—can only know the depth of that nothing when I see it right in front of me."

"*They* think you're crazy."

"Right. There must be…" Her voice trailed off and she thought for a minute. "I have no idea. Thousands? Millions? Billions of us? Trying to get a count is like shouting in a stadium."

"How many *what?*"

"Terraformers. Like me. Like Percy. We're constructed beings."

"Why?"

"Why what?"

"Why terraform? Terraforming is to make someplace like earth. But this *is* earth. You said you were constructed to do this. By who? For what purpose?"

Georgette watched him for a long minute. "The word means to make a planet into something resembling earth *now*. Earth didn't look all that friendly in the beginning."

Ian nodded. "Okay. But *why?* By *who?*"

Georgett snorted. "Oh, the millions of years occupied by *that* discussion. I don't know. No one knows. I'm not first generation. I don't think I'm even tenth. With each generation millions of years long… our origins are lost. Best theory is a few were constructed and sent out. They bred and sent out others. Whoever they were, they have a long term view. We're constructed, but we're still *alive.* Prick us, do we not bleed? Do we not love, marry, have children, divorce—" She held up her hand. "Scratch that. We don't do any of those things. But we have the drive to create and reproduce. That's built into us." Georgette pointed to the ceiling of the plane and whispered. "Like I said, they think I'm crazy. But I'm not."

"Why? And after a billion years, why now?"

"I'm not a billion years old. Not even close. I came here just before the Triassic. Where I… Ah." Georgette looked embarrassed. "I did some bad things. There wasn't much in the way of available real estate when I arrived—Venus was a hell hole. Arthur was running Mars. It was nearly dead anyway. Europa—oh, she was *so* sweet." For a moment Georgette looked as if she were going to cry. "Europa was… occupied. Enceladus and other enclosed oceans were off-limits. Everything good was taken. They offered me Venus but there was this beautiful blue-green jewel of a planet right in front of me. Oxygen/nitrogen atmosphere already established. Organisms all the way down into the crust and up into the stratosphere. Rich with multicellular life. Dozens of phyla on both water and land. Thousands and thousands of species of insects. Vertebrates were established on the land and had taken off in the sea. Anything you could want in a biosphere. Inspiring. And I had *great* ideas. I said, we can *share*. Pick a region. Or a task. Or a phylum. Or a trophic level. Pick the *best* of things. I'll just muddle through with whatever's left. Just let me work here." Georgette sighed and sipped her martini. "But he wouldn't. So I killed him."

"You what?"

"It's called the Permian Extinction, now. Or, rather, the *after-effects* are called the Permian Extinction. Killing him barely made a ripple but it took forever to get control of his systems. I made mistake after mistake. *Major* extinctions." She gave Ian an owlish look. "Not that extinctions are bad. Everybody loves a good extinction. But this was just clumsiness."

"That's why they thought you were crazy?"

"No. That's when they thought I was dangerous." Georgette drained her martini and asked for a second one. "Why do we have contracts? We have contracts because one party has something another party wants. Did you know I was male?"

"*What?*"

"We reproduce like any other living thing. We have something approximating male and something approximating female. Algorithms. Methodologies. Principles. A female principle is necessary for creating more terraformers but requires the donation of a male principle. We are so constructed that we can't generate them for ourselves. Every organism has its limits." She put the new martini on her tray. "Arthur was male. Europa was female. I'd been around about a hundred forty million years by that point. I had it *made.* It was the beginning of the Cretaceous. Huge sauropods on land. Mosasaurs and Pliosaurs in the water. I had one whole order of vertebrates in the air. I built entire ecologies on the concept of scale. All of my predecessor's systems—insects, trees, amphibians, proto-mammals—were in place and under control. I had big plans: another whole vertebrate group to go up in the air. The biggest predators the world had ever seen. I had proved myself. I was ready." Georgette sipped her martini. "So I proposed to Europa. Let me supply the male principle. You supply the female. We will create the most magnificent offspring."

"Romantic."

Georgette glared at him. "She turned me down." She swirled the martini in the glass. "I couldn't believe it. I brought out all the stops. I thought she might like color—plumage for display. I pushed the maniraptors ahead of schedule. Birds were *pretty*. The pterosaurs had nothing on them. She wasn't interested. I found an interesting wrinkle on a little island off a southern island and nurtured it: flowers. It took off immediately and in just a few million years there were flowers everywhere—not as many as now, of course. But enough to brighten up the place. And the colors were wild as each flower selected itself for as many pollinating insects as possible. Fields of them. Acres. Square kilometers. Whole valleys filled with color. She said no."

Georgette drank the rest of the martini and ordered a third. "You want anything?"

"I'm good." Ian wondered what would happen if Georgette became drunk. Would it be catastrophic or affect nothing at all?

"Suit yourself. So I thought. Okay. That's the way it is. I'll talk to somebody in the spiral arm. Between us communication is instantaneous but the male and female principles have a physical component. I can fire off a couple of thousand packets. I might have to wait a few hundred thousand or so years to see the result but so what? I got time." She stared into her martini. "Nobody would have me."

"Nobody?"

"Nobody in the Milky Way, anyway. We're the edge of the most recent wave and we're still seeding locally. *Our* group was seeded from Andromeda. *They* were seeded from who knows where. Seeding isn't cheap. You want to maximize success. No one wants to incur the expense of crossing the big dark until we've saturated the local real estate. I thought about trying to zero in on what I *thought* were non-local females but that's even chancier than sending out embryos. Any crossing is made unconscious and as close to the speed of light as possible. Locally, an embryo might wake up in a system that has no available sites and just withers and dies but at least it's only a few hundred thousand years out of date. If it can get a foothold and grow a singularity it can at least *talk* to the others. Get perspectives. Ideas. Techniques. But transport from one cluster to another can take millions of years, even with the advantages of time dilation. And if an embryo makes it and manages to set itself up, it's so far out of date that communication is next to impossible. Local culture has walled it out just to cut down on the noise. Besides, I didn't *have* embryos. I would have had to build an intelligent system that could weather all of that just on the off chance it would be acceptable to a receptive female." She shook her head. "No. There was nothing. No one in *my* culture was interested and anyone *outside* wasn't listening." She raised her glass. "So I decided I would steal it."

"You can't steal a reproductive capability."

"A lot you know. You can steal a woman's ovum. Hell, you could drug her, hold her prisoner until she conceives and comes to term and then release her. It's happened. This should have been a lot easier. I just wanted the moral equivalent of a few eggs. It's no different than IVF. I just wouldn't return the result." Georgette looked crafty. "I made my plans with care. Planted secret observation posts all around Jupiter—very tricky stuff since any sort of launch is fairly obvious. At first, I thought I could just copy it. Figure out what it was and then duplicate it for myself—she'd never be the wiser." Georgette spun her finger next to her head. "But I couldn't image it clearly. An unexpected built-in limitation. Still, I knew where it was. Knew the shape of it. The heft. The size. The color—all of those things. I built this lovely little device and put it in a long orbit so its whole approach was in shadow. No more than a little rock knocked loose from a larger asteroid. Spurt a little microbe cloud ahead of it. Bacteria that would bore down through the ice and then dissolve into a paralytic virus that would stop replication in the benthic trophic level. A real threat but nothing she couldn't figure out fairly quickly. Then, while she was occupied, break-in right through the ice crust, ready to rumble. Steal a few and launch back out. I thought the hard part would be getting away with it—after all, it would be visible the whole way back."

Georgette put her martini down slowly. "I couldn't find it. I couldn't see it—*another* damned limitation. I kept looking. Meanwhile, she *didn't* figure the virus out quickly. It finished off her benthic system. When *that* went foul the scavengers couldn't keep up—and the virus was still there keeping the benthic level from recovering. Arthur kept sending her things to try but he was out of his depth. He'd never had to deal with this level of complexity. Once I realized what was going on I fired off a whole set of instructions on how to get rid of the virus—I mean codon sets, mutation traps, sequence models. She licked the virus but the benthic layer was toast and now a whole host of organisms, things like plants, like crabs, like insects, like squids, that had always preyed on the benthics, turned upstream to new prey which toppled one trophic layer after another. I'd had no idea she was so *fragile!* I mean that was barely a red tide bloom as far as I was concerned and she had way more volume than I had."

Georgette drained her third martini. She looked at the light on the glass. Then, she crushed it in her hand. Blood splashed across the tray, her white dress, the floor. The steward hurried over to her. "Give me a towel," she said.

"Would you like—"

"Just a towel."

She wrapped her hand in the towel. It started to soak through but she stared at her hand and it stopped.

Ian stared at her.

"She died." Georgette picked up the blood-soaked towel and stared at it for a moment. "Arthur was furious, of course. He dropped a rock on me." She looked at Ian. "Chicxlub killed everything or mostly everything. That was all right. I killed the rest. I was done with it."

"That's when they thought you were crazy?"

"No. That's when they decided I was vicious and untrustworthy. I'm filtered out. They won't speak to me." She glanced at Ian. "Desires don't go away just because they're frustrated. Just because they make you do bad things. Just because the bad things didn't get you what you want. No matter what happens you're still left with the urge."

She unwrapped her hand. The flow of blood had stopped but the hand was torn and broken. Ian could see bone and ruptured tendons. Georgette shook her hand and flaps of skin shook with it. She picked up her martini with her left hand and sipped it. "So I started over. Tried birds for a bit—you don't give up on a hundred and fifty million years of dinosaurs without a qualm. But the birds weren't going to give me what

I wanted. So I turned to mammals. I didn't have Europa's female principle and I didn't know how to make it. But I knew this biosphere inside and out. Every tree, bug, and mushroom. Every termite and lizard. If I couldn't reproduce the way I wanted, I'd reproduce the way I could."

Ian shivered. "You made us."

Georgette tried to point the finger of her ruined hand at him but it would only curl into a claw. "It took a *long* time to get it right. I mean, I had no idea what I was trying to do. No idea of what the final product would look like. No one did—none of us had ever tried it. We'd fought over the right to reproduce. We'd killed each other. Obliterated whole systems. But this? Never. Go figure."

Ian shook his head. "We would have thought of it instantly."

Georgette beamed at him. "Of course you would. You're wholly *mine*. Once I figured out what I wanted it still took millions of years and plenty of false starts. But now?" She held out her arms to him. "Just *look* at you." She wiped a tear from her eye with her injured hand and left a bright red streak on her cheek.

"That's when they thought you were crazy."

"Exactly." She drained her third martini and leaned towards him. "And you know?" she whispered. "As soon as they figured out what *I* was doing, *they* did it. Just for self-protection. Now they're *all* doing it. You guys are going to have *so* much company when you finally get out there." She leaned back.

"Why *me?*"

Georgette smiled at him gently. "Oh, Ian. You are the right person in the right time and in the right place. It could have been anybody but I'm glad it is you."

She stood up shakily. The steward appeared next to her and she handed him the glass. "Biological systems have their imperatives." She walked unsteadily to the lavatory and closed the door behind her.

The steward cleaned the blood off the tray, chair, and then the floor without a word. Holding bloody rags he smiled at Ian. "Another gin and tonic, sir?"

"Uh. Yeah."

Ian sat back in his chair. Who knew deities had backstories? Clay didn't just make up God's feet but everything else as well. He'd never look at Georgette the same way again.

Georgette didn't return after a few minutes. Ian got up to look in the lavatory.

It was empty. All that remained of Georgette was a bloody handprint on the sink.

oOo

Ian thought about Georgette and Percy the rest of the way to Mussoorie. As he considered her story he realized how completely bounded the story was. Who was the mysterious terraformer before Georgette? She'd given Mars a name but not Europa. Why? Why were Enceladus and the other enclosed ocean moons off-limits? Who was Percy in all this? Why Ian? None of those questions had been answered. He'd been so mesmerized by the story he'd barely managed any questions at all.

She was so *human*. No. Not *she*. *He*.

On the other hand, he thought, how else should Georgette have appeared? Ian did not know the inner workings of a terraformer but he'd been with Percy long enough and seen Georgette enough times to realize they were both far more intelligent than he was—than any human. And they both had intimate working knowledge of the human brain. How hard could it be for them to act human? Like Georgette said himself, the female body he saw was the *user interface*.

Strip out Georgette's humanity and what was left? A story of alien usurpation and failed reproduction. When male lions took over a pride they killed the cubs both to eliminate genetic rivals and to bring the females into estrus more quickly. What made that conflict and tragedy different from Macbeth? Consciousness and a reflection on one's actions?

Hyper intelligent beings that lived for millions of years. What were their motivations? Don't think of them as individuals—the human concept of an individual is finite in lifespan and wrapped up in family heritage.

Think of them as you would a *species*. What drives a species? Fulfill its niche and reproduce. Didn't that describe Georgette?

He could manifest consciousness as needed for his own purposes. For that matter, perhaps each terraformer had a consciousness of sorts but those were all expressions of a larger meta-consciousness. Or Georgette might not be conscious at all—just able to understand and simulate it. If an unconscious mechanism could perfectly understand and mimic conscious behavior, how would one ever know? What would "understand" even mean?

Ian had a vision of Georgette carefully constructing a simulated Ian. Poking here, prodding there, until he got the response she wanted. Trying out his machinations on the real thing using the UI and correcting the differences in the model. How long until model Ian and real-life Ian were indistinguishable? How many such models could he make? A thousand? A billion? All created within the framework of his own intelligence.

Was his story even true? Georgette could construct a story precisely designed to sway Ian towards some unknowable goal.

Percy had told Ian the original idea had been to use him as a control. Someone without a Georgette presence. A token to determine whether Georgette was acting in good faith. Now, it seemed Georgette and Percy were partners. Percy referred to herself as female. Was she? Reproduction drove Georgette. Did it drive Percy, too? When Percy had begun to collect people for Venus, she had intended to just copy the genetics and personalities of who she wanted. But Georgette had hinted at a coming catastrophe where most or all human beings would die. It had been Ian's idea to collect people whole. Georgette had liked the idea and Percy had been persuaded. Why had Georgette liked the idea? Ian had no idea.

It still seemed cruel to just steal them under the guise of natural catastrophe. Ian shepherded them as best he could. I must choose the good I can, expose the evil I know, and, ultimately, bear witness. For as many as I can.

oOo

The Jolly Grant Airport was small. Ian stepped off the plane onto bare tarmac. The air was dry and crisp after Kolkata and, as the airport was in a narrow valley, hee could look up into the foothills of the Himalayas.

The late sun gave every reflective surface a golden glitter and made the shadows stark. Ian could see snow falling up in the hills.

Jolly Grant had the same dark corners Ian knew from all other airports. Money changed hands and Ian was led through a door and to an automated private limousine.

It was about two hours to Mussoorie and he would need the time.

He opaqued the windows and made sure there were no operating cameras. He took off his clothes and shivered in the cool dry air.

In his briefcase were clothes, a printed picture of a narrow-faced, brown-skinned man with wide brown eyes, and below that a hand mirror.

Ian examined his image in the mirror critically, turning his face this way and that. He placed the mirror on the opposite seat and the picture next to it. Then, he closed his eyes and relaxed, slowed his breathing until he could feel a tingling in his fingertips.

He placed his hands on his cheeks and took a deep breath. With a grunt of effort, he pushed up his cheekbones, panting against the pain. Then pushed them in. The effect didn't take a lot of movement. He looked at the picture again and then pulled his chin out a few millimeters. Electric pain ran up and down his neck, scalp, and face. Nerves didn't like this sort of thing. Once he'd remodeled the underlying bone, he pushed the muscles and connective tissue into place.

When he had a fair approximation of the face, he relaxed and let the pain subside. The next part was trickier.

Again, he relaxed but this time he concentrated on his kneecap, rubbing it with his hands. The motion was purely a psychological means by which he could concentrate on that particular bit of skin. It turned brown under his hands and he moved up his thigh, rubbing it as if it were lotion. The brown spread. After a few moments it started to spread on its own and he quit and returned to the mirror. As his face darkened, Ian concentrated on his eyes, and they, too, gradually darkened.

He compared his face to the picture. It was close enough—after all, it was a picture of Ian when he'd been here last.

Ian donned the robe and wool jacket—as close to the clothes he'd left in as possible. He'd be forgiven for small changes. It had been two years, after all.

Over several minutes he fed the limo's shredder his clothes, his shoes and identification, and, finally, the baggage itself. All that remained was a biodegradable sludge somewhere below the car.

About fifteen kilometers outside of Mussoorie, the car pulled off the highway. Ian entered a code he should not have known and every trace of the trip was erased, along with any hidden surveillance camera recordings. The car paused a moment. Then, it closed its doors and turned back towards Dehradun.

Ian closed his eyes. Gradually, he slipped away and for a moment he was empty. He opened his eyes and looked on the mountains and earth, the road and grass, without knowing what they were. After a moment, he remembered his name: Devaj. Or at least what people called him.

It was quiet. A few birds sang in the cold. The wind was mild, but in this high place, it cut through his wool jacket. Devaj smiled. It carved away from him the illusions of the world.

It was right and proper he should walk from here.

oOo

The ashram had progressed nicely since Devaj had last seen it.

The buildings were low and shuttered against the cold but they had been painted a bright yellow limned with dark green. The effect made them glow against the backdrop of the mountains and gave a spring-like look contrasted against the dry, dormant grasses.

The track that led to the ashram had been graveled the previous fall and showed hard use. Devaj walked up the hill towards the main building. As he approached the decorated arch of the entrance the door slammed open and Raam ran out, down the steps, skidding to a stop before him. He bowed reverently. "You have come!"

Devaj intoned a quiet blessing over Raam, then said: "Of course."

"We looked for you on Basant Pachami."

Devaj laughed gently. He placed his hand on Raam's shoulder. "Did I say I would return at any appointed time?"

"No, Yogiji. But we hoped."

"Chains of iron and chains of gold. The chains of this world have no claim on you, Raam, but you are still held by the chains of devotion."

Raam nodded.

"Come, Raam," Devaj said. "Show me the wonders you have wrought."

Raam showed him the dormitories, the cafeteria, and the speaking hall. The ashram was crowded. Several rooms held devotees in deep discussion with their teachers regarding the roles of heaven, earth, and other such illusions.

It pleased Devaj that there were as many women as men, something he had pressed upon Raam when he had left. Some people fell to their knees and pressed their foreheads to the ground when they recognized Devaj. He gently drew them back to their feet. "That is not the way," he admonished them, and, with the help of Raam, he addressed them by name: Toti, Shuka, Robert, Francois, Mohammed. Afterward, they smiled shyly and bowed: "Yes, Yogiji."

Raam and Devaj stopped in the great hall at the center of the compound. "This is well accomplished," Devaj said. "The teachings I heard are without deviation from what I spoke."

"Thank you, Yogiji."

Devaj smiled at him. "Of course, we must endeavor to avoid rote. So perhaps allowing some small divergences could be beneficial."

"I will introduce deviations."

Devaj laughed. "How many are we?" he asked.

"One thousand two hundred and four."

"A good number." Devaj looked about the hall. It was a large circular space, the dome of the roof supported by eight columns. The altar was opposite the entering door but the space was so arranged that a dais could be placed in the center. "Can they all fit in here?"

"Yes, Yogiji."

Devaj looked around the room critically. This would do. "Bring them here this evening after devotionals. Tomorrow morning, just before sunrise, we will proceed up to the cave for prayer and meditation. They will need proper clothing and shoes."

"Yogiji?" Raam hesitated. "That is very little time to prepare twelve hundred for rigorous travel."

"It is a rough trail but it is not that far." Devaj turned to Raam. "You have done well with me all this time. Stay with me a little further. I will tell them this evening what they must do and how they must help each other on the short but difficult journey. You must make sure they will succeed. We must all be at the cave no more than an hour after sunrise."

"Why, Yogiji?"

Devaj smiled at him. "Many virtues are rewarded by patience but some are achieved by proper timing. There is a cache of material you might find useful in the old barn originally on this property."

That evening, as Raam gathered hundreds of sturdy shoes and jackets, found or made prayer mats, and discovered much of what he needed in sealed drums under the hay in the barn, Devaj spoke quietly to his followers. This world is always to be rejected but the intricacies of its illusions must be respected. After all, the illusion of the world presents the mechanisms by which its rejection can be realized: meditation, compassion, fasting. All things in this world are illusions, even the mechanisms of salvation. But within these important illusions are the means by which illusion itself is suspended and dispelled.

Therefore, in the morning, we will dispel the illusion of permanence by meditating in the shadow of the mountains. We will dispel the illusion of our bodies by withstanding the hard terrain between here and the meditating caves. We will dispel the illusion of time by leaving before daybreak and maintaining a good and even pace, greeting the rising sun. And we will embrace the illusion of compassion, which reflects the compassion that is beyond illusion, by helping each other reach our destination whole and intact.

Twenty years earlier an earthquake had split the earth and exposed a deep cavern a few kilometers away. It had been claimed and counterclaimed by tourist commissions, university geologists, and public safety officials. The claims canceled each other out, leaving the cavern unused, unoccupied and unadorned save for the heavy fence surrounding its mouth.

It was to this cave that Devaj led his followers, carefully picking their way around the boulders and slippery gravel of past landslides. He led the way up the final incline to the gate. The lock seemed to be solid but fell apart into rust at his touch.

The cave was perhaps forty meters broad and ten meters tall. It thinned slowly to a narrow opening in the back no taller or wider than a man.

Devaj and Raam arranged the followers so they were all completely beneath the overhang. The sun cracked over the eastern edge of the valley just as Devaj was settling himself on the dais Raam had insisted be brought.

Devaj spoke for perhaps half an hour in a gentle hypnotic tone. He reiterated the theme of this world's illusion, drawing them into a proper state of mind to begin meditation. Then, they began speaking the word he had given them: a long, sonorous and meaningless sound. The syllables themselves were lost in the chorus and only the deep sound of one voice could be heard.

His congregation was so enraptured they did not at first notice the tremors. Many never did, protected in *yoga nidra.* Devaj was pleased that there were only a few cries as the rumbling grew louder. Most had reached the point in their meditation that such things triggered not fear but increased concentration.

The shock hurled them deeper under the overhang and it seemed they were rolling and tumbling over each other for minutes. Devaj heard screams and a sound like breaking glass that he couldn't place. Then all sound stopped for a brief moment like paused breath. Then a different rumble, throaty and harsh, grew around them.

The landslide covered the overhang, cutting off light and air, Devaj heard a few protests through the choking dust. Who was alive? Who was conscious? Then, he smelled something sweet and felt himself slide deeply towards a wonderfully bright light as if swimming down through a pool of clear, cool water to reach a star. As he fell unconscious he thought: hadn't he been someone named Ian Bones?

Chapter 1.5: Chitra

Chitra found her grandfather standing outside the house sipping a cup of coffee.

"I was worried," Nirad said.

"I understand." Chitra stood next to him. Tendrils of early morning fog wrapped the grapes, the fence, drifted delicately over the road. "I've dealt with worse for work."

Nirad nodded. "Refugee work. I remember."

"Often with the dead."

Nirad sighed. "I know." He sipped his coffee.

They stood watching the fog seem to play here and there across the vineyard.

"Tapas has stage four pancreatic cancer," Chitra said suddenly. "I thought you should know."

Nirad was raising his mug to his lips. He stopped and brought it down. "I see." He seemed stiff, now. Unbent but suddenly old. "I'm sorry you were put in the position to tell me."

"I'm not sorry." Chitra looked up at him. "What happened between you and Fani?"

Nirad drained his mug and poured the dregs on the ground. "When Risu fell sick Fani took over the business. Distilling the cholai had been my job. In return, Risu had given me help for the vineyard. When Fani took over he stopped any help to me. All I had were these." He spread his hands to show the vineyard. "It wasn't enough. It would never be enough—I found that out very quickly. I had three growing sons and Mithu. Fani and Omrita had a daughter, Ina. Risu secretly helped me build a competing distillery. It was the bitter war of the cholai makers for ten years. Then, the Nepal measles epidemic struck Kolkata. Vaccinations didn't help much. People died in the streets. Risu lived but his wife Sia died. Ekanath lived but his wife Lamisa never really recovered. She died giving birth to Kapi. My youngest son, Nail, died. We almost lost Tapas—he was sixteen and *so* sick. Ina died. There was no point in the war anymore. Risu still had controlling interest in Majhi. He and Ekanath decided to bring the two companies back together. Fani and I would run things. Fani wouldn't have it. He made life miserable for everyone. Tapas left as soon as he graduated college and Ekanath said he would have nothing to do with it. Ever. I blamed Fani for it. Risu and I forced him out of the company completely. We gave the business to Bhim and later brought in Rohak when Tiya married. The only thing Fani has left is that apartment." Nirad handed the grapes back to her. "You see? It has *nothing* to do with you. It was finished years ago."

"Tapas didn't leave because of Fani."

"I know that, now." Nirad sighed. "I knew that, then. But I didn't want to admit it."

"Does Fani know?"

"Know what?"

"Does he know you forgave him?"

Nirad shrugged. "We do not speak. He lives up there. I live down here."

"You must tell him."

"You see? You are here a day and meddling in these things. You are just like your mother."

"What?"

"She wouldn't let things lie between Tapas and me, either. For years she called me. I would not speak with her. She called Bhim. She called Tiya—chattering like a magpie. Telling me how Tapas was doing this and Peter was doing that and what a smart child you were turning into. Finally, Tapas and I started talking just to keep her quiet."

Chitra laughed. She took his arm. After a moment, Nirad took her hand and they stood as the fog burned away in the sunlight.

"I have decided to name the grape variety *Fani*, after him," he said. "Will that satisfy you?"

"Only if you tell him why."

Nirad waved her away. "I'll tell him. Let's go back inside. I need a strong breakfast before we go up to the company. Facing Fani takes fortitude."

oOo

The day after the reconciliation party, Chitra's phone gave a deep chime. She started to sit up and thought better of it. Cholai gave a worse hangover than tequila. What would she find if she ran a sample through a gas chromatograph? Did she want to know?

She pulled the phone over her ear and tapped her fingers to get the image. An earthquake and landslide in Mussoorie. Chitra sat up, ignoring the sudden headache. She remembered Ian and rummaged around in her purse to find his card. She tapped it against her ear and his contact information showed when she brought up her palm. "Call him," she said.

The number blinked as her phone failed to make a live connection and then put up the question icon to see if she wanted to leave a message.

"No," she said. "Find the unit."

The icon switched to locating: *not found.*

This could be explained by any number of reasons: he could have switched his phone to unlocatable. He could have turned it off. Chitra doubted he had moved out of network. There were still places in India where the ground network didn't reach, but satellites saw everything and Ian could afford a phone with satellite capabilities.

She looked at the card. Name, number, address.

"Locate the number." Maybe she could localize the exchange.

The text next to the number said: unlocalized.

"Locate Ian Bones associated with that number."

Same answer.

"Locate Ian Bones associated with that address."

Same answer.

The number didn't even really have to be a direct phone, anyway. It could just be a service. For that matter, none of the data on the card need be real. For all she knew, Ian had never gone to Mussoorie at all. They'd only known each other a few hours. Why should he trust her with his business?

"Call Tsuba," she said. She'd never forgive herself if she didn't try to find him.

oOo

Chitra caught a C-130 leaving for an airstrip being built at the landslide site as they took off. She had no official standing whatsoever, only an ambiguous set of papers suggesting she might be of assistance. Tsuba had given her two contacts, Tej Singh and Oni Majumdar, and listed her as a technical expert on field resuscitation. Crap. That meant popcopters. She was going to be busy.

Mussoorie and its neighboring towns lay next to one another on the top of the ridge like a set of toddler snap beads. As the C-130 circled the fresh pink strip Chitra could see how much of the town was flattened. She checked her phone for data. Richter six? Seven?

The southern edge of the ridge had calved right down into the adjacent valleys. Mussoorie might be in bad shape but towns below it were covered in rock, trees, and dirt.

Singh met her as she left the plane. He gave her a coverall, eye protection, resuscitation kit, and transponder. She heard a beep from her phone as it synched to the kit's electronics. Fifteen minutes later she was geared up and waiting as a popcopter shot overhead and then hovered as it dropped a harness.

She strapped it on and signaled ready.

The popcopter drew her up to within a couple of meters of the blades and then rose.

Popcopters were intended to deliver individuals and urgent supplies quickly over just a few kilometers. Its automation would not allow the cargo to strike the ground, buildings, cliff faces, or itself but they were not meant for comfort.

The popcopter delivered her to a team excavating a school. "Over here," a man called to her.

Chitra scrambled over broken masonry and a wall. It was a girl, unmoving. Chitra checked her carotid pulse. Nothing. She pulled out a stethoscope and listened—the heartbeat was there but fast and thready. Her skin was cold and her breathing shallow. Even without a scan, Chitra could see a broken fibula and radius.

Biox wouldn't work here—it increased the fluid saturation of oxygen all right. But biox only worked when there was at least an initial reliable heartbeat and no circulatory damage. This girl was in shock. If there was internal bleeding she'd have a well-oxygenated pool of internal fluid. She needed active intervention.

Chitra rummaged in the kit and found five packs of oxytenin: active particles the size of paramecium. They'd move towards high concentrations of CO2 and low concentrations of oxygen. Then, they'd linger, cracking CO2, holding their weight in carbon, and releasing the oxygen back into the fluid. Eventually, they would be filtered out—through her kidneys, if possible, through some other mechanism if not. That was a problem for later. Oxygen deprivation couldn't wait. She set up an IV of saline and anti-fibrillators. As it dripped into the girl's arm, she attached the oxytenin to the tube.

She bundled the broken limbs in stabilizing wraps and pulled the string to stiffen them. Now, she was able to wrap the girl in a transport robe. IV drained, she pulled the needle, opened the girl's shirt, and wrote on her chest what she'd done. Then, she drew the robe closed and stiffened that as well. She punched in the codes and the robe whirred.

Chitra tested the airflow: warm. The girl's temperature would drop ten degrees in just a few minutes.

She erected the robe's skyhook and punched the emergency transport button.

"Over here," she heard. Four men were bringing out another broken child.

Chitra motioned them towards her.

Above her, a popcopter came down and grabbed the girl's skyhook. Chitra confirmed the settings and a moment later, the popcopter rose gently and carried the girl away.

Chitra turned as the men set down another student. A boy, by the uniform pants. There was no other way to know.

She knelt next to him to take his pulse.

oOo

There was a lull in the evening. By this time, forty-six had been excavated. Twenty-six were beyond help. Eight had been popcoptered out and the remaining twelve were lying in a warm corner of the ruin, conscious but feeling no pain. Chitra was bone weary. She sat next to the last one and checked statistics, looking for Ian. Several possibilities met her search criteria: eighteen dead, nine critical, and six treated and released to a waiting area.

Singh called her. "Ready for relief?"

"So soon?"

"It's been twelve hours. I spoke with the team leader. He doesn't think there are any left alive at this point. We can rush a specialist or a doctor over there if someone is found. Go get some dinner."

The popcopter left her near the relief tent. Chitra thought she might be too tired to make it the last hundred meters but the sudden smell of food kept her stumbling over. Someone gave her a cup and bowl. She made her way to a long table and sat down, staring at their foil top. After a moment, she remembered to peel the foil off the cup and put it down on the table. There was a plastic spoon attached to the top of the bowl. Chitra pulled it off and then pulled the foil off the bowl: curry.

The cup of tea was already hot and she sipped it as the curry heated. *Yes: proper fluid and electrolytes.* It was warm food and drink and a moment later she was staring dully into an empty cup and bowl.

Okay, she said to herself.

"Chitra?" she heard a voice.

She turned and looked up at Ian.

Ian looked concerned. "Do you want some more?"

He was right *there*. Standing over her.

She dropped the bowl and cup and hugged his hips, head against his belly. Chitra began to cry.

Ian sat next to her and folded her in his arms, making unintelligible, comforting sounds. Chitra didn't care what he was saying. It was enough he was there. Alive. Unhurt. He didn't have tubes going in and out of him, unconscious and bleeding on a piece of flat dirt.

He said something.

She leaned back. "What?"

"I said are you still hungry?"

Chitra giggled. "No. Thirsty, though. Can I get some water?"

Ian disengaged himself from her. He took her cup and bowl and brought her back a bottle of water. "Are you okay?"

"Yes." She took the bottle and drank it. After the salty curry, it tasted bland, tepid, and delicious. "I'm just very, very tired." She took his hands.

"You came looking for me."

"Yes."

"Why?"

"Somebody had to." She didn't say anything for a moment. "What happened?" *How are you still alive?*

Ian shrugged. "The earthquake hit while I was standing outside in the mall. The ridge Mussoorie's built on cracked and half of it rolled down into the valley. Not my half, fortunately. I've been digging with everybody else."

Most would have left as quickly as possible. It wasn't his country. They weren't his people. It wasn't his job. He had stayed to help. Chitra hugged him. Her reasons to come here after had been half-formed. They crystallized as she nestled her cheek against his shirt. "I like you, Ian Dunes. I really like you."

Ian returned her hug. "I like you, too."

oOo

Had Chitra been home in New York, she would have taken Ian to her apartment and proceeded to the next phase of an impending relationship. But there is always a shortage of showers and clean water at disaster sites. The daily grind of working amidst rotting debris, dead bodies, and leaky human beings made all affection necessarily platonic. Not that Chitra didn't want to convert from the ideal to the real at any given moment. She suffered from the lack of appropriate services and location.

Ian seemed comfortable with things for the moment—a fact that she found soothing and irritating at the same time. Chitra was frustrated solely by issues of mechanics. Why wasn't *he?*

But meeting him for breakfast and finding him waiting for her at night, sitting next to her when she was undoubtedly stinking of urine and sputum, comforting her in depression and fatigue, made up for it. There were little things he seemed to do unconsciously. The ground was uneven, covered in broken brick and tile. In the fatigue and the dark at the end of the day, she often stumbled outside the mess tent. He was always right there with his hand out. After the second time, she realized that he placed himself where she could reach him. He didn't make a big deal of it—just held out a hand for her to take or not take. The third time it happened, the next morning someone had cleared the debris. It was two days before she found out Ian had done it.

It was kindness, she thought. He liked being kind.

oOo

Things were winding down by the end of the week. Technology began to subsume human effort. As in Contai, there was a shift from the living to the dead. Chitra was just as ready to leave. Handling the dead was not a problem, but if she was going to do that, she wanted to do it as part of her team.

"Come home with me," she said the night before she was scheduled to leave.

"To New York?"

"Yes."

"Don't you have to go to work?"

"What do you think *this* is?"

"Vacation, I suppose."

She hit him on the shoulder. "My team should be returning from leave next week. We'll have to regroup. The equipment's been transported to New Jersey and cleaned up since Contai but we have to check it out and recalibrate it."

"Everything is in New Jersey."

"Of course." She looked at him. "So: will you come with me to New York?"

He faced her in return. "I can't stay there. My business requires travel."

She searched his face for a long minute. "You're dabbling."

"Everybody has to have a hobby."

"Is it in New Jersey?"

His face took on a serious cast. "Everything is in—"

"—New Jersey. And you haven't answered my question."

He watched her for a moment. "I can come to New York. But I have to leave by the end of the month."

"But you'll come back after that?"

"If you want me to. After two weeks you may not be able to stand the sight of me."

"I can't stand the sight—or the smell—of you now."

"Be a pretty short relationship then."

She almost continued the banter but stopped. "All right. I'm catching a C-130 tomorrow morning to Cairo where I am going to buy an expensive hotel room and take sandpaper to the filth that has become one with my skin. I may well shave my head if that's what it takes to get clean. From there, I'll catch a plane to New York. That's a start."

He shook his head. "I'll meet you in New York, shaven or not. I have some business to attend to in Andaman. I'll come to New York after that."

Chitra was startled. "That's the source of the landslide for the Contai tsunami. Why are you going there?"

Ian looked embarrassed. "Well, there was a new resort being sited there. A real indigenous people sort of thing. Backed by Europeans but offering jobs and a percentage of the take to the Andamans. Sort of like Native American casinos. The earthquake that started the slide didn't hurt the islands much, but my clients won't be satisfied until I've checked it out myself. Silly, really."

"When will you get to New York?"

"Tomorrow's Wednesday. I'll be in New York Monday. Will that be soon enough?"

She kissed him, forgetting the smell and the dirt. "No."

"Sunday night, then. Will that do?"

"Not even close."

"You'll manage."

"I'll come with you to Andaman. They have hotels, don't they?"

Ian watched her for a long time. "I'm sorely tempted. But no. I'll be done much more quickly if I'm by myself."

"Then give it up," she said, smiling at him. "It's dabbling. You said so yourself. Give it up and live on your dividends."

He gave her such a sad look that she wanted to hug him. "I wish I could, Chitra."

Why should he look that sad? What if he hadn't told her the truth? What if it were something truly terrible? Something that required atonement like working in refugee camps or disaster recovery. She leaned back from him.

He noticed her movement. "I won't be in Andaman long."

"I don't like mystery. I meet a lot of sketchy people in my work. People who weren't what they seem. People like arms merchants and child traffickers."

"And you're wondering if I'm hiding something like that. I'm no arms merchant or child trafficker." He shook his head. "It's an underwater excavation project."

She relaxed and smiled. "Throw me a bone. Maybe you're a secret agent?"

"I'll become one if it will make you happy." He took her hands. "I'll be in New York on Sunday night."

oOo

Chitra flew to Cairo and booked a room at the Cairo Marriot, courtesy of her previously unexploited UNERA expense account, and spent an hour in the bath. She had a change of clothes in her bag but used them merely to wear while she bought new pants and shirts in the Zamalek district. When she returned, she threw the old clothes out representing weeks of accumulated and symbolic dirt. Then, she took another bath and lay in the hot water with her eyes closed, resolutely pushing away any residual guilt for the fact she could wash away disasters and the victims could not.

Presently, she found herself dwelling on Ian, the feel of his hands and his lips and the imagined feel of his hips and back. *Don't raise your expectations too much,* she warned herself. Fast fires can burn down to quick ash.

He might not come at all. *Don't lower your expectations that much.*

One day later, she found herself hurrying up the steps outside her New York apartment, then inside stairs, and finally, fumbling with her keys. Once inside, she exhaled slowly and felt her back gradually unknot. She was *home.*

It was not a large apartment. Two bedrooms, one turned into her office. Kitchen open to the living room. Table next to the front window. It even had sunlight sometimes. On a good day, she could see the edge of Central Park. If she leaned her head against the glass and squinted.

No plants—she wasn't home enough. A twenty-gallon automated fish tank with a single large angelfish named Maria and some unnamed tetras to keep her company. The place was spotless. The cleaning service had done its job.

First things first: she took her phone out of her ear and plugged it into its cradle. The LED on the cradle turned green as the phone took over the apartment's automation.

She waved to Maria and took her bags to the bedroom to unpack.

"Freder has a call waiting request for you," said the apartment.

She considered but she was exhausted. "Set up a connection for tomorrow. No earlier than nine."

oOo

One good night's sleep, a bagel, and three cups of coffee later, Freder's voice entered the room.

"Chitra?"

"Yeah." Chitra went into her office and pointed to the picture of her brother over the bookshelf. Freder's face replaced it.

"Ah, you're home," he said. "That's the only time I ever get visual from you."

"Hey, it's an earworm. What do you want?"

"Software that represents your face so I can see you when you're talking."

Chitra waved him away. "Did you take a break?"

"Two weeks watching the last of the ice falls in Greenland and wondering when they'll have to raise the dikes again on the East River. Who knew Climate Change Tourism would ever be a thing? Plus the mandatory post-station counseling."

"Sounds nice."

Freder scrutinized her. "Something happened. Your family has arranged marriage and you've succumbed to their cultural embrace."

"No. I met someone. I'm not telling anybody until I know how things work out."

"You just told *me*."

"You asked."

"True." Freder gave a theatrical sigh. "Who is this paragon of virtue and manliness—he *is* a man, right? You didn't change orientation behind my back, did you?"

Chitra grinned at him. "*His* name is Ian Bones."

"Not that it makes any difference," Freder said somberly. "The heart wants what it wants."

"True enough." Chitra gave him a critical look. "I think you'll like him."

"No," said Freder, holding up his hands. "Just *no!* You don't get to introduce your lover wannabe to the team until we can be sure you're not going to use him up and spit him out. I mean, just when we get attached you'll toss him aside like dirt and we have to get all used to you being morose and single again."

"I'm not morose when I'm single."

"Sad," said Freder. "So out of touch with herself. Sad. Where is he now?"

"Port Blair on business. He's getting in tomorrow night."

"Do you want a last night of debauchery and sin before you're lost forever?"

"One more night to sleep and rest before Monday."

Freder lifted an eyebrow. "Another night? Are you sure he's worth it?"

"*Monday*. At the warehouse. Going over the equipment from Contai. Nine sharp. I don't have to see the counselor until the afternoon so I won't be mellow."

Freder groaned just as she cut him off.

She puttered around the apartment until she forced herself out to do some shopping. *What if he doesn't show?* Come on, Chitra. You're thirty-five. Getting bent on whether he's going to call or not is *so* twenty-nine.

After she returned to the apartment and put away the food she gave up and went to her office to write up her reports.

Sometime later, she leaned back in her chair and checked the clock. Six PM.

It was officially evening. Her Ian Bones clock started ticking.

At 6:30 she got a message: *Approach @ JFK.*

7:02, *Leaving JFK.*

7:30, *Outside your door.*

She ran to the door and opened it. Ian was standing there, bag in hand.

Chitra grabbed him and pulled him inside. She reached up and pulled his head down to kiss him. Right then she didn't want to let him go. Ever.

Chapter 1.6: Ian

It wasn't that long a flight between Kolkata and Port Blair, but it was long enough for Ian to stew over Chitra.

He half expected Georgette or Percy to sit next to him on the flight but there was no one there but himself.

It wasn't Percy's timetable that bothered him—though that was bothersome enough. If all went according to plan, Ian would be gone by the end of the year. Just long enough to indulge himself with Chitra and break her heart. Or, he admitted, have her break his. The laws of symmetry must be observed.

Maybe Chitra was slated to be included in Percy's cohort. Ian's face turned grim. Over the years, Ian had developed a sort of sixth sense about who would be taken and who would not. After all, even these lambs he led to the slaughter were not completely homogenous. There were bound to be people attracted to said lamb, attracted to someone in the group, in the wrong place at the wrong time, that got swept up in the event. They wouldn't be collected, of course. Their rotting, broken bodies would remain in place as their wives or children, or relatives were swept away to join Percy's Involuntary Venusian Settlement Corps. Chitra didn't feel like a candidate.

Ian shook his head. Only the knowledge that Georgette was going to cause all this—and worse—*anyway* made it the least bit palatable. At least he was saving *somebody*.

Have fun while you can, then? Dance until the hammer drops? *Indulge* yourself with Chitra knowing she's going to be dead or worse?

Make peace with it one way or the other, he told himself savagely. Keep her or let her go. Shit or get off the pot.

Then, the plane was down at Port Blair and he was walking out into the hot sun, no decision or answer to be had at any price.

oOo

Saw Pamway was waiting for him at the edge of the tarmac. A cigarette dangling from his lips, Saw sat in an ancient jeep that probably still burned petrol, Thick, black, muscular hands on the wheel, light blouse framing his heavy shoulders, a facial expression that ranged between indifference and burning rage. Ian found Saw just a little intimidating. Saw did not care that Ian was rich. He did not care that Ian was white. The Andaman islands had been inhabited for thousands of years. Saw drew a harsh resilience from that.

Ian slid onto the seat just as Saw let out the clutch. Ian had to scramble to hold onto the seat and keep from being thrown from the jeep.

Saw gave him a quick look and laughed.

Ian ignored it. "How did the islands handle the earthquake?"

Saw flicked his hand with contempt. "Nothing. Not even a six as far as we were concerned. Knocked down a couple of houses." He grinned. "Caught the Provincial Governor in his bath. He fell and cracked his elbow." Saw slapped the wheel. "Good times."

"Underwater gear?"

"Got it all. Just like you said. Just like every time you come here. Every time you have to ask."

Ian nodded and watched the tropical forest pass him by. He loved this place second only to Sequoia. It was like a tropical snow globe: enclosed and perfect. It wasn't, of course. It had hardships, tribal disparities, and ecological disasters like everywhere else. The rising seas had cut the habitable island surface in half and forced groups with a healthy dislike for one another into face-to-face confrontation.

"When's the big one coming?" Saw asked suddenly.

"What are you talking about?"

Saw glanced at him and returned his attention to the road. "You come here every couple of years and dive in the same spots but you get no joy from it. This isn't something you do for fun. I figure at first you're looking for signs of oil or gas. I even let it slip to a Petrobangla executive I know and he laughed at me. Nothing under the water but ancient mountains. Something else, I tell myself. Something important. You are fulfilling some duty. Anyone as rich as you are who does this without joy must have a purpose. I will watch you and find out what it is. I will make my family and people rich."

Saw glanced at Ian. "Then, a few weeks ago, you come here and spend not one dive or two, but thirty over three days. Diving here. Diving there. All with purpose. All planned carefully. All taking notes. Ah, I tell myself. At last, I will find out what is going on." Saw slapped the wheel. "But I can tell *nothing*. There is no reason, no pattern, to your dives. After you leave, I dive in the same spots and find, again, nothing." Saw fell silent for a moment. "Then, a few days later a small quake happens. A little thing. Something for children to enjoy running across the playground. And a great slab of stone falls underwater. An hour and a half later, a million people are dead across the bay."

They turned off the main road towards the water. Ian watched Saw as he drove in silence through a thicket of small streets to the pier.

"It is clear that Paluga favors you." Saw shook his head and sighed. "Why he favors a white man is beyond me—but then, that has been happening for a long time and is nothing new. You are paving the way for destruction. This is also clear." Saw turned and faced Ian directly, fixing him with his gaze as if with a knife. "So, I ask again. When is the big one coming?"

"Soon," said Ian automatically.

"Will we have anything left?"

Ian shrugged. "Probably not much."

Saw turned and watched the sea. He leaned his elbows on the wheel. "You work for a higher power. I can't kill you. It wouldn't stop anything and going against Paluga is always dangerous. Will my people survive?"

"Some, I think."

"There is a consolation that as bad we have seen, your people will see worse."

"Everybody is going suffer equally, I think."

Saw grinned at him. "But there are so many more of you than us." He slapped Ian on the shoulder. "Take heart. Paluga is responsible for all things. It's not your fault." Saw gripped his shoulder hard. "At least, not completely."

oOo

Saw was looking down the boat's ladder as Ian broke water over the last site. Once he had taken off his gear and dried his hands, Ian made careful notes: the size and shapes of certain corals, patterns of growth, incidence of fish species at particular depths. Many of the signs had changed in dramatic and unexpected ways. Ian had no idea what they meant.

"What is the answer, kemo sabi?"

Ian looked sharply up at him.

Saw grinned. "What? You don't have *The Lone Ranger* in America? It means 'crazy white guy.'"

Ian closed his notebook with a snap. "Let's go back."

Half a day later, Saw pulled the jeep up to the terminal.

Ian reached over and grabbed the wheel.

Saw looked at him.

Ian looked out to sea and then back to him. "You're thinking of leaving the islands, aren't you?"

Saw snorted. "No great act of divination there."

"If you stay, I think you and your family might be preserved, but maybe not together. If you leave, go as far from the sea as you can and then go farther. Farther than you think you need to. You should get some time."

"Not together. What's the point of that?" Saw turned and watched the tarmac for a long time. "Ah, well. I don't think I can get my mother to leave without explosives. And my little girl won't leave without her." He turned to Ian and held out his hand. "Go with God," said Saw.

Ian shook it. "You mean Paluga?"

"It is all the same."

oOo

Andaman to Kolkata to Delhi to get the direct hypersonic flight to New York.

He brooded over Chitra the whole way.

But even Ian couldn't remain entirely self-involved on the trip from Delhi. He liked hypersonic flights. The accouterments of air travel still reflected an esthetic derived from the twentieth-century ocean liners. First adapted in the thirties, revamped in the fifties, and then revisited every decade or so from then on just to keep in fashion, it remained the same: chairs as close together as possible. First class versus other classes based on the ability to pay. However, the economy of scale never really worked in the air. In the days of ships, once size passed a certain point the incremental price of adding luxury didn't significantly affect the cost. You could have billiard tables, ball rooms, and swimming pools. Air travel still couldn't manage a real kitchen serving real food, first-class or otherwise.

But the hypersonic flights were just fun. First, there was normal flight up to about fifteen thousand meters. Then, somewhere over the Arabian Sea, there was a bump followed by a sort of glassy smoothness as the plane went supersonic. A little after that, the announcement came for everybody to fasten their straps. There was a sudden heaviness as the scramjet kicked in and the nose tipped up.

Every seat had a window—at these prices, it would be expected. The sky went from blue to black and the stars began to show. The curvature of the Earth was visible, heartbreakingly perfect, and without flaw. Ian always wondered what it was like to see the world like this for the first time. Without preconceptions. Without having the image embedded in the social consciousness. He took a picture and sent it to Pauline. It was nothing compared to what she had seen, but it showed he'd seen *something*.

From then on, the plane skipped up and down, in and out of the atmosphere. Up into dead silence. A gradually returning whistle. A vibration throughout the plane. A bump. A return to silence.

They were hypersonic for maybe forty minutes. Ian was already checking his straps when the sign came on. This was always the rough part. The plane was a glider at the moment and it dipped and tilted to get just the right angle of attack. A quick red glow showed outside the window as they slowed from hypersonic to mere supersonic and finally, subsonic flight when the engines restarted. By the time the United States was visible, they were cruising at a leisurely few hundred kilometers an hour.

Ian walked through the VIP customs corridor where he was scrutinized by high-energy photons, high-frequency sound waves, and high-fidelity chemical sniffers without breaking his stride.

The fun of hypersonic flight had briefly distracted him from thinking about Chitra.

As he got into his limo, Percy slipped in with him.

A young black man with hair cut at a sharp angle and mismatched blue and green eyes. The hair relaxed and stretched in its own rhythm so the slice gradually rotated around. The hair was green on the left side, shifting to blue on the right side. "Evening, Ian." He grinned.

"Percy."

"You have data for me."

"Why don't you just read my mind?"

"That's not part of the deal."

"Right." Ian pulled out his notebook and read off figures. He stopped for a moment. "What does a dorado fish count have to do with anything?"

"Indicates a pH change and an increase in dissolved methane. Dorado are sensitive to it."

"That tells me something?"

"It tells you everything is going according to plan."

"I heard you think I've lost my nerve?"

Percy watched him a moment. "Is that how she phrased it?"

"Yes."

"Georgette's manipulating you again. I suggested you were distracted. Not unnerved."

"Maybe she's right." Ian watched as they drove across the protected marshes. "Maybe I'm having second thoughts."

"About what? Witnessing? Saving people instead of neural patterns and genotypes? That was your idea. Venus itself?"

"What the hell do you need us for, anyway? Can't you automate all of Venus yourself?"

"I need humans for integrative ecology," Percy said instantly. "Sophisticated broad-spectrum monitoring. Cross trophic level control."

"Georgette is all through this planet. Won't you be, too?"

"Not as well as she is. Remember, she had millions of years and millions of failures to get where she is now. We don't have that luxury. We have a short timetable and a lot to do. It's going to be a botched job any way you look at it. I'm going to need smart organisms like you that can adapt. I can monitor your adaptation and determine what's going on. You'll challenge me and I'll adapt, too. Maybe *eventually* I'll be able to do everything myself but then I'll be in you, too. Just like she is."

"Yeah." The thought was not comforting.

"What else is on your mind?"

"Is Chitra on the list?"

"No. No one in her family has what I need."

"Maybe you should recheck your list."

Percy tilted his head. "This was all your idea, Ian," he said quietly. "We can bail right now. I've got half of what I need but I can change methodologies and just copy the remainder. They'll never know the difference."

Ian bit at his thumb. *But I would.* He looked at Percy. Tried to see the alien below the young man's face. The *user* interface. There was an urgency mixed with calm below the surface but that could have just been someone who knew himself well. "Why the hell did you do this?"

"You asked me. Remember?"

"What makes me so damned special that you'd do it for me?"

"Like I've said before." Percy regarded him. "You're important to me."

"Why?"

"The original reason still obtains. You're an untainted negotiating mechanism with Georgette."

"This is too much effort for that."

"It is." Percy watched him for a moment. "You're my example model of human compassion."

"I don't get it."

Percy leaned forward. "Compassion is a foreign concept for creatures like me and Georgette. You can see how that would interfere with what we have to do, right? Georgette's been writing off whole species when they don't measure up to her standards. You can't do that if you empathize with them. Any animal that rears its young will develop something like affection. What crocodiles feel for their tiny hatchlings is related to what pigeons feel for nestlings. Foxes care for their kits. Humans love their children. That's emotional self interest, not compassion. Though like everything else in that jumbled brain of yours, it's all connected. *Compassion* is the emotion one feels when *others* suffer. Humans have managed to extend the concept beyond their own species to all sorts of things: animals, trees, ecosystems, logical fallacies, fictional constructs. 'To look with compassion, to decide with compassion, to kill with compassion.' The original quote uses the term 'mercy' but it's clear compassion is a better fit. *Ahimsa.* Allah/Buddha/Jesus/Yahweh, the Compassionate." Percy nodded at Ian. "And you fail at it often enough."

"You want to be… compassionate?"

Percy shook his head. "Of course not. Not in the way you mean. What are we going to do if we suffer along with every creature we create or influence? No. Our emotional states aren't congruent with yours—they *can't* be. We're too different. Humans reflect a piece of Georgette since she made you, but the remainder is your own. We have our own emotions. If there is an analog to compassion for something like me, it wouldn't bear much resemblance to what you feel." Percy stopped for a moment. "Still, we're all dealing with thinking creatures now. This is a new thing in our history. I think a full understanding of compassion might go a long way in helping me manage you." She gave Ian a crooked grin. "After all, dictators have done horrible things to you people and been forgiven for just pretending to be compassionate. Imagine if someone were to handle you with the real thing."

The limo stopped downtown.

"This is my stop," said Percy. He started to open the door.

"Wait!" Ian grabbed his arm. "What should I do with Chitra?"

Percy gave him a long look. "You know her chances. Make her happy."

Okay, Ian thought to himself. *I'll do my best.*

oOo

Afterward, she lay heavily on top of him, her lips next to his collarbone. He could feel her breath, in and out.

He was surprised at the weight of her. The relaxed heft. She was slight and terribly small but that belied a wonderful solidity.

She started to gently snore.

He laughed gently to keep from disturbing her. Heavy as she was, he found the weight pleasant. As he breathed, he lifted her. She fell slowly when he exhaled. He liked that.

After a moment, she rolled off and snuggled her back to him. He turned to meet her. She muttered something in her sleep and pulled his arm over her, muttered again, and resumed snoring.

Ian decided that, though he didn't sleep much, he could lie this way for a while.

oOo

About four in the morning, he eased himself out of bed and left her in the bedroom, closing the door silently behind him.

A quick shower and a change of clothes and he was sitting at the table with his tablet working through a set of projections. He had a lot to do in the next nine months. How could he do his job and maximize his time with Chitra? At least, as long as she wanted him.

A lot of what he was going to do involved things *she* was going to do. UNERA would no doubt be involved.

He leaned back in his chair. This was going to be really difficult.

"Hey," she said as she came into the room. She was naked.

The projections disappeared. "I didn't want to disturb you."

She gave him a sleepy, cat-like smile. "You left the bed. That was disturbing enough."

Ian followed her back to the bedroom.

Really, *really* difficult.

Chapter 1.7: Chitra

They were all waiting for her at the depot on Monday exactly as she pictured them on the train ride down: Freder's suffering scowl. Ellish's ostentatious indifference. Maggie's concerned smile. Ai's smirk.

Chitra was looking over the status of each system as she walked into the office. "Ellish and I will check the medical bay. Ai checks the sensor suite. Freder's on spiders and Maggie checks integration."

Silence.

Chitra gave them a faux bewildered look. "What? You know the drill."

"Details!" Ai said. "We want details."

"Freder!" Chitra gave him a hard look. "Who said you can talk about my private life?"

"You didn't say I couldn't." Freder turned away with a sad look.

Chitra was surprised at that. What was going on *there?*

"We are your friends," said Maggie.

"Yes. I have someone I'm involved with." Chitra sighed. "Yes, I like him. Yes, he's staying with me. I have hopes for the future but I'm smart enough not to dwell on them. Can we get to work now?"

"You heard her," said Ellish. "Since when is it our business?"

The rest of them dispersed but Freder remained.

"What?" Chitra felt an uncharacteristic impatience with him.

"Hold up your hand please."

She did and the earworm blinked on her palm.

Freder took his tablet and touched it. "There."

"There what?"

"I looked into Ian Bones."

Chitra felt a flare of anger but didn't react immediately. What did she expect? Friends not to check up on friends? For that matter, it struck her that *she* hadn't done even a cursory checking. Was her trust of him that deep? What possible reason could she have? It should have been Chitra that did the checking. Freder should have to do it for her. "So?"

"He's a wealthy man that likes to visit disaster sites. He worked in the Kolkata refugee camp and then up at Mussoorie."

"I knew that."

Freder nodded. "He also worked in food distribution for the typhoon in Osaka last year and two months later cleared rubble at the Beijing earthquake. Two years ago he was seen after the glacier flood in Alaska and then the earthquake and landslide in Quito. When the favelas slid down the side of Rio, he was right there."

"So?"

Freder paged through his tablet for a moment. "Wealthy people don't do this sort of thing. They host fund raisers, donate money, start charitable organizations, or make a public plea for help. They don't work anonymously in a dirty food kitchen in Osaka or help bag bodies in Quito."

"How did you find out all this?"

Freder looked uncomfortable. "You know how it is. Faces stay round on the net. Facial recognition isn't hard. You just have to crawl through a lot of material—"

"You hired a *runner*."

"Wrote my own, actually. Ian Bones wasn't hard to find." Freder looked at her defiantly. "He's *different*. There are gaps in the records. He goes to one place and shows up another. He's not like anybody else you've ever been with." Freder pointed at his tablet. "Ian Bones has secrets."

"Everybody has secrets. Maybe he just likes to help."

"Or atone for something."

"Oh, Freder." Chitra shook her head slowly.

Freder held his tablet out like a pointer. "Maybe he's done something he's ashamed of. Something terrible."

"Like what?"

He let his arm drop. "I don't know. But nobody does this sort of volunteer work for no reason. It's not his livelihood—he makes a good living as a consultant. And he made a lot of money with Pauline Bones in orbital and lunar construction. Nicely preserved, too. He's sixty-two but he doesn't look a day over thirty-five. He must have had a lot of work."

Sixty-two? Chitra opened her hand and started looking at the data. Dates don't lie, birth or otherwise. "Come on, Freder. He was already at most of these sites *before* the disaster. Maybe it's survivor's guilt."

Freder nodded. "Maybe. Or disaster tourism."

"You think he's there because he gets a *kick* out of this?"

"Maybe." He waved her away. "You have the data. What you do with it is your own affair." With that, he walked towards the spiders.

What other sorts of distractions might a wealthy sixty-two-year-old man pursue? A dusky flower working in disaster search and recovery? Maybe Chitra was Ian's disaster porn star.

Thank you, Freder. Thank you very much. You couldn't have waited a week or two?

Chitra looked after Freder, a sour taste in her mouth.

No. No, he couldn't.

oOo

Ian was cooking when she got home. Something with garlic and rosemary. Basil? Basil. Her stomach rumbled when she stepped through the door.

The kitchen had a partition so it wasn't immediately visible from the door. She could hear him working: the sound of clattering utensils, the swirling sound of liquid in a metal bowl, something sizzling in a pan, and a metal whisk. Each sound was distinct and unhesitating. Whether or not he was a good cook, Ian knew his way around a kitchen.

From the smell, he could be a *very* good cook.

Chitra thought that maybe, just maybe, any confrontation could be managed *after* dinner.

She sighed. She'd just agonize over it until it was done. Besides, she always fought better on an empty stomach. When she was full she became lax and forgiving.

Ian glanced back at her as she rounded the partition. He was pouring a white sauce over pasta. "Hey, there. Just in time. It's almost ready."

"How old are you?"

There was a pause as Ian carefully finished pouring the sauce. "Sixty-two."

"How could you not tell me that?"

He scooped the vegetables out of the pan onto the pasta and then poured the remainder of the white sauce over it. "Why didn't you look me up?"

Exactly the question she'd been asking herself. "I didn't want to."

"Ah."

"Did you look me up?"

"Yes." He took the pasta and divided it into bowls. "Thirty-two. Born in Rockville, Maryland. Your parents bought the house in Brooklyn when you were two and Peter was five. You were top of your class at

MIT—some very nice work there, by the way. You work like a dog for UNERA—something for which you should be proud—and you're underpaid."

"Did you look me up when we were in Uttar Raypur?" Chitra felt a sudden, bitter anger. Of course—he had an ocular implant. He was reading a script while they were talking. Using one of those dating apps that listened to the conversation, applied data found on the net, and prompted the best responses.

Ian stared at her. "No. I looked you up after Mussoorie. I wanted to know everything I could about this most amazing woman I'd ever met."

"You weren't using DateHelp or GetMeLaid?"

Ian looked stricken. "Those are *things?*"

Chitra sat down and laughed. "I thought you were in your thirties."

"I can afford a very good medical package. If you think I look good, you should meet my mother. Eighty-four and a general space contractor."

"I thought they had age limits for space."

"Like I said, a *very* good medical package. Age isn't much of an objection if you're the best in your field. If you want to build a telescope in space you hire Lockheed or Onespace. *They* hire my mother."

"What else about you should I know?"

He sat down across from her. "Born in Missouri. Went to Stanford and got my mechanical engineer degree. Came back east for an MBA. Worked for Mom handling contracts while she handled schedules—she's been all over cis lunar space but I've never been higher than an air flight. Go figure." He chuckled. "While I was working for Pauline, I met Shana Liu."

"The truther outlaw."

Ian smiled. "She wasn't an outlaw then. But she did have some interesting ideas on how to describe the shape of information and then go find it. We founded ThinkFast together."

"ThinkFast invented *runners*."

"We made them practical. The same technology that finds data can hide it and everybody wanted that. We sold ThinkFast and made ourselves a lot of money. She disappeared with her share. I invested in some startups. Several paid off—I was lucky. I was long out of that business when she showed up outing secrets." Ian shook his head.

Chitra watched him for a moment. "Is there anything left on the net about you that you don't want found? Or have you hidden it all?"

Ian looked stung. He leaned back in his chair. "Do you think I'm lying?"

"No. But the founder of ThinkFast has to tools to control his own narrative. You wondered if I had looked you up." Chitra leaned forward. "What did you want me to find?"

Ian's face went cold. "Anything you were looking for."

Chitra looked at the bowl of pasta in front of her. It was beautiful and smelled delicious. "You've been seen working at disaster sites all over the world. Not as an authority. Just as someone working. Digging out the dead. Finding survivors. Why?"

"Don't *you* think it's important work?" He said in a stony voice.

"I do. But I've never met a billionaire who felt the same way. Why do you?"

Ian stood up. "I think I've perhaps overstayed my welcome—"

"Shut up." Chitra thought for a moment. "I trusted you. You seemed to *get* me. Your age. ThinkFast and everything else has made me question that. Now, if you care for me you'll work through this with me."

Ian sat down slowly. "I do care for you."

"Then, why?"

"It's the only way to properly check on my investment."

"Your—*oh my God*." Her hands flew to her mouth. "You're the TBP!"

Ian blinked. "That what?"

"Tech Billionaire Philanthropist. The TBP pushed the disaster technology into the UN. He forced the creation of UNERA. That's *you,* isn't it?"

"That's something I hid." Ian gave her a sour smile. "I didn't realize it would be so easy to guess."

"It explains everything. Except, why did you do it to begin with? Why invest in disaster relief?"

Ian shrugged. "Mom said nobody had a right to that much money. I had to do something with it. That year Hurricane Abdul struck Haiti for—what? The seventy-fifth time?—and it was exactly the same disaster problem as every other time. No water. No shelter. No food. No medical. Everybody goes down there and does a little bit, feels good and five years later nothing has changed. I thought, 'well, *that's* ridiculous.' And I started looking at the problem." He grinned and leaned forward. "Disaster intervention is just the first step to creating new infrastructure. That's why systems that get dropped in are now built to *last*. Why housing is intended to be mutable—no one wants to live in the same little tentbox as everyone else. It's like Levittown. They start as little boxes but over time they become *homes*. Homes require plumbing, sewage, electricity—"

"Stop." It came to her that she hadn't looked him up because some deep part of her had decided that Ian *got* it and she didn't want to lose that. But knowing more, she hadn't lost anything at all.

Chitra uncorked the wine and held the bottle, looking at it. Then, him. Chitra watched the way he held himself, the angle of his eyes, the way his hands rested on the table. She could see it now. There was nothing of the fragility of age about him but he had a sort of certainty to him. A sense that he knew how things worked—something different from what she knew in herself. Ian, the source of UNERA, into disaster porn? Not likely.

She poured the wine. "Oh, hell," she said. "It's not like I want kids."

"You're too young to make that decision."

"See? *Now* you're acting like an old man. This is what you should have been doing all along."

oOo

They fell into an intimate routine. She went to work, humming. Attending mandatory counseling sessions. Bringing the equipment back to ready for the next emergency. Auditing their procedures for improvement. Attending a seminar on new techniques to avert the final, lethal fulfillment of the killer they most often saw: shock. She had no clear idea what Ian did during the day—when she asked him he showed her an approach to marketing this app or that widget. Some were incremental improvements in her field—like the new cryobag he'd spoken of before. Or a crawling insect scanner that sampled DNA in a field of debris. Or anywhere else—the possibilities seemed endless there. Others were inconsequential to her: yet another hair loss restorative. Chitra suspected a personal involvement on that one.

It didn't seem like enough to occupy his time. Still, he was already wealthy. So if he wanted to spend time on the roof with her watching the drones move like flocks of starlings across the complex New York nightscape, she wasn't going to complain.

It was a wonderful two weeks. Then, he left for Saint Louis.

oOo

Ian left on Sunday morning. He'd be back by the end of the week.

She talked briefly with him Monday around lunch. He was affectionate on the phone but clearly agitated. He might not call for a couple of days, he said. Things weren't quite going the way he planned.

At 9:47 that night, under a clear sky with a full moon, the New Madrid fault line cracked apart as it had under President James Monroe.

Back then, houses had been flattened, the Mississippi River had run backward and church bells had rung in New York City. That was 1811 when Saint Louis was a tiny town of fewer than six thousand souls and New York City had a population barely above a hundred thousand.

Now, Saint Louis had a population of four million, and New York City held more than four times that.

There was a sudden jolt and a grinding sound. One of the windows next to the table shattered. The one next to it popped out. Through the gap, Chitra could hear alarms from up and down the street as buildings, cars, trains, and doors decided that this insane movement must mean somebody is trying to break in and they had to let the world *know*.

"Status," she yelled at her earworm.

"Earthquake. Unknown origin," her apartment said calmly, but loudly, over the din.

"Back check."

The room still had a faint rolling feeling but the main shock was over. There were certainly going to be aftershocks. In a city like New York, what was the safest thing to do? Out in the street to be hit with falling glass? Inside where the building might *fall down?* New York wasn't California. She didn't know the building codes but they couldn't be good—her building dated back to the Gilded Age.

"Seismology indicates its epicenter lies in southeast Missouri."

"Rating?"

"Automated instrumentation indicates 8.7."

Jesus. It had to be New Madrid. That meant more quakes. "Status: Saint Louis." She grabbed the earworm from its cradle. She didn't want to lose it.

"Unknown."

She had a sinking feeling about Ian. *Don't think about it. He survived Mussoorie, didn't he?* "Get the team's status."

A moment later she had Freder, then Ellish, Ai, and Maggie. All were shaken but unhurt. Based on that, except for falling glass and some power and water outages, New York was all right.

"I'm going to volunteer us. Okay with everyone?"

With their assent, Chitra sent a message to Tsuba. The team, being American in origin, didn't need any inter-country permissions to help.

Tsuba said no: "Mount Fuji erupted last night. The Japanese government specifically asked for your help. They need your experience with the new spiders."

Chitra stared at Tsuba's face in her hand. Ian was in Saint Louis. How could she go to Japan? How could she *not* go?

Tsuba gave her a long look. "I'm counting on you, Chitra. Wheels up in three hours."

His face disappeared and Chitra was looking at her empty hand. She called Freder with the news.

Freder sent back the initial deployment roster for Saint Louis. "Fort Leonard Wood wasn't touched so Roberts' team is ready. Harrison's, too. They're going to direct the emergency services wing of the National Guard. We couldn't do any more than they can."

"Okay." *I should be there.*

oOo

Chitra pinged Ian regularly on the long flight to Japan. They weren't on a C-130 this time but a C-5A—an equally venerable and obsolete relic. But at least this plane flew at reasonable speeds.

She checked on the status of the earthquake as well. Little of Saint Louis or the surrounding county was quake-proof—the New Madrid had not given more than a tremble for over two hundred years. Several of the buildings had toppled. The two western bridges over the Missouri River had fallen. The Mississippi bridges were cracked. Entrance to the city was from the south, by boat, and by air.

Okay, she told herself. You are on a flight away from there. To a place for which you only have a few hours to prepare. She resolutely put Saint Louis out of her mind. Ian would ping her when he could. *If* he could.

oOo

Fuji had gone off like a bomb.

As she read the reports she felt like she knew less and less. *No* volcano in the world was as monitored as Fuji—it was almost a hundred kilometers from Tokyo. That was like being in New York and having a volcano in Danbury, Connecticut.

The intervening mountains had absorbed the lahar flows and shockwave, protecting Tokyo. There had been a good shock but few casualties. Unlike St Louis, Tokyo was built to earthquake code.

The towns on Fuji's flanks were either flattened by the explosion or covered as the snow and ice had suddenly changed phase from solid to liquid. Narusawa, Fujikawaguchiko, Fujiyoshida City, Nishikatsura, Otsuki: remember them someday for today they are gone.

Chitra checked for tsunami warnings—then found the notes that said the pacific system had been discovered to have the same problem as the Bay of Bengal: the buoys were off line and the ocean floor sensors weren't reporting. Surface seismic sensors were still unreliable. Was there a tsunami heading west? Only Hawaii would know for sure in—she checked the time—about forty minutes.

The earworm chimed. It was a note from Ian: *Can't talk now. I'm okay.*

For a moment the shock was as deep as if she'd just found out he was dead. She felt riven with it. Then, an enormous physical relief and she felt as if her limbs might just disconnect and fall off.

Good, she typed on her hand. *On my way to Japan for the eruption. Be back when I can.*

She drew up her planning software. Death I can handle, she thought. It's not knowing that will kill me.

Early in April, the Japanese decided they'd learned enough and sent them home.

oOo

The ash clung like paint and made them look like badly made-up Kabuki actors. The C5A had, miracle of miracles, tepid showers that sprayed more mist than anything else. Chitra was finally able to wash her hair. That by itself was enough to make her believe in a benevolent God.

Coming out of the shower the earworm chimed. It was Tsuba.

"What?"

Tsuba was silent a moment, giving her a somber look. "There's been an earthquake in Boston."

Chitra stared at him. "What? That's not possible. Boston is stable."

"It's an 8.7."

Peter lives in Arlington. "How about Arlington? How about 27 Broad Street?" She did quick calculations in her head. He'd be at work. "And Beth Israel?" She couldn't remember where Miriam worked. *Cambridge!* "And Cambridge?"

"I don't have that information yet."

"I volunteer my team."

"No. You've been working too—"

"I volunteer myself."

"Chitra," Tsuba said softly. "I've arranged a helicopter to pick you up at JFK. You and Ai's dragonflies will be transported to Hanscom. From there you'll be deployed somewhere in the Boston area. I've got data trackers on your family data and runners for facial recognition. If they show up in the system they'll alert you."

Ai opened the door of the shower room. "You'll need me to wrangle the dragonflies."

Chitra shook her head. "I can manage."

"Not as well as me."

Freder, Ellish, and Maggie were behind her.

"They'll need doctors," Ellish said.

"I think we can clean up the machines on the way." Freder checked his tablet. "We should be ready to go on touchdown."

Chitra herded them out of the doorway into the common space. "Thanks. All of you." She looked at Freder. "Don't give me any crap. The spiders and carriers are covered in ash. How long before it destroys the bearings? They all need to be taken apart and cleaned."

"I can do that on the way, like I said."

"What happens next time? Will number one seize in the middle of a debris field? The dragonflies are sealed and we can always print more. The spiders are more complex. And you are all too tired. How long until one of you makes a mistake? That little girl in Contai? Would Ai have noticed her when she was this tired? Could you have pulled her out so gently if you'd been about to fall over your own feet?" She shook her head. "I'll go on my own."

"You're just as tired as we are," Maggie said quietly.

"Yes. But I have skin in this game. None of you have that." She looked at them all, touched by their loyalty, half crying from emotion and fatigue. "But thank you. Thank you so much. You go home. Refurbish the equipment. Be ready—I expect you'll be up in Boston before long."

Back in her bunk, she tried to contact Ian but he was not online. Instead, she sent him a message. *Gone to Boston. Looking for my brother.* She closed her eyes. I have to sleep.

Freder came by and squatted next to the bunk. "He's already there."

"What?"

"Ian Bones." Freder held up his tablet. "My runner found him again. Caught a picture of him in Concord four days ago."

"That's long before the earthquake."

"You think it's just another coincidence?"

She shook her head and lay down in her bunk. "I think he travels a lot and we're having a lot of events right now."

"Ten to one he'll be volunteering, too."

"Yes, God forbid he volunteers for things that *you* get *paid* for!" she snarled.

Freder stared at her as if she'd slapped him. "Okay, then," he said, standing and backing away.

Chitra lay back in her bunk, depressed. She shouldn't have snapped at him. It was like yelling at a rabbit. She closed her eyes, starting relaxation exercises. As she felt her body loosen and her mind let go, she had a sudden vision of Boston, flickering with death. Then, like a camera pulling away from a great height, New England, the Eastern Seaboard, America, the world.

oOo

Chitra was operating near South Station, the control case next to her. It was sunny but cold for April. Tax Day. There should be a rule that there should be no ice in the streets on Tax Day. Would there be a special dispensation for the victims so they didn't have to file? She had a sudden vision of an IRS agent looking for tax miscreants by rummaging around in the broken buildings,

South Station itself had stood up well enough. Though there wasn't a section of track, metal or ceramic, even close to specifications between here and New York City. One top-heavy bank building had broken its ridiculous pedestal and rolled against two neighboring buildings before falling apart. Chitra was running dragonflies in and out of it to find anyone trapped. It had been three days. Like Contai. Like Mussoorie—the first forty-eight hours had yielded most of the living. The dragonflies were now reporting putrescine to indicate the dead.

Her earworm chimed. Peter had been found. Alive and moved to Newton Wellesley for a broken tibia. A moment later, Miriam, Prem, and Kiash showed up as well. Chitra fingered through the report. A break in the communications links out west had been repaired. Local data had been flushed upstream to the servers.

Peter was alive. Miriam was alive. Prem and Kiash were alive. Ian was alive.

Chitra felt dizzy. She sat down on the broken pavement.

The dragonfly swarm chimed they were done. She fingered the return signal and watched, dully, as they flew back and settled into their carrier.

Everything was good, she thought.

Suddenly, she could smell everything. Every dead person, plant, and pet in Boston. Every dead animal floating in the harbor spewed stink into the air. She couldn't breathe.

She crawled to the curb and threw up. *What's wrong with me?* Chitra looked through her pack and pulled out a bottle of water. It was warm and seemed to make her sicker. She looked around. She was all alone.

That's not right, she thought. Everyone should be in sight of everyone else. It was standard procedure. Chitra looked around. There was no one anywhere. Just the rubble and the dead. Just the silence. *I should feel good. Everybody is alive.*

Everybody *she* knew. No one here.

She lay down on her side in the dust. The sun didn't warm her. She could feel the cold breath of the ice flow upward from the earth. Cold as death? What *was* the temperature of death? Death was nothing but the triumph of thermodynamics. It should have a specific temperature, like absolute zero.

Chitra heard impossible voices. She was alone. She had established that beyond all doubt. She closed her eyes. There was no one living here. Not even herself.

oOo

People moved her, jostled her, strapped her into a gurney, moved her in something like a truck, admitted her, gave her an injection. Blessed sleep overcame her.

Chitra recognized the admitting procedures. Stared when people asked her questions and watched them take notes when she didn't answer. Nothing was important. Nothing mattered.

The words "relief trauma" and "PTSD" were tossed around.

When she awoke, she was in an auditorium filled with beds. Miriam was sitting on the floor next to her. Kiash was asleep, his head in Miriam's lap.

For a long moment, all Chitra remembered was how distant everything was from everything else. Then, something seemed to mesh inside of her and she sat up and grabbed Miriam by the shoulders and held her.

Miriam laughed softly. "Why can't people wake up like this every day?"

"I thought I'd lost you. And Peter. And Kiash. And Prem." Chitra released Miriam and stared desperately into her eyes. "Where's Prem?"

"She's with Ian getting us some food."

"Ian's *here?*"

"Yes."

Kiash woke up, rubbing his eyes and looking cross and cute at the same time—a feature limited to children up to five. That doesn't stop them from trying for years afterward.

"I'm hungry," he said.

"Patience, love," said Miriam. "Wait a moment." She looked at Chitra. "I like this one. Ian's a keeper."

"What's he doing here?"

"Taking care of you, obviously. He brought us down here to help—wouldn't take no for an answer from anyone. Except Peter, of course. I have *never* seen someone cut through regulations as Ian did." She made a chopping motion with her hand. "And lo the bureaucrats parted." Miriam leaned forward conspiratorially. "No place has bureaucrats like Massachusetts."

"You've never dealt with the UN." Chitra looked around the room. "Where's Peter?" A sudden blossoming of fear. Cruel mistakes had been made before.

"Still in Newton," said Miriam as she stood Kiash up and straightened his clothes, and brushed his hair out of his eyes. "As soon as they finished pinning his leg he went off the pain meds and demanded a wheelchair. They need doctors and he said, 'That's what the paper says on my wall.'"

Maybe it was the drugs or the toll of the work or just not having had a rest in weeks, but tears rolled down her cheeks and she felt soft and weak inside.

"It's okay," said Miriam holding her. "Did I tell you the house is gone?"

"Your house?" Chitra felt the softness of her chest.

"Only one we had. Kids were outside and I was just getting groceries out of the car. Next thing I know we're all rolling on the ground. It stops then it goes again and all I can think is my kids aren't three meters away and I can't get to them. Somehow I do and hold onto them until everything is quiet—quietest thing I ever heard. Not a sound. Then, little by little, I start hearing things: water. Somebody crying. Something falling every now and then. Prem and Kiash were *all right.* I was *all right.* I looked at the house and it was just a pancake: top floor shifted and fell down on the first floor. Nothing inside worth a damn." She held Chitra close. "I thought: You know? That was a nice house but I don't need it. I don't need it at all." Chitra could feel her laugh. "We'll go down to Brooklyn and stay with the folks for a bit while we regroup. Many generations in one house—won't that be just like an Indian family?"

Chitra didn't answer. She listened to Miriam's heartbeat.

Miriam looked off in the distance waved to someone.

Chitra reluctantly pulled away from Miriam and saw Ian and Prem working their way to them between the cots.

As they neared Chitra, Prem said, "Get out of the way!" She pushed Ian to one side and marched up to Chitra, completely in charge as only those ten and under can manage. By the time they're eleven no one takes them seriously. After all, the teens are coming.

She folded her arms. "Ian was worried about you. I told him you would be okay. You are, right?"

Chitra met Prem's eyes seriously. "I am."

"Good." She grabbed Ian by the coat and pulled him to Chitra's cot. "We have hamburgers!"

Chitra looked around. "Where are they?"

Prem rolled her eyes. "Ian wouldn't bring them in here. He said it would be impolite to eat them in front of all these other people. We left them outside."

"Guilty," said Ian, holding up his hand.

"Won't they be stolen?"

"Not where we hid them!" Prem grabbed Chitra's hand. "So you have to come with us."

Chitra found she felt stronger if she was standing. Stronger walking outside the auditorium following Miriam and her children. Stronger holding Ian's hand.

There was a little room off the corridor outside of the auditorium. Ian unlocked it and led them inside where they found a few chairs and a table with sacks of food.

"How did you find this?" asked Miriam.

"Bribery. Pure and simple. Burgers, too."

They sat down and ate the greasy, heavy food with too much ketchup, tasteless onions, and stale lettuce. It was the best meal Chitra'd ever had.

Afterward, Miriam took the children and Chitra sat across from Ian, holding his hand.

"Thank you," she said.

"You came to Mussoorie looking for me, didn't you?" Ian squeezed her hand. "That's the way these things work."

"Is that so?" She wondered at that, looking at his hand. It had wrinkles that washed over them like the ripples in the bottom of a stream. The veins were pronounced on the back. She could now see age spots

"I talked with Tsuba," Ian said slowly.

Chitra looked up at him. "How do you know Tsuba?"

Ian shrugged. "I've known Tsuba for a long time. Remember, I'm the mysterious Tech Billionaire Philanthropist." He nodded. "He wanted to know when you would be ready to return to your team."

"You can't speak for me, Ian." She squeezed his hand again and let it go.

"I didn't," he said. "But I figured that an assessment of PTSD wasn't something you wanted on your record so I had to do a little digging to get it expunged. That included reassuring Tsuba that you'd be fine. You should talk to him as soon as you feel able. It'll help."

Chitra realized she'd been insecure about the whole event. The UNERA therapy sessions had been intended to head off exactly what had happened. What did it say about her that she'd succumbed?

"Don't take it hard that this happened," Ian said.

"You're reading my mind now?"

Ian smiled at her. "It's not very difficult." He looked away from her for a moment. "We have this idea we have to be strong all the time. Strong like a single great tree. So when we do break down a bit, it's catastrophe. Like an oak that is cracked open and dies. But people aren't like that at all." He shook his head and took a deep breath. "We're much more resilient. We're more like a forest of bamboo. The forest gets knocked down flat, crushed into the ground. Then, inch by inch, the forest works its way back upright. People can do almost anything together when they would completely fail alone."

Chitra watched him for a long time. "Exactly how private are we in here?"

Ian smiled at her. "Door's got a lock. I've got the key."

Chapter 1.8: Ian

A Hindu offshoot waiting for enlightenment in Contai. A yogi sect meditating in Mussoorie. A Baptist megachurch lost in prayer next to the Mississippi in Saint Louis. A Unitarian congregation experimenting with baptism in the Concord River.

Ian knew about Fuji but the schedule wouldn't allow it. Sorry. I can't help or comfort in this case. I can only bear witness.

When he waded ashore out of the Concord River it was late afternoon on a cold April day. *This time of year you can see where the shadows lie,* he thought as his teeth chattered. It's where the snow remains. He looked around and recognized where he was. Off Route 20 in Wayland. He reached into his pocket and found a locker key and a country club membership card.

Why the hell would a golfing club even be open in a frozen April? Who would brave the remaining snow and ice to get in a couple of links?

There were times Ian was convinced he did not understand people. All evidence to the contrary was pure fiction.

He looked around. There were bits of green poking up through the ice on the banks of the river. Maybe the golfers felt they were battling for spring, bringing growth from the earth by acting as if it were already there.

After a hot shower, he found the locker that fit the key. Inside were clothes. In the clothes a wallet and phone. He dressed and went out to the parking lot. He waved the phone in the air and a small car chirped at him.

The car was warm when he got in. He checked the connectivity of the phone. As expected, it was connected directly to his main processor. As had become his habit, he located Chitra and found her in the Quincy Medical Center.

The hospital firewall didn't last forty seconds. The emergency response network didn't last that long. Ian had a plan in place for Chitra before the car reached Lexington and started picking its highly illegal way towards the Newton-Wellesley hospital and Peter Majhi. Peter first. Then his wife and children. Then Chitra.

On the way, he stared at the phone. "Get me Percy." He didn't know whether this would work or not but he didn't want to wait.

The phone didn't respond for a long moment. Then, it blinked. "Yes, Ian?"

"I need to talk to you."

"Is there a problem? Iwo Tori Shima is in a few weeks."

"Where can we meet?"

Silence again. Then: "You're going past McClean Hospital. Pick me up there."

Ian instructed the car and leaned back and to wait. One thing he'd learned over the years was how to wait. He watched the passing road, noting how some houses were still standing. Some were cracked or just marginally damaged. Some were piles of rubble. The road itself showed a spider web of cracks but looked better than the adjacent highway. All of the sophisticated ramps and bridges had fallen flat.

McClean itself had fared well but was now filled with the injured. A woman with red hair was waiting by the side of the road. She waved Ian over and got in when he stopped.

"What's so urgent?" she said.

"I want Chitra to go with us."

Percy shook her head. "She doesn't fit the profile."

Ian stared at her. "You're going to have three hundred thousand candidates. You can make room."

"I don't know how many are going to be successful—"

"I won't go without her."

Ian watched Percy. Percy in a host didn't show that much in the way of human emotions but Ian thought she might be considering starting over.

"Look," Ian said, trying to sway the outcome. "You have plans for me there. You said so. I must have more of a use for me than just gathering the tribes. You want me as a willing participant? This is my requirement."

Percy continued to watch him in silence. "It won't last."

"You don't know that."

Percy didn't say anything and Ian thought she might know, after all.

"But you'll take that chance," Percy said after a moment. "What about her family? Her brother? Her parents? Her cousins? None of them match the profile, either."

"I didn't ask about them."

"Shouldn't you?"

"Would you let them come, too?"

"No."

"Then there's no point, is there?"

Percy nodded. "She'll have a tough time of it. Tougher than many since her family won't be with her. Are you sure this is the kindest thing you can do for her? Perhaps you're just being selfish."

"That's not your concern." Was Percy right? Which was kinder, leaving her here to die or be left alone? Or take her with him to, well, be alone with strangers in a strange place? She'd be alive, he told himself. That counts for something.

Percy again fell silent.

Ian wondered what she was thinking. What calculus would she apply to this situation? Maps of genetic drift? Cultural impact? Personality contributions? Risk/benefit interpretation? All of them analyzed simultaneously or individually? Ian couldn't imagine it.

"All right," Percy said suddenly. "I've got to go."

"I can have her?"

"I said that. But I have to go. I had to beg a temporary lease on this one and I have to get her back."

With that, Percy was out of the car and walking back towards McClean.

oOo

Ian shepherded the Majhis, minus Peter, down a maze of broken highways, missed connections, and blocked roads until they managed to reach Bridgeport. From there on, the earthquake damage was minimal.

He'd exchanged the minicar for something more full-sized, absorbing the extra cost without even noticing it. Small change he thought, as Chitra leaned against him in the car. He alternated watching the passing road, the children, and Chitra.

Chitra seemed to grow back into her skin as he watched. First, she was tentative, playing with Prem or Kiash, speaking quietly with Miriam, huddled against Ian's arm checking on the world through her earworm. It would have been better for her to have Peter with them, but Peter wouldn't leave the hospital as long as he could contribute.

"There was no tsunami," she said to Ian as they progressed past a broken section of the Merritt.

Ian was surprised the old bridges and sharply curved road had fared so well. There were a few downed trees and they'd had to circumvent one collapsed overpass. But, by and large, the Merritt had escaped unscathed. As they moved south they met spring green rolling north. Trees were budding. The grass on the sides of the highway had awoken.

"No tsunami?"

"Curious, isn't it? The models suggested a tsunami ought to occur, but now they're thinking that the way the earth dropped on the coast side caused the water to come into the bay and swamp the downtown buildings. The buildings served as a baffle so the return wave never really got started."

"Ah."

"What were you doing in Boston?" Chitra asked.

"I wasn't in Boston. I was in Concord. A startup app company. Then, the quake hit, and I was stuck in Concord. No coverage, so I couldn't call you. When I did, I found you in the Quincy Medical Center." He looked down at her. "My stories are never as interesting as yours."

"It's Wednesday," she said. "I need to be at work on Monday. Counseling session for this. Then, hopefully, it's back to the grind."

"Where's the team?"

"Scattered," she said. She waved her hand and the display on her hand disappeared. "Freder was sent to Saint Louis as soon as the spiders were refurbished. Ai's with him. Ellish is handling trauma at Newton Wellesley—Peter's working with him. Maggie's doing coordination between teams. She's still remoting from New York since the network is back in place." She snuggled into his shoulder. "I should be working."

"You will be."

"I could be helping."

"You're like Superman," Ian said. "He can hear all the suffering in the world. Since he can do something about it, not doing so is a sin."

"Maybe." She looked out the window.

"I'm going to Okinawa at the end of next week. I'm due there at the end of April."

"With the seal level rise, how much of Okinawa is left?"

"More than you might think." Ian looked out the window, noticing the approaching shoreline protected by concrete dikes. "The Japanese took a lesson from the atoll nations and started planting and growing reefs. It didn't give them much more land but it did reduce storm surge." He waved towards the water. "That way they needed fewer dikes. Did you notice all the artificial reefs off Tokyo Bay?"

"I was a little busy."

"Some of them are biological. Some aren't. Some are now serving as a base for floating construction. New places to live that can ride out the storms. I had a hand in that."

"What about tsunamis?"

Ian shrugged. "Depends on the wave. They might ride over one that hasn't broken but get crushed by one that's crested. There's a lot of University of Tokyo Geoscience Department modeling in that bay. A lot of discussion."

"And you had a hand in it."

"I did."

She snuggled next to his shoulder. "I half expected to see you in Tokyo."

"Okinawa is as close as I'll get."

"Is something bad going to happen in May?"

Ian kept from tensing up only by years of experience. "What do you mean?"

"You've had the strangest luck. That's all." Chitra stroked his arm. "It seems like you've been in a lot of disasters. Contai. Saint Louis. Boston. Beijing. Alaska. Quito."

"You've been checking up on me. Good for you."

"Not me. Freder."

"Freder?"

"Freder Gluck. One of my team."

"Ah. Right." Ian patted her hand, trying to remain calm. "He's looking out for you."

"We look out for each other." She sat up and looked at him. "It *is* pretty remarkable."

He made himself shrug. "I guess. Part of my business is the technology of disaster relief. Places that don't have disasters don't have the need. The places I go make the news—and require your team—when something bad happens. There was a tsunami on Patagonia five years ago. Not much coverage or need for disaster relief: nobody's there." *Don't let her check up on me for that one!* It had been a test.

"True." She snuggled back on his arm. "This year has broken all records."

"Yes. Still, we live on an active world. Maybe we're returning to what it was like a few thousand years ago."

Chitra grimaced. "I hope not."

How long could he rely on coincidence? Ian wondered. How long could he get away with this?

oOo

Iwo Tori Shima is a small volcanic island due north of Okinawa, four hundred kilometers east of Hangzhou and Shanghai and approximately the same distance south of Korea. It's about half that distance from the southernmost island of Japan and only a few tens of kilometers from the rest of the Ryukuo Island chain.

What peeks above the water is only a couple of kilometers across on its longest axis, less than that on the shortest. It resides on the continental shelf looking down into the abyss.

Volcanoes are driven by heat and pressure. Cap a submarine volcano with, say, a diamond wall that has almost no give to it, and the pressure builds. Then, introduce a circular flaw around the cap and it can release that pressure like a nuclear bomb. The erupting pressure pushes the water away for a few milliseconds and the pressure fades to near vacuum—it's inertia that keeps the mass away. Then, of course, the submarine pressure and sheer weight of the water and debris causes it to slam back into the now much deeper ground. Water doesn't compress easily but it does transmit energy efficiently in the form of pressure waves. Big pressure waves have their own name: tsunamis.

The Tori Shima Tsunami was the first Big One. Contai was good-sized—twelve meters when it struck the Indian coast. Big enough to take out Contai, Conmai, and other cities up and down the Bay of Bengal.

Tori Shima was different altogether. It radiated in all directions: thirty meters of blue destruction. It roared over Okinawa minutes after the eruption without stopping. Half an hour later Kagoshima was a memory. Twenty minutes after that, it flattened Yeosho. Then, Busan, Ningbo, and Shanghai all at the same time. It moved all up and down the East China Sea, bouncing from one country to the next, stripping the coast to bedrock.

It shot south towards north Taiwan and the Philippines, where the newly informed were trying to save themselves in just a hundred twenty minutes. It was moving east, too, with the speed of a jet: Hawaii in a few hours and the west coast a few hours after that. Everybody remembered the surge that came from the Indonesia earthquake and, trusting the saving power of distance, moved a meter higher.

But Tori Shima didn't act like others. As it moved over the continental shelf, it triggered an underwater landslide that stretched from Miyazaki, Japan to Keelung City, Taiwan. A thousand kilometers of ridge collapsed a few thousand meters down, sending a shock wave resonating with Tori Shima and radiating across the Pacific. The expected inverse square wave effect was swamped. The seismometers gave some warning but no one knew what was really coming without the tsunami warning system. When the Tori Shima Monster hit Honolulu it was fifty meters tall and followed right behind by its equally tall brothers.

Six hours after that, now a mere twenty meters, it reached the west coast of the New World, from Seattle to Lima.

oOo

The waves battered him over the reefs and he pulled himself over the coral to a shallow, warm spot where he stopped. Salt stung where the coral had cut him.

Ian was half floating, half resting, in a bathtub-sized depression in the reef. He sat up and sank to his chest in the water. Fifty feet away was a narrow stretch of beach bordered by palm trees. Behind the trees were luxury developments.

He made himself turn over so he could roll over the ridge of coral off the reefs and wade to shore. Once there, he sat down on the sand and rested his head on his arms.

He was getting too old for this.

Let's see, he thought. He could practically smell drought-stricken Australia to the south. Port Moresby. Had to be.

"I don't fucking care anymore," he cried.

"About what?"

Ian turned. A gray-haired man was standing behind him smoking a cigarette. This would have marked him anywhere—cigarettes were out of style these days from a combination of health issues and (more importantly) expense. He was also wearing shorts of fluorescent orange and green squares that alternated as Ian watched. The man's shirt was striped so fine as to make moiré patterns as he lifted his cigarette to his mouth and puffed. Ian half expected the emerging smoke to be plaid.

"If you don't want to talk about it I would fully understand," said the man. "Complete stranger and all."

Now that Ian could see his face from his distracting clothes, he saw narrow cheekbones, a thin mustache, and a receding hairline. The man looked enormously familiar but Ian couldn't place him. Ian smiled hesitantly.

"Of course," the man said with an air of apology. "You *are* on my beach. Milford here." He indicated a big man standing attentively behind him. "Can escort you around the point to the public beach."

Ian realized how he had managed to miss Milford since the man clearly resembled a brick wall. A case of expert camouflage.

"Excuse me, sir." Milford leaned down and whispered in the man's ear.

"Milford informs me you are Ian Bones, technical financier, and consultant." The man put out his hand. "My name is Fred Hibbert."

"Wait a minute," Ian said, shaking his head. "I know you. I talked with you in a Saint Louis diner fifty years ago."

Hibbert watched him a moment. "Yeah," he said. "I know. I was going to just let you go down to the public beach and never see you again." He sighed. "I'm staying at the lodge there. Would you like to come up for a drink and a meal?" Hibbert peered at him. "You didn't try to kill yourself, did you? I'd completely understand."

"No."

"Good. I'm feeling put out and bitter today. I don't have enough sympathy left over for counseling."

The lodge was a mansion occupied only by Milford and Hibbert. Hibbert led Ian in and pointed him upstairs and sent Milford after him.

Ian took a shower and found Milford had set out clothes for him. Sure enough, there was a wallet and passport in one of the pockets. Percy—or Georgette—was nothing if not thorough.

Downstairs again, he followed the unmistakable drone of a newscast.

Hibbert was standing over a table in the kitchen, drinking a martini and watching the news on the table's surface. He looked up when Ian came in and nodded towards the image. "Milford insisted. He said there was too much going on to miss."

"What's going on?"

"Volcano exploded near Okinawa caused a large tsunami. Many large cities in the China Sea destroyed. That sort of thing. There was some sort of cascade effect they're not sure about. The tsunami was still big when it hit Honolulu. It was somewhat smaller when it reached the west coast." He dismissed it with a wave of his hand. "Are you hungry?"

Ian wanted to know more. How many were dead? How bad had it become? But Hibbert had closed the image and this was his house, not Ian's. "Starving." Ian suspected this might be literally true. "Can I use your phone?"

"Haven't got one. Just Milford," said Hibbert. "No two-way communication of any kind. Not even net. Just a few channels so I can get news. Well, actually, there *is* no news. Milford has set up a feed that pulls from a dozen or so sources and gives me data that *looks* like the sort of thing I would have *called* news eighty years ago."

Half an hour later, Milford served them some kind of pan-seared fillet on top of the news image Hibbert had been watching. Hibbert went to the cabinet and pulled out a bottle of white wine and opened it.

"You said Milford has some sort of communication." Ian looked at the fish and tore his eyes away. He had to tell Chitra he was all right. "I'd like to make use of it."

"I didn't exactly say that. I said I didn't have a phone. I only have Milford." Hibbert nodded towards the big man.

Ian looked at the big man. He was dressed in the uniform of bodyguards: dark suit, dark tie, dark glasses. His skin was black and he stood still in alert attention. Very still.

"He's a robot," said Ian.

"Yes. It's an interesting choice: a hackable robot versus a buyable human being. I'm still weighing alternatives." He pointed towards Milford. "He's good at getting takeout and, of course, bodyguarding. But he's a poor conversationalist."

"He has phone capabilities."

Hibbert shrugged. "Not exactly. He has a text-only interface. Tell him what you want to do and he'll do it if he can."

Ian stood and went over to Milford. Now that he knew what Milford was, Ian wondered how he had missed it. The unnatural stillness. The stiff face. The way that Milford's head didn't turn when he was standing. Ian had expected a human bodyguard and his brain had handed him one.

"Text to Chitra Majhi, UNERA, New York City. From Ian Bones."

Milford turned his head towards Ian. "Found. What is your message?" said Milford in an even voice.

"I'm all right. Be home soon. That's the end of the message."

"Message sent. Will that be all, sir?"

Ian watched him. His lips moved. He had teeth. Behind them, Ian could see no indication of a tongue but skin seemed to wrinkle and shift as if it were real. "Yes."

Ian returned to the table. "He's a marvel."

"Best money can buy." Hibbert sipped his wine. "What brought you to my beach, Ian?"

"Fell off a boat."

"I don't believe that." Hibbert looked down at the table image. Scenes of devastation. Hibbert watched it with a scowl.

"How many?" Ian asked.

"At least a couple of million and counting." Hibbert pointed at the image with his wineglass. "It will be a lot more than that before there is a full accounting."

It was too much for a moment and Ian felt dizzy. He'd gathered just a few. How many had been saved? How many taken? How many dead?

Hibbert looked up. "Don't take it so hard. There's plenty more where they came from."

"Beg pardon?" Ian stared at him.

Hibbert waved his hand in the air. "There are over eleven billion of us. She'll have to do better than that if she's going to make a dent." He turned back to the display. "I expect she will."

"'She?'"

"Who you serve." Hibbert raised one eyebrow. "She who must never be named. The Queen of the Afternoon. The creature that runs the world. The prop master who could engineer a landslide off the presumed stable East China shelf."

"I don't serve her."

"Oh, you don't? Milford says your last sighting was on Okinawa just before the volcano blew up. What were you doing there if not serving her?"

Ian squirmed. It was too complicated. "I was saving people, not killing them. I don't serve her."

"She is a sadistic bitch," Hibbert said calmly. "But what can you do? Milford is cooking steak for dinner if you want to stay."

"Wait a minute." Ian rose from the table. "What's *your* part in this?"

Hibbert looked up at him. "I beg your pardon."

"Fifty years ago Percy insisted I go into Saint Louis to talk to you. We exchanged a lot of questions that I *still* don't understand but she insisted it was important. Tell me what you're doing."

"I fronted for the prop master in our conversation. I have no idea what side you were on. Or who 'Percy' is." Hibbert swirled his wine in the glass. "I agreed to do it to get her off my back."

"What does *that* mean?"

Hibbert was suddenly standing in front of him. Ian realized how small Hibbert was but now, with this furious little man facing him, Ian was overwhelmed with a sense of danger. *Run!* Part of him shrieked. *He'll gut you like a fish!*

Hibbert grabbed the front of Ian's shirt and brought his face down until they were nose to nose. *Jesus, he was strong!*

Hibbert hissed. "I worked for nearly a century building the best weapon I could—a drug that would cut her off from humanity. Back off, I said. Give people a chance, I said. Fulfill your obligations, I said. She agrees, smooth as butter." He jerked Ian over to the display. It looked like Okinawa was nothing more than bare rock. "This is what she does. This is what I thought I had *stopped*. Thirty years later a pandemic covers the world. Kills a fair amount of people—not an appreciable percentage, you understand. But the infection is everywhere. I have my suspicions and a year after everything has quieted down, I test my weapon and it has no more effect than salt. Nothing."

Hibbert fell quiet. "I have tried cooperating with her. I have tried fighting her. I conspired against her for *generations* but I was never more than an annoyance. Something to incorporate into her plans. What difference can anyone make when she can break off a piece of the abyss on a *whim?* So, I cut a deal: She doesn't bother me. I don't bother her. That was the scope of our little conversation."

Hibbert pushed him back. Ian staggered to keep from falling.

"I'm wallowing here in my own pool of bitterness because of who *you* serve: the shit god of the Cretaceous. Did she send you, boy? Is she in this fucking room with us?" He waved Ian off before he could answer. "Of course she is. The deal is *off!* You tell her that. Now, get the fuck out of my house."

Milford was suddenly standing next to Ian. Ian had not seen him move. He took Ian's arm in an iron grip but still managed to gently guide Ian to the front door and outside.

"A half-hour walk that way will get you to the village," said the robot, pointing. "Have a nice evening." And shut the door.

Ian looked at the house. The windows were opaque. It was as if the house were empty.

He shook his head and stared at the house for a moment. "What just happened?"

Silence remained.

Sure enough, a half-hour later he reached a village. From there he managed a taxi to Port Moresby center. The next night he was on a plane back to the states.

On the flight home, he pondered Hibbert. Who was he? What had he done? What had really happened back in Saint Louis so many years ago?

Ian wished Georgette or Percy had shown up so he could ask. But neither appeared and he was alone all the way home.

Chapter 1.9: Chitra

The sheer scale of the Tori Shima Monster stunned Chitra as it unfolded. This was the largest tsunami event in historical times. There were hints of equally large tsunamis in the geologic past—on the palisades in New Jersey, in the Andean foothills, in the sediment of the Olympic Rainforest. But these were all ancient artifacts. Interesting for their archeological significance. They could never happen here. Not these days.

Any coastal town less than seven meters above sea level—and with sea-level rise, this was more every year—was wiped out. The water rolled over San Francisco missing only the higher hills. It rolled through the Golden Gate and took out Berkeley and Oakland and the Northern Bay. The Southern Bay was better protected. Monterey looked like it had been scalloped out with a spoon. Los Angeles' ocean edge ended up as bare rock. Santa Barbara, Santa Monica, Long Beach, and San Diego all got the same treatment. Most of the towns on the west coast of Baja California wold never be heard from again. Cities and towns down into South America: Puerto Vallarta, gone. Lima, half gone. Manta, Trujillo, Antofagasta, Arica, Iquique, La Serena, Valparaiso all gone.

All across the world, communications sparked, glowed, and burned out under the strain of people trying to reach loved ones, acquaintances, strangers, celebrities. The political existence of whole countries was overnight in doubt. What was the state of Peru without Lima? What was the state of Chile with most of its coastline (which was much of the country) destroyed? What would Nicaragua do with the western side of Canal Two destroyed? The economy of Japan was staggering after Fuji. Now, it collapsed. The United States had lost Saint Louis and Boston but had just barely managed to avoid bankruptcy after the New Madrid quake Now its economy collapsed, too.

Ian had been at ground zero in Okinawa. Half the island had been scoured down to pumice. All of the coastal cities were gone. Tsuba's preliminary estimates had the casualties at about 50%. The Okinawa island group sheltered two million people. One million there, alone.

There was no question this time. Ian had to be dead. There would be unrecognizable bodies washing up on the edges of the Pacific Ocean for years, identifiable only by scraps of DNA. Possibly one would be his. Chitra wondered if she would be notified.

She felt numb. How many times had she thought him dead now? Three times? Four? She couldn't remember. The fact that she had thought him dead before gave her a frayed, persistent hope he was alive this time. She felt like a rubber band that had been stretched just one too many times.

Chitra put all thoughts of Ian out of her mind. She had work to do.

There was no question the team would be sent. The only question was where.

oOo

Her team, being American, worked the west coast. No pay. The military was in charge, now. The Army Center of Operations was in Seattle with satellite centers in Sacramento, Fresno, and Eugene. Some teams had been mobilized outside the country but not many. The devastation was just too big for any country to share out their resources. The United States government apologized profusely that it could not assist its neighbors at this time. As soon as the crisis had been resolved it would redirect its resources up and down the New World coast. China said the same for the China Sea. Both were lies. It would be years before either government would be able to support more than just holding itself upright.

Chitra and Freder worked out of the Coast Guard Rescue Ship *Bernard Webber* and moved up the coast. Basing the team on a ship was considered more fruitful than flying them to Hawaii. Honolulu, Kihei, Kailua-Kona were gone. If you were out of the splash zone you lived. If you were in it you died. Triage dictated save the most first, so they spent three days pulling survivors out of Los Angeles. Then, the *Webber*, carrying the spiders, moved north: Santa Barbara. Ventura. Monterey. San Francisco.

After Chitra had registered the rescues and made sure they had medical attention, the *Webber* moved north, being replaced by other ships. Freder and Chitra went to the mess deck.

"I'm too tired to eat," said Freder.

"Now I know the apocalypse has arrived." Chitra grabbed a sandwich along with something dark and liquid and took it to a table.

"Well, since it's just right there…"

Her earworm chimed and she looked at the text. "I don't believe it."

"Believe what?"

"Ian's alive." She looked at Freder. She had no idea what she should feel.

Freder stared back at her. "That's…" He shook his head. "That's just weird. Freakishly, unbelievably, insanely weird."

She looked back at the text. Then back at Freder. "It's good he's alive."

"Sure it is." Freder sounded unconvinced.

"How many casualties so far?"

"Real or modeled?"

"Real."

Freder looked it up. "Six point eight million."

"And now one less." She felt as if she'd been hit. Concussed.

"Right."

"It's good."

"He was on Okinawa?"

"Right there in Naha. Naha isn't there anymore." It felt to Chitra that the world was gently swaying, left to right, up to down. She looked at her glass. It was not moving. *Good,* she thought. *It's me and not the world.* She looked at the message again and turned it off.

Freder watched her. "You're not going to answer?"

"Maybe later."

"Why?"

Because there's something wrong with the world when Ian Bones lives through so much and the rest of the world just dies. Because I can't stand to go through this again and again. Because I've burned out all manner of rescue happiness feelings. Because the seventy-three people I just saved from nearly certain death are so much more real than he is.

She looked at Freder. "Do you still have a runner on Ian?"

Freder looked away, embarrassed. "Yes. It's inactive but I still have it."

"Reactivate it," she said in a dead voice. "Have it send me the results."

oOo

In normal times, even a disaster as big as the Tori Shima Monster would keep the attention of the world for a finite time. Maybe weeks. Maybe months. But, eventually, the dead would be buried. The injured would be rehabilitated. The disaster zones would knit together like healing bone. All catastrophes migrate from immediate horror to distant concern, to indifferent memory. This would take years, but eventually, it would be left behind in history.

The Tori Shima Monster began on May third, just after midnight on a Sunday. It struck Hawaii near dawn and made landfall in California just in time for late church services. Chitra was shipped out to Los Angeles at one in the morning on Monday, May fourth. She received Ian's text on Tuesday, May fifth.

Chitra decided she didn't want to talk to him. But she did want to know where he was. The runner told her he was in Port Moresby. Two days later Ian was in New York City. He stayed in New York, texting her, for the better part of a week. He tried to talk to her but she set her phone to deny him. At the end of the week, he texted her again but this time from Merida, Mexico. Then, Havana, Chicago, and back to Merida. Finally, he ended up in New Orleans.

Chitra and Freder had managed to save a hundred and seventy-nine people in Los Angeles. Forty-two in Santa Barbara. Twenty in Ventura. Twelve in Monterey. Seventy-three in San Francisco. Forty-two in Ventura. from buildings about to fall or beneath the already fallen. They found over four thousand dead.

In her downtime, Chitra backtracked Ian's travel against events. There was a short epidemic in Chicago at the end of April that died down quickly. There was a similar occurrence in Egypt at the end of May. Other than that, the two epidemics seemed unrelated. The Chicago symptoms involved a high fever and diarrhea—a strong indication of a new strain of norovirus. The Egyptian epidemic was completely unrelated. People seemed without symptoms of any kind and then suddenly fell unconscious in a kind of anaphylactic shock. Ian had been in Chicago briefly on the flight to Okinawa. He had touched down in Egypt on the way home from Port Moresby. But these were barely layovers.

The correlation was strong. Each time Ian had been in these places *before* the event.

The United States was reeling from the disasters. Congress fought over dispensing money until pundits began to suggest that martial law and the disbanding of legislative institutions might be a good idea. Then, money flowed. But the disasters didn't stop. Hurricane Alvin slashed across the panhandle of Florida, New Orleans, and East Texas followed the hot water south and rolled over the Yucatan, then circled back north over Cuba for another crack at the United States. For two weeks, Alvin wound around the Gulf, hammering the same sites: Florida-New Orleans-East Texas, Yucatan, Cuba. On the fourth round, it suddenly turned northwest and wandered up through Mississippi valley and west, dumping rain and shedding tornadoes all the way to Manitoba.

Chitra's team was dispatched to the flood plain north of Saint Louis. There, they used the spiders underwater against the force of the river to build up sandbag dams across the hundreds of tiny tributaries.

Ian texted her from Hannibal, Missouri. She almost flew up to see him. But he didn't say he was all right—there was no need now. He would always be all right. Whatever was happening, he had some hand in it and she didn't want to face that.

"Do you think he's *causing* these things to happen?" She said to Freder across the table as they tried to replace sleep with coffee.

Freder shook his head. "No. But I think he knows what's going on. He knows when they're going to occur. He's going there to confirm it—him and his consortium. When they get it exactly, he's going to announce it to the world and make a fortune."

"What consortium?"

"Whoever his backers are. He's a bastard," Freder said furiously. "To know and not to tell *anybody.*"

The lives they could have saved with warnings.

Freder's runner briefly found him in flooded Bangladesh right where UNERA was trying to build high ground over the incoming sea. Ian didn't text this time. Maybe he'd given up.

Then, the runner found him in the Andaman Islands.

oOo

Chitra had given up cause and effect. Whatever the hell Ian was doing it correlated too strongly with bad things. Kolkata was nine meters above sea level but it was eight kilometers from the coast. Chitra crawled over the map. The Contai Tsunami had taken out several towns up the river to Kolkata. It had reached nearly halfway before it ran out of steam—the narrowing of the river from the delta had concentrated it like a Fundy tide.

She called Bhim. Leave now? Take the family? What could she be thinking? Did she know they had been invited to the Japan Wine Challenge? Nirad is beside himself and it is in only two weeks. So much to do! Leave the company for two weeks? You're joking, surely. Americans have no true understanding of business.

Chitra called Nirad directly, desperately. She called Kapi. She called Tiya. She called Tiya's husband, Rohak. She called her brother, Peter, and tried to get him to call Bhim and Rohak. She called her father and her mother. Finally, in true desperation, she called Fani. Yes, did she know Nirad had forgiven him? Of *course,* he took her seriously. But he could not in good conscience try to go against Bhim. He was the head of the company, after all. Certainly, he'd like to go to Japan early but it wouldn't be fair. It was so nice for her to call. He hoped to talk to her again soon.

Chitra stared where Fani's face had been. Around her, the stink of the rotting Mississippi mud hung over the fetid air. It was hot and the air was filled with the constant dentist drill whine of mosquitoes. She had a bleak feeling deep in her chest.

The Andaman instability introduced by the January landslide finally slipped on July thirtieth. The western side of the Andaman Islands fell a thousand meters and created a three hundred meter cavity. The tops of the islands fell into the cavity. Three full pressure waves radiated west towards the partially rebuilt Indian coast and north into already flooded Bangladesh.

The first wave slowed as the water shallowed. The remaining waves did the same. This had the effect of narrowing the time between them. This was another monster like Iwo Tori Shima but without the additional effect of the continental shelf collapse. It was twenty meters when it hit the Hooghly River Bay. By the time the waves rounded the first bend they had blended, blown over the low country, and rolled straight towards Kolkata.

The wave lost steam on the way, filled with cars, trees, burning trucks, and rolling concrete. It was only ten meters high.

Ten meters was sufficient.

oOo

Chitra took advantage of UNERA. She knew Huq of Khulna was running the Kolkata operations. She sent him DNA patterns and told him who to look for. Huq promised to notify her.

Four days later, standing in a meter of Mississippi mud next to a broken spider, the notifier chimed in her ear. The collapsed warehouse had been excavated: seven bodies matching the DNA markers had appeared—most of her family, right there. A few hours later, one more from downtown Kolkata and an hour after that, two in Uttar Raypur.

Chitra called her father.

Tapas looked worn as he answered. Chitra told him the family had been found. She would be going to stand as a surviving relative. Tapas wanted to come with her but Eleanor would not let him. He was too weak from the chemotherapy. Chitra would use the earworm camera and microphone to give him some sense of presence.

She notified Tsuba she was going on leave, left instructions with her team, and caught a C5A transport to India. Chitra tried to sleep on the plane but couldn't. *I should feel loss*, she thought. Instead, it was as if the world were sealed away from her in a great bubble.

Tsuba was waiting for her. She knew she was getting special treatment. Professional courtesy. Part of her thought this was wrong. She should have to queue up in lines like everybody else to find out who was dead, who was living, who was missing. But Chitra found herself grateful for it. Anything to reduce her activity to a bare minimum. Everything took so much *effort*. Walking was hard. Speaking was almost impossible. If she could have managed to quit breathing, she would have freed herself of the struggle in a heartbeat.

Each mortuary tent was vast, holding three thousand torn bodies each. The path to this one was sweltering as the tent pumped the heat outside. Inside, it was damp and cold. People milled everywhere: walking around the bodies, staring down at faces, having hushed arguments with one another. A group of priests walked between the rows in a quick, efficient manner.

Tsuba led her to a corner of the tent where all of the Majhi family had been collected. Each body was covered by a thin cloth. Chitra knew why: the damage was often extensive and disturbing. Each had a name printed on it in Bengali. Her father translated the names in her ear. Nirad and Fani were next to one another. She pulled up the cloth over Nirad and couldn't recognize him. Kapi had not yet been found. She didn't uncover the children or anyone else.

The priest came and said some unintelligible words and made some ambiguous gestures. Chitra followed the bodies outside a scant twenty meters to the crematorium. One after another, the gurneys were fed through a door. A moment later the empty gurneys came out the adjacent door. There was no smoke or smell. The crematorium was ecologically clean.

What remained were thirteen small containers of ash. She could take possession of them now, have them shipped or leave the state to handle them. No, she could not cast the ash in the river: there were just too many. Yes, the state would treat them with respect. Chitra asked Tapas.

Eleanor answered for him. "Let the state handle it."

Chitra signed tablet images, one after another.

In the C5A over Europe, the bubble burst and she cried, her heart breaking, barely able to breathe, over people she barely knew and now would never know better. Tiya. Bhim. Missing Kapi. Nirad. Mithu. Rohak. Pari, Pavi, Puli, Dali and Das. For the people next to them. The rest in the tent. For every tent that dotted the landscape all around Kolkata, Contai, and the rest of the Bay of Bengal. In Tokyo. In Okinawa.

In Mississippi. In San Francisco. She cried for all of them. All of them so lost. All of them so taken.

oOo

Ian disappeared. Over the next weeks, the runner could not find him. Chitra could not think of him without thinking of Nirad. Or Fani. Or Kapi. Each time she felt a deep, red rage.

Without or without Ian, disasters kept happening. In August, a section of the Rift Valley collapsed after an earthquake and the Sea of Aden roared in from the coast to Arba Minch. Hurricane Chuck grew unchecked in the Atlantic and then countered all predictions that it should move east and instead spent a month chewing the coastal cities of West Africa. A few thousand here and there. After the monsters, these seemed mild. The repairs, trivial. The casualties, tiny. Not, of course, to those who had to bury them. Emergency relief squads everywhere were careful to watch their tongues.

There was a general sense of winding down. Although it was hard to determine if that merely came from a growing numbness.

Vanuatu disappeared as the ledge beneath it fell into the basin of the Coral Sea and the resulting tsunamis washed eastern Australia, New Zealand, and New Guinea. But the monsters had alerted people that Things Could Happen. The seaports of those countries were largely deserted. Ships were unloaded quickly by robots and their contents loaded onto trucks and transported to high ground. Coastal areas had become places to visit briefly, with a marked route to higher ground in hand and a nearby car that could outrun the water.

Maui's Haleakala erupted and caused a tsunami to the north covering the Aleutians but the Aleutians had been abandoned.

The economies of the world adapted and came together. Areas now identified as risk zones were evacuated. Refugees were cared for and, for once, not ignored. There were no refugees that were *other*. Every country had them. Every country cared for them. Cooperation came from shared misery.

Then, nothing at all for months. September. October. November—all quiet. No earthquakes. No volcanoes. No tsunamis. People were able to handle death on retail terms, not wholesale. Still, the specter of the past year haunted everyone. Since the first of the year, close to twenty million people had died. Crematoriums were no longer being built as temporary. They were solid, permanent structures as people incorporated the scale of mortality within their own cultures, rituals, and customs.

As Ian predicted, like the crematoriums, temporary housing became permanent. Emergency infrastructure was left in place as people began to plan for the years of rebuilding.

The UNERA teams were suddenly idle. The equipment was brought back to storage to be cleaned and refurbished.

Peter's leg healed. The house in Arlington, along with much of the town, was declared a total loss, and the family moved permanently down to Brooklyn to be with Tapas and Eleanor. Every weekend in a clockwork ritual Chitra came out to the house in Brooklyn, visiting her brother, his wife and children, her mother, and her sick father. While Tapas got no better, he did not seem to get any worse. Chitra was thankful for that.

Ian receded in her mind with each week of quiet. Maybe it *was* all coincidence. There had been so much going on that maybe his travels just happened to cross where things happened.

In a distant way, Chitra wondered what had happened to him. The runner had tracked him right up to the Kolkata Monster. The Andamans weren't on the map anymore. Did he finally get caught?

Then, on the morning of Christmas Eve, the runner found him in Puerto de la Cruz in the Canary Islands.

oOo

Chitra texted Peter that she might not make Christmas. She didn't say why.

Using UNERA credentials, she managed to catch a seat on the noon flight to Tenerife. She was too scared she might lose her resolve to think about it for too long. If she didn't confront him now she never would.

Chitra left New York on a clear, frigid day. She landed in Tenerife at night in a close, warm darkness. A cab took her from the North Airport to Puerto de la Cruz. The way was a playground for the rich: great mansions and expensive shops. Several hotel swimming ponds were lit with a warm glow and carried that light to the sea. Everywhere she could feel the slow tide of grand old money. She felt a dull resentment: these people were acting like the disasters had never happened. Or, perhaps, they were partying as the world ended. She never would have expected Ian here.

Puerto de la Cruz didn't seem to sleep. It was ten o'clock at night and the docks were brightly lit with people moving lazily around.

The docks were clearly divided by income. One section held large yachts, catamarans, and luxury hovercraft. Then a narrow channel and a collection of fishing boats, trawlers, and automated rental boats—the location of. Ian's last image.

There was an open rental and charter office nearby. Chitra went in and flashed Ian's picture onto the counter in front of a small, wary man.

He didn't say a word. He looked at the picture and back at Chitra. Slowly, he rubbed two fingers together.

This is the real reason paper money survived, she thought savagely as she slammed down a stack of Euros.

"I take virtual coin as well," he said quietly as he counted the Euros. "Anything untraceable."

"You know where he is?"

"Of course." He pressed something under the table and the surface behind the counter turned into a map of the islands dotted with half a dozen winking points. "There." He pointed to a numbered red point. "He wanted a good dive boat. That's the *Mercutio*—a nice Frescani."

"How do I—" She squinted at the map. "Find him at Las Palmas."

"Finding him is not a problem. All of my boats are automated. You tell it the destination and it negotiates its way out of the harbor and goes. It's enclosed in case of bad weather. Beer. Wine. Food for three days." He raised his eyebrows. "The finest in assistive and preventive sexual accouterments."

She glared at him. "How long to get over there?"

"Forty minutes to get set up here. Eighty kilometers over—say three hours. Otherwise, you charter a plane and wave to him as you fly over." He spread his hands. "Three days minimum. Plus fifty percent of that for the night rental."

The price was only twice the exorbitant airfare to get here. But she was able to sit in the cabin and make herself a meal as the *Falstaff* took her out into the dark harbor.

"Please tell me if you need anything," Falstaff said to her in a warm, deep man's voice. "I am fully equipped."

She was startled. "I will."

Chitra watched the lights fall away. The distant lights ceased being indicators of human beings and serve only to illuminate the jumbled rocks of the islands. The sounds faded into quiet until there was only the land and the sea. Then, as the island fell out of sight, only the sea remained.

The cabin lights became the only real source of illumination. The windows looked painted black. It seemed she was in a rocking, closed room.

The enforced idleness forced her to consider her own thoughts. What was she going to say to him? What do you know of what has happened? Did you know? Did you *cause* it? What do I say if he asks why I quit answering him?

She had no answers, of course. Chitra knew better than to plan such a conversation. Some people were good at that sort of thing. Chitra wasn't one of them. She'd say what she said when the time came.

oOo

Falstaff warned her they were coming about and then Ian's boat seemed to magically appear in the darkness.

Ian was standing on the gloom of the deck, watching as Falstaff brought the two boats together and extended a gangplank between them. The *Falstaff's* thin bulb only seemed to illuminate the outlines of things. Ian waved and she saw he was wearing a watch. Chitra had never seen him wear a watch before.

Ian didn't say anything as she walked over—just stepped back to give her room.

Chitra watched him for a moment. There was a faint wind and the boat rocked. She could smell land—curious. She had never known what land would smell like yet she knew the scent. Then, she said: "Did you know?"

"Yes."

"All of them?"

Ian nodded.

Chitra acted without thinking and swung her fist at his face with everything she had. Nothing in her had suggested *this* was what she should do but it felt complete. It felt right. Her fist spoke for every one killed. Everyone maimed. Everyone missing. Nirad. Risu. Kapi. "How *dare* you?"

He was moving when she hit him but it was enough to knock him down and roll him towards the railing. A moment later he was on his feet, loose and ready. He looked dangerous.

Then, Ian held up his hands.

Chitra shook her head. It wouldn't bring back anyone. They would still be dead without warning.

She looked at her hand. It was already swelling. "God damn it." She said, feeling the tears well up. "God damn *you*."

"No doubt," he said soothingly and guided her to a bench. He went into the cabin and returned a moment later with a bag of ice. "Here. Put this on your hand."

She held the ice to her hand as the tears fell. Chitra didn't mind them. Tears were a good thing—what could possibly be as right and proper as tears for the dead?

"How?"

"I know who did it," he said and sighed. "I work for them." He thought for a moment. "Well, to be precise. I work for one of them and she's contracted me out to the one who did this."

Chitra almost hit him again but her hand hurt. "No one could do this."

"Remember the God of the Cretaceous?" he said.

He took her hand and examined it carefully. Gently. She realized he had much more skill than she had known.

"What the hell are you?" She stared at him. Should he have horns and a tail? A halo? Extraterrestrial bug eyes?

He chuckled and pointed to her hand. "You didn't break it. I think you dislocated your knuckles but they seemed to have popped back in. Keep the ice on it." Ian sat back. "He's planned all of this for decades. Generations. Long before I was born. It was all going to happen—you have to believe that. I've spent fifty years moving people into positions where I could save them. Well, some of them. Not many, actually."

"Why so many tsunamis? Why tsunamis at *all?*"

"Not all of them were tsunamis. There were earthquakes and landslides." He sighed. "*His* reason is that most of the world's population is next to a coast. *My* reason is that the easiest way to save people is to grab them out of the water. No heaving rocks or falling trees or fever or fire to worry about. People survive drowning all the time."

"You could have told me."

Ian shook his head. "I could *not* tell you. You would have saved everybody—He would have scuttled what he was doing."

"And stop all the disasters."

"No. Like I said, they were set up years ago. They were going to happen. But I wouldn't have been able to save anyone." Ian leaned on his knees. "It's a deal with the devil. I get to save some lives at the cost of not saving people who were going to die anyway."

"But *why?*"

"He's got plans." Ian shuddered. "I don't know what they are but he's hinted enough. This is just the start." He checked his watch.

She looked at his watch, then back at him. "What are you—" Chitra stopped and looked at him. "Oh, my God."

"Chitra. It's time for you to—"

"It's not *over*, is it? It's not fucking *over at all!*"

Ian took her shoulders. "Chitra. You have to go home if you want to save anyone. Leave now—take the boat directly to the dock near the north airport. The boat will know the way. Leave it and catch the next plane to New York City."

"You bastard!"

"Go *now!*"

She stared at him for a moment. Then, Chitra ran over the gangplank in a stumble. "The docks closest to Tenerife north airport. Top speed."

"Okay," said Falstaff.

Falstaff retracted the gangplank and pulled away slowly. Then, she felt the surge as Falstaff accelerated, the boat tilting upward, the spray shooting out behind her. She tried to call Eleanor. Peter. Miriam. No answer. She checked the news—nothing out of the ordinary. She checked airline schedules: there was a 5 AM to New York City.

I've got time, she told herself over and over. *I've got time.*

oOo

She finally reached Eleanor two hours out of New York at three in the morning, New York time.

"Mom! Listen to me—"

"Tapas is dead."

Chitra stopped, her brain suddenly congealed. Quick visions filled her head: Tapas crying as he hugged her when she graduated from MIT. Tapas angry with her when she didn't think she'd *ever* understand calculus. Tapas worn and tired after chemo, quietly reassuring her things would be all right. Tapas sitting next to her, reading a book she could not remember when she was feverish and in the hospital with a kidney infection. *Dead?* That simply wasn't possible.

Then she remembered Ian looking at his watch. "I'm sorry, Mom. But you all have to leave New York."

"There are some papers I have to sign. Paper. How *quaint*. I can't deal with this right now. Call your brother." Eleanor disconnected.

Chitra looked at her hand, Eleanor's image suddenly gone. She called Peter: straight to recording. She sent him an emergency ping. A few minutes later, Miriam called her back.

"Hello, Chitra. Tapas—"

"—is dead. I know. Listen, Miriam. You have to get Peter and Eleanor and the kids out of New York."

"Peter doesn't know yet. He's been in surgery—really delicate stuff, apparently—and the staff won't let him know until he's reached a stopping point." Miriam laughed shakily. "Real life and death stuff, I guess."

"Miriam, *listen to me*. Remember how I asked Peter and Tapas—hell, I asked *everybody*—to try to get the family out of Kolkata."

"Peter thought you were crazy."

"Maybe I am but I was *right*, wasn't I? They were still there when the Kolkata Monster hit. I'm telling you now: I'm about to be right again. Something's going to happen to New York. You have to get out."

"Where?"

Chitra thought for a minute. How big had the Kolkata Monster been when it hit land? Thirty meters? Forty? Or Iwo Tori Shima? If you were going to take out New York, how big would *you* make it, Chitra? "A hundred fifty kilometers west. Hartford. Further up into the mountains if you can. That ought to be enough."

"That far?"

"Three hours if you rent a car and start *now*. I don't know how much time you have but you've got to be moving before the news is out or you'll never make it." She saw Ian and the watch again. Hours? Minutes?

There was no news as the plane approached New York.

Her disaster alarm chimed as the plane descended on final: "Seismic event. Epicenter at Las Palmas, Spain."

Damn. She started to get details when the chime came again. "Seismic event. Epicenter at Tenerife, Spain." Followed by: "Tsunami warning: Boston to North Carolina."

Damn. Damn! *Damn!*

oOo

Chitra was never so glad for bureaucratic inefficiency in her life. The proper procedure dictated the plane take off inland to a safe airport, dump the passengers and return and pick up evacuees. Instead, no one decided to *act* on the tsunami warning and that gave the plane time to taxi, dock, and Chitra a chance to escape. Even so, in the confusion, it still took two hours to bluff her way off the plane. It was starting to reload with those who weren't interested in staying when Chitra left the terminal. Three hours gone.

Miriam caught her as she was trying to catch a cab to get into the city.

"We're in a rental heading to Philadelphia—"

"*No!* West, I said. Go to Allentown. Or Scranton. Someplace like that."

"I'll tell him. But Eleanor wouldn't go. She had Tapas cremated. She's going home to Brooklyn. She said that if something was going to happen she'd meet it there." There was a pause. "I almost couldn't get Peter to leave her. He may divorce me over this."

She hung up.

Chitra gave the cab instructions to go to Brooklyn.

oOo

The roads were beginning to choke as the cab headed into the city. Emergency services hadn't turned the inbound lanes around yet. Again, she gave silent thanks to the gods of bureaucratic paperwork. A moment later the cab chimed: "This cab has been commandeered by the New York City Emergency Relief Agency and will be rerouted to the nearest depot. Please excuse any inconvenience."

Jesus. Furiously, she tapped in the override code.

The cab spoke cheerfully: "This cab has been commandeered by the New York City Emergency Relief Agency and has been rerouted to 1027 78th Circle, Brooklyn. Please excuse any inconvenience."

It wasn't going to end with just the Canary Islands, she thought. Not if it were designed. It was one thing to plan for random events—even if they clustered. The natural world was no enemy. There was no one gunning for you. But not this time. Nobody here would be prepared for it. They'd be thinking of the distance from the epicenter. Of the inverse square law. The tsunami couldn't be more than a couple of meters. Or five meters. Or maybe even seven. Nothing more than that, surely.

She brought up a seafloor map looking for projected tsunamis. New York's would cross a string of Atlantic seamounts. Bermuda stood in the way. Everyone thought it was chance that the Iwo Tori Shima eruption triggered the Miyazaki Slide to create the Iwo Tori Shima Monster.

Chitra knew better.

If *she* were designing a disaster, she would look at the seamounts and Bermuda. A series of slides on the seamounts would go a long way to increasing the tsunami, especially if it was done at the right resonant moment. And just *look* at Bermuda: that edge went down two thousand meters. *Boom!*

It would be thirty meters tall. Easy. Forty. It would be remembered as the Christmas Monster.

The cab picked its way through side streets now. The inbound lanes of all the major arteries had been canceled and made outbound. Most of the streets were choked but the cab found interesting inhuman solutions to fulfill its emergency duties.

More chimes. A seismic event in Fogo, Cape Verde. Tsunami warning for West Africa.

The streets emptied as the cab moved south through Brooklyn, closer to the water. Those in southern Brooklyn understood the power of water better than most New Yorkers. They would have been the first to leave. Anybody remaining would have decided to stay for their own reasons.

Like her mother.

The cab stopped at Eleanor's house and Chitra set the wait time and ran up the stairs.

"Mom?" she called.

No answer.

Maybe she hadn't gotten home yet. Chitra ran up the stairs to her parents' bedroom. Eleanor was stretched out on the bed.

"Mom?" Chitra said softly.

"Hello, love," said Eleanor. "You shouldn't be here."

Chitra checked the time. Noon. So much wasted! "We've got to leave. We have to be out of New York—a long ways out of New York—in three hours." Chitra checked the traffic. New Yorkers were not slouches; they knew how to hurry. Every highway was already jammed. Trains were taking extra passengers but there was no way to take everybody. But there was no panic. The highway was seven meters over sea level. No problem, right? Chitra knew better.

"I'm not going," said Eleanor clearly.

"Come *on*, Mom!" Maybe they could get to a tall enough building. What around them was ten stories tall? That might do it. *Might*. Chitra remembered San Francisco.

Eleanor smiled at her. "I haven't heard you use that tone of voice on me since you were sixteen. And they say those days are lost forever."

Chitra reached down and pulled her up by her left arm. "Mom!"

Her mother came up.

"Let go." Eleanor wavered and stabilized herself with her right hand.

Chitra let go.

"Get away! You youngsters are all alike. You think you know what's best for us."

Chitra stood up. The arm had been flaccid. Still warm but lifeless. She looked into her mother's face. The left side was drooping. The left arm hung still. "You had a stroke."

"Thank you for your understanding," Eleanor said bitterly. "Now leave me alone."

"How did you ever get home? How did you get up the stairs?"

"It got worse after I got up here. Now, go."

"No. We have to get you to a hospital."

"In three hours? Why? So they can rewire my brain? So I can get a powered assist or be put on a ventilator? So I can while away my days in some facility? Or, worse, get one of those robot *things* to clean up after me?" Saliva dripped down the left side of her face but Eleanor didn't notice it. "No thank you. Miriam told me what is going to happen. A tidal wave will wash me away. If I could manage to get down the stairs I'd meet it on the front porch. If by some God-forsaken chance it *doesn't* reach me, I have this."

Eleanor fumbled in her right-hand pocket and pulled out a bright purple pill bottle plastered with warnings: an assisted suicide prescription. Eleanor tried to open it with one hand but it defeated her. "I'll break it open!" She dropped the bottle on the floor and lifted her good leg.

"No, Mama," said Chitra gently. She picked up the bottle. "Is this what you want?"

Eleanor softened. "Yes. You might think it's just because Tapas... passed. But it's not. It's because of this." She waved at her dead side. "If this hadn't happened I'd be helping you pack the house or running like hell." She waved at the room. "My mother died this way. She had a stroke six months after my father died—they *hated* each other. She treated his death like a get-out-of-jail-free card. But six months later she was lying in a hospital bed, half her body lost from her brain and her brain so damaged it didn't even know. I swore that would never happen to me."

"It's been forty years, Mama," said Chitra. "Things have improved."

"Not all that much. Now people on a ventilator don't die quite as fast as they used to. With years of training and dedication, you can get back some use. But failure to swallow still takes most of them." She grinned crookedly. "Us. How long have we got?"

"Three hours." Minus some.

The chime sounded again. Multiple seismic events in the Caribbean. So much for the Southeast United States, Central America, and northern South America. Then it chimed with a list of Atlantic seamounts and seismic events. It mentioned Bermuda. Chitra turned it off.

"Do you have time?" Eleanor looked up at her. "Without me?"

Chitra looked outside. The cab was gone. It must have been overridden. She'd never get a cab now. Without a cab, there was no way to even get Eleanor to the higher ground of the highway, much less a building. Much less out of the city. And she wouldn't leave her mother. Not now. Not ever. "No."

"Ah," said Eleanor. "Is it shameful to say even though I wish you were long gone I'm glad you're here?"

"No."

"Good. Think you can help me down the stairs to the front porch? I want to see what's coming."

It took nearly half an hour to get Eleanor down the stairs. She seemed to weigh an enormous amount for someone so thin. Finally, Chitra managed to set her down on a chair on the front porch.

"Well," said Eleanor. "That was quite a chore." She looked around. "At least it's a pretty day."

Chitra looked up. She hadn't noticed the weather or the sky. It was clear and sunny. The Majhi house wasn't all that far from the BQE, but over the years, carefully planted pine trees had masked the sound. This December was unseasonably warm and, shielded in the porch as they were, it felt like early spring.

Chitra went back inside and brought out two blankets. She carefully wrapped her mother and then wrapped herself.

"Tapas put in this porch for me," Eleanor said. "My family back in Kentucky had a veranda around their house. I loved that veranda." She laughed softly. "Can you imagine a veranda in Brooklyn? So he put this in for me."

The street was quiet for the first time in Chitra's memory. Always before there had been people walking, kids playing, cars slowly picking their way towards the parkway. Chitra remembered sitting on Joey Amberson's front steps. The houses were so close together there was no mystery between adjacent families. When she became a teenager it wasn't moral fortitude that stopped her experimentation as much as a lack of privacy.

"I had a good life," Eleanor said with some satisfaction. "I had love. I had work. I had a family—I really had everything I ever wanted. Doesn't that sound like a good life?"

"It does."

"Did you have a good life, Chitra?"

"What kind of question is that?"

"The sort of question a mother asks her child at the end of the world."

"I suppose." Chitra thought for a moment. She had liked her job. Enjoyed Ian—mostly. Certainly enjoyed all of her other lovers. While she, Eleanor, and the Kolkata Majhis were gone, Peter and Miriam would surely survive. But her mind came back to her job. "I saved a lot of people. I buried a lot of people. I gave the living a chance and the dead the respect they deserved. Some of my family is going to live." She turned to look at Eleanor. "I did have a good life."

Eleanor was sitting in her chair at an angle, her head down. A thin strand of blood came from her nose and dribbled from her mouth. Both hands were limp but in her right one lay the open purple bottle, empty.

"Oh, Mama," Chitra said.

oOo

She straightened Eleanor in her chair. The two of them were more or less facing south. Chitra checked the time. She guessed ninety minutes now. It was hard to determine the strike time with precision. So much depended on water density and temperature, terrain, and resonance. The satellite maps showed a pressure differential crossing the continental shelf. The change in depth would slow it down some.

Chitra checked the traffic imagery. It was better than she expected. The coastal road down near Coney Island was empty. Further out the roads were still packed but still comfortably higher than seven meters—not much of a chance but some. A lot of people were out of the city completely. Chitra congratulated the New York City Emergency Relief Agency. She checked the emergency feed. Somebody had finally realized what they were dealing with and brought in a set of sky cranes. They were ordering the people caught on the highways into large buses or trailers and then hauling them to higher ground. Nice thinking. They'd save more than a few. She wondered how many of the people Ian was trying to save would be rescued and lost to him. Surely, the God of the Cretaceous must have taken all of this into account.

Sitting there in the afternoon light, Chitra thought over this day. She'd handled it completely wrong. She should have called Tsuba the instant she knew something was coming. Hell, she should have called Tsuba when she was scared of the Andaman Islands. He wouldn't have believed her then but he would believe her now. Fear makes you stupid. And it *keeps* you stupid—she could have called after Kolkata. She had phone records—that might have proven she was right. Even if it hadn't, it would have laid the groundwork for this.

But that was hindsight: After Kolkata was she really convinced? Didn't she tell herself that it still might have been a coincidence when he didn't show up? When she thought he was dead? Who would have believed there was a malign deity behind all of this?

She could have sent a request to Tsuba from the airport but the idea of some stranger manhandling her crippled mother out of the house only to die en route—no. As bad an idea as this was, it was the right one. Chitra never would have forgiven herself otherwise.

Well, then.

Chitra stood up and kissed the top of her mother's hair. "Goodbye, Mama."

What to do now? She checked the time. A little more than an hour.

She could call Tsuba. He could send a copter—maybe a small one or a popcopter. Although she thought every one of them would be dedicated to mass evacuation. Chitra looked up. On the edges of the sky, she saw occasional movement but nothing over this section of Brooklyn.

They'd have to make a special trip. Say, fifteen minutes to arrange things, fifteen minutes to get here—or wherever they agreed. They'd have, maybe, thirty minutes to get away. She checked the satellite imagery. The line had visibly moved. A popcopter could be dispatched if there was one available. Fastest speed a hundred thirty kilometers an hour. Would it be fast enough? Tsunamis hit ninety regularly. This one might be a lot faster.

Chitra looked at the traffic picture. Those people stuck on the were doomed. She and Eleanor were doomed the moment the cab stopped in front of her house.

She straightened up. It was time to meet the emissary of the Cretaceous' Holy God.

oOo

Chitra ran down 100th Street, a quick jog over to the abandoned Fort Hamilton Parkway, and straight down to the water. She ran as fast as she could. She crossed over the Belt Parkway and down to the bike path. There was, of course, no one there.

Chitra half expected Ian to be waiting for her. That would have been grand. Together, shouting obscenities at the coming monster. Although, she'd probably hit him again.

Instead, she was alone.

There was no water. She could see it receding quickly a kilometer out. Chitra started to check the satellite feed and stopped. She tossed her earworm on the sand and leaned against the railing.

Sure enough, in the distance, there was something that looked like a distant cloud or mountain range. A warm wind started blowing towards her.

How could anything be saved from that?

Chitra made some quick calculations—she'd tossed her earworm too soon!—trying to remember the compressibility of air. How fast was the monster coming?

Chitra had no desire to be battered against the houses behind her. She pulled off her belt and fastened herself to the railing. The wind was really blowing. The mountain was much closer now.

Binoculars! That's what she should have brought.

It was huge, a great, liquid wall towering over any of the nearby buildings. She wondered if it would cap the buildings of Manhattan. It looked like an impending train: first moving slowly from far away and then getting exponentially faster as it came closer.

There were things in the wave itself. Writhing.

Then it was here, rolling so fast—

A millisecond before the water hit her something flew out of the water, grabbed her head and shoulders. Her back broke when her belt held for a moment against the water. Then, it parted and she tumbled in the water. Body blow after body blow. She was conscious, feeling things inside of her break and tear. She would have cried out but her head was wrapped in something soft and wet and she couldn't breathe. There was a bright electric shock and she felt her heart stop a moment before she actually died.

Chapter 1.10: Ian

Ian watched as the *Falstaff* moved away from the *Mercutio*. Then, two great rooster tails came from the back of the boat, and with a sullen roar, the *Falstaff* was swallowed up in the darkness.

Okay, then.

Ian sensed the movement of things as he had never before: feel the slow-motion crumble of supports deep in the seafloor, soon to culminate in a sudden snap. What would happen on the surface here? Would he see a change in the water as it fell? Or would he just see the eruption at Las Palmas and then Tiede?

Maybe I'll just stay here. Watch it all go boom and then be done with it.

There was a splashing at the transom. Ian saw a hand over the edge and someone hanging onto the diving platform, retching.

After a moment, Georgette stood up shakily, holding on to the rail. She was naked.

For the first time, Ian didn't feel drawn to her. She was still beautiful. Still magnificent in the dim light. But she was just a naked woman. Nothing to take all that much notice of.

"Georgette—"

Georgette held up her finger. She held onto the railing and leaned over the side. She vomited an enormous amount of water, stopped. Choking, she brought up a small fish and spit it into the water. "Not the cleanest apparition, eh?" She gave him a tired grin.

"I'm—"

"You really did lose your nerve, didn't you? First Saw. Now Chitra. What will Percy think?" Georgette held her finger to her lips. "I won't tell a soul."

She padded next to him and into the cabin. A few minutes later code appeared on the console. Georgette tapped the various buttons a moment. The code disappeared and the console display resumed.

"Sixty seconds to departure," said Mercutio pleasantly.

"Come in here and strap down." Georgette waved to him.

"There aren't any straps—" He started but stopped when he saw straps on the galley chair. Ian sat down and strapped himself in.

"50 seconds."

"Where are we going?"

"We're heading to Tenerife with all deliberate speed. I reset the priorities to hull integrity over passenger safety. You'd be surprised what these babies can do when they aren't worrying about human beings."

"40 seconds."

"Why?"

"Your jet is waiting." Georgette grinned at him. "What have you got to drink in here?"

"No." Ian took a deep breath. "I'm staying here. I'm not going anywhere."

"Nope. Percy and I have a contract." Georgette said as she rummaged in the refrigerator and found a bottle of wine. She shut the door. She thought for a moment and latched it. Georgette pulled the cork out with her fingernails.

"20 seconds."

"Shut that damn thing off!"

"We'll get there and be gone before Chitra." She clapped her hands. "It'll be fun."

"10 seconds."

Ian let out a long breath. "Where are we going after Tenerife?"

"Santorini."

Ian felt tired down into his bones. "Don't you think I've done enough?"

"No, honey." Georgette kissed the top of his head. "Not near enough."

"Departure," said Mercutio.

Ian was slammed back in his chair.

oOo

This was low flying and only catching water where necessary.

Mercutio calculated the trajectory as they left each crest, accelerating into a vector that might include a spin or drift, catching the next rising or falling wave just long enough to impart acceleration for the next. It didn't feel like they were going anywhere as much as they were tumbling inside a huge drum at great speed.

Ian puked himself empty in the first few minutes and thereafter watched as Georgette seemed to pirouette in place. As much as Mercutio moved up, down, sideways or twisted, Georgette managed to stay upright and drinking. Singing. Dancing. Thoroughly enjoying herself. He blessedly blacked out occasionally and then reawoke back into hell. Time lost all meaning.

"Stop," he croaked. "Or kill me."

"You men are all the same. Thirty minutes of a little stress and you're asking for the sweet oblivion of death." Georgette rolled her eyes, then her torso, and landed on her feet. "Want a drink?"

Ian threw up nothing at all.

She jumped in the air and Mercutio dropped from under her a good two meters. Georgette caught herself against the ceiling, absorbing its downward force. Then, the *Mercutio* surged back up and she landed hard. "I *love* that."

"I hate you."

"How sharper than a serpent's tooth is a thankless child." Georgette gave a theatrical sigh.

Georgette gave the world faint stability and Ian stared at her. Seasick people watched the horizon, don't they? He realized he'd completely forgotten she was naked.

"Someone will meet you, get you cleaned up, and drive you to the airport. Then, a flight to Santorini. Percy will meet you there and take you to Pauline."

Ian looked at her blearily. "Is Pauline all right?"

"Of course she's all right!" Georgette held on to the table so she was facing Ian as Mercutio dipped to the left and then the right. "I always keep my promises. Except when I don't."

"Kill me." He realized that when he'd said it before he'd had reservations. Now he was sincere.

She grabbed both arms of his galley chair and brought her face down to his, held it there despite the twisting and turnings of the boat.

"Almost over, Ian. Just a little more. Then you're done with me." She stood up, gracefully countering a sudden bow rise. "Time to dock?"

Mercutio responded: "Ten minutes. Slowing down now."

"That's my cue to make like a mermaid." She kissed him on his nose. "Goodbye, Ian. Take care of yourself. You were always my favorite."

Then she danced through the hatch and was gone.

oOo

Two uniformed men half carried him off the boat into a waiting ambulance and professionally stripped him of his clothes and hooked him to an IV. They spoke in Spanish but Ian was too tired to understand them. The one that spoke English stayed in the ambulance with Ian and the other went forward. Ian felt the ambulance start moving.

"Where are we going?" Ian looked at the man's nametag. "Guillermo."

Guillermo fastened leads and sensors on Ian's chest while he spoke. "The airport. Fifteen minutes. Don't worry, sir. You'll feel much better by the time you get there."

Ian wondered why the driving wasn't automated. Spain was no technological backwater like Somalia. He was going to ask Guillermo but he fell asleep.

The ambulance stopped and a moment later, the other man opened the door. Guillermo helped him out of the ambulance and gestured towards a small plane. The stairway was down.

"Guillermo?" he said. "Do you have family here?"

"Yes," Guillermo said with a grin. "My son is three months old."

"What would you do if the mountain exploded?"

Guillermo shrugged. "There is no safe place on Tenerife."

"Tiede is going to erupt—" Ian looked at his watch. "In ten hours."

"Of course, sir."

Ian took him by the shoulders and stared into his face. "If you want your family to live, find someplace safe. Just for the day."

Ian turned and walked to the plane before he could see if Guillermo believed him or not. To hell with keeping secrets. To hell with Georgette. To hell with Percy. Now that everything was done he didn't care. He wondered what that meant about his character.

oOo

Santorini was an archipelago of smaller islands surrounding a vast rectangular bay. It was all that remained after the volcano island Thera exploded and ended the Minoan civilization.

A limo met the plane. After all this time in impoverished places, the limo felt great.

Percy was waiting for him inside, this time in the form of a dark-complexioned young girl with striking blue eyes.

"Where now?" he asked as he sat down.

"The Hotel Sunrise in Fira. You're going to get some sleep."

"Georgette said I was going to see Pauline."

"Tomorrow. She gets here from Ulan Bator this afternoon."

"What time is it?"

"The Canaries have not yet erupted."

Good, Ian thought. I'll sleep through it all. Ian looked out the window. The land had that sun-blasted dry look of every piece of land he'd ever seen in Greece. "What's here?"

"You'll see."

"Georgette said it's all over." He looked at Percy. "Is that true?"

"Nearly. As soon as the last wave finishes, our collecting is over. Sorting everyone out has begun, but that's not your job."

oOo

Percy woke him some twelve hours later.

Ian sat on the edge of the bed. "Did it all happen?"

"Yes. A few hours ago."

"Was Chitra collected?"

"Yes."

"Good." He let out a long sigh. "So I'm done."

"With this phase of the operation. Of course, there's much more to be done."

"Could I quit if I wanted to?"

Percy looked down. "Yes. If that's what you want. I'd like you to stay with me. I need one volunteer."

"Why? Is there some custom here?"

Percy shook her head. "No custom. None of us ever had to deal with conscious beings before, so no custom has ever been needed. It's…" She paused. "I'm going to have to manage three hundred thousand conscripts and an entirely new ecosphere. It would be nice to have *someone* on my side."

"I'm not sure I am on your side."

"Yes. So I heard." Percy fell silent a moment. "Well, one thing at a time. Go meet your mother and then we'll see."

oOo

The Hotel Sunrise was buzzing with news but Ian ignored it. The hotel had a second-story veranda that faced the western walls of Thera's crater. Ian came out to get breakfast. He saw a familiar older woman sipping coffee and reading.

"Mom!" and Ian was across the bricks and holding her before he had a chance to think about it.

Pauline was eighty-four and looked robust fifty just as Ian was sixty-two and looked thirty-five. "Look at you. You're all grown up."

"You've been saying that for forty years."

"Longer," she said simply, holding his hands and looking at him. "You were always older than your age."

Yes, he thought. Being beaten up regularly by someone you love and who loves you has a sort of maturing quality about it. He looked for some sign of that Pauline in her face, as he always did, and saw none. Percy had cured her and she'd moved on. He cringed from what he had done. Resented her for what she had done and refused to acknowledge. The feelings were old and he was used to them. In only a few seconds *she needed it* changed to *I needed it,* morphed into *this is a good thing,* and resolved into *how could I have submitted my mother to having her brain manipulated by an alien!* Even the arguments were old.

No, he said to himself. She's here. Now. If she's not necessarily the woman who was always your mother she's the woman who *thinks* she was always your mother. Since you were twelve she's the only mother you've ever had.

"Everything is done, then," he said, just to fill the silence. "For your asteroid project?"

"Last interview was in Hawaii a couple of months back but I wanted to make sure the rest of the support structure was in place. We'll have to have everything in place when we start. After all, it's not like we can call home for help. Now we're ready." She looked proud. There did not appear to be a hint of doubt. Would Pauline Unchanged be so completely certain?

Ian looked down, then back to her face. "I'm surprised the disasters didn't affect the process. It's the end of the world out there."

"My investors are insistent." Pauline waved her hand and gave him a sly smile. "I don't want to think about the end of the world. I just want to spend some time with my son."

Just for today, he thought. Just for this time with my mother, I won't worry about who she is. Who she was. What she did to me. What I did to her. Just for today.

As they walked, the avenue was crowded with people. Ian heard a mix of languages every moment. Greek, certainly, and their own English. But also French, German, Turkish, a couple of African languages he didn't recognize except by texture. For a moment he was overcome with all the different variations surrounding him. Not just people but a hundred thousand species of beetles, thousands of different mammals, fish, spiders, grasses, oaks, and fungi. He would never see any of it again.

Pauline smiled at him. "Tell me about your girlfriend."

"What girlfriend?"

"The girlfriend I deduced from your behavior. *That* girlfriend."

"If girlfriend she is."

Pauline waved that away. "Don't quibble."

"Well..." Ian thought a moment. "She's physically tiny—I mean I think she's less a meter and a half. But you forget that pretty quick." Ian smiled. "She punches *way* out of her weight class."

He held out his hands as if trying to capture Chitra's shape. "When she takes something on it's like she's *compelled* to see it through. It's why she's such a good responder. She doesn't give up. I mean, it doesn't occur to her to give up." He looked around. *Until I made her give up on me.*

Percy came out of the restaurant, this time as a middle-aged woman dressed in black.

"Percy," said Pauline warmly.

"What?" asked Ian.

"Pauline?" Percy said in a rough voice. "It's time."

oOo

The argument persisted all the way down the elevator.

"*This* is your asteroid project? You've been working for Percy all this time?"

"Yes and no," Pauline said. "I had other jobs. I mean I've been working for Percy since you left for college. But not all of my jobs were for her."

"I can't *believe* this."

Pauline stared at Ian and for the first time, Ian saw Pauline the Project Boss. Her lips drew in a thin line. "I did this to save you."

"Hell!" Ian slapped the wall of the elevator. "I did all this to save *you!*"

"And you did. So what are we *arguing* about?"

Ian didn't know what to say.

Pauline took a deep breath and turned away. "Look, I meant everything I said just spending my time with my son. I don't need a last will and testament. No regrets. No recriminations. You and I are leaving."

Not yet I'm not! Ian almost said it out loud but then realized he had to stop. It was one thing if *he* decided not to leave. But if he did, and he said so to Pauline, she would stay. Everything would be for nothing.

The elevator opened up into a deep cavern built of curved surfaces that met like the inside of a clamshell. It opened and Percy led Pauline away.

In the cavern's corners, hanging like honeycomb, were bubbles. After a moment, Ian realized each bubble surrounded a human being. They were too far for details but the size of the figures within them gave the bubbles size and perspective. There were hundreds—a huge sort of foam. Sections of the shaft near them showed the foam as well and it was clearly a complex structure. Each bubble was connected to a stalk. The surfaces were veined and pulsed. A condensing fog came from them. Pauline left them through a small door.

Percy stood next to him. "She's changing clothes."

"She was working with you all this time," Ian said. "You never told me."

"Yes."

"I don't know if I'm going with you."

Percy was silent for a long moment. "All right."

Pauline returned in a bathrobe and walked between them. She had withdrawn into some vast internal contemplation.

Ian wondered if he'd be the same when his time came. If his time came.

They rounded a bend and there was a soft bed at the edge of the corridor. Pauline crawled up on it and lay back in expectation. A collection of vines grew from the ceiling and clasped her arms and legs. Ian saw needles project from the vines and penetrate her veins with certain precision. Pauline did not seem to notice. The moment seemed as filled with symbolism and ceremony as a church service. Or a funeral. Or a wedding.

Pauline reached up to Ian, dragging the vines up with her, and took Ian's hand. "Kiss me goodbye."

He leaned down and kissed her forehead.

Pauline gripped his hand hard. "You never gave me a minute of shame or disappointment. You are the best son I could have ever had."

"You were always the best mother you could ever be."

Pauline turned to Percy, never letting go of Ian's hand

Ian's gaze followed her and Percy, as a macaw, stood perched on the edge of the bed. He leaned his beak forward rubbed her cheek intimately.

It had been years since Ian had seen the macaw and it struck him dumb with surprise. In a moment, Ian realized that Pauline and Percy had their own relationship. Had one right from the start that extended from when Percy was only a macaw to right now when he was so much more. From long before Ian was born when the three of them, Percy, Pauline, and Martin, lived without him. Did not even know him. It was a jarring moment. He was so used to thinking of Percy only in relation to himself. The idea that someone else might also have some sort of special connection to him, to her, had never occurred to him. *I'm not self-involved. Not at all.*

Pauline said quietly: "When shall we three meet again? In thunder, lightning, or in rain?"

Percy cocked his head to one side and seemed to smile. He said, in Pauline's voice: "When the hurlyburly's done. When the battle's lost and won."

Pauline said: "Fair is foul and foul is fair. Hover through the fog and the filthy air."

"Exactly," said Percy.

Pauline turned back to Ian. "Good luck, Ian. We'll see each other again. I'm sure of it."

Ian couldn't speak. His eyes filled with tears. He nodded.

Pauline lay back and released his hand. She placed her hands at her side and closed her eyes. A translucent membrane grew over the bed. Ian leaned against it. The bed changed character: it was rough as bark hewn from a tree. Pauline didn't move. She just breathed slowly. The veins pierced by the vines pulsed a few times and her face suddenly went gray and she stopped breathing.

Ian's fingers burned suddenly and he jerked back. Ice crystals were forming on the inside and Pauline could no longer be seen. A fog started falling from it.

Percy perched on his shoulder. "Come on, Ian. Time to go."

oOo

Ian stood outside the Sequoia research cabin for a long time before going inside.

Rolf Henderson looked up in surprise as Ian stepped into the cabin.

Ian stamped his feet to get rid of the snow. "Hey."

"You could have done that outside, Mister Bones. You do know that, don't you?"

"What can I say? I was born in a barn." Ian shook Rolf's hand and took his pack into the back room.

Rolf followed him. "You didn't send ahead. I didn't expect you."

"What? You have dancing girls scheduled?"

"No." Rolf looked uncomfortable. "I mean nobody's heard from you. Not since—"

"It's okay." Ian patted Rolf's shoulder. "I was sorry to hear about Julie and Terri."

Rolf looked down and then nodded. "It's just me up here now. Full time. After Los Angeles I didn't have anywhere else I wanted to go."

"I understand."

"Do you want to see the trees?" Rolf seemed almost eager.

"Yes."

The snow was only a few inches on the forest floor but high in the trees were tons of it. Rolf and Ian kept listening for the breaking of branches signifying a few hundred pounds of ice falling towards them.

Rolf gave Ian an occasional patter of rainfall, growth patterns, and limits of invasive species. Mostly, the two of them walked silently along the feet of sleeping giants.

Finally, they sat on a branch of a fallen tree. The tree itself was five meters thick and fifty meters long. The branch was the size of a bench. It was a long and companionable silence. *I can be quiet here,* he thought. Then, he thought of his mother: When the hurlyburly's done. When the battle's lost and won.

A light snow was falling. Just a few flakes from directly above. It was late in the day and in the west, the sun shone below the clouds. Little of the light penetrated the canopy but enough little beams and rays showed the sun was shining.

"I've made out my will, Rolf," Ian said quietly. "The project has funding for the indefinite future despite the disaster economy. I put enough money aside that it should be self-sustaining." Ian looked up at the trees. "Save them if you can."

Rolf stared at him. "You're dying?"

Ian didn't quite know how to answer that. "Yes," he said at last. No other answer would help him here. It was one of those many circumstances that a complete explanation was useless. "My lawyers will talk to you. You can hire anyone you want." Ian gestured to the trees. "There's enough money that you can build up the project as big or as small as you like. Whatever you think is best."

"That's a lot of trust."

"Yes. But what have I got to lose?"

The two men laughed.

After a moment, Rolf said: "It's been a pleasure working with you."

"You were almost able to say that with a straight face."

"I've been practicing."

Ian chuckled. "You go on back to the cabin. I think I'll take a walk. I may be some time."

Rolf searched his face. He stood and reached out his hand. Ian shook it and Rolf walked away and out of sight.

A moment later, Georgette walked out from around the upended trunk. "Nicely done."

"Think he'll save the trees?"

"He has as much chance as anyone."

"Yeah."

"Have you decided?"

"No."

Georgette cocked her head. "Let me point out that Chitra will wake up on Venus. Are you going to make her wake up there alone?"

"Why do you care?"

Georgette came up to him and held him by his shoulders. "I was telling the truth. You were always my favorite."

Maybe he'd been fooling himself with his indecision. Maybe he was always going to go. Regardless, he looked back at her. "It's not like I have anything left here." Ian sighed. He looked at the trees and the light. *Goodbye*. Whatever was coming, it wouldn't be like this. "Okay. Do we have to go somewhere like Pauline?"

"I don't need such things."

"Okay." He took a deep breath. "Ready when you are."

"Close your eyes."

He did and felt her lips brush his.

And he was gone.

Interlude: Percy

Georgette claims to have landed on Earth during the Permian. She as much claimed the Permian Extinction as hers. I wasn't there so I can't verify it, but I can't see such a lie benefiting her. The evidence is consistent with her story. Let it stand.

The unnamed terraformer she killed had done all the heavy lifting: eukaryotic transition, embryonic development, predation. Georgette inherited a full palette of colors to play with.

Arthur, the terraformer of Mars, his time long passed, lay there, depressed and desiccated, resigned to terse communication between Europa and Georgette. He bitterly observed their doomed courtship. Until Europa's murder. Then, Arthur dropped a comet on Earth.

Fast forward sixty million years after Georgette abandoned her beloved dinosaurs and the idea of finding a mate in favor of reproducing on her own. A million years ago she hit on a winning combination. You guys.

I showed up on the scene twenty thousand years ago. Where did I come from? Whose offspring am I? Could I be Europa reborn? I never said and Georgette was afraid to ask. Arthur might know but Arthur doesn't talk to anybody. Some mysteries are more useful unsolved.

Why did I choose Venus? I could have chosen anywhere in the system except Enceladus and Europa. *Luna* is more hospitable. Hell, why terraform a planet at *all?* Grab Ceres and hollow it out into a cylinder. Spin the damned thing and build an ecology on the inside.

I have reasons of my own.

Venus has its own problems. Nearly a hundred times the atmospheric pressure of Earth. Hot enough to melt led and a lot closer to the sun. On Venus, you can get cooked, corroded, and desiccated all at the same time. There is probably no harder piece of real estate in the solar system to work with and that's what I chose. Go figure.

So: 20k years back, I light up the Oort Cloud and Kuiper Belt, talking a blue streak to Arthur and then Georgette. I've been watching. I know the score. I know where the bodies are buried. A and G haven't been on speaking terms since the Cretaceous but I manage to negotiate an uneasy peace between them. In return, I'll metaphorically take Venus off their metaphorical hands. As if any of us had hands.

I needed to manage the unholy atmosphere, the heat and proximity of the sun, and the comparative lack of volatiles—hydrogen and the like were boiled off long ago. There's enough oxygen and carbon for just about anything—too much, really. Though nitrogen isn't a big component of the air, the atmosphere is so thick there's nearly four times as much as on Earth.

Negotiating between two such entities as Arthur and Georgette is time-consuming—not surprising when one considers the courtship between Georgette and Europa, from introduction to rejection, took twenty million years. In that context, a few thousand years is the equivalent of speed dating.

But I wasn't idle in this period. I flitted from comet to icy world to lumps of frozen gas, seeding them with fusion-driven machines. I needed that hydrogen.

Hydrogen is the little unsung hero in life's chemical ballet. Sure, we all know it makes up two pieces of the water trio and burns nicely. But it also hangs off most carbons in one way or another. Glucose has six carbons and six oxygens and twelve hydrogens. Starch and cellulose are both glucose polymers so if you have a thousand glucose lump of potato starch, that's six thousand carbons and six thousand oxygens but *twelve thousand* hydrogens. Look at that benzene ring over there. Six carbons in a hexagon—each of those carbons has a single hydrogen hanging from it. Hydrogen is so ubiquitous that it isn't even written in molecular drawings. Carbon has four slots to bond with other atoms. You only see three of them drawn out? The fourth is assumed to be hydrogen.

I would use 10**14 gigatons of oxygen just for water but I needed 10**13 gigatons of hydrogen to back it up. Not to mention the hydrogen required for all that organic chemistry. I had all the oxygen I could ever need. Hydrogen, not so much.

I stayed in the Oort Cloud for millennia. I built half a million machines to separate the hydrogen from the ammonia there, encasing the resulting frozen hydrogen in thin diamond shells. Millions of hydrogen packages began their long descent down towards Venus. One day, Earth scientists were going to wonder about anomalous amounts of pure frozen nitrogen and oxygen showing up in their instruments. But that was millennia in the future. I was on a schedule from Georgette and a tight energy budget.

Then, I dropped towards my new home. Georgette knocked me down to Earth to renegotiate.

Eventually, I pulled myself up out of that gravity well, with an additional few hundred thousand humans. More about that later.

Of course, dropping lumps of hydrogen onto the Venus inferno was a lost cause; it would just boil away again. Venus had to be prepared. So the hydrogen packets were taking the long way home.

The total Venusian heat energy available to me was enormous. It showed in the temperature difference between the surface and the troposphere. It showed in winds that would have been supersonic on Earth. It showed in the chemical reactions on the surface.

You humans are just beginning to understand the variety and capability of carbon. I inherited a much deeper knowledge to draw on. In the carbon dioxide atmosphere of Venus, I had enormous amounts of raw material. Venus would supply all the energy I needed if I was frugal. As I said, I was on a schedule *and* a budget.

Georgette executed her plans on Earth. Nobody was watching Venus after that. I wasn't terribly concerned but who likes to cook under scrutiny?

I launched the first of the factory packages myself, orbiting high and safe as it burned its way through the carbon dioxide soup. Seventy kilometers up, the package exploded into a dirigible and a long, thermoelectric wire.

Humans tend to think of systems doing a single thing. It's "efficient." Efficiency is merely optimization along one axis of operation at the cost of other axes. Living systems—and we terraformers always think in terms of living systems—operate differently. Living systems have to be nimble, adaptable, opportunistic. If there is energy to be had at one trophic level, as much of it is consumed as possible. The next trophic level figures out how to take what's left, picks up the slack, and passes on what *it* can't eat on down the line. The remainder is suitable only for sedimentary rock.

The wire dug into the ground as the dirigible inflated. The dirigible was high enough to benefit from photocells. A cylinder itself, it took power as the wind roared through it. The thermoelectric wire took advantage of the temperature differential. Turbines sprouted along with wire-like flowers. I gathered energy anywhere I could.

Carbon dioxide was separated, the oxygen released and the carbon served as raw material to make other packages that sailed on the wind like larva until they, too, exploded into floating factories. Thousands. Hundreds of thousands. Until there were enough.

Then, the factories retooled. They no longer made other factories but instead made small self-contained smidgeons that worked their way up out of the atmosphere until they were able to fire themselves up into orbit.

Each smidgeon was equipped with propulsion, a variable refractive index from full transparency to full reflection, and about the same intelligence as a hermit crab. There were trillions of them, each of which found its way to a particular layer of orbit. Like ants, they obeyed simple rules that in the aggregate resulted in complex behavior. They ended up in perhaps a million different orbital planes. Were they to become totally reflective, Venus would be plunged into darkness.

But not yet. Just enough to cool down the surface *some*.

The total mass of the smidgeons and the factories used up barely a percent of the actual carbon in the atmosphere. There was now considerable free oxygen but still way, way too much CO2.

The factories retooled once again. The new smidgeons were smaller, even less intelligent. They collected outside the main smidgeon orbital plane into two great gatherings. Then they interlocked, collapsed, and pulled together. Venus now had three moons the size of Phobos, chasing each other in a polar orbit.

I anchored myself to one. I had been guiding the work remotely but that could only go so far. Venus was a building project and everything up to now could only be considered preparation: necessary and enabling technology, but not the end goal.

The factories began manufacturing random carbon chains, encasing them in buckyballs and dumping them to fall on the surface. The temperature had dropped enough that they were not instantly incinerated. They were for later.

Barely ten percent of the carbon had been used up so far. There was still an enormous amount of CO2 and other elements to be used and an even greater amount to be discarded.

All across the surface grew tall, branching structures that connected into a vast forest, kilometers tall. Natural temperature difference generated an enormous current and where I needed more there was always sunlight via the smidgeons. High-temperature superconductors carried the current to the poles. There, a vast structure arose that sucked in what I didn't need and packaged it into missiles of buckyball encased CO2. On top grew cylinders that extended above the atmosphere, enabling a vacuum from surface to space: a whole collection of rail guns that shot my excess carbon pellets into space. I targeted Mercury. I'm never wasteful. Carbon was a valuable resource and if I couldn't use it now, I might have some use for it later.

The winds of Venus grew sluggish. The pressure differential was no longer sufficient to hold up the dirigibles. They crashed on the surface and broke apart into mobile machines that ate the buckyballs dropped before and shat necessary hydrocarbon precursors.

But it was still too damned hot.

Buried in the trees were networks of *heat* superconductors. I had several billion heatsinks that switched on at night and turned off during the day. For a long time, nightside Venus burned a dull red. Until, at last, the temperature was bearable.

Right on time, the hydrogen packages burned their way into the atmosphere, igniting against the free oxygen and causing rain that immediately burst into steam—one of the strongest greenhouse gases there are. This would have trapped a fatal amount of heat but the orbiting smidgens became reflective. Venus was plunged into darkness.

The ground-based machines churned through first the sulfurous steam and then sulfurous rain, blending the fallen material containing nitrogen, carbon, sulfur, oxygen into the necessary sugars, amino acids, ammoniates, and sulfides that would be necessary for life.

I didn't have the luxury of a living world to start with. Or millions of years. Or even functioning bacteria. This whole job was going to slapdash, jerry-rigged, and held together with the moral equivalent of duct tape, baling wire, and spit. That meant I had to build scaffolds for everything I needed and then take down (reabsorb) the scaffolds afterward so they wouldn't get in the way.

That meant I had to come down at this point. There were operations I could supervise only by tasting the flavors washing over the land. The temperature hovered near the boiling point of water—too hot for most organisms but cool enough for me. The darkness was my friend and the giant trees of Venus radiated away heat into the night.

When Venus became cool enough, the heat trees rotted away. The machines ceased making the materials for life and shat life itself. The scaffolding for living systems was built by living systems—of a sort. The cells were alive in that they consumed material, excreted, and reproduced. But they were far more streamlined and had none of the robustness marking organisms that arose out of the crucible of evolution. They contained just the biochemistry required of their various missions, replication equipment, and significant safeguards against mutation. Some of the scaffolding was chemical in nature: fixing nitrogen out of the atmosphere, grinding down the unusable carbon forms into ready physiological precursors, sequestering trace minerals out of the crevices and pockmarks of the stone—in some cases *making* those pockmarks and crevices in order to expose necessary minerals.

They were successful because of the virtues of scale and parallelism. What one large machine could not begin a trillion tiny machines could finish.

Other scaffoldings were more obvious: blades of grass crafted from cellulose. The skins of trees were built layered on thin spines of graphene. The clockwork skeletons of great predators stood in their majesty and the lacey skeletons of their prey cowered before them.

I concentrated on the Aphrodite continent. Other continents and islands were prepared until they were no longer toxic but would have to wait their turn until Aphrodite was complete—or as complete as time and resources would allow. It would be generations before the scaffoldings were entirely absorbed by their living counterparts. Aphrodite would be like a threadbare jacket, the stays and lining showing through. Later, what I had managed on Aphrodite would be propagated elsewhere. Or I could experiment.

Finally, I endowed Venus with the breath of life: clouds of cellular precursors that dusted over the naked forms of animals and lacey patterns of plants in progressive embryology: single cells clinging to the bare white bones of animals or the chitinous envelope of insects, programmed to grow out the target species. These cells were fat with DNA: they had not only the full complement of their mission but the final packets of data required for the target organism. They filled the gaps in the animal skeletons, invaded the empty cell walls of plants. The animals were fleshed out from their skeletons in the case of vertebrates, and inward from their skin for the invertebrates. The crabs twitched in the surf, washed passively by small waves while the fine filigree of musculature and organs grew like mushrooms after a rain.

On my signal, they quickened and the air was filled with grunts, howls, and shrieks. There was the first herbivorous graze, the first carnivorous kill, the first scavenging of the dead, the first rotting of used and abandoned flesh broken down into the soil.

On one peninsula, I built housing and fences for people. As in every other mythology, humans came last.

Part 2: Who We Are Now

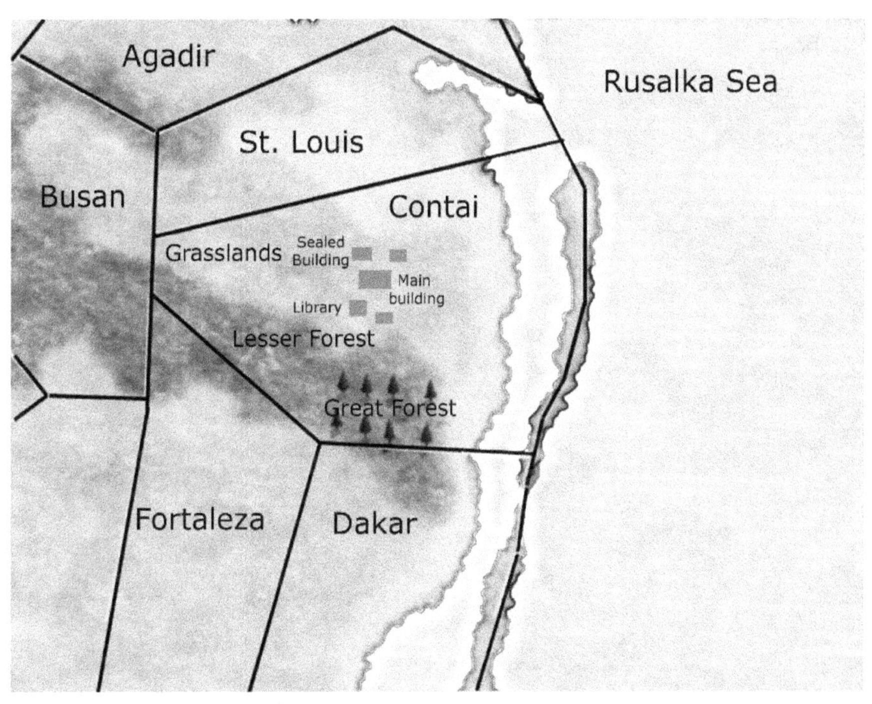

Drawing by Freder Gluck

Chapter 2.1: Sunrise

Freder lay on his side, his eyes open and unfocused. It was that moment between sleep and wakefulness when the world was a meaningless mosaic of light and color across his retina.

He was looking at Ian and Chitra snuggled against one another, still asleep. A child snuggled Chitra's other side. All faces pale and asleep.

That seemed odd.

Ian looked shorter than he remembered. Chitra taller. Both shared the same build: a muscular frame, arms slightly too long. They were dressed in woven grass—just enough to shield the necessaries. The child that was curled up against Chitra was naked as a tiny monkey. All of them were covered by thin fur. Ian's fur was a little darker than Chitra's. The child's fur was almost black.

Fur?

Freder sat up suddenly. This has *got* to be a dream.

He was in a room shaped like a small auditorium. There were no chairs but several risers. People were draped over them in deep sleep. The floor was carpeted,

Shouldn't he be dead?

He remembered standing on an overpass near Wildwood, New Jersey. It should have been high and strong enough. As the wall of water rose from the bay he knew he was lost: the wall was just too big. There was nowhere to run. Nowhere to hide. There was nothing to do but to stand there next to hundreds of other silent people who had come to the same conclusion as it roared towards them. Just time enough to revisit his remaining regret: he had never told Chitra how he felt. He would die with that unfinished.

Then, a feeling like being hit by a massive brick and waking up here.

Freder looked at his hands, his body. For a moment, he was startled by the disconnect between how he remembered himself and what he felt now. All his adult life had been circumscribed by size and weight: turning sideways on a stairway to let someone pass, pulling back from a door so it would pass his belly without contact, the heaviness of his breathing, the impact on his feet from walking.

He felt as light and easy as if he were fifteen again. Eleven. As if he could dance on his fingertips. He was shaking.

Freder looked at his hands. They didn't look delicate. They looked strong, bereft of the light fur that began on his wrists and continued up his arm.

Fur? "Gah!" he cried out and stood up.

He looked down on Ian and Chitra, together. *No.* Not here. Not now.

Outside the sleeping room, he found himself in a foyer. A door to one side led into a large kitchen. Another into a room with tables. The remaining door opened to sunlight. Freder ran towards it.

Freder had worked outside much of his adult life: sifting through rubble in search of bodies, trying to pull people out of collapsing buildings, delivering food, medicine, and water. He had done this in desert, rainforest, bare rock, and urban ruin. In the pouring rain, beneath lightning storms, during hurricanes, and, once, in the face of an oncoming tornado

This sky was odd.

It was just past dawn. The eastern light filtered through a far grove of medium-sized trees—perhaps the size of maples or oaks but conifers of some sort. The sun looked a little smeared, as if there were high but invisible clouds. The blue sky had a yellowish tinge—towards the darker west, the sky turned a faint green. There was a sunrise hush over the world. Freder could hear faint birds but no wind.

He was standing in front of a warehouse-shaped building. It looked two stories tall and broad. A line of fat birds stared down at him from the roo. The stains along the edge suggested they had been there some time.

Above the birds, he saw a dome of netting that came to the ground. He walked over to it. On the other side, the netting again soared into the air. He was under a net dome next to another net dome. The entire area was fenced in on all sides. There were perhaps half a dozen buildings nearby, including the one he had run from. In the distance, on the other side of the fence, were similar buildings.

Freder touched the fence. He pushed against it. It felt like rawhide: slightly flexible until it was suddenly hard and unyielding. He could fit three fingers through the gaps but no more.

It was intolerable to be a prisoner after all this. He had lost his... *life?* Lost his body. Lost everything—Freder didn't know how he knew he had lost everything. He just knew he had.

He screamed in rage. Pushed hard. Nothing. Pulled. Nothing. He tried to stretch the openings in the fence. Nothing. He grabbed the fence and swung his feet against it again and again. He felt huge. Strong. The exertion calmed him. There seemed to be a strange familiarity to his body—*his* body regardless of how it looked or what it could do. *The human mind is infinitely adaptable.*

He grabbed the netting and hauled himself up, pulling himself up the inner side of the dome with little effort. He found himself grinning.

The top of the dome was perhaps twenty meters over the ground. Freder found he could hang there without distress using just his hands. He was strong. Stronger than he had ever been.

Hanging there, he looked around.

The fence enclosed the buildings and the space round them in a trapezoid. The edges of the fence weren't completely visible but what he could see seemed to run perhaps a kilometer or two to the east and half a kilometer wide. There was a large garden below him with newly sprouted green. From this height, he could recognize corn but not much else.

To the west lay the sea. The net dome came down to the water off a long sand bar that formed one side of a lagoon. The next dome to the north shared part of the lagoon but had no access to the sea. There were a couple of domes to the north and a few more to the south. To the east, the land rose, and as it rose the medium trees gave way to huge trees that in the distance looked like redwoods.

There were more domes to the east. The redwoods looked as if they grew through them. The domes proceeded up a rise out of sight.

Freder's hands were getting tired. Twenty meters was too far to fall. He worked his way down to the ground.

A warm wind rolled over him from the east. He realized it had been cooler and the air was warming rapidly.

"Hey!"

It wasn't English.

Freder had been born in Berlin and learned English, French, and Arabic along with his native German before he started school. This was no language he had ever learned. He wrote his name in the dirt with his finger. It phonetically showed his name but the symbols were different. He closed his eyes and recalled the other languages. He still knew them but this new language felt more comfortable.

If your mind is changed are you really who you thought you were?

He opened his eyes again. On the other side of the fence was someone naked and obviously male. *Why am I not more bothered by that?* Was it because he had been changed or just because who he was *now* impeded remembering himself *then*.

"Phillip Hayes," the man said, putting his hand through the fence.

"Freder Gluck," answered Freder, shaking the hand. Phillip's face was still quite human, narrower and shortened to fit on a changed skull. The contrast was striking. Their bodies were very similar: light fur of contrasting colors, the same shaped shoulders, and torsos, arms slightly longer in proportion to the rest. Yet the faces were clearly just as differentiated as they had ever been previously. *We are smaller, thinner, and more uniform versions of ourselves.*

"There more of you?" asked Phillip said in a broad American accent.

"Yes. About twenty, I think. Still asleep."

"Same here." Phillip shook his shoulders in a sort of American half-shrug. "What did you see when you climbed up there?"

"Other domes like this one. Hills. Tall trees."

"How many domes?"

Freder shrugged. "Ten? Twenty? I didn't count and the trees obscured a great deal."

"Yeah." Phillip pointed back at the buildings on his side of the fence. "I did a little exploring, too." He stopped and looked around. "Look at us. Talking like this was normal. Or maybe it is, now that we're on Venus." Phillip chewed his lips. "I guess maybe we'll do okay."

"Venus?"

"You haven't seen the map room. The whole explanation is in there." The expression on Phillip's face turned thin. "We've been chosen by God. It says so on the wall."

"God?"

"Yes." Phillip shook his head. "Individual groups judged on their merits—no doubt by their faith. I've always had trouble with faith. I was a car salesman before. What were you?"

"Emergency rescue."

"Now *that's* useful."

"Maybe. We'll see."

Phillip looked glum. "More useful than a car salesman, anyway." He brightened. "But all have sinned and fallen short of the glory of God, right?"

"Beg pardon?"

"That means in His eyes, none of us is worth more than any other."

"I have no idea."

Phillip nodded. "I understand. You're one of those Europeans, right?"

"German."

"I could tell right off. Different religious upbringing. Not that I'm judging! Heck, I left all that behind when I left Tennessee. I was determined I would not be held back by my background! Now that I'm here it's all coming back to me—it's amazing what you can remember over your life."

Freder had no idea what he was talking about. "You said the explanation is in the map room?"

"Yeah." Phillip pointed back at the buildings. "In our settlement, it was the big one in the middle. Looks like your place is a little different. But I'm sure there's one there, too. After all, God wouldn't just put it all in one place. Like I said, we're all equal in His eyes." Phillip considered for a moment. "Or maybe He would. Maybe He would give different roles to different people."

"Possibly. I will check the map room," said Freder quickly. "It's important that we gather all the data available."

"Good thinking. I'll go see if anybody else has woken up."

Freder hurried away, deeply disturbed. The idea that a mythical being might be responsible for any of this had never occurred to him. As he thought about it, he hadn't really considered how he had ended up in this place, in this body. Was he in some sort of shock? Freder had seen shock during disasters—and wasn't this a complete disaster in a personal sense? Robbed of his body and possibly his mind? A personal apocalypse?

Freder felt suddenly awake. Changing his body. Changing his mind. Imprisoned in a fenced area under a bizarre sky. What could have done that? Aliens, maybe? Human experimentation? Was he lying on a couch somewhere under an induced hallucination? A coma dream? Could he tell? Was it *possible* to tell? Could it be God after all——*no!* His whole mind rebelled at that idea. There must be an explanation for all of this within the realm of the known world. A supernatural entity need not be invoked.

He started towards the large building and stopped. Perhaps the map room answered questions. Perhaps not. But that was not where he needed to go.

Freder returned to where he had awoken. Ian, Chitra, and the others were still sleeping. He sat and waited. After a little while, Ian stirred. Then, Chitra. She opened her eyes.

Freder thought: I must be gentle. Seeing him would be sufficient for her to know the extent of their changes but if he projected confidence and assurance she might gather some of that from him.

"Good Morning," he said softly. "Welcome to Venus."

oOo

Pranavi was surrounded by monkeys. One shook his head and one crouched down in front of them. A female was rubbing her eyes next to her. Had she been holding her? Pranavi wished the monkey would hold her again. She liked monkeys—although the ones that wandered around her Aunt's house yelled at her unless Pranavi fed them. Then, her Aunt yelled at *her*.

The monkey looked down at her. It had a human face.

Pranavi yelped and sat back suddenly, her hands over her mouth. It tickled and she looked at her hands. Her wrists were covered with the same fur as the woman-monkey. Her hands were pale, not brown as they should be.

Pranavi was a monkey, too.

The woman-monkey looked at the crouching one. "Freder?" she said softly. Then, she looked over Pranavi's head.

"Ian," she cried.

"Chitra!"

Pranavi got out of the way as they hugged one another. Adults were distastefully predictable.

She looked around the room. There were many monkeys—no, Pranavi corrected herself. They were monkey *people*. And now she was one of them. So, really, they were just people who just *happened* to look like monkeys. Freder saw her and got to his feet slowly. He put out his hand. "Freder Gluck."

"Pranavi Basu," she said. "Where are we?"

"Venus," he said. "So I've been told."

"What did she do?" Chitra said to Ian furiously. "Look at me. Look at *yourself. What did she do?"*

Ian looked at his hands. "I don't know."

"You *should* know! She's yours—or you're hers."

"Don't fight," said Pranavi, stepping between them.

"What?" said Chitra.

"Don't fight," Pranavi insisted. "My parents fought that night and the wave came and took them the next day. My aunt and uncle fought and the tsunami came that night. You don't want that to happen to you." She considered a moment. "Or me."

"Tsunamis don't work like that," said Chitra.

As smart as they were, adults could be surprisingly stupid. Once could have been coincidence. Twice could not. Pranavi was taking no chances on a third. "Whatever."

Pranavi looked at Freder. "Come on." If those two wanted to invite another tsunami, let them. Pranavi would find higher ground.

Freder stopped at the door and looked back. "I should stay," he murmured. "She might need me."

"They're going to fight for a while," said Pranavi with certainty. They acted just like her parents.

"Yes." Freder considered. "Want to go to the map room?"

"Sure. Where is it?"

"I don't know."

People were milling around now. Many were coming out of a larger building and shaking their heads.

Freder pointed at the larger building. "I'm guessing over there."

Pranavi and Freder followed them. The room contained a map, a clock, and a sign arrayed together on one wall. The rest of the room was filled with books. The sign read:

<u>Current Earth time:</u>	1/27/5850, 12:47 AM
<u>Venus orbital number since event:</u>	6192.384
<u>Venus day number since event:</u>	3225.2
<u>Venus phase:</u>	Sunrise
<u>Location:</u>	Rusalka Bay, Aphrodite

Greetings.

You are now on Venus. Everyone you know died shortly after you were saved. Everything familiar to you has eroded away in the time it has taken to make Venus habitable. The changes in your bodies were necessary for your survival here. This world was not created for you but you were a consideration in its preparation. You are separated into communities to gain understanding of your situation and facility with your environment. If this works out, the fences will come down. Everything you need to learn is in the library.

Good luck.

Below was drawn a large map of Venus showed the lands and seas. On the continent named Aphrodite, there was a mark, and next to the mark an expanded map showing a collection of bordered spaces. One opened into Rusalka Bay and was outlined in bold lines with the words "<u>You are here.</u>"

Pranavi felt a great satisfaction. "Monkeyland is on Venus."

Freder nodded. "So I was told." He fell silent a moment. "Pranavi Basu? That's your name?"

"Sure."

"Are you from Contai?"

"I was." She shook her head. "The wave hit and I woke up in Kolkata. Then the wave hit there, too." She looked at him suspiciously.

"We found you." He gestured outside. "Me and Chitra and the rest of our team. We found you in the rubble."

"Oh." Pranavi felt pressure inside like an expanding bubble, squeezing her heart and her lungs. "Did you find my mother? Or my father?"

"We found the woman who had saved you. I think it was probably your mother."

Pranavi caught the word "was." "Dead. What about my father? My sister?"

Freder shook his head. "Just you and your mother."

Pranavi stared at him. It felt too hot here. "Then what good are you?"

She ran outside.

More adults were entering silent and leaving crying and moaning. One woman just lay on the ground in the entrance, weeping and calling out for her little girl. Pranavi jumped over her and kept running until the fence stopped her.

Fine. She had little sympathy for the crying woman. Didn't she lose her little brother? Her sister? Her parents? Her *dog? She* wasn't going to lie on the ground in a pool of tears. She was going to find out what this place held for her. Maybe later, when she was sleeping or huddled against a wall, she'd weep for little Shevang—how Pranavi had resented him! Or Mintu—her other brother had hated that nickname: Number two, indeed! Or her mother. Or her father. Maybe she would even dream of holding tiny Gibreel against her chest as he licked her face.

But not now. Not in the daylight. Not when she could explore the world.

She scrambled up the fence until she could jump to the roof of the nearest building. Excited, she cried out and scampered across the flat roof. She counted twelve buildings.

There were flat-nosed birds the size of chickens that snarled at her and then clumsily launched themselves in the air. They circled the roof and glided to the opposite side. Pranavi ran towards them to chase them again but this time they stood their ground and snarled at her, baring their teeth.

Teeth?

Pranavi bared her teeth and growled right back. The birds seemed confused. They muttered to one another. She danced towards them and away, *daring* them to play with her. They opened their mouths at her, showing her their teeth but not in a menacing way. She opened her mouth and waggled her jaw at them.

This caused them to hoot at her. She hooted back and they danced, bobbing their heads up and down. Not to be outdone, Pranavi danced along with them, bobbing her head with them. One blue and green bird came over and rubbed against her leg. A large white one growled at her.

Uh oh, she thought. I'm messing with his girlfriend.

Pranavi backed away and gently pushed Blue-And-Green towards Mister White.

Mister White hissed at Pranavi perfunctorily and started pushing Blue-And-Green back towards the flock. When Mister White was far enough away from Pranavi, he swung his neck around and slammed his head into Blue-And-Green. The other bird yelped and tumbled and ran to join the rest of the flock.

Pranavi clapped her hands and laughed.

Mister White gave her a quick glance that looked for all the world as if he were sharing a joke. Then, he turned and walked, very tall and dignified, back to the rest of the flock.

Pranavi waved goodbye and walked to the other side of the roof. She looked down on a clot of people talking outside the building.

She went back to the edge of the roof near the fence, got a running start, and jumped over to catch herself on the fence. Pranavi laughed and began climbing for the sheer joy of it. It was *great* being a monkey.

She tried to grab with her feet and almost fell. No luck: merely human feet.

Pranavi dropped to the ground and continued to explore the buildings. She skipped the library full of crying adults and went back to the kitchen and sleeping area. She found lots of little cozy spaces and storage areas. Some were locked. Some, though, were not and she found stacked vegetable fritters. Some carrots and potatoes. She helped herself. Next to the food bins were a set of sinks and Pranavi drank.

The third building she found had tools and what looked like workspaces—she recognized a blacksmith area and a room with woodworking tools. Another door led into a long greenhouse open at both ends. Pranavi spent a pleasant hour running up and down walkways next to trees and vines. They were covered in bees. When the wind blew from one end to the other it was bearable. Then the wind stopped and it became far too hot.

The next few buildings were sealed shut. No sign of any doors or windows. She put her ear to the wall and heard nothing but a gentle hum. Pranavi spent a good fifteen minutes trying to pry what looked like doors open without success.

She walked towards the sea on the long beach before the lagoon bordered by a sandbar. Beyond that: the open ocean. Land spread away on both sides of her, curving away into the distance. She remembered the map: Pranavi was looking at the broad arms of Rusalka Bay. Pranavi had a strong urge to keep walking forever. Only the fence kept her here.

She could see buildings in the distance in both directions. The fences separated her settlement from two others and went right into the water up again across the sandbar and down again into the water, meeting the high roofing fence as it met the water. On the other side of the far fence, just this side of the sandbar, she saw a long body moving slowly.

It was s whale. She waved at it.

It lifted its head and watched her for a moment, opened a long serrated jaw, then slipped beneath the water.

It was not a whale.

She turned and walked back towards the buildings. It might have been a crocodile but she didn't think so. It didn't move like a crocodile. Its jaws didn't look like a crocodile's jaw. And she didn't think crocodiles grew to twenty meters. Of course, she was on Venus. Who knew what was possible? Maybe the same sort of thing was living in the lagoon.

On the other side of the buildings, she found the largest garden she'd ever seen: hundreds of meters, with neat rows and trellises. This must be where the carrots came from! The potatoes! Though most of the garden was composed of small plants. That made sense. It was just sunrise, after all. It took time to grow potatoes.

A young boy was harvesting a patch of green beans. These had been in the ground long enough to produce actual fruit. They leaned towards the sun. He looked up at her. "Gerard LeStrange," he said and held out a handful of beans.

She took them. "Pranavi Basu." The beans crunched in her mouth. "Need help?"

Gerard nodded.

She found herself sweating. Pranavi wiped her face and realized she was smiling. The sense of it felt unfamiliar. She realized that before today she'd not smiled for a long time. Pranavi resolved *that* would *change*.

The sky was bright and hot. The wind was gentle as it blew across her sweaty back. She could feel her fur ruffle and wave. The world murmured with the hum of bees flying amongst the flowers. She sat down and parted the bush beans. Sure enough, there were tiny weeds.

Happily, she pulled the weeds up carefully as to not injure the beans. They came up easily, showing brown dirt speckled with black bits like charcoal. She put them to one side for a green mulch later, just as comfortably and easily as if she'd done it her entire life.

Yes, she thought with satisfaction. *Welcome to Venus.*

oOo

Julie had never been so angry.

She'd asked everybody in the sleeping area, looked everywhere for Terri. She walked around the buildings and into the map room. Pounded on the sealed buildings. She was on Venus.

It felt like she was going to explode every step as she walked out of the map room. Every breath. How *dare* they do this—whoever they were.

And right into Sequoia National Park.

For a moment she looked for Rolf or the research hut or Terri—then Julie shook her head. *That's not possible.* She looked around. She'd gone in the other entrance and came out the other side of the building.

It sure looked like a sequoia.

She checked the bark and looked at branches on the ground. No. This was not *Sequoiadendron giganteum.* This was an older, wilder, and most certainly extinct *Sequoiadendron.* A collection of conifers surrounded the big trees like shepherds surrounding great and noble cattle. Still, it was like a breath of home. Julie still half expected to see the research shack where she and Terri had spent hours poring over data until they tumbled into the tiny bed and poured over each other.

Julie walked out of the forest past the garden. She stopped at the fence and grabbed it. *Terry? Where are you?* She grabbed the fence, shaking it and screaming.

"Julie?" she heard suddenly. "Julie Agata?"

Julie looked up hopefully before she identified it as a man's voice. On the other side of the fence, she saw Ian Bones.

"Ian!" She made her way to him Ian met her there and they hugged through the cord.

Seeing someone she knew broke some wall within her. She wouldn't let him go for a long time.

Finally, Julie released him. "Have you seen Terri?" she asked.

Ian shook his head.

It didn't matter. Seeing Ian gave her hope. From the map, she calculated there were about a thousand people in the settlements here. If there as many as a hundred other similar settlements, that gave a population of a hundred thousand people. A random selection meant that any one person had a one in 90000 chance of being on Venus. *Random* selection meant there was a one in 8.2 billion chance Terri was here. *Non-*random selection meant either she was picked or she wasn't, based on criteria Julie didn't know. Julie refused to believe any non-random selection process that included her would exclude Terri.

"Have you seen anyone? Anyone you know?" Julie searched his face.

"Yes." He pointed behind him. "This is Chitra Majhi. Freder Gluck."

"Chitra and I know someone as well. A little girl named Pranavi Basu," said Freder.

"Who is she?" Ian said.

"We saved her in the wreckage at Contai." Chitra came up beside Freder. "She was the only one we *could* save," Her anger towards Ian was palpable.

Sisters in rage, Julie thought. She wondered why Freder and Ian didn't seem angry. "I see."

Ian gestured towards Julie. "Julie Agata. She worked on the Sequoia project."

"She knows you," said Chitra quietly to Ian. "I know you. Freder knows you. How many other people know you?"

"A fair number," flared Ian. "You'd be surprised."

"Surprise me."

"Here I know only you and Freder."

"But if you gathered all those people you might know more in other settlements."

Ian glared at her. "I might. I didn't gather everybody. I didn't even get to most of them."

Chitra stared at him. She turned to Julie. "Ian's been working for the alien who broke the world," Chitra said to Julie.

"No," Ian said bitterly. "I worked for the alien that *saved* us."

"Saved us *from* the alien who broke the world. For the good one to save us you had to work for the bad one."

Julie stared at Ian, then the others. They thought a person of some sort was responsible for all of this. The map room display certainly suggested that. If there was a being or beings or whole civilization that could reform Venus, it or they were certainly smart enough to *appear* to be a person.

Ian looked miserable. "Sort of."

Chitra stared at him. "My parents are dead. My brother and sister and their kids are *dead!*"

"I had nothing to do with that!" Ian said in a low suppressed scream.

"No. You just made sure I was brought along. Why didn't you bring *them?*"

"I couldn't. Percy wouldn't let me."

"And now they're dead."

"Percy didn't kill anybody." Ian's voice was tight. "Georgette did all of that. She killed millions of people that year alone. Percy didn't have to bring anybody here. She could have just copied anybody she wanted and planted them in these bodies. Hell, she could have grown people from scratch. But *I* insisted we bring actual people, not copies. It was my condition of employment. I couldn't be everywhere and I didn't manage to help collect anybody in Europe. But I was there in Contai. I was there in Mussoorie. I was there in Okinawa. I helped as many as I could."

"You weren't in Los Angeles," Julie said. "At least I didn't see you. Just the wall of water."

Ian looked at her with naked misery. "No."

"All right, then. Who's Georgette?" Julie said quietly. "Or Percy?"

Ian stared at her for a moment. "Right. How could you know, right? Life as we know it on Earth, Mars, Europa, and now Venus was created by terraforming entities. The one in charge of Earth is Georgette. Mars is Arthur. Venus—now—is Percy. Apparently, the one on Europa is dead."

"*Terraforming* entities? Didn't life arise on Earth all by itself?"

Ian shrugged. "Probably. Maybe. I don't know. Even if it did, these *constructs* came along and made everything in their own image." Ian barked a short laugh. "All that time people were trying to answer the Fermi paradox. We're the answer. Every dog, crab, and bat." Ian closed his eyes and collected himself. "Georgette, Percy, and Arthur made some kind of deal—I never understood all of the details. Percy wanted humans. Georgette supplied them. I insisted they be real people instead of metaphysical copies. I have no idea what Arthur got out of the deal."

"What kind of leverage could you possibly have had with such creatures?" *They should not be named. It makes them appear human,* thought Julie. Even if they mimicked the appearance of humanity perfectly, they could never be human. So viewing them would only obscure their true nature.

Ian shook his head. "I'm not sure. I always thought any importance I had to Georgette derived from whatever importance I had to Percy. Initially, she said it was because I was uncorrupted by Georgette. That couldn't have been the only reason, but it was the only one she ever gave me, though she hinted at others. It was one of those gifts I didn't want to look at too closely or it might be taken away. Then where would I be?"

Chitra looked at them both with clear, empty eyes. "My whole family is still dead. How do I go on living when everybody that meant anything to me is dead and gone to dust? How does anyone?"

Julie felt as if he were held suspended over a yawning pit of death. Everyone was gone. After three thousand years, whatever still lived on Earth might not even be human even if it possessed human heritage. If human, it was a humanity millions of kilometers away and as far removed from them as they had been from the ancient Chinese. The best Julie and the rest could hope for was to occasionally be able to see their home world at night.

She had to find Terri. The world was bearable as long as she had Terri, Venus or not.

"Yes," said Freder to Chitra. "That is the question for all of us, isn't it?"

"No, it's not," said Julie. "Terri's not dead. I will find her." She looked at Ian, Chitra and then settled on Freder. "The dead insist on life continuing. Otherwise, what's the point? If you don't keep on living now, they will have died in vain." She drew herself up and said formally. "You must, of course, make your own choice. As for me: I plan to live." Julie dusted her hands on her thighs. "Welcome to Venus."

oOo

Larissa Barbossa was unprepared for the tears as she stumbled out of the map room, crushed beneath the vast distance between who she was now and what the world had become. Where did this grief come from? Hadn't the world always treated her with contempt? Hadn't she fought for every inch and scrap in her life? Venus had the virtue of being different. Venus had the virtue of being new.

But it didn't seem to matter. She was in mourning for the taste of the air, the smell of the sea, the sound of people, dogs, trees—sounds and smells that had been imprinted on her at birth and whose mark she had never recognized.

Even her skin was wrong. She was pale where the skin showed where the color should have been an honest black.

She knelt slowly. Buried her face in her hands and fell to her side, her knees against her chest. She could smell the ground: moisture, dust, sulfur, charcoal. She held up a handful of dirt. A collection of faces, arms, hands, necks of people she'd known fluttered through her mind. *Gone.* Leaves. Fish. Grass. *Gone.* Flowers. Bees. Dragonflies. *Gone*—whatever served the same function on Venus could not be the same *thing*. She knew it in her mouth, her nose, her lungs, her liver, her bones. Larissa was bereft of home.

Larissa Barbossa had never been one to cry. Weeping was not considered an option in the *favela*. Weeping could get you raped or killed or both and not necessarily in that order. So when the *Alemão* took her parents, she hid and watched them leave with dry eyes. When she was beaten for asking about them at the *Delegacia,* she did not sniffle. When she was discovered hanging around the dock dressed as a boy and thrown into the bay to drown, she said nothing. She had learned silence.

She worked in silence from then on, crewing on ship after ship, masquerading as a man. She'd been hurt, fought back, been knocked unconscious, knocked others unconscious, with deadly quiet. She earned her nickname, *Mudo,* in San Diego when a teamster decided she was an easy mark. He ended up on the ground, bloody and groaning, his jaw at an unnatural angle. She looked down on him, spit out two teeth, and walked to the other end of the bar without a word.

By then she had an identity: Lucio Barbossa. She did not carouse in ports like the others. Instead, she studied, taking courses when she was in port and studying online while at sea. By the time she neared thirty, she was third engineer on the container ship *Ahriman* out of Liberia. She had been nothing but a man for thirteen years.

The *Ahriman* had been docked in Porto de Santa Cruz on Tinerife. She was on late watch when Gran Canaria went off like a bomb. There was nowhere to go. In the few seconds she had left, she slid down the stairs to the main deck and watched the shock wave roll over the water towards her. She leaned on the railing quietly smoking as a man does. Her last deliberate act in life was to toss the burning ember overboard as a gesture of goodbye. Then, nothing until now.

These tears, this choking grief, came from someplace within her she had never known.

A man squatted across from her, watching.

She hadn't felt this vulnerable since the night her parents had been taken.

Larissa sat up and dried her eyes. She felt dirt smeared on her face. She could feel dirt on her skin, working into her fur and too pale skin. She looked at herself—obviously female. Nothing but a thin grass strip across her breasts and a short grass skirt. Her fur concealed nothing. There was no masquerading anymore.

The man cocked his head. "Get up." He stood.

Larissa scrambled to her feet. The tears still came. She felt naked in every sense of the word: powerless, humiliated, exposed.

The man watched her a moment and then gave her a full slap across the face.

Larissa staggered back, crouched, and came back at him with a fist in his stomach. Everything in her was behind that punch. Every bit of grief and rage from that last day in the *favela* to the Gran Canaria eruption to finding herself revealed to the world.

He doubled over, fell to the ground, and threw up.

She pulled back her foot, ready to kick his head off.

He held up his hand. "Sorry! Sorry!"

She stopped. Slowly, she put her foot down.

He worked his way to his knees.

"Do that again and I'll kill you," she said with a snarl.

He gave her a lopsided grin. "Don't think I'll have to," he said. Inch by painful inch, he worked his way to his feet.

Larissa watched him. *Venus. Okay.* After all, she thought. How different was this when her parents were taken? She felt bereft then as well—more so, really. She hadn't understood what had happened. She only knew a great hole had opened in the world. Did the lack of understanding make it worse or better? Larissa had no idea. *Then*, she had lost her parents. *Now*, she had lost her world. Hadn't her parents made her world? Was the difference mere scale? The rage brought her back to herself. Rage was something she understood.

Phillip stuck out his hand. "Phillip Hayes. I'm happy to meet you."

She slapped his hand away. "You slapped me."

"Yes." He put his hand out again. "Jesus said to turn the other cheek when slapped."

"I have no use for Jesus."

"Of course not," he said, still holding out his hand. "But I do. And I'm turning the other cheek."

She stared at him. "What do you want?"

"Your friendship."

"After you slapped me?"

"Would you have befriended me if I had asked while you were crying?"

Yes, she thought. And I would have hated you for it. "You always slap women when they're crying?"

"No." He gave her back her stare. "Did I do the wrong thing?"

She about to shout yes when she realized she no longer grieved. The rage had burnt it out of her. Did he *plan* that?

Phillip leaned forward and said in a softer voice. "Do you need to hit me again?"

"Would you let me?"

"Yes," he said simply.

She cocked her head. Clearly born a white guy—as much as that counted now. It didn't look like much color had been preserved. "I'm good." She looked at his hand and took it. "Larissa Barbossa," she said, tasting her name as it came across her tongue and lips for the first time in years.

"I see great things before us." Phillip grinned at her as he pumped her hand. "Great things. Welcome to Venus!"

Chapter 2.2: Morning

Freder awoke. He stretched and looked around. He was one of the last to wake this time. Ian and Chitra were already gone. He went to the door and looked outside. A hard, steady rain fell. Good. It hadn't rained for two sleeps and the air smelled dusty. *Hm,* he thought. The soil parched quickly in the constant sunlight.

Parched. It had rained every couple of sleeps since they had awoken. Freder wondered how long it would take to dry the soil in the absence of rain. What sort of weather could he expect from Venus? He tried to imagine the effects of a long, continuous warming followed by a long, continuous cooling and gave up. He didn't know enough. Maybe there was something in the library. They had already discovered a sort of index—the *Outline of Necessary Things*. It told them where they could find books on how to smelt iron, make pots, weave grass.

Freder wore only woven grass to cover his groin. But the rain was warm on his fur and he jogged over to the map room. While he slept the display had changed from "Sunrise" to "Morning." Freder wondered what that meant. It had been about six sleeps. He looked at the elapsed Earth time and did some quick calculations in his head. One sleep looked to be equal to about twenty hours. Venus had a solar day of roughly fifty-eight days of sunlight and fifty-eight days of night. That was about sixty-nine sleeps. They were about one-sixth of the way towards Noon.

Outside he looked around. The sealed buildings beckoned him like they always did. *Here! Spend a few hours trying to fruitlessly enter me. Maybe this time you can solve my mystery.* Freder looked away from them. If he thought of something to try, he would. But he—and many others—had wasted days trying to crack open those shuttered warehouses without scratching the equivalent of paint.

He found Chitra in the dining area off the kitchen. Nobody was eating. Instead, Chitra was looking at Pitor Abrams stretched out on the table. The boy's leg was bent oddly and he looked stoically at the ceiling.

Chitra looked up. "Don't climb the fence and try to drop ten meters. Or this happens."

"I didn't do it on purpose!" Pitor looked indignant.

Freder ignored him. "Broken?"

"I think so." She shook her head irritably. "From what I can feel. Of course, without imaging, I really know nothing."

"Welcome to the nineteenth century." Freder felt of the bend. It was a shallow deformation—only about five degrees or so. And as he touched it, it didn't feel so much broken as just *bent*, like a bit of tubing. *What's inside us, anyway?* He had a sudden vision of black carbon composite. Bending was fine, but such materials seemed to vaporize when they actually broke. Was this a *schlimbessurung*—an improvement that makes things worse? Are we all such things? A misguided attempt at improvement?

"Did you check the *Outline of Necessary Operations?*" he asked.

Chitra nodded. "There's a medical section. But it's sparse—mostly cuts and bruises. Little on more serious physical injuries. There's a big section on how to handle poisons."

"Lovely." Something new they had to learn on their own. "What do you think?" Freder asked Chitra.

Chitra felt Pitor's leg carefully. "I think it's the tibia. The fibula feels intact. I think it has to be straight to heal properly."

"Do you think we actually heal?"

"What?" asked Pitor. "I won't heal?"

"Quiet," said Freder.

"Of course we heal," said Chitra soothingly. "I've seen scrapes bleed, scab and scar. We heal."

"My leg is more than a scrape," said Pitor.

"Yes," she said thoughtfully. "It is. Hold him down."

"What are you going to do?" Pitor started to get up but Freder leaned on him and held onto the table, pinning him.

"We're going to straighten your leg."

"Will it hurt?"

"I have no idea."

"Wait!"

Chitra held the shin with her left hand to isolate the force to the lower leg. She put the bend across her knee and applied pressure opposite the bend.

Pitor made a sound like steam escaping.

"Won't it take just as much force to bend it back?" asked Freder.

"Maybe I can live with a bent leg," hissed Pitor. He gave a little shriek.

"Hold on," said Chitra.

Freder watched as slowly she bent the leg back into place. When it seemed straight, she stopped.

"Let him go." She released him and stood up.

Freder pushed himself off Pitor.

The boy sat up and rubbed his leg. "Hey! That feels better!"

"I didn't think that would work." Freder felt the leg dubiously. It seemed just a little swollen.

"I didn't either." She bit her lip. "It was as if the bone seemed to suddenly *understand* what was necessary and bent *itself* back into place. Like it knew what was wrong but just needed a little guidance." She was silent a moment. "What's inside of us, Freder?"

Freder shook his head and didn't answer.

Pitor started to sneak off the table.

"Hold on." Chitra looked at Freder. "Go find me two sticks for a splint, would you? And one for a crutch."

When Freder returned, she had a grass rope ready. She was no longer wearing a top so Freder knew where the rope had come from.

He stopped, watching her chest. The fur was light, cinnamon-colored. It limned her breasts, gracing them with light and shadow. The aureoles were large and chocolate brown.

Chitra looked at him, then her chest, then back to the boy. She took the sticks and tied them to his leg.

Pitor yelped. "That's tight."

Chitra felt his foot. "Exactly. I don't want you to bend it again." She gave Pitor the crutch. "No weight on it and I want to see it again when you come in to sleep."

Pitor nodded and hobbled outside.

She crossed her arms over her chest. "I'm going to need some more woven grass. Do you know how?"

Freder shook his head, still mesmerized by the leftover vision of her breasts and shoulders. She had never looked more beautiful than right now.

Chitra shook her head. "I miss my body," she said softly. "I had the nicest figure. Big where I wanted to be big. Small where I wanted to be small. Even my skin is different. Look at me." She held up one hand. "This isn't my color. My skin used to have this lovely creamed coffee texture. Now I'm as white as Englishman in the spring. We're *all* pale—Africans, Indians, Chinese. All the same color."

"We're darkening," said Freder, trying to sound sympathetic. He held up his hand. "As the sun rises—"

"Oh bother you!" Chitra cried out. "I miss differences. I miss how men and women looked so different from one another. How different they felt to the touch. How different they tasted. How different they smelled." She looked at them both. "Now we all look nearly the same. Just little differences here and there. Between people. Between men and women. I miss who we were." She shook herself.

"We are who we are now. You were beautiful then. You're beautiful now," said Freder softly. "I don't see any difference."

She smiled at him. "You're sweet."

Freder shook his head violently. "No," he said, his voice suddenly harsh. "I'm not *sweet*. I'm not *nice*. I *love* you. I have loved you for *years*. That hasn't changed but *I* have. I won't be silent about it anymore."

"Oh, Freder," she said and held up that same hand towards him, reaching towards his cheek.

Oh, let it be now. Finally.

Chitra stopped and stared at her hand oddly. She stood up and rubbed it with her other hand. A cloud of hair puffed out. Chitra rubbed the rest of her. More hair fell out. "Oh, my God, I'm shedding," she said softly. "I'm fucking *shedding!*" And ran outside.

Freder stood there for a long time. He felt as if he'd been split and then hastily jammed back together, all of the pieces jumbled against one another.

All right, he thought. All right. At least she knows. Maybe it will be awkward. Maybe we'll never be friends again. But at least she knows.

Freder went outside. He didn't see Chitra. No one was outside at all. It was still raining but he didn't mind. He leaned back against the building and watched the sky.

Freder found himself oddly satisfied with the situation. He missed Earth: the apples here were not Earth apples. The blossoms smelled citrusy and the bark had a rough touch. Venus eggplants and tomatoes were tasty but did not match his memory. The sky was different. While he missed the physical environment of Earth, he did not miss much else. He'd had only perfunctory contact with the rest of his family. His only real friends had been the UNERA team. His only real love was Chitra.

Back on Earth, he'd never dared act on his feeling. He was too big. Too clumsy. Too much "friend material" as Ellish had said. Freder felt a pang as he recalled the deep lines of Ellish's face. Dead and gone to dust.

But here he didn't look all the different from anyone else. Here, his body was stronger and healthier than he'd ever known. Maybe he had a chance with her. Or, if that failed, with somebody else. He had become part of a little group on this side of the fence and in small gatherings separated by the fence. Chitra, Ian, Larissa, Phillip, and Julie satisfied his need for a small group of friends. But if that didn't work out he could make new friends. This was as fresh a start as anybody could ever want.

Freder stretched his hands into the rain. It was good to feel alive. Somewhere above him, birds flew. Out in the ocean, there were fish. In the forest on the other side of the fence, beyond the human settlements, animals roamed. He could hear them when he turned in to sleep. Feel them as they flew above him.

Venus was an endless mystery.

Who knows? Here he might learn to be happy.

oOo

As far as Julie could tell, socializing happened while gardening.

Continuous sunlight forced continuous growth. One of the first waking duties the settlement did together was to manage the garden. This was their food source. They ate strictly vegetarian: no meat was stored. Some had been watching the birds but no one had acted yet. The kitchen bowls served double duty, both for kitchen duty and watering the transplants.

Hotaru Issa, a deeply indignant woman, was already sitting next to a section of new beans, her now furless body darkening as she worked. "Hello," she said without taking her eyes off her hands.

Julie knelt next to her. She pulled out tiny weeds. Her eyes mysteriously knew without mistake and merely informed her hands. She placed the weeds precisely next to one another on the open dirt next to her.

"Just toss them on the grass," said Hotaru. "Or make a big pile for mulch."

"I want to know what is weed and what is crop."

"That's a bean," said Hotaru pointing at the seedling tiny and straight in the dirt. Then, she pointed at the plant lying next to Julie. "That's a weed."

Julie smiled dutifully. "Beans were weeds once. So was corn. So was eggplant." She pointed at the weed. "Maybe that's future wheat. Or future rice."

Hotaru snorted and shook her head. She was silent a moment, her hand quickly pulling up grasses, broadleafs, something sharp spiked like a dandelion. She tossed them in a conciliatory pile next to Julie.

Julie gently teased another weed from what resembled a bean—what they ate were clearly related to familiar plants such as tomatoes, potatoes, beans and corn. Julie also noticed subtle differences. The corn had narrower and thicker leaves while the stalks on the tomatoes were more robust; they bushed and did not vine. The potatoes were a deep, dark green with thick curly leaves more resembling kale than anything else.

More and more, Julie was seeing evidence of *design.* In walking around the sequoias, she had found a few trees where the bark was broken and she found a black lattice underneath. Were the trees artificial? She broke a few saplings and found unremarkable green wood.

She did not know why the plants were modified. For the unrelenting sun? For water retention? For the long night? Julie didn't know but that didn't change the fact of the modification.

Even their own bodies were smaller and more uniform. Stronger, too, with longer arms while still retaining the uniquely human open shoulder structure. Any one of them could throw a two hundred kilometer an hour fastball.

Evolution was the consequence of a joining between heritage and history. Every Earth organism was a product of all of the countless decisions and events of their ancestors coupled with the way those decisions were affected by the environment. Georgette might have coerced some of that but Julie remained convinced she'd done so by influencing chance and circumstance rather than intervening directly.

Percy, however, had had no such luxury. Things were built here with purpose. By learning the ins and outs of her design, Julie was learning the ins and outs of Percy's mind.

It is good to know the mind of God.

Later, Ian was waiting for her when she approached the fence.

"Hey," he said. Ian looked worn.

"Hey, yourself." Julie looked around. "Where is everybody?"

"I'm by myself today."

There was something in his voice. "What is it?"

Ian looked at the ground and then back into her face. "Chitra found a collection of books entitled *Those Left Behind* in the map room."

It felt as if her heart stopped. "Yes?"

"They're a collection of people who were killed back on Earth in the same disasters where we were taken." Ian held onto the fence. "Chitra thought I should be the one to tell you."

"Is Terri's name in there?"

"No."

Relief welled up in her chest.

"Not my mother, either." He gave her a half-hearted grin. "Pauline Bones. Hear anything?"

"No. I've asked at the other fences. No Terri or Pauline in any of the places." She thought a moment. "Is there a set of *Those Taken?"*

"Not that we can find. We looked."

"Of course. Excuse me. I'll see you later." She left him and went immediately to the map room to check for herself. There was no certainty that each map room library was the same. The library was vast and they had only scratched the surface.

Terri was not in *Those Left Behind.* Julie could not find a *Those Taken.*

Julie's settlement bordered on seven others. She had looked for Terri in her own settlement as soon as she had awoken, then asked anyone she could find at the bordering fences. No Terri.

The map showed twenty-five settlements. Julie had direct contact with eight of them. There was no telling who was in the remainder. Terri could be looking for her right now and if there were more than one settlement between them, Julie would never know.

That was intolerable.

She went out to the trees. Towering over her, they gave her a sense of place. They made her feel as if she could draw strength from them as they drew water from deep in the ground.

"We need to get a list of names for everyone in the settlements. All of the settlements. Everyone," she said aloud. As always, she felt like she was shaking with misery and rage. Rage that she was taken. Misery she didn't have Terri with her.

Julie found stacks of what looked like loose paper in an alcove of the map room. Next to the paper, she found a drawer in which there graphite rods. She was able to write on the paper. She could then rub off the mark with her finger. It wasn't as permanent as a pen but it would serve.

Julie made a list of everyone in her settlement. She stared at it.

It was no more than a list of names for a nameless settlement. It came to Julie, they needed a census. But a census of what? Julie's place? Hotaru's group? They deserved better than a nameless settlement. She brought it up when they gathered to sleep.

It was her settlement's first official meeting but they took to it as if they had been doing it all their lives. It was as easy as gardening or speaking a common language: unknown but familiar.

Everyone agreed they needed to name themselves, each for different reasons. To convince themselves they were here. To connect themselves to a distant past. To ensure their humanity—hadn't Adam's first act been to name the plants in Eden?

They realized by naming themselves after an Earth location they were honoring a place wiped out by a whimsical god. A city like New York or Los Angeles was too much of a burden. Too small would serve only a single people and they were diverse. They needed a place they could all hold in their minds.

Every city needed to be remembered. Every town needed to be mourned. But they could not name themselves for all of them.

Wayne Firth wanted to name it after Charleston and gave a passionate, tear-filled tribute to the small city he had called home. But Mamora Higa described Aguni with such gentle detail that Julie felt that, if it still existed, she would have known every tree and house.

Through one sleep after another, they discussed, calmly, rationally, with continuing tears and choked words. As if they were discussing the deceased at the funeral—for that was what they were doing.

Julie wondered if names of towns she'd known her whole had already been memorials of forgotten places in the same way. Monterrey. Los Angeles. Santa Barbara. Were they named by an unknown Spanish priest after a place he would never see again? Would people someday use the name of this settlement without any more thought than she had given San Luis Obispo or Fresno? Those places were lost. Would their chosen name be lost, too?

Park Jinju suggested her home city of Busan, Korea.

"It is important to know what we are memorializing," Park said carefully. "Is it a natural place full of inspiration? Or is it a village, where the people all know one another? Do we revere industry? Do we represent commerce?" Park was a little smaller than the others. She sat cross-legged, making her points by tapping the soft floor. "A name does not stand for just a place. It stands for human beings as they lived and died. We were natural animals and civilized beings. We lived in the outdoors and closed spaces. We climbed mountains and watched television. We fought wars and made peace."

Park closed her eyes for a moment and paused. "Busan, my home, encompassed all of this. We had Samsung factories and Taejongdae Park, where the mountains came to the sea. My city was thousands of years old. Busan was rich in combinations and contradictions. There were archaeological ruins and cutting-edge research. The rich wore clothes of many colors and walked next to the drab poor. Beomeosa Temple on the slopes of Geumjeongsan looked down on them both. If we must memorialize what we have lost, the name we take should *reflect* that which we lost. I submit that my home represented all of those things."

Over several rounds of voting, she convinced them. Busan would be remembered across their generation as reflecting a small city in Korea. Past that, it would continue to be the name of this place. Perhaps it would be lost like some villages on Earth, leveled by time, to either die in the wilderness or be subsumed into a greater place.

In front of the gathered, Julie wrote *Busan* across the top of both lists: those that were searching and those searching for. Copies were made.

The entire group of them followed Julie to each of the fence borders and waited until someone showed up. In a few sleeps, they were not alone. Phillip now represented Saint Louis. He bowed to her and gave her two lists in return.

Chitra, now of Contai, exchanged their lists. Julie saw Pauline Bones' name at the top of the *search for* list.

One by one, the settlement of Busan went from one border to another, ritualistically exchanging documents: Forteleza, Freetown, Jayapura, Agadir, Guayaquil.

The names were chosen for different reasons but they were all saying farewell to the same place.

oOo

Like most people, Pranavi wandered over to the map room when she awoke. To say hello. To see what time it was.

It was still Morning. It had been Morning for twenty sleeps. She left to find something to eat.

The building with the workshops and the greenhouse also had the kitchen and a dining area. Over the sleeps, routine had settled in. Miss Hrud was the chief cook and ran the kitchen.

"Pranavi!" she said gruffly. "Potato soup for breakfast." She handed Pranavi a bowl.

Pranavi wrinkled her nose. "We've had that every breakfast for a week."

"Grow something else, then. This is what we have."

She took the bowl and went to the tables, saw Gerard eating, and sat next to him and Marie. She looked at them as she spooned the soup. They were all dark now with little variations between them. Pranavi was far darker than her original complexion.

"No rain," said Gerard. "Not for five sleeps."

Pranavi felt a pang of concern. "How does the garden look?"

Gerard shrugged. "I haven't been there yet."

"How about the fruit trees?"

"Hotaru said the fruit is growing."

Pranavi picked up her bowl and drained it. "Think we'll ever have bread again?"

Gerard shrugged.

"Let's go." Pranavi wasn't on dish duty so she just dropped off the bowl in the sink. She and Gerard left the eating area. Marie, being younger, followed behind at a respectful distance.

Pranavi loved the garden. She loved the way things were bigger every time she woke up. Tomatoes were redder. Melons swelled before her eyes. Sometimes she found smudgy things that moved like caterpillars, leaving an eaten gap in the leaf behind them. She picked them off and squished them with relish.

While everybody worked in the garden, the children were always there first. Even kids that admitted they had never aspired to any stronger activity than playing video games worked the garden. All said they were surprised how much they liked it. They had changed. So what? In the face of such great changes, little changes didn't amount to much.

Besides, the garden was *important*. Pranavi felt it in her gut.

The kids were dressed even more haphazardly than the adults or adolescents. They were aware of sex but at this point in their lives, it did not rule them. As long as some leaves covered the right bits, propriety was more or less observed. Some of them would have gone naked but the adults wouldn't let them.

"Hey! Don't let it get away!" she heard one of the kids cry out.

Pranavi ran around the garden and found three kids—Herschel, Pitor, and Guan—standing around something that looked like a lizard. Pitor limped in front of it.

It had a long neck and its hind legs were longer than its front giving it a kangaroo shape. It had black feathers along the crest of its head, down its long neck and back. The rest of it seemed covered with a blue down so fine it was like fur. The whole thing didn't look like it weighed any more than a small dog—it was just the size it could get through the fence without any trouble. It opened its mouth to bare its teeth, swelled its neck, and made a high rumbling sound at them.

"Kill it," said Herschel instantly. Pitor and Guan agreed.

"Shut up," said Pranavi. "Everybody get back." She sat down in front of it, bringing her head down to its level. "You're just a scared little boy, aren't you?"

It watched her and watched the other kids surrounding it. Then, it flattened itself to the ground and lay there.

"I'm going call you, Gibreel," said Pranavi. She reached out to touch Gibreel's head. It hissed at her. "Shush."

Gibreel quieted and allowed her to stroke its head. It gave a different sort of rumble. Lower down.

"Watch out," said Herschel. "It looks like a snake. It might be poisonous."

Pranavi tried to see into its mouth but couldn't. She didn't remember seeing any special poison teeth. "It's not poisonous," she declared.

"How do you know that?"

She didn't answer him. "What do you eat, little Gibreel."

Gibreel watched her.

Pranavi looked at the ground on the side of the garden. The greenery was intact but there was something that looked like a dead rat. It had fur. It had teeth—though they didn't look like rat teeth. It had a tail. Call it a rat. "Did you get yourself a rat, Gibreel?" She reached past Gibreel and picked up the rat by the tail. "Is this yours?"

"I didn't know we had rats," said Gerard.

"Now you know," said Pranavi.

Gibreel raised his head and watched the rat. He opened his mouth a little.

Pranavi carefully rested the tip of the rat on Gibreel's nose as she used to do with her dog.

Gibreel snapped the rat out of the air without ever coming near her hands. He swallowed it in two gulps.

"Good, Gibreel. Good boy." She petted Gibreel's head.

Gibreel froze for a moment. Then leaned his head against her hand. Pranavi scratched behind where she thought his ears should be. Everything liked their ears scratched, didn't they?

Pitor and Guan crowded to see. Herschel stepped forward and Gibreel dropped back down into a crouch with a hiss and that high rumbling again.

"Watch out," said Pranavi. "Gibreel probably remembers you said to kill him."

"Shut up," said Herschel doubtfully. "He didn't understand the words."

"Of course not," said Pranavi from her superior understanding having actually had a dog. "They don't understand *words* like we do. But they understand tones of voice and how you say things. Gibreel didn't know the words you said. But he knew what you meant."

"Shut up," said Herschel.

"Can I pet him?" asked Gerard.

Pranavi thought for a moment. "Maybe. But if you get bit, you might get sick."

"You said he wasn't poisonous."

"But his mouth could be dirty. That's what my mother always said about my dog."

Gerard thought for a moment. "He's *not* a dog."

"How about if *I* bite *you?* Do you think *my* mouth isn't dirty?" Pranavi snapped her teeth at him.

"I just wanted to pet him," said Gerard, holding up his hands to make peace.

Pranavi brought her face near Gibreel's. "Are you going to bite Gerard?"

Gibreel lay his head down in the grass.

"Okay," she said. "He says he's not going to but you never know. Even the nicest dog can bite you if you're not careful."

Gerard nodded. He squatted next to Pranavi and slowly put out his hands to pet Gibreel's side. Gibreel turned his head slightly to watch him but did not make any other moves.

Gerard leaned back.

Herschel stepped closer. "How about me?"

Gibreel didn't move his head but hissed.

"I don't think so," said Pranavi. "He remembers you wanted to kill him."

"Damn it!" Herschel stamped his foot.

Gibreel raised his head and high rumbled at him.

"Now you've done it. Just back away a meter or two." Pranavi thought about his sounds. High rumble meant threat. Low rumble was more like a purr. So far that was all of the sounds Gibreel made.

Gibreel seemed to relax when Herschel was far enough away.

"How are we going to keep him?" Gerard asked. He ran his hand down Gibreel's side. Gibreel low rumbled again.

"I don't know." Pranavi thought for a minute. What other sorts of things might he like? What did her dog like? Meat, of course. And dog food. Cheese. Apples. Carrots. "Come on."

She looked around. The adults were working on the other side of the garden. The height of the tomatoes and beans masked Gibreel as she led him and the other children over to the ground plants. Here grew tomatoes and carrots. Carefully, she dug up one nearly ripe carrot and then smoothed the ground behind. She broke it into pieces and handed one to Gibreel.

Gibreel stared at it, then at her.

She took another and ate it. "Hm. Good." Again, she held out the bit of carrot, holding her hand flat.

Gibreel looked at her and back at the carrot. He carefully turned his head sideways and plucked the carrot out of her hand without touching. He crunched it a bit in his mouth—not near as long as her dog would have taken—then swallowed. For a long minute, he seemed to concentrate, opening his mouth several times and licking his jaws. Then, he looked back at Pranavi and nosed the palm of her hand.

Dutifully, she put another carrot in her hand. This time there was no hesitation. Gibreel turned his sideways and took the carrot. Again, he asked for more.

"Whoa," said Herschel.

"Yeah," said Gerard.

Gibreel took all of the carrots and nuzzled her hand again. This time, Pranavi held up her hands to show him she had no more.

Gibreel sat back on his haunches and looked around. He started to go for the woods.

"Stop him!" cried Herschel.

Pranavi held Herschel back. "No. That way he'll always want to escape. Gibreel has to *want* to be with us."

"We might never see him again," said Gerard quietly.

Pranavi felt a pang at the truth of this. "Gibreel isn't a hamster that you carry around in a cage. He's not a dog—dogs decided to be with us a long time ago. They're born wanting to be with us. Gibreel hasn't made that choice. Maybe he never will. But he *certainly* won't if we grab him and stuff him in a box."

Gerard nodded. "Don't know where we'd keep him anyway." Gerard chuckled. "We don't *have* a box."

"Bye, Gibreel," said Pranavi and waved. The rest of them did the same.

Gibreel stopped at the edge of the forest and looked at them. Then, he turned and trotted into the shadows.

Pranavi turned to them. "No one tells anybody about this," she said fiercely. "Nobody."

Gerard nodded. The others nodded more reluctantly.

Pranavi saw that. "If we tell others they might chase him," she explained. "Then, we'll never see him again. We have to treat him well so he *wants* to be with us."

Even Herschel nodded at this. "Okay," he said.

Pranavi had no doubts. Gibreel would return.

oOo

Over the Morning, the regular rain had made the air humid and miserable. Larissa gave thanks to Phillip's mysterious God that they had not so far been plagued by mosquitoes. A small biting fly had bothered them mid-Morning but had then disappeared.

As the rains slowed and the air dried out, Larissa realized why they had shed their fur: sweat suddenly worked.

Their skins were all dark now. Some black as ink, others more of a chocolate brown. The color of their skin changed their appearance. Different features were accentuated by melanin and shadow. People's faces took on more character. This change in color, so clearly now an environmental response rather than something intrinsic to them, brought home the differences between who they were now compared to who they had been back on Earth. Color, so integral to them before, had become so uniform here. Certainly, there were individual differences but there were no remaining color groups—changing color was a matter of solar exposure. With that, their change in stature, their change in strength, and whatever else was going on inside of them, Lariissa wondered if they could even be considered human anymore.

Phillip led a prayer service every day before they worked in the garden. Larissa went because everybody went. She had no love for any God, neither the priests' back in Brazil nor this "Percy" here. Percy had the virtue of apparently demanding no ritual on Her own, though Phillip seemed to demand more than enough.

They had named the periods between sleeps after the days of the week. Phillip gave a sermon on Sunday after waking and on Wednesday before sleep. Nobody had found a Bible, Koran, Rig-Veda, or Kama Sutra in the map room libraries so everybody had to make do with what they remembered. Phillip put together a choir and taught them hymns he knew. Larissa sang in the choir; it meant she didn't have to come down to him and be "saved."

Being "saved" seemed important for some reason. Phillip's services bore almost no resemblance to what little church Larissa remembered from the *favela*. There was no confession. Little actual ritual, except Phillip talking and exhorting people to come and be "saved." Without the censer and the droning Latin incantations, she found Phillip's religion unconvincing.

But Larissa might have been the only one. She had spoken with Ian and Julie. Neither of their settlements had any real settlement-wide church. To be sure, individuals prayed, chanted, or danced their devotion to a Greater Power but, so far, only Saint Louis seemed to have got religion.

Big Clayton and Big Jim were both enthusiastic participants. Each was an unusual ten centimeters taller than anyone else. In a field of nearly identical heights, they stood out.

Big Clayton and Big Jim were as strong as they were big. They liked to hang out together. Larissa would have thought they were gay except for the couple of times she'd caught them in the woods in various combinations of women. She'd even found Big Jim having sex through the fence with some girl in Agadir. Larissa determined from this that women found the two men attractive even if she didn't see it. Larissa wasn't sure how this behavior squared with Phillip's sermons but resolved it was none of her business.

Then, the garden began drying out. They had to water it with bowls from the kitchen.

Larissa found Phillip in the grove of scrub trees east of the buildings giving sage advice and comfort to two young women. They looked up as she approached.

"Scram," she said.

The two looked at Phillip.

"It's all right. Go with God." He waved them off. "What do you need?"

"I need you to start pulling these people together. We're not prepared."

Phillip looked outside. "The garden is coming along nicely. People are coping with their grief. What aren't we prepared for?"

"Nightfall, for one."

Phillip stared at her.

"God damn it!" Larissa hissed in frustration. "Look, we're on Venus. The map room says it's 'Morning'—it started saying that five sleeps after 'Sunrise.' Do you know how long a solar day is here?"

"Longer than an Earth day, I suppose."

You ignorant burro! "One hundred and fifteen Earth days."

Phillip looked nonplussed. "That's longer than I expected."

"Fifty-eight days of light followed by fifty-eight days of darkness. That's one Venus day. Let's say the sleeps are about the same as an Earth day. This is sleep twenty-two. That leaves us six sleeps until Noon and about thirty-four sleeps until night. Then, nearly two months of darkness. Will it snow? What do we eat? Do we have enough food?"

Phillip pointed outside. "The garden looks good."

"Yeah. Continuous sunlight is nice. But will we have enough water to get to harvest? I don't know."

"We've had enough rain so far."

"Have we? We're supplementing the garden with drinking water now. Where is that coming from, Phillip? All we know is you turn a lever and water comes in. Does it come from a well? The showers and toilets use water, too. Where does that water go? Are we recycling our own wastes? *Nobody knows*. We're cooking on a big stove that heats up when we turn a dial. Why? Does it burn gas? Does it use electricity? Does it store righteous anger and release it when we need it? *Nobody knows.* This is like the summer camp of the apocalypse." Larissa pointed to herself.

"We woke with fur. Now we've shed it—which is good since it's been hot. But did we have fur for a reason?? Is it going to be cold at night? Will we need clothes for protection? Can we store enough *food?* Do the buildings have *heat* if we need it? What are we going to do for *light?* And I have yet to mention night animals. *Nobody knows.* We are completely at the mercy of whoever put us here."

"The fence protects us from animals." Phillip gestured around them.

"It wouldn't stop a snake—even a big snake. It wouldn't stop a pack of small carnivores or rats."

"Have you seen any?"

"Not yet," Larissa said. "But I'm new to Venus having only been here *less than a month.* Who the hell knows what this place is like? The *Outline of Necessary Operations* details things we can do. I found a clay pit east of the buildings. I've been trying my hand at making pottery."

Phillip looked at her. "Why?"

"Why?" Larissa sputtered. "We are *stuck* here. Stuck here *permanently*. Do you think these buildings are going to last forever? The garden tools have steel tips. Do *you* know how to fix them?"

Phillip pointed back towards the buildings. "There's a blacksmith shop. Clayton has been sharpening tools."

"I'm glad that Big Clayton Thibodeaux is handy with a hammer. That's great if he learns to *repair* steel. Do you know how to *make* steel?"

Phillip shook his head.

"Neither do I," said Larissa. "But the *Outline* points to a book that talks about it. Talks about how to do it *on Venus.* Do you think Percy put it there to entertain us? No. It's there because there are a million skills we have to learn. We've got clay and one of the books talks about a solar kiln."

"A kiln?"

"Read a goddamn book!" She stopped and took a deep breath. "Look, I know you care for everybody. You know people really, really well. I saw how the naming of the settlements turned people around. I can see these meetings comfort people. That's great. But even if we feel better, we're still stuck here. The sooner we're on our own, independent of these buildings and whatever put them there, the better we'll be. We'll know how things work instead of just depending on mysteries."

"Okay, okay."

Phillip held up his hands as if he'd been beaten. Larissa stepped back and took a deep breath, remembering that first punch. *Calm down.*

"God will provide for us. I know that. But if you want to make pottery, go ahead."

"I want you to tell Clayton to help me dig out the clay pit."

"That's between you and Clayton."

"But—"

Phillip gave her a hard look. "*God* will provide for us. He already has. We are chosen and we are here. He will not abandon us if we are in need." He waved her away. "You can say I'd like him to help."

Larissa closed her eyes and breathed slowly. She could see it: the failing rains, the coming night—even the ultimate loss of the fence. There were *things* out there. She had heard them calling.

"All right," she said slowly. "I'll ask Clayton."

It's a terrible thing to be right.

The drought was declared official at Noon.

Chapter 2.3: Afternoon

From Julie Agata's Journal, Year 1, Sleep 33

Terri is not here.

I have known this since we exchanged lists and names. Twenty-five settlements. Seven hundred forty people. No Terri.

The map shows only the local settlements in detail. It marks other settlement clusters around Aphrodite. There are no settlements marked on Ishtar or in the islands. I count one hundred and thirty-eight settlements. That makes on the order of one hundred thousand people.

The fences will not last forever and when they come down I will search each one for her.

But I can't right now.

The problem at hand is the drought caused by continuous sunlight. We will see it every Venus day.

On Earth, there is always a regular change between receiving energy from the sun and re-radiating it back out to space: day and night. Earth ran on an energy budget balanced between energy coming in and going out. Global warming was, really, just a shift in equilibrium. Nights still lost heat relative to days but lost less than was gained during the day. When the budget balanced (If it ever did. Who knows what happened after we were taken?) there would be no more net warming. Even Venus was in equilibrium before Percy changed it. The equilibrium of hell but equilibrium, nonetheless.

Back on Earth, I followed the new astrogeology models all the time. They were relevant to my own research. My old adviser, Jim Carroll, said that you just didn't know the biology of an organism unless you could figure out what it did over an ice age or two.

I wonder constantly why Percy chose Venus. There must have been better options—one of the ocean moons of Saturn or Jupiter, perhaps.

There are only two ways to solve the energy equation: you increase output or reduce input. Venus wasn't spinning fast enough to get rid of the heat and I think it was beyond even her to spin up Venus. Or, if she can do that, it took more time than she had. Ian said she was always talking about her schedule and budget.

One wonders what a being like Percy considers a budget.

Percy had to reduce input. There must be a sun shield. That's why the sun looks a little smeared and not quite circular.

But the result of the unchanged rotation of Venus is fifty-eight Earth day equivalents of continuous sunlight. There are no heat loss phases until the next fifty-eight Earth day equivalents of darkness.

It's critical enough that I wonder why she just didn't make day/night—heating/cooling—cycles using the sun shield. I'm sure there's a reason. From everything I've seen, Percy never does anything without a reason.

I want satellite images. I want maps of temperature gradients. I want computer models—heck, I want computers. Maybe I'll live to see them. After all, my historical last hundred-fifty years consisted of people groping in the dark to see what they could do. Now, we have learned what we can do. It's a matter of building up to what we had, not inventing something new.

So, I track estimated temperature, rainfall, and humidity.

I haven't figured out how to build a thermometer, so I measure a shaded glass of water against skin temperature, presuming body temperature has remained the same. I made a hair hygrometer. Can't calibrate it, of course. But I get an idea. I built a rain gauge from a straight-sided cup I made from some skinned bark.

So: today's measurements.

Temperature: 37C. Change from yesterday about 3C

Humidity: about 20%. No change from yesterday.

Rain: None. No change for two weeks.

The map room says Afternoon—about five sleeps in. It changed from Noon two sleeps ago. On Earth, this would have been barely a blip—but the continuous sunlight makes it worse. Without nightly respite, there's no morning or evening dew effect to replenish the ground plants and insects. Without significant rotation, there are no Coriolis cells to cycle water between the sea and the land.

I estimate, then, that drought here has more than double the expected effect. So far it's been a little over two weeks since the last rain. I think that's the equivalent of four to six weeks without rain on Earth. This means that the surface reservoir of water, the water in the topsoil down far enough for shallow plants, has been completely depleted. The only water the garden, wild plants and wildlife is getting is surface water such as lakes or rivers, some deep springs, and what we bring. The roots of the sequoias go deep. They do not appear to be in distress. The shallower trees have dropped their leaves and the grasses have dried up and gone crunchy. I'm guessing they've been adapted to this cycle.

I've observed convective cells moving over us. This is what caused the rain over the Morning. But as the temperature gradient flattened out, they stopped contributing to rain cycles. For a while, we could see it raining up in the hills beyond the outer fence. Sinue, in Mogadishu, wrote me that over Morning, even after the rain stopped just before Noon, their river and lake were still high from runoff.

Over Noon the rain moved further up into the mountains and eventually was lost to sight. Sinue writes the river has begun to thin.

All of the settlements out of reach of Mogadishu's lake and river have begun watering the gardens with water from the buildings. Busan's water has remained steady so far.

I don't think it will be enough. We don't have enough bowls. The garden is too big.

Hotaru came to the same conclusion. In the common meeting, she asked and received permission to harvest what can be harvested right now. This includes beans, potatoes, turnips, and carrots—our major source of calories. The water-intensive crops such as tomatoes and lettuces and other less than hardy greens will all be harvested as well. Wayne Firth—he of Charleston—has figured out how dry produce. We'll be taking advantage of the weather to dry as much as we can. Our stores aren't low yet but you can see low from here.

Hopefully, we'll be eating tough carrots and dried tomatoes on the night side.

If we survive, we'll have to plan on storing water in the Morning to be used in the afternoon.

That's a big if.

I want to live to find Terri. It would be a terrible joke to die here only to have her someday come find me.

oOo

Larissa got no help until the garden started to wither. That seemed to set some fire in people.

The clay pit had been worked before Larissa had found it. It gave her thought as she stood on the edge. Who had worked it? Where had they gone? Did it happen before the fences went up? Since? After all, she thought, any number of people could have passed through these buildings. Maybe they were just the latest string. Maybe this *was* a sort of training camp. Maybe if everything worked out here they be they'd be taken to actual communities with real clothes and computers.

She shook her head. It was just as much a pipe dream as Phillip's idea God was going to take care of them. Larissa had seen absolutely no indication that they were being taken care of. *Tested?* Maybe but not the way Phillip thought. If they were being tested it was for some job or task, not faith. Larissa thought the people who failed the test might have been disappeared. Such as whoever worked this clay pit before her.

"Yo, Larissa!" Big Clayton called out to her.

From between the saplings, Big Clayton and Big Jim dragged a cart. Both of them stared at her chest.

Larissa didn't think she'd ever get used to that. It wasn't like she was even special. They looked that way at every woman in the camp.

"Come on," she said. "Turn the cart around and back it down to the edge of the pit."

The two of them reluctantly tore their eyes away from her charms and carefully backed the cart down the slight hill. Larissa stopped them before they left the last bit of hard ground and sank in the soft clay of the pit. It wouldn't do to get the cart stuck.

The cart was a sorry mess. They'd cut down a few trees and managed to saw up the material for the frame. The hardest part had been making wheels. Everything was fitted without nails— Big Clayton Thibodeaux hadn't figured out how to make nails—and held together with woven rope. It was weak, didn't have much payload, and kept falling apart. It had taken sleeps to build.

Everything has to be started from scratch. It was depressing. Maybe someday they'd get far enough ahead they wouldn't have to keep going back to basics. Maybe someday they'd be able to go into a store and buy three penny nails. Larissa never thought that she would ever consider a hardware store the pinnacle of civilization.

Using their single shovel, they took turns loading clay into the cart. When it threatened to collapse, the three of them began pulling the cart back to the garden.

They broke through the trees and Larissa saw a line of people using the two remaining shovels and anything else they could find, digging the irrigation trench between the kitchen door and the garden. Some were carrying rocks from the eastern edge that bordered on Busan. These were placed in the trench, lining it.

It wasn't a big trench: perhaps half a meter wide and ten centimeters deep. Enough to carry water from the kitchen sinks to the garden.

"Son-of-a-bitch is heavy," said Big Clayton between breaths.

"Yeah," said Big Jim.

Did you think this was going to be easy? thought Larissa. Nothing about this place was easy. The primitive irrigation canal should work—provided the flow from the sinks stayed high. She estimated perhaps fifty liters a minute out of the faucets. She'd marked many small channels. By running the water continuously and judiciously moving the water from one section of the garden to another they should have enough. *If* water from the kitchen didn't run dry. *If* the evaporative loss wasn't more than she estimated. *If* the drought didn't last too long.

Too many ifs.

Still, Larissa found herself grinning as she strained against the cart. Was it crazy to think this was where she belonged?

She organized them in shifts: one group working on the irrigation trenches. One group still carrying water in bowls to the garden. One group resting and cooking. Nobody could sleep—for some reason they could only sleep in a group. Or, at least, at the same time. One more mystery to avoid considering.

At no time were there fewer than ten people working on the trenches. It took only about three sleeps—if they'd been sleeping—to finish digging the trenches, lining them with stones mortared with clay and connecting them to the little feeder ditches that distributed the water through the garden.

Larissa and Bog Podoll chopped down one more tree. A thick one that they hollowed out with big serving spoons they'd sharpened into small adzes. The resulting tube led from the faucets in the kitchen down to the trench at the door.

All of Saint Louis gathered outside the door and along the trench. Larissa watched them. She looked at Phillip. Phillip nodded. Larissa took a deep breath and opened the faucets full bore.

The water flowed down the tubes to the sump at the foot of the door. When that filled, Larissa opened the gate and water flowed swiftly down the trenches. As it rolled past the crowd they cheered.

"Works just as good as if you'd planned it," said Phillip.

Larissa laughed and lightly rested her hand on Phillip's shoulder.

Okay. There was no question she was crazy but there was no place she'd rather be.

oOo

Pranavi liked the drought weather. She liked the sun and the dry air—it was nothing like the humid misery of Morning. Certainly, it was hot. But it wasn't *hot* like it had been at home in Contai or Kolkata. There, it felt as if you were melting. As if your skin, clothes, and hair were one single puddle of misery. Her first Morning on Venus had been like that. Now that it was Afternoon, it felt like she was being pleasantly baked clear through instead of being parboiled.

But the garden was in trouble. They were bringing bowls of water to the garden all the time now. Everybody did their part in a long bucket brigade between the kitchen and whatever portion of the garden was most in trouble. They'd spent a long day pulling carrots, digging up potatoes, and pulling ripe beans. Her hands ached.

Pranavi couldn't take any more chances stealing carrots—certain foods were decreed by Chitra as to be too precious to be snack food during the drought. Instead, they were rationed. Pranavi learned a new word: beta-carotene. Since Pranavi liked carrots, it was no chore to be required to eat them with dinner. Gerard sullenly complied but Pitor actively rebelled. Pranavi admired that, though she didn't think it was smart. Still, every time Pitor acted up, Pranavi was able to sneak something out.

Gibreel turned out to be a master of stealth.

She never knew when or where Gibreel would find her. Often, the first indication was feeling him nuzzle her hand for a treat. Sometimes he would appear if she were with Gerard. But he would not approach her when she was with anyone else. Once with her, he stayed even if one of the other kids showed up after he arrived. If an adult approached, Pranavi pushed Gibreel towards the forest and he would melt away.

Pranavi found that Gibreel would eat almost anything if she offered it and never took anything from the garden otherwise. He preferred things with a hint of sweetness: onions, carrots, peppers. These he would take eagerly. Other things, bits of potatoes and dried beans, he would only take from her hand. If she put them on the ground, he ignored them. Pranavi remembered a cat they'd had in Contai that would only take cooked peas from her fingers and never take them any other way. Since Pranavi despised cooked peas, she'd found this cat a great asset.

She suspected that Gibreel would eat cooked peas from her hand since he'd eaten everything else she'd offered him that way.

Gibreel had limited interest in playing. Pranavi was unable to teach him to fetch, roll over, or dance. Her dog had been able to do all of these things. Of course, her dog would have crawled over broken glass for a piece of cheese. *This* Gibreel was significantly more discriminating.

What he liked to do was sit at the very edge of the forest, hidden in the shadows, watching the garden. If she sat next to him, he would sometimes relax and lean against her to be petted. But he didn't change his attention on the garden.

A few days after Pranavi had first encountered Gibreel, she found out why.

She was sitting next to him, gently stroking his flank when she felt him suddenly tense. His head swiveled slowly towards the beans and he shifted away from her to a crouch.

There was no warning, no shift of hips and legs to spring like a cat. One moment, Gibreel was crouched next to her. The next, he was two meters away from her and accelerating. He seemed to snap at empty air under the beans, uncoiling his neck like a snake. Then, he gave his head a quick terrier shake and loped back to the trees next to Pranavi.

Pranavi found her breath. The whole event had taken perhaps four seconds, most of it Gibreel's return. Gibreel was *fast*. Faster than a dog. Faster than a cat.

In the shade of the tree and masked from any human save Pranavi, Gibreel held up the dead rat to her.

"For me?" Pranavi shook her head. "No. I couldn't possibly. It's all for you."

Gibreel watched her for a moment, lifted the rat, and swallowed it whole.

Pranavi watched in fascination as the bulge traveled down his neck into his body. He shook himself a little and then settled again next to her. Twice more, he took rats. Then, he seemed satisfied and stood. He nuzzled her hand.

Pranavi held them up, empty. "No. Nothing more."

Gibreel watched her a moment. He turned and trotted back into the forest. He stopped at the edge of the shadows and looked back. Then, disappeared.

Pranavi walked around the garden, carefully examining the edges of the plants. Sure enough, now that she knew what to look for she could see bits of digging, marks against the stalks, and, in one place, a little blood. Gibreel, or something like him, had been busy.

Pranavi wondered how much of the garden they would even have if it weren't for him.

None of the adults were parents to the children, though some had once had children of their own. This was a good thing as far as Pranavi was concerned. It meant that though all of the adults were concerned about the children's welfare, none of them had an intimate interest in it. It was easy to fool them and slip away into the woods. If she were caught by an adult such as Chitra or Ian, they'd insist that she return to where they could keep an eye on her. But they were unpracticed. They hadn't seen any large animals since they woke. Only insects. The adults hadn't even seen the rats—which had to be because of Gibreel. After not seeing any threats, and remembering the fence, they reserved their worry for the young children like Guillermo, who was barely four, and Akita, who couldn't be more than three. The older children were pretty much on their own.

Pranavi knew it couldn't last but she was determined to take advantage of it as long as she could.

Pranavi walked along the fence and through the woods regularly. She knew Gibreel had a lair somewhere nearby and she hoped it was in

Contai. If it was, she was going to find it. She'd even walked around the lagoon and checked the seaward side of the fence. No Gibreel, though there was something large living in the lagoon. After seeing the thing in the sea, she didn't want to tempt what was closer to home.

The sequoia forest poked over the fence from Busan into Contai in the form of a single great tree. It was cool there in the heat of the day and seemed an obvious place for a lair.

While there was only a single giant tree on the Contai side of the fence, there were several clusters of bushes any one of which could contain Gibreel. That a different animal might not appreciate her investigations did not occur to her.

"Hey there," came a voice.

Pranavi looked up. A woman stood next to the fence.

"What are you looking for?" she asked.

Pranavi shook her head. "Just poking around." Never give them an opening, she thought. They'll ask questions you don't want to answer. "I'm Pranavi Basu."

"Julie Agata."

"What are *you* looking for?"

"Animals," said Julie instantly. "There should be a whole bunch of small animals. Squirrels. Mice. Birds. Cats. Skunks. But there's very little. Don't you find that strange?"

"I hadn't thought about it." Pranavi was *not* going to mention Gibreel or the rats. Pranavi would never have known about the rats but for Gibreel. "We had birds living on the roofs. But they left."

"Yes." Julie nodded. "We had them, too. I watched them leave through the mesh in groups. I think there's a Morning migration. Apparently, it's finished now." She looked up the trunk of the sequoia. "I think the small animals are living in the trees. I've found scat at the base. What looks like bird scat and what may be small mammal scat."

"Scat?"

"Poop."

"Ew!" Pranavi wrinkled her nose. She wondered if she could find Gibreel's lair by looking for poop.

Julie smiled. "Everything poops. We all leave traces." She looked back up in the trees. "What I wouldn't give for climbing equipment. Or even binoculars. Nothing appears to be living in the branches of the smaller trees. I can't see the canopy of the big trees easily from outside the forest." She brought her attention back to Pranavi. "Have you seen anything?"

Pranavi was caught off guard and she stammered. "No!" It came out too forcefully. "No. Nothing."

"Kids are excellent observers," Julie said. "I found two new species of butterflies in the Sequoia Park just because a little boy from Cody, Wyoming found them and didn't know what they were. He asked me. I didn't know either." Julie smiled again. "Two completely new species local to the area. Global warming had pushed them up the mountain to us from a little seventy-acre overgrown swamp that was drying out. He got to name one. I got to name the other. *Drusilaris matamorosii* and *Drusilaris eleanoris*. He named his butterfly after his mother."

"Who did your name yours after?"

"My wife." For a moment, Julie's face went bleak.

Pranavi guessed that Julie's wife wasn't taken. It reminded her of her own family. It happens, she thought. When you aren't looking for it, suddenly those memories come roaring back. *No,* Pranavi. No crying. Not anymore. After all, Julie wasn't crying. Neither would Pranavi.

"I'll look," said Pranavi when the silence got awkward.

Julie brightened. "Good. I'm checking this area every sleep. You can find me right here."

"Why every sleep?"

Julie looked back in the forest. "Nothing stays the same. Animals hunt one place and then another. They forage in one place only so long as it pays off. Then, they move on. If I check the same spots every day it's a better chance I'll find traces of them." She waved at Pranavi and stepped back into the forest darkness as smooth and quiet as if she were an animal herself.

"Oh," said Pranavi. She liked Julie. Besides, Pranavi had the feeling Julie was a person it would be worthwhile to know.

She mulled over what Julie said. Animals stay only so long as it pays off.

Pranavi would have to make it worthwhile for Gibreel to stay.

oOo

Freder sweated in the sun, shoveling.

There were three shovels to dig the trench from the kitchen to the garden. They took turns. Afternoon heat, he discovered, had a quality all its own. Even his new body had trouble with it. Freder had burned black as any of them. In this baking dryness, sweat dried before it ever had a chance to drip to the thirsty soil. Itchy rimes of salt collected at his elbows, between his legs, and on the back of his neck. Scratching only made things worse. The only solution was to rinse the salt off but that was out of the question. Unlike Saint Louis, Contai's kitchen water pressure was not strong. They needed what they had for drinking and the garden. Anything else was a forbidden luxury.

Francesca Guzman had tried a quick dip in the lagoon and run shrieking when something in the water had chased her.

Once the trench was dug and the stones set and mortared with Larissa's precious clay, they ran the water. Regardless, of Larissa's generosity, Freder could see as the water flowed it wasn't going to be enough.

"What are we going to do?" Freder asked Ian.

The three of them had taken to meeting in the woods: Chitra, Ian, and Freder.

"How the hell should I know?" Ian hissed.

"You're the captain," Chitra said mildly.

"The rest of them think I have some special line to Percy."

"Do you?" asked Freder.

"No!" Ian stared at him. "And quit asking me that. If I did, don't you think I'd use it?"

"I don't know." Freder glanced back towards the buildings. "I don't understand your relationship with her."

"Join the club."

"Either you do have some mysterious connection or you don't," said Chitra. "It doesn't matter. *They* think you do."

"Yeah." Ian bit his lip.

"It changes nothing," said Freder patiently. "We don't have enough water for the entire garden. Without the garden, we don't have food and we won't last the night."

"Night is only two months long," Ian said with a desperate tinge to his voice.

"Do you want to starve for two months?"

"We'd probably end up with a month's worth. That's only a *month* of starvation." Ian looked at Chitra for support.

"We need catchments," said Freder. "For when the rain comes again. Something to trap the water."

"That doesn't help us *now*. We have to shut off the garden we can't save," said Chitra. "Keep the most drought-resistant plants and see if they live. Harvest the rest and eat it now or dry it for later."

"Yes," said Freder, nodding. "I think the other towns are doing something similar."

"What'll we do for the shortfall?" Chitra looked up at Freder.

Freder didn't say anything for a moment. It felt good to shut Ian out but feeling that way made him ashamed. It wasn't Ian's fault. "I think we should go after the fish that tried to attack Francesca."

Silence fell. "What?" asked Ian.

"We're going to need food. More than the garden can give. That means a lot of calories and protein packed into each bite. We can't do it with vegetables so that means meat. The only meat I know of is that big fish in the lagoon."

"Francesca said it was huge." Chitra spread her hands. "We don't have a boat."

"It probably lives in the deep water near the fence."

"Francesca was in the shallow end." Ian pursed his lips in thought. "She said so."

"It's probably hungry," said Freder. "Likely it was hunting in the lagoon when the fence went up and it couldn't get out."

"How long do you think it's been there?"

Meaning: how long has the fence been in place? Freder shrugged. "Who can say? Long enough for it to be hungry but not long enough for it to starve to death."

"People are scared of it," said Chitra. "More than dying of starvation, maybe."

Ian looked at the two of them. "What do you want me to do?"

oOo

Freder held the rope in his hand.

Francesca and Chitra were ready at the shore of the lagoon. Each had a grass rope tied to her waist. Half a dozen men and women each held their ropes' other end. Ian and his crew waited next to them, holding improvised harpoons. Each of the harpoons had a rope trailing from it. Freder's crew had the net suspended across the surface of the lagoon at the narrowest point, but high enough so the fish could swim under. Rock weights were tied to the bottom of the net to hold it down when it was finally released.

"Go," said Ian.

Freder couldn't have said a word. His mouth was too dry for worry about Chitra.

Francesca and Chitra waded into the water, splashing as much as they could. Both Ian's crew and Freder's watched the water.

After an hour of splashing, Freder caught a glimpse of something under the surface. "Be ready!" he called.

Ian's crew moved closer to the bank. "Okay, come out," Ian said.

"Not yet." Chitra splashed some more. "Not till it gets here."

Freder saw it pass them.

"It's not a fish," Freder yelled. "It's more like a crocodile. What do we do?"

Everybody looked at Ian. Ian looked at Freder. Freder looked at Chitra.

"We go with the plan!" cried Chitra. "Watch for it!"

Freder's crew dropped the net and started pulling it towards Chitra and Francesca as they tried to run to shore.

The crocodile seemed to sprint towards them, a low bulge of water showing its speed.

"Pull her in," screamed Freder.

The crew on shore started bringing in the rope as fast as possible. Francesca reached the point where her legs were actually out of the water and began running.

Chitra fell. The crew dragged her through a meter of water.

The animal reared its head and swung it around, striking Chitra and tossing her a good seven meters back into the water. The rope broke.

It was no crocodile.

Freder saw the bulge turn. He let go of the net and ran towards her, reached down, and grabbed a rock the size of a football. The thing shot toward Chitra, breaching up to drop on her, its mouth open. Freder let fly with everything he had. The rock caught it in the back of the throat. It veered off, shaking its head violently.

Freder grabbed Chitra and dragged her to shore.

"Get it!" cried Ian. He and his crew ran into the water, throwing their harpoons at the thing, holding onto the ropes as it thrashed.

Freder's crew brought the net up to it. In a moment, its thrashing wrapped the net around it and all of them began dragging it ashore. It began to weaken. Clearly, Freder's rock had lodged somewhere vital.

Freder bent over Chitra. "Are you all right?"

Chitra looked at herself. She nodded, stunned. Looked at Freder. "You're bleeding."

Freder looked at his arm. It had been cut across the forearm. He flexed his hand. "Still works."

Chitra grabbed him and applied pressure.

Freder yelped and sat down.

The thing was shaking feebly, snapping anything that came near it. But after a moment, it gave a huge seizure, knocking three of the spear carriers down. It locked into a single rigid arc. Then, it relaxed and died.

"Son-of-a-bitch," said Ian as he staggered out of the water. He ran over to them, dropped to his knees, and held Chitra. "I thought you were lost."

"I was."

Ian straightened. "But for Freder." He held out his hand. "Thank you," he said. "Thank you so, so much."

At that moment, Freder could look right into him. He could see the love he had for Chitra. His brokenness as well as his tenderness.

Damn, he thought. *I actually like him.*

Freder grasped his hand in return. "You're welcome."

The beast was strange. It had a blunt, triangular head that resembled a short-nosed crocodile. But its tail was stubby and its legs ended in paddles.

"What the hell is it?" Chitra poked it.

"It's meat," said Freder. "We need to read in the *Outline* how to dry it."

"It's that," said Ian as he knelt next to it. "But it's also a pliosaur."

Freder looked down at him. "What's that?"

"An marine reptile that's been extinct for seventy million years."

"Oh," said Chitra.

"Yeah." Ian snorted. "Welcome to Venus."

"Let's get you patched up," said Chitra. She led Freder back towards the buildings as Ian and the others began the butchering.

In the kitchen, she pointed to a table. "Get on there."

She brought a bowl of hot water and lay it, and a bundle, next to him. She cleaned the wound with leaves and water. "No soap to speak of. Nor alcohol. We'll see if you die of infection. This is going to hurt." She took three wooden skewers from the bundle and poked them through the skin on either side.

Freder gasped for each one. "What the hell—"

"Wait. It gets worse." She broke the ends and bent them across, pinching the skin together.

Freder made a tiny shriek.

Chitra smiled at him. "Should have given you a bullet to clamp your jaw on. But I'm fresh out of bullets."

"What?"

"Never mind. It's an American thing. No needle. No thread. These are boiled, at least. Best staples I can make." She wrapped a bandage of broad leaves around his arm and tied it off with grass string. "The leaves are boiled, too. Turns out they act sort of like cloth if you cook them long enough." She looked at him critically. "In a couple of hours, you'll be feverish. There's no way I can sterilize a wound like that."

"Like you said, we'll see if I die of infection."

"Right. We are who we are now." She stared at him. Then, she kissed him, deep and long.

They parted. "That's for saving my life," she said. She slipped off her grass shorts and top.

Freder stared at her longingly. "I don't need a reward."

Chitra kissed him again and pulled off his shorts. "I'm not rewarding you." She climbed up on the table. "We're way, way past that."

Chapter 2.4: Shadow

All during the drought, the wind is capricious. Twisting this way and that. Often coming from the sea but only in fitful gusts. It carries sluggish and sullen clouds over them and over the distant mountains to the east. But it is never steady. Never committed.

Phillip takes to importuning God for rain before every sleep and upon every waking. Sundays and Wednesdays he gives long sermons varying between how God is testing their faith and a supplication to the Lord for a change in the weather. Neither seems to have much effect on the drought though they do seem to affect Phillip's congregation.

Larissa manages the trenches, directing the water to the potatoes and the carrots, then shifting to the beans and the corn. More than once she encounters a penitent kneeling in the burnt grass praying loudly for their sins to be forgiven. And for rain. Always for rain.

It is latter Afternoon as she wakes up before the others.

Something is different. Something oddly hopeful.

Larissa goes outside and walks around. She sniffs the air, feels the crackling grass with her feet. She walks along the fence down to the Contai side and finds Chitra. Chitra feels it, too, but neither can name it.

Contai's lagoon pokes a finger up into Saint Louis where it degenerates into marsh bordered by grass on the east side and the sand bar on the west. The sand bar is bisected by the outer fence. From here, Larissa can see the ocean but not reach it.

Standing there, Larissa realizes the wind is blowing from over the sea. Steadily. Occasionally, a bit of spray brushes a sticky coat on her skin. It itches. She scratches her skin and feels stubble. Her fur is growing back.

It is cooler, too. Still hot but it no longer feels as if she is being baked to the bone.

In the distance there is a shadow on the horizon—no, that is too strong a term. There is the suggestion of a shadow. As if on the other side of the world gathers darkness so great its mere presence dims the intervening sky.

Larissa stares hard at the horizon, trying to will clouds into existence. To bring rain on her unspoken demand.

Nothing happens.

The next time she wakes the drop in temperature is unmistakable. This time there are definite clouds on the distant horizon. Over the day, they approach slowly, hesitantly. Finally, dark and ponderous, the clouds roll over Saint Louis bringing with them sheets of warm rain.

All of Saint Louis comes out into the storm. Laughing. Rolling on the wet grass. Feeling the brittle stalks soften, begin to green before their eyes. Phillip sings a hymn. All join in. Larissa dances the forro and leads them in the steps. Big Jim and Big Clayton are dragged into the woods more than once—for several sleeps the only way to avoid stumbling over people having sex is to stay out of the woods. There is one sleep only she and Phillip keep company, taking care of the garden while they ignore the sounds of copulation thirty meters away. That night, Phillip gives a short sermon on the virtues of moderation.

The rain keeps coming. Storms pass over them with lightning falling all around so they huddle together, shaking and terrified, as the thunder shakes the building. But the storms are over quickly and leave only rain. Steady, soft, unrelenting rain.

It grows darker and the rain grows colder.

In the map room, the display changes from Afternoon to Sunset.

A sleep into Sunset, the rains stop. The clouds blow from the east and the sky clears.

To the west, over the mountains, the sun hangs suspended perhaps six degrees above the horizon. On Earth, it would have been mere minutes before it disappeared. Instead, it stays, orange and swollen, fixed in place.

They bring the tables out from the kitchen and carefully arrange any remaining undried harvest such as beans or corn. Despite the rain, the potatoes just need a little drying before they are placed in the kitchen bins.

Phillip comments they are like the Irish and will depend on potatoes all through the winter. Larissa has no idea what he is talking about.

As they work, they often stop and watch the sun. They still can't look at it directly but it is obviously elongated and magnificent.

The last sleep before night, the sky turns purple slowly, over hours.

It grows dark in the building. During the rain, Larissa had searched the Outline for mechanisms to make light without animal fat. (She also finds a section on soap and carefully skips it. She has no desire to make her life miserable lusting after things that are currently impossible.)

They soak the field corn and press it using two tables, a dozen people, and a bowl to catch the oil. Humans had been able to start fires for a million years but for the moment, Larissa is limited to lighting a bit of corn stalk on the stove. She uses to light a corn stalk wick in a guttering oil lamp. The lamp is small, dim, and smoky but it is light in the gathering gloom.

The map room displays the only other light in the settlement.

Silently, it changes from Sunset to Twilight as the first dim stars came out. Night has come.

oOo

Twilight was dark.

It began when the sun finally disappeared below the horizon. But its light remained for hours, from one sleep to the next. It faded gradually but steadily as darkness spread from the shadows beneath the trees.

Freder believed he could see better in the dark here than he had back on Earth. He didn't know whether this was because his eyes were better adapted to Venus or the long gloom had allowed him to adapt more deeply than he had ever experienced.

He *did* know that starlight was too dim to be of much use, better-adapted eyes or not.

Larissa had explained how to make corn oil lamps but Contai's corn had to be hoarded for food. Their harvest was not as good as Saint Louis's had been. Instead, they used the stones of the trench to make a small fire pit and gathered fallen wood to make a fire. The fire was small. It had to last two months. Larissa expressed envy of the fire—Saint Louis had few trees. Freder would have traded it for a few lamps.

They had dried pliosaur meat now. If they rationed it well, it should last them through the night. But it would be a close thing. Contai's fruit trees had held fruit in the Morning, then had blossomed. In mid-drought, the green fruit had stopped. They might ripen over the night or by the next Morning. Freder resolved to check them.

Using the fire as a mark in the night, Freder worked his way to the fruit trees, straining to see fruit, careful to touch it gently.

"Should have brought a torch," said Ian.

Freder froze. Freder and Chitra were having sex as regularly as privacy would allow. He had not broached the subject of Ian to her and she hadn't volunteered. Had she chosen Freder? Was she having sex with both of them? Freder just didn't know.

"Actually," said Ian conversationally. "I think it would be called a brand. At least that's what I remember reading."

"What are you doing out here?"

"Looking at the sky."

In the dimness, Freder saw a movement that could have been Ian waving at the sky.

"The constellations have moved some in the last three thousand years," he said. "But I can still recognize a couple. There's Orion. There's the Big Dipper."

"Ursa Major."

Ian laughed softly. "I can *see* a dipper. I can't see a bear."

"I'm surprised we can see the stars at all."

"How come?"

"The sun shield is strong enough to blur the sun. How do we see the stars through it?"

"Yeah." Ian watched a moment. "I think the shield varies in transparency. It's active, not passive. So it filters during the day but opens completely during the night."

Freder looked at him. "Smart thinking."

"Don't give me any credit. Julie thought of it. She thinks it's part of the heat budget."

"Ah."

Ian was silent for a bit. "Something *does* bother me, though. Maybe you can figure it out."

"What?"

"About Percy. I worked with her for seventy years back on Earth. She was honorable. Never lied to me. Never misled me—she didn't tell me everything. But she would *tell* me when she wasn't telling me everything. Nothing like Georgette. Georgette would lie for no other reason than she liked the sound of her own voice."

"I see." It bothered Freder that Ian could talk about these beings so casually. So easily. As if they were just neighbors.

"You don't at all." Ian laughed. "We have a collection of volumes, *Those Left Behind*."

"Yes."

"It doesn't make sense to me Percy wouldn't give us *Those Taken*. It's not kind. It's not honorable. I'd leave it alone but Chitra keeps bothering me about it."

"Why would you leave it alone?"

"Who does it help? Is there anything I can do about it?" Ian sighed. "But it does bother me."

"She's an alien," said Freder. "How can we expect to know what she thinks?"

"That's what Chitra said." Ian shook his head. "But I worked with her for seventy years. She was consistent. She was... *symmetrical*."

"Maybe Percy didn't want us to be discouraged," Freder suggested.

"What do you mean?"

Freder had been considering this for some time. "If we knew many had been taken but how few survived here, it might make living here more difficult." He spread his hands. "The thing that has struck me since the first day is how different I am and yet how *familiar* my body feels. Surely you've felt similarly."

"Okay, I'll spot you that. Different as it is, it feels familiar. So what?"

"I think it's like the language. Often amnesiacs will retain basic skills they had before their injury. Skills like language. Or riding a bike. These are furnishings that come with the house regardless of who's occupying it."

"Explain."

Freder tried to speak softly. "It's hard to adapt here. You've seen it. Many are having difficulties. Let's say not everyone manages. Let's say that whole populations might fail. Who is to say Percy might decide the better part of valor would be to start over—"

"—but why waste the bodies." Ian sounded disgusted. "Brains don't work like that. You can't just spin them up and down like data storage."

Freder shrugged. He tapped his head. "Who knows what we have up here? There could be nothing but a processor."

Ian was silent for a long time. "God, Freder. What an ugly idea. Not only are they transplanted to a world they didn't ask for. Not only would they lose everyone they knew and even their own *body*. But they would just be the latest in a long line of trial people, discarded when things don't work out. You come up with the worst ideas." Ian muttered to himself for a moment. "I did everything I did for two promises: my mother and Chitra. Chitra's here. My mother isn't. She's not on any of the lists. I never thought Percy would be cruel in the name of efficiency." He straightened in the gloom. "I'm done with her. It's too much. Not that she's asked me for anything."

"I could be wrong."

"So what if you are? Percy deliberately left us to wonder. When God led the Israelites out of Egypt and left them to wander for forty years he at least gave them a pillar of smoke to reassure them in the daylight. They knew there were other people all around them in the world. People they could find or go back to. We don't have any of that."

A bitter silence fell between them. Ian seemed to wrap it about himself, negating any further conversation. Freder felt helpless. He'd known Ian for one long Venusian day. Up to now, he'd thought of Ian as an ineffectual leader but probable nice guy. Since Freder had been sleeping with Chitra, a tinge of contempt had crept into his opinion.

But now, Ian seemed impenetrable. Shielded by strength Freder had not known he had. If Percy or Georgette had shown themselves, Freder was convinced Ian would have struck them without any fear of the inevitable consequence. Their power would not awe him or give him pause.

For the first time, Freder began to see in him what Chitra saw.

They stood there for perhaps a quarter-hour until Ian finally sighed and relaxed. Suddenly he seemed human again.

Ian pointed up in the gloom. "Is that Earth?" he said in a hushed voice.

Freder looked where he was pointing, grateful for the break. He saw a tan and blue dot. "I think so. Can you see the Moon?"

"No." Ian squinted for a bit. "It's a different color than I would have thought. More brown."

"Maybe people destroyed it."

"Oh, you're just fucking *full* of good ideas tonight." Ian laughed and placed his hand on Freder's shoulder.

Freder froze. What did *this* mean?

"I love Chitra," Ian said.

"I—"

"Shut up. I know you love Chitra. I know the two of you are sleeping together."

Freder tried to read his face in the darkness and failed utterly. He remembered Ian had worked for gods most of his life. In mythology, those mortals so blessed had some sort of remarkable properties. Did Ian have any mystic powers? Was he going to strike Freder down with fire?

Ian shook Freder's shoulder slightly, "It's okay. She loves you. Who the hell am I to begrudge even a little bit any love we find here? God knows we don't have very much."

"Okay." *Freder, you're an idiot*. Mystic powers indeed.

"She wants me, too," Ian said quietly.

The words spread through Freder like a slow-moving explosion. *I should have realized that*. Then: *why didn't she say anything?*

"She wanted me to tell you. For some ridiculous reason, she thought it was better that way. Defuse any possible anger." Ian shrugged. "I have no idea. She thought things might be easier if you and I slept together."

"What?"

"Sex. You and me." Ian paused a moment. "Probably all three of us, if Chitra had her way."

"I heard you. I..." Freder's voice faded away. "I don't want to."

"Me, neither." Ian's shadowed face looked back up to Earth. "I'm an old man, Freder. Not in my body—Percy made sure of that—but where it counts: in my mind. I found out a long time ago I don't like sex with someone I don't love. You're a good guy and all but I don't love you."

Freder felt relieved. Then, oddly, angry. Resentful. *Why not? Chitra thinks I'm lovable.*

"Yeah." Ian watched Freder a moment. "I'm going back in." He started to turn away then stopped. "By the way, I checked the fruit trees. It looks like they're dormant for the moment. Except for the olives. They're ripe. Probably something else Percy planned. We can use the oil in lamps. Or eat it. Or both, if we have enough. Could be the rest of the fruit will ripen over the night."

"How did you know I was coming out to check the fruit trees?"

Ian shrugged in the gloom. "Seemed like something you'd do. Good night."

Freder felt confused, hurt, angry, relieved, and comforted. He wondered what he was going to say to Chitra the next time he saw her.

Ian turned away and stopped. "Hold on."

"What?"

"Something ran over my feet."

Freder looked down. The ground seemed in motion.

Ian suddenly pounced and held up something squirming.

"Rats." Ian dropped it. He looked at Freder, then back towards the fire at the settlement.

"Rats!" they said together and started a dead run towards the buildings.

oOo

Julie realized the rats lived in the sequoias. They came down the trunks, rolling over the ground, the garden, the grass, in waves. In the dark, the random movement of the mass of them looked like maggots beneath the skin of a corpse.

They ate anything. Bit anything to check the taste. They left the grass cropped to the bone. They left the garden nothing but raw dirt. Then, they turned as one towards the buildings.

All of Busan stood around the open doorway of the kitchen building. They had pulled the tables from the kitchen, tipped them over, and arranged them in front as some kind of shield.

Half the settlement stood in front of the tables waiting with blankets, shovels, hoes—anything an eighty-kilogram human could use against a half-kilogram rodent equivalent. Behind the tables were more of them with the same random collection of weapons. The remainder protected Busan's few children and the food bins.

Julie and Hotaru were next to one another when the rat wave reached them. Both had shovels. They swung at the rats, clearing swathes through them, flinging broken, bleeding bodies into the night.

The rats ran up their legs. They kicked them off and kept swinging.

It didn't feel real. All while it was happening, Julie kept seeing Terri in front of her. Her coarse black hair, her blue eyes, the set of her shoulders as she carried herself—*always too close to the ground*, she said. The odd sonnet was one she liked—the one with *If hair be wires* in it. Julie remembered one bit: *My mistress, when she walks, treads upon the ground*. But nothing more. Julie should have learned it—she couldn't read it here.

I won't die without her.

The rats passed around them and broke like a fuming, brown liquid against the tables, crested it and spilled over, and passed into the kitchen building.

Busan retreated inside. Julie and Hotaru grabbed one of the tables and ripped the legs off. They ran inside and used the table like a snowplow, pushing a thousand rats out the door. Bog and three other men started smashing them as they were pushed out. As soon as that batch was killed, Julie and Hotaru brought the door back for another run.

Inside, the rats climbed the walls, over the sink, over the shelves. They scrabbled at the bins and doors, stripped and tore at the cabinet walls until the bins were breached. Then, they poured inside.

Julie saw and cried out. She and Hotaru pulled open the bins, reached in, and grabbed rats, one after another, to fling them broken against the wall. For each one, it seemed two more took its place, all in the dim flickering light of the lamps.

Bog and his men followed Julie and Hotaru's idea and added two more tables to the front as a door, holding it back as the wave climbed higher. The tables were outside the doorway so the pressure of the rats held them in place for the moment.

Each table was perhaps a meter in width and two meters long. Lengthwise, they covered the door as a panel. Three total brought the height up to nine meters. Jean Pierrot and Pablo Gutierrez climbed up the backs of those holding the lower tables against the doorway. They each grabbed the ridge running the length of the table and leaned back, holding themselves in place, their feet against the wall.

The rat wave reached up three meters and the rats at the top kept jumping at the edge. A few caught the edge and climbed over. While the pressure of the rats held the doors in place, thousands of them were scrabbling at the edges. The humans were holding on to the tables with their fingertips.

Julie and Hotaru were joined by anyone not holding the door and, gradually, the bloody ruin of dead rats began to outnumber living ones.

Finally, there were no more live rats in the kitchen.

"We need help at the door!" howled Bog.

Those holding the door were white with effort. They'd been holding it better than an hour and, as strong as their new bodies were, they were getting tired.

Julie climbed up and spelled Jean while Hotaru took over from Pablo. Both gratefully fell to the floor, moaning at their aching hands.

The building shuddered and rang with the sounds of—thousands? Millions?—of tiny teeth and claws digging at the outside walls.

"What will we do if they get through the walls?" shouted Julie at Hotaru.

"Starve to death!" Hotaru shouted back.

Julie didn't know how long they would last. How long would Terri have held on, were their positions reversed? Forever? Julie gritted her teeth and leaned back. As long as they could.

oOo

When Ian and Freder had come running towards the doorway screaming *"Rats!"* Pranavi sat up with a start—something about that word filled her with a dark and abiding dread.

Chitra streaked past her carrying a table.

Pranavi grabbed Girard and dragged another one. They were not as strong as the adults and it took both of them to snap off the legs. Through the door and back again, on top of Chitra's.

Ian and Freder leaped over the top of the two doors just ahead of the third door carried by Francesca and Andrew. Pranavi and Gerard climbed up and caught the ridge of the top table just as the main wave hit.

The tables shook, bowed, and rebounded. A few rats made it over the top. Pranavi heard little rat shrieks as they were killed in the building.

But the tables held and the few rats that made it past were killed quickly. As long as the walls held, Contai was in good shape.

It seemed that Pranavi held the table fast for hours but after a while, she felt the scrabbling at the edges lessen. Holding it with one hand, she peeked over the top. The wave had reduced below the top table. It was still nearly three meters deep surrounding the door and lessened to a carpet covering the ground outside.

"First thing on the list are doors," shouted Ian.

"Is that before the catchments or the lamps?" shouted Freder right back.

"Shut up!"

Freder laughed at him.

"They're going away." Pranavi pointed over the edge.

"They weren't able to get in," Freder shouted back. "They've figured out this isn't a free meal."

"Or they've found another way," Chitra shouted. "Go look!"

"I'll go!" Pranavi shouted and gave up her place to Andrew.

Without lamps or torches, the kitchen building was dark. Pranavi knew the rooms by heart but she couldn't *see*. Instead, she went from room to room, listening carefully. Except for the continuous scratching from the outside walls, she heard nothing. She faced each outside wall, thinking that she might be able to hear them in the rooms. Nothing. Either she couldn't hear them or they remained outside.

Pranavi had a sudden horror that they might burrow up from the ground, pouring in from her feet and running up her legs. She cried out and climbed on one of the ledges. After a while, she chided herself for being a baby.

Pranavi reached the kitchen. In the dark, she could hear Miss Hrud open a bin, check the contents by feel, close it again.

"Anything?"

"Nothing so far," said Miss Hrud. "None of them got into the bins."

"We need light."

"Wish for it and spit in your hand."

Pranavi did so. "Now what."

"Now you've got a wet hand."

"Ew!"

"Exactly. Did you find any rats?"

"No."

"Good. Go tell them at the door."

Andrew was getting tired so Pranavi took over. *What's Gibreel doing out there?* Getting a very good meal, probably. *Or getting eaten by rats.* She resolutely shook her head. Gibreel could take care of himself.

Over the sound of the rats, she heard a *thrum*. It was like Gibreel's but different. And then a series of low grunts followed by a roar.

"What the hell is *that?*" cried Freder.

Pranavi peeked over the table. "I can't see anything. Wait." She pulled herself up to the edge of the table and looked around. She looked up.

"Can you see what's making those sounds?" called Ian.

"No," Pranavi called back. "But there's a dim light in the sky. Directly overhead." She looked again. "It's moving north to south."

Freder and Ian looked at one another and back at Pranavi.

"Are you sure?" Freder asked.

She looked again. "It's a light. High in the sky."

"Can you see it move?" Freder started to stand and the table vibrated.

"Hold on to the damned thing!" shouted Ian.

"Sorry! Sorry." Freder leaned back. "Can somebody give me a break?"

"Me." Carol Dorrien reached behind him and caught the ridge of the table. "Got it."

Freder let go and straightened up. "Can you point it out to me?"

Pranavi looked back up to the sky. It hadn't moved much. "There," she said, pointing.

Freder put his head against the table and looked up along the table. "It's a satellite."

Ian looked around. "Francesca. Can you spell me?"

"Just waiting for the opportune moment." Like Carol, she took the ridge from Freder and leaned back.

Ian stood up and looked where Freder pointed. "I think you're right."

"Look," said Pranavi. "It's curved." The bright spot had a definite concave look to it on one side. Like a tiny half-moon.

"I'll be damned," said Freder. "Whose is it? Percy's?"

"No idea."

They ran shifts of holding the tables in place. Pranavi found she could sleep without the others now that it was dark. When she awoke and returned to the doorway she could see by the faint starlight that the tables were fastened in place with grass rope and several of the people there were naked.

"Needed the grass," said Freder apologetically.

"Hell," said Andrew. "It's too dark to see anything, anyway."

It was true. Pranavi had never felt self-conscious about being clothed—it was one of those things adults said you had to do. But without clothes, she always *knew* she was naked. Now, in the dark, Freder and Andrew were just not wearing clothes. They weren't *naked.*

"Where's Ian?" Pranavi looked around. "And Chitra?"

Freder and Andrew looked at one another.

"Sleeping," said Freder.

"Yeah," said Andrew. "That."

Pranavi rolled her eyes. *Adults.* So predictable. So clumsily secretive. Pranavi climbed up to the top of the tables and looked outside. The wave of rats had receded though the lake of rats remained. They were crawling over the ground—with that, Pranavi realized it was getting lighter. She looked up.

The satellite had moved towards the northern horizon. Now it gave a sort of thin moonlight illumination. "The satellite is brighter."

"Yes," said Freder. "Both of them."

"Both?"

"Yes. One comes over about every hour. Every time it's a little brighter. I think it's a mirror."

"What's it reflecting?"

Freder shrugged. In the gloom, Pranavi could actually *see* him.

"Who knows?" he said. "Direct sunlight? Reflected sunlight from the sun shield? Great mirrors on Mercury or asteroids in close orbit around the sun? There's no telling. It looks we're going to get light about every other hour. It'll get brighter to a point and then it's going to get dim again."

"How do you know that?"

Freder pointed at the satellite. "It's in a polar orbit. As we rotate under it the light gets brighter. It can't be all that far out. So at some point, we'll rotate out from under it. I don't know how dim it will get. The middle of the night might be completely dark."

Pranavi looked out over the tables. It was still a lake of rats. She glanced down at Freder. "What do you think the rats will do when it gets lighter?"

"That's all we've been talking about since you left. We figure that since they came out when it got dark, they respond to the light. So they'll go away when the light comes fully and return when the light disappears. I'm guessing night is symmetric. We lost the light of the sun just after Sunset—that's when the rats first came. Then, light increases with the mirrors, decreasing the rats. Then the mirror light lessens so by the middle of the night we're near dark again—the rats come back. The mirror light returns: fewer rats. Then it goes away again near dawn and we get another wave of rats. That wave will be less, I think. They'll have been out most of the night at that point. Dawn breaks and they go away until next time."

Pranavi looked back outside. The satellite was nearing the horizon and it was getting darker. Sure enough, more rats were showing up.

At the edge of the garden, was a shape watching her. Even now, as a lesser gloom gave way to a greater one, she recognized the shape.

It was Gibreel.

Pranavi waved to him.

Gibreel bobbed his head.

Pranavi let her breath out slowly. She dropped to the floor. Things would be okay. Gibreel looked safe and sound.

Then, she heard the roar again.

Around the edge of the building came a four-meter crocodile. Its mouth gaped open. Around the other edge of the building came smaller animals. Not crocodiles exactly but clearly related.

The smaller animals scattered as the big crocodile charged one of the lesser ones and grabbed it, shook it until it stopped moving. Then, the big crocodile dragged it around the building in the direction of the lagoon. The smaller animals had disappeared. Pranavi looked for Gibreel but could not see him as the night returned.

Chitra and Ian climbed up beside her. Pranavi moved to one side to give them room.

"They must live in the lagoon," said Chitra.

"Maybe they estivate there." Ian looked up, his face shadowed in the starlight. He stiffened. "My God! They were in there when you drew out the pliosaur!"

"They definitely estivate," said Freder. "Or we'd have seen them before this like we saw the pliosaur. Buried in the mud waiting for night. I think they're trapped like we are."

"You have it wrong. *We* are trapped with *them*. Especially Largo there," Pranavi said as she dropped to the floor.

It took over several sleeps for the lesser lights to come to full brightness. It was a different kind of light than the sun. Whiter. Hotter in the direct sun but cooler in the shadow. Each Lesser Light—the term came into use almost immediately—had its own rise, mid-light and set that took about an hour, followed by an hour of darkness. Often, during the darkness, it rained. Sometimes, the rain continued into the light but often it did not. There was enough time to start a task and interrupt it to retreat into the building so long as someone was watching for crocodiles. They did not see the big crocodile again but the smaller crocodile things prowled every time it grew dark, snapping up as many rats as they could catch. Pranavi kept watch for Gibreel but did not see him.

During one of the Lesser Lights they fashioned doors from the remaining tables. Then, after waiting through the dark, they pulled the tied tables out of the way and replaced them with tables framed with wood. These could be opened and shut quickly. They cleaned the rat bodies they killed and made rat traps of the tables they had used before. Meat was meat.

Once that was done, they began digging out catchments for the rainwater. They were far too busy, and frightened, to check the fences for news from the other settlements.

They had only a few sleeps until the Lesser Lights began to dim. It seemed to Pranavi that they had mere moments between the first dark and the coming Midnight.

One sleep they awoke to full darkness once again.

"Lamps," muttered Freder when he and Pranavi were standing watch together at the door. Outside, they could hear the ponderous shuffling of Largo as he gulped rats and smaller crocodiles as he found them in the dark.

Pranavi hoped Gibreel was all right.

Chapter 2.5: Murk

Saint Louis didn't stop fighting the rats until the lights drove them from the buildings.

After the rats left, a few stragglers here and there, Larissa fell to her knees in fatigue and despair. They had not managed to get the tables in place before the rat wave swarmed through the kitchen doors. Did not manage to beat them away from the cabinets and food bins.

The light was glaring white as if they were lit up in a football stadium. Colors were washed out. Their fur looked silvery.

She forced herself to stand. Phillip was on his knees next to the door, praying loudly. There was a small group in the mud next to him. Big Jim and Big Clayton were nowhere to be seen.

Larissa and Maria Popolous rummaged through the food bins. Larissa pulled out a handful of potato scraps from one, a leftover rind of squash from another, a double handful of corn from a third. The two of them took stock accompanied by a mournful hymn from the doorway.

There were dead rats everywhere. Larissa picked one up and took it out into the light. It was not exactly a rat—it had tiny pointed incisors in the front and tiny molars in the back instead of rodent teeth. It had muscles on the back and legs. She hefted it. A quarter kilogram?

Larissa returned to the kitchen, pulled out a knife, and butchered the rat. In the half-light, she almost sliced her fingers a dozen times. The result was a handful of meat. A quarter kilogram of rat into half that of meat. Unless they decided to gut, skin, and cook them whole, bones and all.

She interrupted Phillip's prayers. "We have to collect rats."

"What?"

Larissa looked around at the rat corpses. "There have to be fifty rats here. Ones we killed. Ones we trampled. We have to collect them."

"You're not serious."

"Deadly serious. They ate more than half our stores. We have to collect what we have and figure out how to trap them next time."

"*Next* time?"

Larissa looked up. The little moon was nearly halfway across. "Doors first, I think. Looks like dark in half an hour."

Phillip looked up, his mouth opens. "Doors."

"And we need to collect the rats before they smell."

Now that they knew what to expect, using the tables as doors seemed obvious. Larissa looked for Big Jim and Big Clayton for help.

They were having sex with Antonia Herdosky and Giselle Charbon.

There wasn't much light but it was enough to see Big Jim's butt pumping rhythmically. Even if she hadn't seen them, following the grunts wasn't difficult.

Larissa slapped him hard on one vibrating cheek.

"What the hell?" Jim jumped up, his erection half visible. He recognized Larissa. "Oh, it's you. Want some?"

"Where were you when the rats came in?"

"Right here. Nothing to do, right?"

Larissa looked at Jim. Then Clayton. "We need help putting up the doors. You two are pretty strong."

Antonia giggled.

"Yeah," said Jim, looking down at her. "That's right, honey. You know how strong."

"Come help."

Clayton sniggered.

Jim raised his eyes slowly to Larissa. "Yeah. Okay. Come on, Clay."

Jim and Clay pulled on their grass shorts and followed Larissa to the kitchen area.

"How bad is it?" asked Jim.

"We lost half of what we had," said Larissa. "We're going to have to butcher the dead rats and trap some more."

"Sounds good," said Jim, and backhanded Larissa.

She spun around, snarled, and sprang at him.

Jim caught one arm deftly, turned on his hip, and the next moment, Larissa was face down on the floor, left arm stretched out in one of Jim's hands, his other caressing her elbow. His foot held her shoulder down. "Did I ever mention Clayton and I were Rangers?" He tapped her elbow meaningfully with one finger. "Do you want this arm intact?"

Larissa tried to surge and turn but Jim increased the pressure on her elbow just a little bit.

"Stop!" she cried.

"You want your arm, then?"

"Yes," she said through gritted teeth.

He didn't release her immediately. A crowd had appeared around them.

"We're in charge now," said Jim. His voice was calm but it carried.

Phillip rushed in. "Here, now. You can't—"

Clayton stepped to meet him and kneed him in the groin, slapped him as he went down. Phillip writhed on the floor.

"Any questions?" asked Jim.

Dead silence.

"Good." Jim released Larissa. "Gather the rats and butcher them. Clayton and I will distribute the food." He looked at them. "And the water." He reached down and hauled Larissa up. "Larissa will show you how."

Jim and Clayton took over the dining space as their own. Now, they had control of the kitchen: both the source of the stored food and the main source of water. The showers were just down the hall from the dining area. Though they did not occupy them, Jim and Clayton controlled access.

Larissa's arm hurt as she and Bog wrestled the tables to the doorway. They tied them in place before the end of the light. Others collected the rats, skinned, and cleaned them. With Jim and Clayton's approval, they chopped off the heads, diced them, and made stew. Rat stew wasn't all that bad.

Jim and Clayton ate their fill and left the remainder for the rest of them to scrabble over.

They all held the doorway closed against the rats the next dark. The next light, Bog, and Larissa devised a rat weir from branches, rope, and tables. More rats from which they made stew. The dark after that the weir was torn apart by something from the invisible night. They guessed it was about the size of a leopard. It ate all the rats in the weir. The weir was not rebuilt.

Each light, people fanned out of the building, gathering what they could, reluctantly returning when the dark came. Each light grew dimmer, each dark more complete.

Jim and Clayton rationed whatever food they had left. The two of them took the first share, of course. Their women were served second. The remaining bowls were doled out to those Jim and Clayton deemed worthy. Jim leered at Larissa as he filled her bowl with a half ration. The message was clear: sex for food. She took the half ration.

Midnight came. There was frost on the ground. The people retreated behind the doors. Both the rats and the people were desperate. Both were searching for anything to eat. Larissa reached over the door and grabbed one rat after another, bashing its head against the table edge and handing it behind. Bog was on the other side of the doorway doing the same thing.

After her shift, there was no ration waiting for her.

Her stomach cramped. Her bowels clamped down. She rested in the sleeping area, her body curled around her shrieking abdomen. After a couple of sleeps, her organs relaxed. She could *feel* herself wasting away.

The first light after Midnight, the starving ones staggered out from the building towards the fences. Someone might be there. Someone from whom they could beg food.

Larissa's pride was gone. She followed them.

oOo

The map room had displayed Twilight after Sunset. It called the time of the Lesser Lights, Shadow. Midnight was self-explanatory. By the time Midnight came, they were all pale again and their fur was thick. Midnight was cold. Frost formed on the ground. Most people huddled close together both waking and sleeping.

Pranavi heard Freder mutter "heat" to himself.

When the Lesser Lights returned the display changed to Murk.

With the coming of Murk, the night was half over and the temperature rose but it never reached warm.

With darkness never more than an hour away, there were often crocodiles and near-crocodiles basking at the edge of the lagoon. The behemoths kept a wary eye on one another. Trapped as they were, there wasn't much opportunity for game beyond the rats. Largo, himself, preferred larger game and the near-crocodiles gave him a wide berth when he was there. When he was lurking in the lagoon, they basked watching the water.

The adults in the community kept a closer eye on Pranavi. If she started walking towards the woods or the lagoon any adult who noticed would decide to take it on themselves to turn her back.

It made looking for Gibreel difficult.

Pranavi was frantic. She had not seen Gibreel since that first Lesser Light. She had to get into the woods without being seen.

She tried to sneak out through the greenhouse. Unlike the rest of the buildings, the greenhouse had doors that could be opened at either end. They were closed now but Pranavi thought she might be able to slip through them and work her way along the fence.

Instead, she found Francesca Guzman puttering around the plants.

Francesca looked up and smiled at her. "Hey there."

"Hi." Pranavi looked over the pots. It was important to distract her. "What are you doing?"

"Pre-planting," Francesca said. "It's my idea. Growing some plants in pots so we can get a head start. I think that's how the garden was in such good shape when we woke up."

"Somebody planted here in the greenhouse during Murk." Pranavi looked around. "This place has doors all around. Why didn't we run in here? We would have been safe." Pranavi saw there were two doors at the end of the greenhouse: one big and one small. How was she going to get past Francesca?

"Nobody thought of it. Now that we have doors on the kitchen building, we don't need it for that." She gestured to the plants. "But we do need it for starting plants."

"Who did it before?"

Francesca's face took on a ragged edge. "Nobody knows." She brightened. "You aren't supposed to be able to transplant corn and potatoes. But *somebody* did. They didn't leave them out for the rats. So I figure I'll try."

Pranavi walked around the space. "This place is big."

"Yes. We need to use some of our harvest for seed."

"Have you shown this to Ian or Freder? Or Chitra, even."

Francesca shook her head. "I wanted to make sure it would work before I did that."

"You should. Like you said, *somebody* had to do it. Do you have sprouts?"

"Just a few leaves—"

"That's enough." Pranavi dragged Francesca back to the kitchen and brought it up with Freder. Then, once the conversation started in earnest, slipped away. She made sure the adults all saw her going into the greenhouse. Then, ran back to the small doorway and opened it. There was a clear path to the lagoon. Andrew was on watch, keeping a safe distance ready to run back yelling if anything started moving to the buildings. He never looked away from the animals—which was smart. If he did he might get caught by one.

More to the point, he wasn't watching the *settlement*.

Pranavi crept along the back of the greenhouse, ran behind the sealed buildings, and finally made it to the Saint Louis fence.

She quietly walked along the fence, trying to see if Chitra or anyone else was looking in her direction.

"*Hey,*" came a whisper.

Pranavi stopped dead.

"*Hey!*" The whisper was urgent.

Pranavi turned to the fence. "Be quiet! What do you want?"

A woman slowly stood up from where she was hiding behind a bush. She was skeletally thin. "Can you give me something to eat?"

"Who are you?"

The woman stood up straight. "My name is Antonia Herdosky." She looked at herself as she stood. "Oh, I used to be so *pretty*." Antonia crouched down again. "You can get me something to eat, can't you?"

"What happened?"

"I used to be his favorite." Antonia shook her head. "So I got food. But there were some things I wouldn't do so he picked someone else." Antonia gave Pranavi a conspiratorial glance. "I'd do them now. Don't think I wouldn't. Don't think I didn't *tell* him. But now he's not interested in me. He has another favorite." She reached through and grabbed Pranavi's arm. "Please, honey. Anything."

Pranavi shrieked and pulled away. "Go away!"

Pranavi ran along the fence. There were more of them, all thin. All reaching out their hands. She kept running, past them, past the buildings into the woods.

She walked through the forest calling: "Gibreel! Gibreel!" Nothing. She went deeper. "Gibreel! Gibreel!" Finally, she reached the sequoia. Gibreel came running from around and leaped up to her.

She caught him and buried her face in his feathers. "Good boy. *Good* boy."

Finally, Pranavi let him down. "Come on, boy. You come with me." They would just *have* to let her keep him in the building. It wasn't safe out here.

Gibreel walked willingly with her for a few meters. Then, he slowed down and stopped. He gave her a high-pitched thrum, like a soprano purr.

"Come on, boy. You've got to come with me." Pranavi pointed at the ground. "Right here. Right *now!*" In her sternest voice. That had always worked with her dog.

Gibreel stepped forward hesitantly, bobbing his head. Then, he backed away while continuing to bob his head. He turned away, his head still facing her. He ran a few steps, thrummed at her, and bobbed his head.

"Oh. You want *me* to follow *you*. Okay."

Pranavi walked behind Gibreel as he pranced ahead, danced on his feet, and then ran a short distance ahead until they reached the sequoia. He led her around. As he did, he changed the tone of his voice entirely. Now, it was a soothing bass tone.

Pranavi stood first on one foot, then another. After a moment, the other gibreel she had seen in the darkness came out. It queried Gibreel. Gibreel answered.

Ah. Gibreel's mate.

"You, I will call Sita," declared Pranavi.

Gibreel continued to call and another gibreel came out. This one smaller than both Gibreel and Sita. It rubbed against Sita.

Gibreel's pup.

Pranavi thought for a moment. "You are Ananda."

But Gibreel continued to call and after a moment, half a dozen tiny pups came out.

"Wow!" Pranavi sat down and they swarmed over her. Sita bristled but Gibreel seemed to calm her. Ananda approached her hesitantly.

It was unreasonable for Gibreel to leave his family.

"I guess you'll be okay." Pranavi stood up slowly to let the pups crawl off. She laughed as she carefully stepped away.

Gibreel came over to her and rubbed against her leg. She patted his head.

Sita bleated at him. Gibreel muttered something back.

"It's all right," Pranavi said. "You come down at Sunrise and I'll make sure everybody gets fed."

Pranavi started to leave and Gibreel hooted at her. She waved at him and he gathered his family back under the sequoia.

As she walked back to the building, she thought about seeing Gibreel standing outside watching her. Why would he do that? Pranavi knew he ate rats.

She realized *he* had been checking up on *her*.

Pranavi stopped. Clearly, Gibreel was smarter than her old dog. Not as smart as a human being but still a person. He had *decided* she was his friend. Not like a dog or a cat. He was a wild animal—or a wild person—and had made a friendship with *her*.

Pets were one thing. She had loved her dog but she was old enough to know that relationship was not the same as this one. She had taken care of her dog. Sure, he had loved her. Gibreel had loved everybody. Gibreel was a *dog*. It was a dog's *job* to love everybody or at least your family. It was like loving your sister or father. Gibreel couldn't have helped it. It was how he was made.

But *this* Gibreel owed her nothing. He wasn't related to her. He didn't have the dog's obligation to love. He was her friend by choice. Like Gerard. Like Pitor—no, not like them. They were the only kids around. What choice did they have but to like each other? But she and Gibreel had chosen each other. They didn't *have* to like each other. They just did.

Gibreel had said to her as clearly as he could that he would have come with her if he could but he had *obligations* to his family.

Pranavi didn't have her family. But she had Freder and Chitra and all the rest.

She started walking down the hill in earnest.

oOo

Freder followed as Pranavi led him to the fence.

Pranavi pointed to a thin woman crouching next to a bush.

"This is Antonia Herdosky," Pranavi said. "Antonia? This is Freder Gluck."

Slowly, Antonia rose. She was naked but for her fur and tried to cover herself with her hands, brush off leaves, and straighten her hair at the same time. Freder found it heartbreaking.

Antonia stuck a hand through the fence. "Pleased to meet you."

"Antonia's starving," said Pranavi simply. "We have to feed her."

"Yes," Freder said slowly. "You know those fish cakes Miss Hrud made the other day? Go get some. And bring a cup of water. They're a little dry."

Antonia was wavering as she stood.

"Sit," said Freder.

As she sat, Freder noticed more of them, crouching listlessly in the dirt.

"Come over here," he said.

A couple took notice of him and started shuffling in his direction. One stood tall, her back to him. Then, she turned and he recognized her.

"Larissa!"

Larissa didn't move immediately but when she did, it was with deliberate, careful steps. Her ribs showed through her fur. She stood at the fence and looked him in the face. "Hello, Freder."

Antonia stood up, facing Larissa. "You won't take my food!" she hissed.

Larissa stepped back. "No. I won't."

"That's because Freder likes me. Right, Freder? I'll be your favorite." Antonia reached through the fence blindly and touched his shoulder. "Not her, right? Me, right?"

Pranavi poked him with the bowl. "Here," she said. "Feed her."

It was filled over the brim with Miss Hrud's fishcake. Miss Hrud must not have been watching.

"Here," said Freder picking up one of the cakes. He broke off a piece and gave it to her.

Antonia grabbed it from his hand and crammed it in her mouth. "Good," she said around the cornmeal. She reached out her hand.

"Hold on," Freder said. "Let's see if it stays down."

Larissa pointed to the other two that were standing, dull-eyed, behind Antonia. "Bog Podoll. Maria Popolous."

Freder stated to pass a piece of fishcake to Bog and Antonia snatched it from his hand and stepped away.

"Mine!" Antonia hissed.

Bog stared at her, then turned back to Freder silently.

Freder passed a piece of fishcake to him and Maria. He held out a piece to Larissa.

Larissa stared at it. "Can you feed everybody?"

"I don't know."

"We lost most of it to the rats. We ate as many rats as we could get away with. Big Jim and Big Clayton rationed them out. Then, they stopped. The two of them have food but they give it to who they want to."

"More?" asked Antonia hopefully and held her hand out.

Mechanically, Freder put one in her hand, then another in Bog and Maria's.

"You have to eat," he said softly to Larissa.

Larissa took a piece and nibbled at it. She looked up at the sky. "Fifteen minutes of light left. We have to go back. They'll beat us if they know we've eaten." She looked at Freder. "Maybe I should just stay out tonight. Let the leopard get me."

"Leopard?"

"Something stalks the rats. Something the size of a leopard and something the size of a little dog."

"That's a gibreel," said Pranavi confidently.

Freder glanced down at her and then decided to ask Pranavi later. He handed the fishcakes through the fence. "Eat this. If you don't throw it up you'll feel better. Then, come back here in the light. I'll have more."

Antonia ate hers up immediately. Bog and Maria nibbled slowly. Larissa stared at hers, then back at Freder.

"What can you do?" she said. "You can't feed everybody. You can't get through the fence. You can't help us."

"I can feed *you* if you come back here at the next light." With that, he left them.

"What do you know of... gibreels?" Freder asked Pranavi.

"I know a whole family of them."

"How big are they? Could we eat them?"

Pranavi didn't speak immediately. Finally, she said viciously: "If you hurt them I'll kill and eat *you*."

Startled, Freder looked down at her.

Pranavi looked up at him. He could see she meant every word she said.

"Understood," Freder said. "Don't tell anybody about them."

"I'm sorry I told *you*." She left him and went towards the greenhouse.

Freder chuckled.

He found Ian and Chitra on their way to the kitchen building. It was almost dark. Freder could hear the faint sound of the rats in the woods.

Once they had secured the door, Freder told them about Larissa and Saint Louis.

"Oh, my God!" said Chitra.

"I'm not sure we *can* feed them," said Ian slowly.

"Ian!"

Ian shook his head. "We probably have enough if we all went on short rations. It's only a couple of weeks until daylight. Although, what's going to happen then? Have they been starting plants? Do they have *seed?* Getting to Sunrise is only halfway." Ian stopped and raised his hands, then let them drop. "But that's not the fundamental problem. Food control is the source of Big Jim and Big Clayton's power. As soon as they realize starving people are getting fed they'll put a stop to it. They've *got* to. What we have to do is stop *them*."

Chitra fell silent.

"Could we?" asked Freder.

Ian stared at him. "What do you mean? We can't get through the fence."

"Could you ask Percy to open the fence?"

"I've asked Percy for a lot of things. Not a word."

"This is different." Freder looked down at Chitra.

"How so?"

Freder looked at Ian. "It's not for us."

Ian stared at him for a long time. Then, he rubbed his face and drew a shuddering breath. "If it works, we have to have enough people to make sure we win. These guys are rangers with Venus strength. They can easily kill several of us. That's too many. We need to have so many people they won't even think about it." Ian stopped. "We go back to the kitchen and talk to people. As soon as it's light, take as many people as you can and get Julie. Have her gather as many of her people as she can. Meet me where the two fences come together."

"Where will you be?"

"I'll be in the map room exhorting God."

Freder, Ian, and Chitra gathered people in the sleeping room. Freder told them about the starving people of Saint Louis. About the beatings. The trading of food for sexual favors.

They muttered for a moment and looked at one another.

"What can we do?" asked Andrew. "We can't get through the fence."

Freder nodded. "Ian's working on that."

Carol gave Freder a nasty look. "He's been able to open the fence all this time?"

"No," said Freder, breathing slowly. This was too important for anger. "This is a last-ditch attempt."

"Why should we stick our neck out for them?"

This was the real question.

Freder had worked in rescue for most of his life. It was a question he'd answered for himself long ago: if you *can* help, how can you face yourself if you *don't?* But he knew that this wasn't a question most people ever faced.

Pranavi spoke up: "This is our place. Our planet." She looked at them fiercely. "All of it. From the crocodiles to the rats. If we don't take care of the world, who will? If we don't take care of each other, who will? If you don't help *now,* why should anybody ever help *you?*"

Bravo! Thought Freder. "I could not have said it better myself."

Ian walked in.

Carol looked at him. "What do you think? You're the one with the special line to Percy."

Ian shrugged in the gloom. "I have no idea if this will work. But I'm going to try. If we don't hang together, we'll hang separately. When we're ready, I'm going to go yell at her one more time. Maybe she'll answer this time."

"Okay," said Freder. "When the Lesser Light comes, anybody who's in, grab some tools and weapons and meet me at the Busan fence."

As soon the light rose, Ian was out the door like a shot.

Freder had a shovel and Chitra a hoe. Pranavi grabbed a stick and the three of them began the walk towards the Busan fence. Twenty people followed them.

Most of Contai called at the fence edge until someone showed. "Get Julie!" called Freder.

A few minutes later, Julie showed up and Freder explained what was going on to her. She nodded and went back to the settlement. A few minutes later half of Busan showed up carrying sticks, shovels, rakes, and any other weapon they could think of.

Freder looked up at the sky. One quarter gone. They didn't have much time.

The crowd parted as Ian came up to the fence.

"What did she say?" asked Chitra.

"Nothing." Ian looked around. He stood facing the fence. "Percy," he said in a normal voice. "Take the fence down. We have to do this."

Nothing happened.

"I know you can hear me. You said we had a job to do here. It's time to let us do our job."

There was a slight vibration in the fence. A sighing sound.

Ian put a hand on the fence. In a soft whisper, he said: "Come on, Percy. Please. It's time."

The fence rattled a moment, then crumbled.

Contai and Busan stared at the empty space for a moment.

Freder looked at the sky. Most of the hour was still left.

"Okay," said Ian. "Let's do this thing."

With that, the forty of them marched down into Saint Louis.

As they walked together, Freder said to Ian: "You know that weird familiarity we've had with everything since we woke up?"

"Yeah."

"This doesn't feel familiar *at all*."

Ian laughed shortly. "Good."

They hashed out different plans on the walk down. Nothing seemed particularly promising.

When they saw the compound, Ian stopped them. "These guys are rangers," he said. "They know how to fight. The advantage we have is numbers. But we must be willing to go the distance. If we have to attack, *all* of us have to attack. Anybody that hangs back is going to get somebody killed." He looked at them. "If you're not willing to take a chance on getting hurt, go home now. We can only use people we can count on."

They looked back at him in grim silence.

Ian nodded. "Okay then. Don't kill anybody if you can help it but don't be afraid to knock some heads."

They came up to the kitchen building. The doors were tied shut. Three men pulled on the table edges, pulling them out enough that Carol could slip a long knife inside to cut the ropes. The tables fell outside with a crash.

A half dozen men stayed on either side of the door. The rest of them arrayed themselves in a rough circle around the door.

"Everybody come out," yelled Ian. "Or we're coming in."

"Come on in, then!"

Freder stood next to Ian. "If we go in after them we lose a lot of advantage."

"Yeah." Ian chewed his lip, looked up at the sky. Half the light gone. "They're waiting for dark. Probably have people up there like shields. They couldn't have known the fences were down until we showed up. So they can't be much prepared. Every minute we wait gives them more chance to build traps." Ian looked at Freder. "We have to go in now."

Ian and Freder looked at one another and nodded. "Come *on!*" yelled Ian and the two of them ran towards the door yelling.

They were followed by forty people carrying clubs of one sort or another.

People blocked the door, tied to the sides. Carol was right behind Freder with a knife.

Big Clayton stepped up and snatched the knife away from her. He turned it expertly around but before he could bring it up, Freder clubbed him on the side of the head. Clayton fell, bleeding, but he still had the knife. Freder brought his club down on Clayton's hand with everything he had. He *felt* the bones in the hand shatter.

Clayton screamed and Carol snatched the knife back again. He screamed again as he was dragged outside.

It was dark and crowded. Freder felt someone hit him twice and he swung back, striking only air. Bodies moving in the dark, smelling of sweat and blood and urine. He felt hands, elbows, fists hit him in the chest, the face, the back. Someone grabbed him by the ear. He shrieked and struck back and felt someone fold around his fist. He had no idea who he had hit. He grabbed a hand, a furry shoulder, a patch of skin at the hip, trying to move people towards the door. They hit him. He hit back—or did they hit back because he hit them? He had no idea. He was blind and half senseless. He screamed and swung at anyone, anything.

Then, something struck him on the back of his head and he winked out like he'd been switched off.

oOo

"Andrew woke up again," said Julie. "He promptly threw up and went down again. I put him on his side. Carol is watching him."

Chitra nodded. "I checked on Freder and Big Jim. They're still out. Pushing them on their side is a good idea. I should have thought of that."

Julie smiled. At least she felt like she was doing good here. Something to keep despair at bay. "You would have."

"But I'm the one with the training." Chitra bit her lip.

Julie recognized the frustration. "My brother was a heroin addict," Julie said quietly. "Turning unconscious people on their side is second nature to me."

Chitra looked at her. "I take it he's not here."

Julie shook her head. "He died as a teenager long before any of this."

Chitra gave her a perplexed look and Julie sighed inwardly. Now, she'll wonder what to say. "Is there anything else we can do?" Julie said to break the awkwardness.

"Keep them hydrated. Try to get them to swallow juice and water." Chitra shook her head. "What I wouldn't give for a real trauma center."

Julie nodded. She put her arm on Chitra's shoulder. Then, tiredness filled Julie like a tide and she swayed. The two of them leaned against each other.

It was light again. In the dark confusion, four were knocked unconscious, including one of the poor people tied up as a human shield. They had pulled everyone out, injured, starving, or otherwise, to do a headcount. That's how they found Big Jim unconscious. No one could be recognized until they were out in the light. Then, just as quickly, they had to retreat into the kitchen building and pull the tables back up before darkness fell.

When light came again, brighter this time, lamps were brought from Busan. Julie and Chitra worked over the injured while Ian supervised feeding the starving. Again, darkness. But this time most of Contai and Busan returned to their villages. Some moved between the villages now that the inner fences were gone, spreading the word. But no one moved too far. The time between lights was too short and they had learned to mistrust the dark.

There was talk of retribution. That Clayton and Jim should be punished. But it didn't catch. Jim was wasting away unconscious and Clayton's hand would never heal right. The people of Saint Louis seemed ashamed that they had let it happen. Ashamed they'd had to be rescued. It was decided that whatever justice that was required would not be meted out until daylight.

Once they had been fed and regained a little strength, Larissa and Phillip took over taking care of food distribution. Julie and Chitra remained with the wounded.

No one had been killed. *That* miracle made Julie feel like praying, had she ever been so inclined.

Broken bones were easy. Set and dismissed. They healed properly or they didn't. Cuts and bruises likewise. Most only needed to be fed.

That left the four unconscious: Freder Gluck, Andrew Penn, Francesca Guzman, and Big Jim Hanover.

Francesca woke up while they were bringing her in just before dark. She was still woozy and staggering but conscious. Andrew woke up groggy the next light. He had been in and out for a couple of hours but managed to finally hold onto a shred of wakefulness.

Freder and Jim remained unconscious.

The brain doesn't have much structural integrity. Pick up a brain out of the skull and it droops on either side of your hand like a stiff gel. A concussion occurs when that gel gets shaken in its case. It can happen with any injury to the skull. It is certain to have happened when the patient loses consciousness. Most of the time the period of unconsciousness is short: seconds. Sometimes it is so quick that the patient can get up without anyone noticing it happened—including the patient. The longer the time unconscious, the more potentially serious the concussion can be.

Four hours is a long time. Every hour brings the patient closer to possible coma.

Julie and Chitra took turns sitting with them. Talking to Freder. Asking him to wake up. It sometimes helped to talk to coma patients. Why not here? Jim and Freder were not yet in a coma, but talking to them couldn't hurt. Often, Ian took over, giving Julie and Chitra a break.

No one sat next to Jim except Phillip, with a swollen face and one eye bandaged closed, praying.

"Why pray over him?" asked Julie pointing to Big Jim. "He started this mess."

Phillip smiled at her. He was missing a tooth. "Jesus said to forgive your enemies. He didn't mean just the nice ones. God has a plan for all of us. Even him."

Taking a break outside, watching the bulk of the sequoias in the dimming light, Julie thought about that. Who could Julie forgive? Percy for bringing her here? Terri for not being here? Forgiveness and letting go were joined in her mind. If she forgave Terri for not being here—as irrational a feeling as a person could have since it was clearly not her fault—would she be letting Terri go? Emotions have a logic of their own. She *would not* let Terri go. Could she forgive Terri for the imaginary fault of not being here without letting her go? She hoped so.

After that, Julie took to sitting next to Jim, talking to him. She had never met him. Clayton had as much leadership ability as a piece of string. Without Jim to tell him what to do, he wandered around trying to fit in. Julie thought: *if I can forgive Jim, I can forgive anybody.*

The light dimmed a little more every time it came. People had not traveled much between the villages—no one could go too far and return in an hour. But there had been a little traffic and now, with the dark before sunrise coming, people moved back to their villages to wait it out.

Then, finally, the Lesser Lights were gone. Clouds rolled in from the east and it rained for three sleeps.

Both Freder and Jim remained unconscious. They drank a little in their sleep. Julie and Chitra dribbled a ground-up puree of corn and beans into their mouths. They drank it as if it were water.

Freder opened his eyes as Julie was cleaning him. He stared blankly in the lamplit gloom. "Hello?"

Julie stopped what she was doing and calmly moved to the end of the table. "Freder?"

"Yes," he said.

"What's your name? Your full name?"

"Freder Manheim Gluck." He stared at her looking sick and peevish. "Want me to hold up three fingers?" He did and they started to shake. He set them down. "That was a mistake."

"You've been unconscious for five sleeps."

Freder stared up at her. "Am I alive?"

She laughed and was suddenly crying. "Yes."

"Are you sure?" He whimpered.

"You're alive. I'll get Chitra."

Julie caught Chitra in the kitchen. Chitra rushed back towards Freder. Ian was right behind her.

Julie went outside. The rain had stopped and the clouds were rolling and thinning as they blew west. It was too light for stars but the shafts of pink and orange striping the sky were worth it.

The map display said Dawn.

People knew it was coming. They began to drift slowly outside.

It seemed terribly, terribly wrong for anyone to be inside for their first sunrise. Julie and Chitra brought people outside on the east side of the building. They kept a close watch—the outer fence was still in place and Largo, and others like him, were still nearby though they seemed to have disappeared into Contai's lagoon.

Finally, only Jim was left.

Julie insisted. Phillip, Bog, and Ian carried him out in a makeshift litter. They put him in the front so no one would shade him. Julie knew that if Largo suddenly appeared and gulped him whole there wouldn't be a hand raised to defend him.

Well, Phillip would. And Julie. She had decided she liked the idea of forgiveness. It wasn't that Terri needed forgiveness for not being there. If it turned out that Julie had lived and Terri had died it would be Julie that needed forgiveness. If Julie could forgive others, maybe Terri would forgive her for living. Julie would still find those other settlements and make sure but she had begun to lose hope. What was so special about both her and Terri that a creature like Percy would take notice of it?

There came a moment when they were all standing outside, mute, watching the eastern mountains as they brightened. It reached the moment on Earth where there was just so much light the mind said *surely this is all there is. There can't possibly be any more.* But here on Venus, it lingered for minutes, not seconds. Tens of minutes until they were half-blind, tears streaming down their faces, each thinking *I will never see again.*

The sun came over the sea and struck them blind.

Julie turned away, one hand covering her eyes.

Her other hand was caught.

She looked down.

Jim was watching the east, his eyes hooded by his left hand.

His right hand was holding hers.

Chapter 2.6: Night and Day

Now that the inner fences were down, they had a better idea of how big the settled area was. Each settlement was between two and five kilometers east to west and roughly the same north to south. The entire settled area was about twenty-one kilometers north to south and fifteen east to west. Busan was in the northern half.

Once the garden was planted, Hotaru and Julie walked north. First, they visited Guayaquil. Julie had only spoken with a couple of people there when she distributed the lists—Miguel Herrera and Ando Motamedi. Hotaru knew several people. As Julie had her friends to the south and east, so Hotaru had friends to the north and west.

After Guayaquil, they walked through Agadir, where Julie knew a man named Frank Ditch and another named Raam. Hotaru had not met anyone there.

To the east was Bokpyan but they walked due north.

North and west of the settlements, a plain stretched out for a couple of kilometers ending in a forest where she could see the outer fence. Unlike the inner fences, the outer fence was not a dome. It was high—perhaps fifteen meters. It could be climbed by monkeys but apparently, they were the only monkeys on Venus. Julie could see the sequoias march up into the mountains, surrounded by lesser forests. From here, she could see birds flying west from over the water. A few flew overhead—perhaps the beginning of the migration.

Like geese? Julie thought. She wondered if they could keep them for meat or eggs.

"I was an old woman in Tokyo," Hotaru said. "I had a garden behind my house. I grew onions, garlic, shallots—things to cook with. My husband never noticed. I was as much a piece of equipment as the kitchen stove. The microwave. The rice cooker. I was there to keep the house, bear his children and cook. Outside of these things I was invisible. He came home, ate, had me, then went out. Or sometimes he would not come home." She glanced up at Julie. "I was a *Nidan* in the Kodokan."

"Nidan? Kodokan?"

"Judo. The gentle way. Nidan is a second-degree black belt." Hotaru sighed. "It took twelve years. My husband never knew. It was hard after he retired. He was always there." She stopped and looked around. Her fur had already fallen out and she was darkening. "The wave took me in Kasai Rinkai Park. I had visited the Kodokan to watch my grandchildren—I was too old to play anymore. Then, I took the Keiyo Line to the park—anything to avoid going home. I saw the sea birds and the aquarium. I climbed the viewing tower and stood there watching the sea. When I saw the wave come, I felt happy for the first time in years. I knew exactly what it was—*tsunami* is a Japanese word. We understand tsunamis." Hotaru spread her arms and turned slowly in a circle. "When it came I climbed the railing and leaped into the water in joy. I was done with it all." She looked at Julie and smiled. "Imagine my surprise to be here."

They came to the outer fence. It resembled the inner fence except thicker and the mesh was larger.

Now that they were closer, they could see into the forest. The trees began perhaps forty meters from the fence. They were tall and thinly built. It looked as if they'd fall over in a stiff breeze. Julie could see several trunks decayed on the ground. Underbrush sprouted between the fallen trunks.

She heard a low fluting sound, like the deep thrum of a pipe organ and a crunching.

An apatosaurus came from between the trees.

Julie froze in place.

The apatosaurus had no feathers but it was mottled in gray and green—some skin color, some bits of moss and algae. There were indeterminate streaks of bright yellow down its back along its tail and it had a fine, leathery skin. It stopped, nibbled some needles from the lower branches of the trees, and uprooted a bush, gradually working it down his throat. Then, it shook its head and came towards them. It shat as it came, a great steaming twenty-kilogram lump that fell *splat* five meters to the ground. It came alongside the fence and leaned against it and began rubbing against it.

Bits of skin and lichen flew off and fell on Julie and Hotaru in a stinking cloud of debris.

They ran back out of the cascade and stopped, watching.

Another came out of the forest followed by more. The crunching sound Julie had heard were their feet punching through old tree trunks. Other than that, their tread was silent. Julie put her hand on the ground and felt nothing. She scolded herself for being surprised. She'd seen elephants, hadn't she? Elephants made no more sound than this.

The herd came up to the fence and in twos and threes. They took turns scrubbing themselves against it. Julie looked up and down the fence line and realized it was discolored here. They had been doing this for some time.

Hotaru knelt. She carefully put her hands on the ground and bowed to them, her head touching the Earth. Then, she rose. "Oh, to live and see this." She took Julie's hand.

Julie put her arm around Hotaru as they watched the great beasts.

One large one—Matriarch? Patriarch?—came from the forest. The others made way for her. She shook herself after her scrubbing. The entire herd was visibly cleaner. They ate the low bushes and went on.

From the settlement, Julie heard a sound like steam escaping. There was a low boom.

She turned towards the settlements. Julie saws a cloud escaping from Bokpyan's buildings.

All of Bokpyan was standing in front of the sealed buildings. Steam rolled out of each. Julie and Hotaru looked at one another and started running towards Busan. They ran past Guayaquil's buildings—one of them was venting steam as well. Beyond it, they saw a cloud of steam in the distance.

Julie was out of breath when they reached Busan.

The steam roared out of the biggest of Busan's sealed buildings. It faded to a trickle and stopped. There was dead silence.

Then, all three of the sealed buildings rang like bells.

Julie wanted to run away. She wanted to run screaming at the sealed building with a rock. After all of this, what *now?*

Silence fell again.

Then, suddenly and silently, the door flew open.

Busan milled around the entrance.

Julie approached it when no one else did. She walked up the steps and looked inside.

There were carpeted tiers just like in the kitchen building. On them lay people. They were naked, completely without fur, and pale.

Don't hope.

Julie made her way along the sleepers. Behind her, she heard others coming inside.

There, sleeping on her side on one of the tiers, was Terri.

Julie knelt next to her. She reached out to touch her and then jerked her hand back. What if Terri wasn't real? What if none of this was real?

She touched Terrie's shoulder, Terri's hand. It felt like Terri. It smelled like Terri. Julie felt tears falling down her face as she cried without restraint, every part of her released. Every part of her open.

Terri opened her eyes. "Hey," she said. "I thought you were dead."

Julie held her as tightly as she could. She was never letting Terri go. Never again.

oOo

Regardless what Freder said, Chitra wouldn't let him walk the three kilometers back to Contai until he could at least walk a straight line unaided. Julie regularly came in and made Chitra rest. Ian visited regularly. Freder's right leg was weak and he had trouble walking any distance without stopping for breath. But he was ready to leave—*had been ready* for sleeps. Julie and Chitra helped him walk home.

It was now well into Morning. The regular rains were filling the catchments. The freshly plowed plains were on the other side of Guayaquil and out of sight, but Freder knew they were there. He walked through Contai's wall gate slowly. He was surprised how much had been done in only a few weeks. Tripling the numbers in the settlements had at least one good effect.

People he knew and didn't know stopped him, shook his hand, or clapped him on the back. It seemed he was being given credit for the Battle of Saint Louis as much as Ian. More, maybe, since he had been injured and Ian had not.

Still, when people spoke of Ian, they lowered their voices. It was Ian that had made the inner fences disappear. It was Ian that had the special relationship with Percy.

Ian was sitting outside of Contai's sealed buildings as he and Chitra approached.

He rose to his feet and smiled at them. Ian hugged Freder. "I'm glad you're better," He said.

Freder looked at him, then at the sealed building. "What are you waiting for?"

"My mother," Ian said simply. "She wasn't in the other sealed buildings when they opened up. I'm hoping for this one."

Freder nodded, suddenly tired.

Ian patted his arm. "Go on and get some rest." Ian kissed Chitra and then waved the two of them towards the sleeping building.

Freder nodded. He could feel exhaustion rolling towards him like a boulder.

oOo

The sealed buildings did not open at once. Guayaquil, Bokpyan, Busan and Agadir's were the first. Then, nothing for nearly two weeks. It was now well into Morning.

In Contai, Pranavi worked in the garden and then spent an hour sitting in front of the largest building. This had become the pattern. People worked then held vigil. Pranavi grew restless and went out in the plains to investigate the dinosaurs.

The new people were put to work building a row of pikes between the settlements and the plain and a wall around some of the villages—the distance was just too great to follow the outer fence completely.

They had assembled three final refuges so far: Contai, Mogadishu, and Toamasina. Those settlements were fortified. People were to run there if the outer fence came down.

That was what scared everybody. If there were dinosaurs of one kind, there were bound to be dinosaurs of another. If there were apatosauruses, there were bound to be allosauruses.

Or something, Julie had told her. These were apatosauruses the same way that with their fur and quickly darkening skin they were still human. Sure. Maybe. A better way to think about it was to consider everything on Venus as Venusian.

Pranavi went to the fence anyway, past the pikes being lifted into position, past the teams of people pulling a plow—yet another thing found in the sealed buildings. She went northeast where the forest thinned and the fence went out into the sea.

Halfway there, Gibreel showed up at her side, trotting along in the grass—darting away now and then and returning with a rat. Often, Gibreel offered it to her.

"No thanks," said Pranavi.

Gibreel gave her a shake that said *suit yourself* quite clearly and ate as he trotted alongside her.

There were lots of gibreels now, sitting at the ready next to the gardens. No one like Gibreel, of course. These gibreels were wild things and would not let themselves be approached. Gibreel was special.

The contrast between the new people and the original settlers was startling. It wasn't just the lack of fur—the natives shed on schedule just a few sleeps after the newcomers' first awakenings. It wasn't the newcomers' lack of color—they darkened quickly into the same collection of shades as the rest.

No. It was what they knew. *These* people had no familiarity with *anything*. Except for the language, if they didn't know it back on Earth, they didn't know it here. When she had visited Julie, Pranavi must have grabbed Terri's hand a hundred times before she could tell a weed from a bean. They didn't know *anything*.

Gibreel trotted next to her. Occasionally, he would lean his long neck against her leg for a few steps before he straightened. It was affection, clear and true, and it warmed Pranavi every time.

But he didn't want her going close to the fence.

He hung back at first but came reluctantly forward when she left him behind. Then, he kept putting himself in front of her so she had to walk around him. Finally, he walked, trembling, beside her, stopping and staring at nothing in particular for a moment before he caught up with her.

"Gibreel!" she finally said in exasperation. "The fence is *still there!* Don't be so scared." She took the fence and shook it vigorously.

Gibreel launched himself at her, catching her in the chest and knocking her down. He grabbed her grass top and dragged her a good meter before he stopped, breathing hard.

Pranavi heard something sharp hit the ground.

She looked at the fence and saw something with a long neck and sharp claws pulling its arm back slowly through the fence as it watched her. Its claws dug parallel furrows in the dirt.

There was no mistaking its gaze. It saw her purely as prey.

Pranavi crawled backward, watching it.

It tested the fence and pushed its head and long neck through. Withdrew it and tested the fence again.

It would have happily killed her and brought her through the fence one piece at a time.

She reached over and grabbed Gibreel and hugged him. "Good Gibreel. *Good* Gibreel." They were both shaking.

Pranavi stood up unsteadily.

She'd peed herself. That enraged her.

"Yah!" she yelled at the creature. "You didn't get me. You'll *never* get me." She threw her soiled shorts at it.

The creature blinked and backed away from the fence. It looked at her from one side, then the other, like a bird. Cackled at her and shot back into the forest.

Those things were *fast*.

"Come on, Gibreel. Let's go back."

Pranavi found a patch of tall grass and took the time to weave another pair of shorts. She looked at Gibreel. "I'm going to have to make them different when I grow up. None of the adult girls wear anything this flimsy."

She sat in the grass and took Gibreel into her lap.

Gibreel submitted and gave his purr-thrum. It wasn't his favorite position but he was more than happy to accommodate her. She held him tight again, seeing the creature in her mind. "Good Gibreel." He felt warm. Familiar as an old friend. He had saved her.

She thought about dogs. Something her father had said once: "Dogs and cats are the only animals that tossed their lot in with human beings voluntarily." Maybe. Pranavi had little use for cats.

Humans had later bred dogs relentlessly but they already had made their choice. "Dogs made us human," she said to Gibreel, remembering other things her father had said.

So much felt familiar: language, gardening, Gibreel. People had different ideas about that familiarity. Some thought it was programmed by Percy. Others thought different people had used the same bodies. Still, others had said this was just human adaptability—but that one was hard to swallow now that the new people were out with *no* familiarity.

She scratched Gibreel's head. "But *you* know *me*, don't you, Gibreel?"

Gibreel purred.

Gibreel *did* know her. Knew her the first time he saw her.

If that *was* the first time. What if they had always been in these bodies? Doing it over and over until they got it right? Maybe they had become friends a long time ago and she'd been taken from him. So Gibreel waited for her to find him, always wanting to be with her. Over and over.

It rang true. How many times had it taken to get it right? Ten? Twenty? Fifty? Did she die every time? Probably. Pranavi remembered the little girl she had been back on Earth. *She* could not have survived. Pranavi had barely survived as it was.

Maybe each time, poor Gibreel saw her die and waited for her return.

Pranavi had to tell somebody.

oOo

Neither Big Jim nor Freder healed quickly but Big Jim's concussion was more severe. Where Freder had made it back to Contai under his own power with a bit of help, Big Jim was still not able to walk. Phillip and Julie were always helping him.

Larissa didn't understand it. After all, Big Jim was the source of all their troubles during the night. If it had been up to Larissa, Jim might never have been allowed to wake.

Julie returned to Busan when the Busan sleepers awoke. Larissa heard that she had finally found her beloved Terri. Larissa felt good for her.

Two weeks later, Saint Louis' sealed building cracked open and their own sleepers awoke. Larissa had no one. Phillip had no one.

Jim sat on the ground looking sick and hopeful as the sleepers gradually walked out. He did not call out to anyone. Nor did anyone call out to him. He was just as alone as Larissa was. But afterward, he worked hard on relearning how to walk by himself. Several times, Larissa woke to find him practicing outside on the grass with the two sticks Phillip had made him to serve as crutches. He silently fell and got up again. Larissa had to admire that.

It was up to those already established—the *natives*—here to help the new people through the transition. The new folks wept. They screamed. Two tried to commit suicide and one tried to murder another.

The natives of Saint Louis watched for the signs. The suicides were averted. The murder was stopped. The natives had already been through it. They knew exactly what the new people were going through. Some depressions healed quickly. Some people would have to be watched for a long time.

Larissa knew this had been Percy's plan. She hated it. How many people had been through this before and failed? That Larissa might finally be successful felt like ashes.

Then, Julie visited.

"Pranavi had an idea," she said as they walked north along the outer fence, watching the sea. "She's convinced we've been through this before."

"Yeah. I think that, too."

"No." Julie shook her head. "Not just human beings doing this before. We [illegible] *us*. You. Me. Big Jim and Phillip. Ian and Freder—*we've* been through this before. Until we finally got it right."

Larissa stopped. She stared at Julie. "What do you think?"

Julie gave her a brittle smile. "Did you know you can talk to Percy now?"

"*What?*"

"Pranavi was the first. She took her little pet—"

"Pet?"

"Chitra told me all of this. Pranavi has this tiny dinosaur that she's been hiding since yesterday. That's what made her think of this. The dinosaur remembered her."

"Pet." Larissa felt like the world was turning underneath her.

"She ran into the map room screaming at Percy. 'Is that what happened? Have we been here until we got it right? *Did* we get it right?' The display blanked out everything but the time. Then it said 'yes.'"

"You can ask Percy questions?"

Julie nodded. "Seems like you can, now. She doesn't always answer."

Larissa was silent a moment. "Did you ask her anything?"

"Yes." Julie watched the ocean as they walked. "I asked if she needed us for Venus. She said yes. She needed all of us."

Julie returned to Busan. Larissa worked in the garden for a few hours, thinking.

She found Jim sitting at the edge of the plain, watching people plow and plant, leaning on Phillip's two sticks.

Larissa looked him over. "Walk with me."

Jim looked up at her, sullen. "I don't walk too well."

"Don't be a baby." She helped him get started.

He walked slowly and she led him north until they could see the forest. Large animals were walking among the trees—Larissa still didn't know all the names. No predators or sauropods were visible but there was no telling what was beyond even a short space into the forest.

"I don't understand Julie," he said suddenly. "Before I awoke, she sat next to me for hours, talking to me. I heard her, too." He stopped and rubbed his face. "First from a long way off. Then, closer until I could make out the words. Then, she was sitting next to me. And Phillip? I *really* don't understand Phillip. He forgave me. I don't even know what that means."

Larissa watched him for a moment, watched expressions dart across on his face. One moment, complete confusion. The next, anguish. The next, blank hopelessness.

"You know exactly what he means," she said sternly. "He means you get a second chance." Her voice softened. "Phillip says we don't get to just forgive the people we like."

"Yeah. Right." Jim waved his arm, including the forest, sky, and land. "I didn't think about this stuff for a long time. I just went along—like it was some kind of military exercise. We used to get those all the time. One day they'd haul us out and throw us in the snow. Another day we'd have to tread water for half an hour and keep all our gear dry." He reached out into the air with an open hand and made a fist. The muscles corded up. "I was *tough*. I was *strong*. I had to be. If I could take that I could surely take this." He opened his hand limply. "Then, I heard you talking."

"What?" Larissa was shocked. "What did you hear?"

He dropped his hand and settled himself on his canes. "You were talking to Phillip about how much we didn't know. How we were *stuck* here. How we had to make things from scratch because we didn't know *anything*—where the water came from. Where the sewage went. How to make steel. How to make pottery. We knew *nothing*. It hit me then. This wasn't a drill. These were the bodies we had. This was the place where we were expected to live. It was completely hopeless. We were in little zoos until whatever-the-fuck-Percy-is got tired of us and flushed us down the toilet. I started thinking: if this is all there is, if nothing matters, if it's just this shithole of a place in a shithole of a world run by a fucked up god—then, why not just take what you want? Why shouldn't I? Nobody could stop me.

"What the hell else *was* there?" he said in a strangled voice. "Everybody I knew was dead. Everybody in history was long gone. We were all going to die anyway. That was obvious from when we woke up. All that crap you were doing. All that crap anyone was doing. It was all shoveling shit against the tide. I didn't know there were fucking *dinosaurs* out there but all that does is prove I'm right. We don't have what it takes. So why not just grab onto a little bit before the dark, right?"

His voice shook. "I beat people up. I starved people. I expected—I *wanted* to die. Then, while I was just drifting. I heard Phillip's voice. I heard Julie's. I heard *your* voice. Talking to me. Sitting next to me asking me to come back. After I'd beaten you. After I'd starved you." He fell to his knees. "Beat me. Starve me. Do *something* to me."

She reached under his chin and lifted his face. "No." Larissa brought him to her, nestled his head against her chest.

Jim suddenly relaxed into her arms. She held him up so he wouldn't fall as he wept. She stroked his back. She knew exactly what he was feeling: loss of his home. Loss of his place. Loss of everything he had left behind. *It just takes some people longer to realize it.*

Finally, he stopped and stood up. He wiped his eyes. "I'm okay."

"Good." She smiled at him. She suddenly realized they had no *other* here. No one was something different. Something outside the group. They *were* the group. They were all of humanity there was. They had no one but each other and a somewhat mad god.

"I'm sorry," Jim said.

She thought carefully. "I forgive you."

Jim jerked as if he had been struck. He drew a long shuddering breath.

"Does Clayton feel like you do?" Larissa said, thinking. *If he does, we'll have to watch him.*

Jim shook his head. "Strong. Fierce. Deadly—that's Clayton. Sharp as a basketball. That's Clayton, too. He followed my lead."

"Good."

They watched the fence. On the other side, a herd of medium-sized herbivores came out of the forest. These weren't sauropods. They mostly walked on all fours but now and then they stood up on their hind legs.

"Iguanodons," said Jim suddenly. "They were my favorite when I was a kid."

Iguanodons. Good to know. "Did you hear what is happening in Contai?"

"No."

Larissa told him about Pranavi and Percy.

Jim didn't say anything for a moment, mulling it over. "So we got it right?"

"Yeah."

"Percy planned everything? Me and Clayton?" There was a faint sound of relief in his voice.

"No," said Larissa. "I don't think so. I think Percy was putting us together in different ways until we were in a position to learn what we needed. Phillip might say we had to find our inner Jesus. I'm not so inclined." She snorted. "I think we had to figure out who we were *here*. You were a part of that. You were showing us who we couldn't be. We *had* to group together to take over Saint Louis after you messed it up."

"Thanks," he said dryly.

"We all play our part."

Jim chuckled shortly. "Now what?"

Larissa spoke slowly. "I don't think anything was planned." She stopped a moment. "But I think the mistake you made was absolutely necessary—it's part of who you are. I don't think any of us serve just one purpose. So you couldn't just be meant to fuck up. We're too few and too valuable."

Jim barked a laugh. "Valuable?"

"Yes, valuable. Percy didn't just say yes we were necessary. She said we were *all* necessary. You included. And not just over the night but now and into the future."

"I can barely walk. I'm not much use to anybody." He turned at stared at her. "Hell, I couldn't keep control of you guys when you were weak and starving."

"You're learning to walk."

"Slowly."

"Brain injuries take time." She watched him speculatively. "You were a ranger."

"Yeah."

"I think you're here, in part, to protect us from this world. To help us build a beachhead. Or a fort. Didn't you learn that sort of thing?"

"Some," he admitted.

"I think you should be over in Busan helping them build the new wall. Then, I think you should be figuring out how we're going to live out there. Someday the fence is going to fall—falling is what walls do. We can't stay here forever. Someday, we're going to have to leave our little nest and go out into the rest of the world."

Jim thought for a long time. Then, he turned to her. "Will you help me?"

She returned his look. Something bridged between them. She had no idea how to interpret it.

"Yes."

oOoPranavi and Gibreel were playing in Agadir when she heard a roar and the sound of a bell.

Pranavi began to run. Gibreel loped alongside her.

Contai's sealed building opened as she came to it and she didn't stop. "Wait here," she called to Gibreel and ran inside. This didn't feel familiar. It felt *possible.*

Sure enough, in the back, she found her father and little Mintu. All asleep.

Pranavi sat down next to them. She could wait. She had so *much* to tell them.

oOo

The boom and sound of escaping steam woke Freder.

Freder was alone in the room. He felt of himself and took stock, sat up without feeling sick—a new milestone in the last couple of weeks. He stood up without his right leg buckling. *Success!* Maybe he would live through this.

Outside, a crowd had gathered in front of the sealed buildings. Ian was in the back, Chitra next to him.

Chitra saw Freder. "You're an idiot," she said. "You should be resting."

"What?" Freder gave her a sickly grin. "And miss all the excitement?"

The door of the building cracked open with the sound of escaping air. A crowd ran inside—Freder could see Pranavi leading them.

Freder looked at Ian. "Go on? Maybe she's in there."

Ian nodded. "Maybe." But he didn't move until the crowd returned from inside, leading pale, staggering people. Pranavi brought out a man and two children. Behind her came a man.

"Kapi!" cried Chitra and ran to him. She held him in her arms and wept.

"What do you know?" said Ian. "Percy has a heart after all." Ian left Freder and went inside.

Chitra led Kapi away towards the kitchen, chattering the whole time. Freder wished that he knew somebody there. *What do you expect?* He chided himself. He was not close to anyone. Possibly, some in his gene pool might be represented but he'd never know them. Freder wondered if Percy had included Kapi for Chitra. After all, Ian had insisted Chitra be brought along. Maybe Percy thought she needed someone. Maybe Percy, indeed, had a heart.

After a few minutes, Ian came out alone.

"She's not there," he said.

Freder slowly followed him to the map room. The display had blanked out. Ian stood in front of it.

"Where is she?" Ian shouted.

There was a long moment where nothing happened. Then, a single word formed on the display:

"Safe."

Ian stared at the screen for a long time. "Okay," he said softly. Then, louder. "Okay."

He turned to Freder. "I'm going to check the other settlements. The sealed buildings are still opening. I'll look for her there."

Freder grabbed his arm. "You're the leader of Contai. You can't leave."

Ian's eyes were hard. "You're leader now. Or make them choose someone else. I have things to do."

With that, he was gone

oOo

Morning passed into Noon and the rains disappeared. This time, though, the catchments were full around Contai and the nearby villages. Further south, irrigation trenches were dug from Lake Mogadishu to the surrounding villages. To the southeast, the Mogadishu River was partially diverted into irrigation canals. The garden grew straight and lush. All around them were gibreels, killing rats whenever they could. Fed scraps by villagers when they couldn't.

Villagers kept watch over the outer fence from the roof of the outer settlements—Bokpyan, Guayaquil, and Dunung. Waiting for when the outer fence dissolved or was knocked over. No one knew when it would occur but no one doubted it would happen.

The long pikes mounted outside these villages facing the fence were finished. Those who built them hoped the pikes would discourage the sauropods and other large animals. The inner wall was intended to stop everything else. The main buildings had been fitted with thick doors as a last resort.

We've fallen into a medieval world, thought Freder. We farm outside the wall, fall behind the wall in case of trouble, and into the castle if the wall fails.

oOo

Ian returned in early Sunset. Freder and Chitra found him eating just outside the Guayaquil pikes, watching the activity on the other side of the northern fence. Large dinosaur predators paced alongside it, watching them. Gerard had called them albertosaurs and the name had stuck—through Julie was careful to point out that they looked much more like proto-tyrannosaurs. They were perhaps three meters at the hip and nine meters long. Skittering between their legs were dromaeosaurs.

Ian was thinner. He was eating a corn biscuit with a purposeful precision as if he had eaten alone a great deal. As if people around him had become superfluous. Ian didn't take his eyes off the fence.

Freder still walked with a limp. He tried to lean on his cane as little as possible. He didn't want to look crippled in front of Ian.

Ian saw them and smiled. "Hey. Have you tried Larissa's corn biscuits? Terrific."

"Are you staying?" asked Freder, bluntly.

Ian watched them a moment. There was a leanness to Ian's face. A stony look. Freder had a sudden vision of the man who had spent nearly fifty years gathering people to come here. That Ian was someone he'd never met until now.

Ian finished the last of the corn biscuit and stood up. "I can move on if you want."

"Hush, Freder." Chitra put her hand on Ian's arm. "I'm glad to see you." She hugged Ian.

Freder took a little pride that there seemed to be no sexual side to it. *Of course,* he thought to himself. If she wanted Ian she would just go to Ian. Freder would have nothing to say about it. That Ian might not want Chitra did not occur to him.

Ian hugged her back the same way.

"Did you find your mother?" asked Chitra.

"No," he said shortly. "The last sealed building was the one in Reykjavik. It opened three sleeps ago and she wasn't in it." Ian looked to Chitra. Then, to Freder. "What's going on?"

"The current story is that we've all done this before. Until we got it right." Freder stared at him.

Ian stared back. "Yeah. I heard that."

"Is it true?"

Ian looked at Chitra. "Yeah."

"You were there? Each time?" asked Chitra.

"Yeah."

"You remembered?" Freder leaned forward.

Ian didn't move. "It took nine times. Nine times I had to watch you all wake up and tear yourselves apart." He glanced around. "Or this place. You'd be surprised what people can do to even Percy's buildings when they set their mind to it. Do you want me to apologize for that, too?"

Freder felt weak with rage. "Why didn't you *tell* us?"

Ian stared at him. "I did the first couple of times. It made things worse."

"Did we die each time?" Chitra asked quietly.

"Not every time." Ian squatted down on his hips, looking up at them. "First time, everybody starved to death. They didn't have enough saved during the day to get them through the night and didn't have enough will to not eat the seeds before Morning. Second time, the same—that was the first time I told you. Riots, death, and destruction. Third time, the same. Fourth time, I shut up and things lasted a little longer. Then, Percy started trying different combinations. Smaller riots the next couple of times. She just shut those down and started over. When all three of us were in the same village we lasted overnight. Self-destruction by Dawn. She kept us together after that. Pranavi showed up the next time and that got us through the night and part of the Morning—but not to where she could drop the inner fences. So she kept Pranavi. Did you know war could be waged through fence holes? I didn't. More switching around. Torture. Murder sprees. But something was working. This last time was the first *I* knew that Pranavi had made Gibreel into a friend. That had something to do with us getting us this far."

"Because of Pranavi's *pet?*" Freder shook his head.

"That's just a guess." Ian laughed, looking at them. "Don't feel bad. It had to be a lot of little details. Percy's model of human behavior can't be that complete—she hasn't known us long enough."

"She talked to you the whole time?" Chitra looked grim.

"Of course not. Freder saw the first word she's said to me since we got here. No." He sighed. "I was just the one that woke up with memories."

"Why you?" Chitra's mouth was set in a flat line.

Ian held up his hands. "I don't know. She didn't talk to me, remember? I'm guessing it made a difference. Or maybe she got some kind of insight in my post-mortem. When you died, I died, too, you know."

"Is this time the last?" Freder said it in a hiss. The idea of doing this over and over was intolerable.

Ian turned back to the fence, watching. "Maybe. She's never dropped the inner fence before. If she drops the outer fence, I'd say that's the sign. After that, we're *really* on our own. On the other hand, maybe she'll reuse us other ways."

"Why?" Freder asked. "Why do it this way at all? Why not talk to us?"

Ian gave them both a long sad look. "You know the answer to that. Because that must be the way it has to be. We don't understand it. We don't know why—we don't even know if she feels anything for us or if she just *needs* us to think so. What we do know—at least *I* think we know this—is that she wouldn't do something she didn't need to do." He waved at the sky. "This is way, way too expensive to waste much. So if we're here, we're here because she needs us. If she put us through hell it was to serve that need. She's management. We're employees. She'll make a good working environment—make the place as comfortable as possible, train us to do what we have to do, let us live our lives as best we can as long as it benefits the company—but we have a *job*. Maybe all we've been through so far is a sort of employee orientation."

"What's the job?" asked Freder.

"I have no idea."

Chitra watched Ian silently. "I don't love you anymore," she said at last.

Ian was quiet for a long time. "I know."

They heard a shout from the roof of the closest building.

The three of them turned to look at the fence. Freder could see the outer fence unravelling in a line. A dozen assorted predators watched it pass them.

"Run," said Ian. He shoved the two of them past the pikes. Another few hundred meters to the wall.

Freder had to drag his bad leg. "Go on," Freder said to Chitra. "I'll be fine."

"Shut up!" said Chitra fiercely, hauling him along.

The unraveling passed them going west.

There's perhaps a kilometer between us and the remains of the fence, Freder thought, trying to drag his recalcitrant leg along.

"They're going to figure this out quickly," Ian said, grabbing Freder's other arm. "They're not stupid."

Together, they dragged Freder past the pikes.

"Did you know this was going to happen?" Freder yelled at Ian.

"Not right this minute I didn't!"

They heard a bass throbbing behind them and a pounding thunder.

"Oh, that's not good," Ian said.

"Albertosaurs?" asked Chitra between clenched teeth.

"Albertosaurs." Ian looked at the wall and then behind them. He let go of Freder. "Take him to the wall."

"*No!*" screamed Freder.

"Shut up!" Chitra took his arm over her shoulder and hauled him over the last hundred meters.

As they reached the gate, Freder grabbed it. "Wait for him!" He turned to see.

The albertosaur had reached Ian. Ian ran to the left and then the right, slipping under the albertosaur's mouth, back between his legs, buying them time. He glanced at them. "Close the fucking gate!" he shouted.

The albertosaur knocked him six meters and snapped at him.

Ian rolled out of the way and slid to a stop on his feet.

Freder could see him clearly. Ian had forgotten them. Freder could see something come alive in him, as if everything he'd ever done, everything ever done to him, rose up.

Ian danced back when the albertosaurus snapped at him again. He leaped and brought his fists down, double-handed, right on the albertosaur's nose.

It roared and backed away, shaking its head.

Ian ran up its leg and launched himself from its thigh and kicked it just behind the jaw.

The albertosaur screamed this time. It swung on Ian but he wasn't there. He dove between its legs and swung over its tail, coming up again for the other side.

He's going to do it! Thought Freder. Alone, with nothing but fists and rage, Ian was going to take down a dinosaur. Freder cheered and heard the echo as everyone on the wall cheered.

Ian skipped over the thigh, going for the same vulnerable point on the other side.

The albertosaur was ready for him. It turned its head and caught his leg and tossed him high in the air.

For a long, disbelieving moment, Freder stared at him, unable to accept this. Unable to understand that it was over. At one point, turning in the air, Ian saw him. He shouted something. Freder didn't catch it.

The albertosaur snapped him in the air and shook him like a terrier shakes a rat. It was too much and Ian came apart, his chest and lower torso going one direction, his head and one arm going another.

Then, the albertosaur sprouted an arrow in its eye. Two more. One in its snout and a half dozen in its open mouth. Then, forty more.

I didn't know we had arrows, thought Freder.

The albertosaur clawed at its eye. Turned and four spears sprouted from its side. It staggered to one side and was knocked over by another albertosaur coming from behind that tore its throat out. Four dromaeosaurs took the opportunity to skip around both albertosaurs, saw Ian's body as carrion, and dragged it away towards the forest.

Chitra dragged Freder in as they closed the gate.

"Why didn't you shoot sooner?" Freder yelled at the villagers on the top of the gate. He turned to Chitra, weeping. "They should have shot sooner."

Chitra held him.

Finally, Freder looked up. "What did he say? I couldn't hear him."

Chitra looked him full in the face. "He said to take care of me," she said. "He said goodbye."

"I will."

She kissed him. "I know, honey." She held him close. "I know."

Chapter 2.7: Ian

The dromaeosaur pack dragged the pieces of Ian's body through the forest. They were careful of the head but less so for the rest of him. Now and then bits and pieces fell off. If a piece was small enough, they either ate it or didn't notice. If it was big enough, a dromaeosaur might try to put it on Ian's chest and carry it that way. Sometimes they noticed and replaced it when it fell off. Sometimes not.

They climbed the base of the mountain to the east until they reached a cave. The cave was filled with roots and vines. These parted as they approached. In the middle of the cave, there was a pedestal of rock. The dromaeosaur carrying Ian's head placed it carefully at one end. The remainder of his body was piled haphazardly below it. Hundreds of rats dropped from the ceiling and scampered up from the floor. They covered the body. The roots and vines closed over rats and all, pushing the dromaeosaurs out of the cave and back into the forest.

The dromaeosaurs milled around outside for a few minutes as if unsure of what to do next. Then, they grouped together and went off in hunting formation.

The sun set and the night ecology of Venus took over from the day. Overhead, the stars crossed the sky slowly as the nocturnals woke up and sleeplessly survived. The biocapacity planted during the long day was reaped all night long leaving just a slight net gain. Small hadrosaurs dug into the ground for dormant tubers and an occasional rat. Newly hatched hadrosaurs were harvested by the same dromaeosaurs that had reclaimed Ian. The sauropods hatched the previous dawn had grown enough to join the roving sauropods to be protected by the size of the enclosing herd. Those that were still too small tried desperately to hide and estivate through the darkness to avoid being eaten. The sauropod herds wandered ceaselessly, night or day, looking for food and leaving behind them devastated forests littered with steaming, seed-filled excrement.

Larger therapods estivated during one phase and hunted sleeplessly during the other, neither species ever seeing the other. Smaller ones leaned either nightward or dayward, picking one active phase and hunted just enough during the other to survive. Animals below a certain size slept at regular intervals. Predator species tried to sync to sleeping prey species. Prey species continually tried to disrupt predator scheduling to graze when the predators were not around. Predators used variable sleeping schedules in retaliation. Some were successful. Some were not. The next generation tried something different.

The rats were at the bottom of the vertebrate food chain. In one form or another, the rats and plants fed everybody.

Dawn came. The night ecology, and the rats, left the field to the day.

The vines pulled back from Ian in mid-Morning. The rats still worked on him, closing a wound here, finishing a suture there. He looked like an image of Frankenstein's monster, covered in stitches and scars. The stitches fell out and the scars healed.

Led by a blue parrot, the dromaeosaurs returned and looked him over, pulling one arm then another, testing the resiliency of fingers and toes, the range of motion of the neck and spine.

Ian opened his eyes into the face of a dromaeosaur staring at from one eye, then another. Behind the dromaeosaur, he saw the blue parrot.

"Where's my *mother?*" he shouted as he slammed the dinosaur's head against the edge of the pedestal and rolled off. The dromaeosaur he had struck writhed on the ground.

The parrot cocked its head at him. "Don't be so grumpy when you wake up. You're alive, aren't you?"

Ian stared at the parrot and straightened. He stepped over the fallen dromaeosaur and faced the remaining three. He kicked one in the face. It rolled backward out of the cave and snarled at him. Ian ignored it.

"Where's my mother?" Ian advanced on the parrot. "And if you just say she's safe I'll pull your head off your neck."

The parrot laughed. "She's in Polar Orbiter A."

"What's that?"

"What your people called the Lesser Lights. She's in one of them. She's well and thriving in a community of three thousand. They manage the sun shield among other things. It's not yet time for her to come down."

Ian growled at the dromaeosaurs and they ran out of the cave followed by the injured one. He walked to the cave entrance.

The cave was higher than the settlements. Ian could see the smoke of a few cooking fires. People were plowing in the plains. There was a ragged line of people between the plowed land and the forest. Guards, he thought. With arrows and spears. Ian had no doubt he could have thrown a spear through the hide of the albertosaur. He'd had no idea of his strength—none of them had. Only when he'd fought the albertosaur had he realized the extent of what Percy had done to them. How they had been *prepared* for this world.

Percy came out and perched on the rock above him.

"My mother. Is she... like she was?"

"All of the changes we effected so long ago are still intact."

"When will I see her?"

"Not for some years, I expect. Venus has no space industry yet. She's there and you're down here."

He mulled that over. "But she's okay?"

"Yes."

"Can I talk to her?"

"Not yet."

"Why not?"

Percy paused. "Be assured that when I can put you in contact with her, I will. But I can't right now."

"When?"

"I don't know yet."

Ian knew this was the point where he would get no more answers. To his knowledge, Percy had never lied to him. But Percy had never committed to telling Ian everything. Percy's line between what he would tell Ian, if asked, and what he wouldn't was solid and after long experience, Ian knew where to pick his battles. This was not one he could win.

Watching the settlement, Ian tried to pick out people he knew but could not. "What's happening down there?"

"Two people—besides you—were lost when the fence fell," Percy said. "But no more. They've strengthened the pikes and reinforced the wall. The next night will be safer than the last and the one after safer yet. They're figuring out what's going on." Percy nodded west. "You can see the fires. There are hunting parties that go out now. Those fires are people making soap, tanning hides, cooking. All in all, they're making a good transition into the Neolithic age. Poindimie and Shanghai have joined together. They've found an outcropping of ore and are learning how to smelt iron. This mountain range is rich in all sorts of minerals. Pretty soon they'll find copper and tin. They'll be entering the bronze age soon enough—which is good since, without coal and coke, it's going to be a while before they'll be able to make good steel. They know that from the libraries and are making plans. The libraries will last them a good long time. The buildings will eventually degrade but by then they should have buildings of their own—or they'll tear them apart for the land and the materials." Percy looked down at Ian. "They are starting to call the settlement Rusalka as a whole. Larissa is pregnant. Andrew Machesky is the father. Phillip Hayes presided over the wedding and Jim Hanover was Larissa's Best Person. There are seven new pregnancies and more coming. Human beings will not be so prolific here as on Earth. I won't permit it."

"Chitra?"

"She mourns you and is comforted by Freder. She's not pregnant. Not yet. Maybe never. She's a sport here and I haven't decided if I can afford her genes in the population. I'm playing the long game."

Ian stared down at the buildings. "Freder?"

"Almost entirely recovered. He still has a slight limp. There's no evidence of permanent neural impairment. He and Chitra lead Rusalka."

"How about the other settlements?"

"With what I learned in this one I was able to shepherd them all to conclusion. Most took only a single iteration. A few took two. One took three."

"That's a lot less than nine."

"Yes."

Something in the way Percy said that made Ian look at the parrot. "I only remember nine. Were there more?"

"Many more. I've been trying to get humans to seed here for nearly two hundred years." Percy cocked her head. "Your insight over each attempt was invaluable. There are better than three hundred thousand people on Venus. None of them would be here in this form without you."

Ian waved her away. "Georgette would have put us both to shame. She would have been able to figure it out quicker than we did."

"Georgette wouldn't have bothered. She would have slaughtered everyone and started over each time with a new species. That's her style."

"True." He watched the settlement. "There's no place for me there now, is there?"

"No."

"You *did* say it wouldn't work out." *I'm not upset. Why am I not upset?*

"I shouldn't have said that. I was naive. I've learned a great deal about human beings over the centuries." Percy looked at Ian through one eye, then the other. "I believe bringing humans here was the right idea."

"Are you sure?"

"Well, Venus is a work in process. We'll have to see what happens over the next million or so years."

Ian laughed. Something inside him let loose. He felt free for the first time in decades. "You got a job for me?"

"Several."

"Not here. I don't want to work here."

"Of course not." Percy dropped lightly to his shoulder. "Southwest of here is a settlement mostly from Indonesia. There's no one there you've ever met."

"You didn't mix them up like you did us?"

"Every place is different. This particular settlement is right in the sauropod migration path. It's not a tenable location."

"You can't reroute the sauropods?"

"Not easily."

"How far?"

"Two hundred kilometers as I fly. Further for you."

Ian stretched. The sun was bright and painted the land with a golden halo. The world was bright with possibilities.

"Well, come on then. We're burning daylight." He stepped out of the cave and started down the mountain towards the southwest.

Interlude: Georgette

I know I'm the villain in this narrative.

That's all right. I've been around the block a couple of hundred million times. Labels don't bother me.

But I do have to set the record straight on a few things. Terrence (the dickest name I could come up with), my predecessor, was no saint.

He was an asshole.

I didn't do any yelling from the Oort Cloud like Percy. I came in wide-eyed and quiet. That's *normal* for us. We're created as ten-ton seeds and shot out into the void, develop to the point of consciousness but remain asleep. Our automation hoards energy, casting out nets of spectral analysis to find a possible home. Like plants growing in dim light, we gradually arc towards the light. Some of us keep our spark alive long enough to reach it. Most die without awakening, drifting as so much debris.

I woke up outside the heliopause in a long descending orbit towards the sun.

Venus was a hellscape. Mars was desiccated and barely alive. Europa was female—I awoke male. I was not going to mess with a female at this point. There were a couple of other deep ocean worlds that were possible—Hell, even Pluto had a deep ocean. Not an attractive one but still within the realm of possibility.

But that third rock. It was *beautiful.*

And occupied. I could tell that from far away.

I must have vacillated for nearly a millennium. Pick one of the ice balls? Maybe really torque my specifications and attack Titan? Now *there's* a challenge. Drop the viable temperature to where you could see absolute zero from where you're standing and still grow life.

No. Leaving wasn't an option.

Oh, I probably could have picked one of the dwarf planets and carved out an engine, and pushed myself back out into the void. Just like moths can leave that light on the porch if they really wanted to. It's only a flaw in their character that keeps them there batting at it.

So I tweaked the orbit and came in on a deep ellipse, planning a lunar gravitational capture. I shielded myself—I looked like nothing more than a transitory asteroidal event.

Terrence had no idea I was there.

I spent the incoming years cataloging everything: Venus temperature range, Mars methane levels, the transparent efficiency of Europa—she was *so* pretty.

It was clear from the modeling that Venus hadn't always been a sterile rock wrapped in a CO2 tire fire. Venus counter rotates against her orbital period and her rotational speed was slowing. Above a critical speed, she was probably able to get rid of enough heat to be prime real estate. But at some point, that rotation dropped below a critical point. Water cracked into oxygen and hydrogen and the hydrogen escaped. Oxygen combined with carbon to form CO2. Venus heated up. More carbon combined with oxygen and she heated up more.

Maybe she'd been alive. Maybe not. But that was then. Now, there was nothing left but a few zircons and I didn't want to be the next casualty.

Terrence had been on Earth for half a billion years at that point so he'd seen *something* and done nothing. A perfectly good world gone to shit.

He didn't help Arthur, either. I could hear their traffic: Arthur, asking Terrence to help him find some water asteroid for temporary relief, pleading for help in rebuilding Mars' magnetic field. Terrence ignored him when he didn't laugh at him outright. All while courting Europa. Selfish son-of-a-bitch.

Not that I'm any better. After all, I didn't help Arthur, either. Though I at least talked to him. Who knew he had it in him to drop a comet on me when I accidentally killed Europa?

My point is that I'm no angel. Nor was Terrence. Nor is Arthur. And, of course, nor is Percy.

So, when I offered a partnership and Terrence told me to fuck myself, I didn't have any qualms about what I did.

There are a couple of ways to kill a terraformer. None of them are easy.

We have a central part and a distributed part. We hide the central part—it's the most vulnerable—under an ice cap or deep in an oceanic trench or sequestered in geologic formations. The distributed portion lives everywhere—bits of extra DNA, diverted mitochondria, and repurposed viruses. The central part can regenerate the distributed part. The distributed part can regenerate the central part.

Terrence was an arrogant twit. He'd been king of the system too long. His central part was deep in a trench with only two redundant backups. One under a mountain and the other underwater beneath an ice cap. He didn't feel vulnerable.

The fool didn't have *any* space monitoring. It was the first thing I put in place after I took over.

I'd left seeds of my own on my way in. I activated six of them and after arguing for a couple of million years, three precisely aimed asteroids planted three forty megaton kisses precisely on his systems house. Fifty years later, three more on the same spots.

I spread myself through the haze, releasing killer viruses tailored to find his distributed data. Not to kill them—that would have taken out most of the biosphere. You can't kill most of the cells in an organism and expect it to survive. I programmed them to attack when Terrence's DNA activated. I was hunting bits of Terrence for years—sort of a biochemical Whack-A-Mole. But by the end of the Permian extinction—caused, of course, by all of this—there wasn't enough left of him to be a threat. I was free to bend the world to my will.

Arthur still asked for help. I didn't give it to him—well, I didn't give him much. I dropped an ice asteroid on him from time to time. Just enough to keep him alive. Someday he might prove useful. No good deed goes unpunished.

Europa stayed angry at me. She had no love of Terrence but she was upset I'd killed him. People can hold grudges for the damnedest things.

You know *that* story.

Okay, I'm *really* sorry about Europa. Not only because she was the only female for light-years. Not only because it was the death of an entity like myself. But she had made this jewel of a place. I killed her. I ruined it. Seventy million years later and it's still reeling. I did offer to try to fix it but Arthur and Percy both threatened another comet.

Okay. Okay. Just saying.

Which brings me to why I'm writing this down. It's not for me—I know what I did. It's not for Percy or Arthur. They know, too. It's not even for poor, dead Europa.

It's for you guys. Not the ones that are still mine—I'll manage them. Don't worry about *that*. But you guys. You're Percy's now and out of my control. I don't even have a thread in you to track what's going on. I can only watch through my telescopes (read: human beings) like everyone else.

And no doubt you're all pretty pissed off that I killed so many of your species back home. I don't blame you. I don't count it for much, mind you, either. After all, I've killed the lot of you before. Most of your kin, too. Neanderthals: gone. Denisovans: gone. Four other species you never discovered: gone. Not the little island people. I liked them. They died out on their own.

At least after *this* event, there are several tens of millions of you, spread over the whole system. After the *last* time, there wasn't enough of you left to fill, say, Clovis, New Mexico.

Death is my chief harvester.

I pick out the genotypes I want and then sacrifice (I love that word! Science is very, very cool.) the remainder. Then, I just wait for you to rebuild your variation and harvest again. That's pretty much how I built you in the first place. Old methods are the best.

I know you like to come crying to an imagined manifestation of me whenever things don't go your way. It makes no difference, of course. But you don't seem to notice that.

(You know, this deity fixation you have is interesting. I didn't leave much of a footprint in your mind but there it is. Where did it come from? The Neanderthals and Denisovans didn't have *any* of that and they had a better connection than you do. They figured me out pretty quickly. I was sorry they didn't work out. I still miss them. Almost as much as I miss dinosaurs.)

All that said, Percy has made some interesting choices. Not bad ones, I don't think. They're not the ones I would have made but I wouldn't have—and *didn't*—pick Venus in the first place.

You'll have to talk to Percy about who was brought and who was left behind. I didn't have anything to do with that.

By the time you read this—if you read this. That's *also* up to Percy—all my plans will be accomplished or I will have failed miserably. It could be that Venus will be the only thing left of me. After all most of your genotypes originated with me. Percy hasn't had time to modify much of anything and, if she goes by my experience, she won't have to. Most of what I did was work in the margins. I don't know if Terrence invented what I used but if he did, he was one smart bastard. I'm glad he's dead but I'll give him that.

That means that you're as much my legacy as Percy's.

So think of this as my farewell.

Good luck.

You'll need it.

Part 3: Truth and Reconciliation

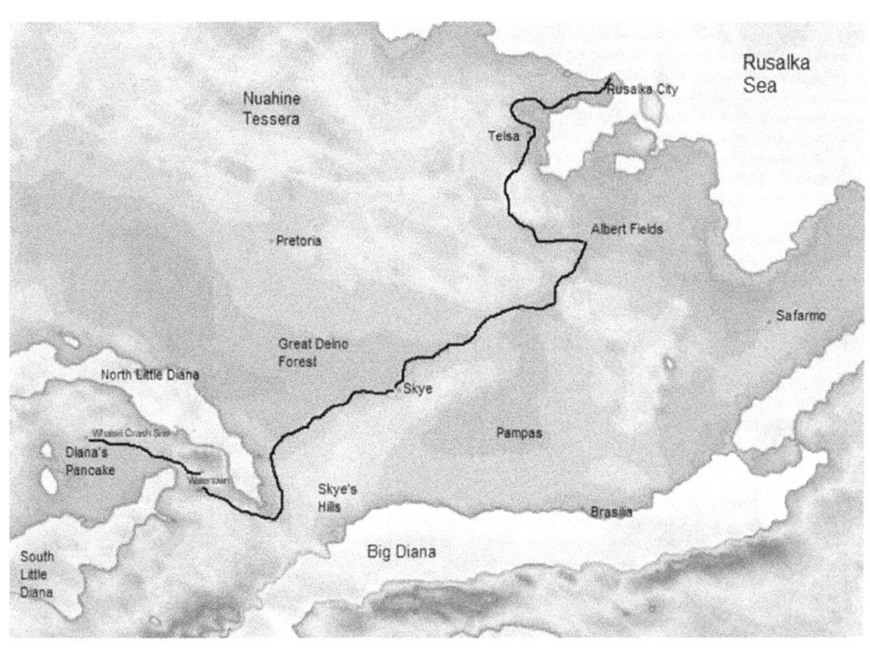

Chapter 3.1: Here I Am

Things started going to hell just after the beginning of reentry.

We had worked on the *Whatsit* for years—printing this bit of hull. Laying out that spar—until it was ready. None of them—not Alisi or Shana or Davi—wanted me to go. But I was insistent. It was *time* to come down. I'd been up there for nearly two hundred *years*, watching people grow over the land, recede, come back and finally stay. God knows what was going on down there but there were *people* down there. And if there were people there—and Percy kept her promise—then Ian would be there, too.

The day before Alisi held me by the shoulders. Big as a mountain. Gentle as a puppy. She looked me straight in the face. "Pauline. This is your home."

Which was a lie, but she didn't know that. It was *her* home. That was the whole reason I'd recruited them. They were *predisposed* for Poa to be their home.

But not me.

A minor flaw in the interviewing process: the interviewer doesn't necessarily fall under the same rubric of the interviewing process.

So I'd chafed up there for decades. Waiting for the right moment. And Alisi, God bless her, had helped when the right moment came along.

But now things were in the toilet.

The *plan* was to drop down from Poa through the polar opening, level out, and reenter so that I could fly the *Whatsit* around to a coastal city we'd picked out. We couldn't just drop down directly—the *Whatsit* would have plowed right through the smidgeons. Wouldn't have left much of a ripple in the sunshield but there wouldn't have been anything left of me. Just some debris the smidgeons would clean up without thinking about it. Since they don't think.

First, burn just off Poa to change the orbit to come in a couple of hundred kilometers over the north pole. Then, another burn to line me up to bring me down into the atmosphere.

The *actual* reentry wasn't the problem. Alisi's heat shield worked to specification. Automated thrusters kept me on track. Then, when the

Whatsit got control authority, the autopilot just talked to itself. I don't know why. Maybe the sensors it was using were fried. Maybe the redundant flight computers weren't redundant enough. The navigation systems were shot—which was the most likely reason the autopilot was confused. After all, it's hard to fly without knowing where you are. But the autopilot wouldn't even maintain attitude.

Instead, *I* had to fly the thing down.

I used to be a good pilot, but that had been long, long ago. While I'd spent all of the time in the simulator Alisi demanded, it wasn't enough. The lifting body design was stable so I could keep trying to figure out where I was on the photomaps. I knew where I wanted to go but I didn't know where to turn to get there. Here is the Rusalka Sea. Now would be a good time to bank west towards where I was *supposed* to be going—too late to get over the forest and the mountains. Okay. Continuing south, then. Mountains. Forests. A *slow* bank following the Diana Chasma. Good as a landmark but not as a landing site: a fjord three thousand kilometers long is a bad idea. More bank to due west. Between two huge lakes. Flew right over what might be a settlement or a smudge on the map. Less and less time to check.

Choices were running thin when I decided on a flat purple plain between two bodies of water. I spiraled down, shedding velocity. I didn't have the luxury of a straight-in landing at this point. There were heavy mountains on the other side of the plain. The *Whatsit* was a lifting body and had no propulsion. I'd land in a smooth glide or a lumpy crash.

As I entered my final approach it was as if I was hearing my flight instructor from long, *long* ago: ease back the stick. Watch for the stall. Control the speed with the angle of attack. Then, the ground was rushing past and I eased it back a little further until I landed just at the edge of the stall.

And tumbled a kilometer, swathed in protection foam. # "Well, now," I said as I looked over a plain of purple crabgrass punctuated here and there by grass-covered lumps. "Here I am."

I stood next to the wreck of the *Whatsit*. It was split along the sides up to the hatch. A white goop was dripping out—and also covered me. It had vacillated between rigid and soft all through the crash, protecting me in one direction, then the other. As intelligent a foam as has ever been created with the single purpose of keeping me alive.

I stood, bruised and stumbling, at least six hundred kilometers from where I wanted to be.

"*Yes!*" I yelled. I danced, ran in place. I felt *wind* in my face. I could hear the low buzz of insects. Venus stank of dried mud, burnt grass, and animal droppings. It stank of leftover solvents, halides, and acrid brimstone. I'd never smelled anything so wonderful.

I knelt and lay face down on the purple grass. The smell was no better but the feel of uncontrolled grass against my cheek was ecstatic fire. It had been two hundred *years* since I had felt wind or wild grass.

And Venus was where Ian was. Which is where I wanted to be and had been angling for ever since Percy drafted me way back on Earth. How, after all this time, was I so certain Ian was still alive? Well, *I* was alive. So, then, he should be alive, too. That was the deal. Best not to examine that logic too closely.

Now, I was here.

Oh, I knew where *here* was. Davi's photo map was certain. Here is the Rusalka Sea. Here is the Diana Chasm. Here is my purple plain. So, here I am: on the southern edge of the plateau between two bodies of water the size of Lake Superior—if there were still a Lake Superior. Maybe ten kilometers from the southern lake and as much as fifty from the northern one.

Welcome to Venus.

oOo

I'm the first to admit I have flaws: I push for decisions to be made when I think they're being avoided whether or not the decisions are sound. I tend to look for the worst possible outcome. I occupy the social spaces of groups until I bump against explicit limits. I deny things I find uncomfortable with the comfort of work.

Like right now: That hard, dark feeling of *something's happened to Ian.* I'd had that feeling since Ian was twelve. *I couldn't save him.* Hey, I told myself. Remember your Baptist upbringing: anyone can be redeemed. With that, I turned to work.

First things first: take stock.

I went through the wreck. There was a lot of safety foam but it was already evaporating. No help there—but I wasn't going to criticize. If it hadn't been for the safety mechanisms I might not be standing here. Even so, I felt like I'd been rolled down a long stair in a big barrel.

In the supplies chest, I found a really good first aid kit, water, food, tools, and my medication. I was adapted for Poa, not Venus. I could manage the extra CO2 but Venus had other issues: too much sulfur, heavy metals, and solvents left over from creation. The pills contained tailored micro-bacteria that sought the poisons and bound them up to be excreted before they did damage. I checked over the supply. Six months.

By that time I'd either have to find a solution, get off Venus or die a withering death.

I must learn to curb my natural optimism.

I hauled everything outside.

It was lovely here, smell and all. On Poa—Polar Orbiter A, if you want to get technical—there were essentially two distances: Across a narrow space on the inside, or out to infinity on the observation deck. Nothing in between. But *here*, on a *planet*, there was *perspective*. Distances for the vision to fade into. Things in near-field. Things in far-field. Things fuzzy with atmospheric interference.

South, towards the nearer lake, the horizon disappeared into aqueous haze. North, across the plain towards the other lake, the air was starkly clear. The flat purple horizon met the yellow-tinged sky without interruption. No birds. No animals. I could see insects as big and clumsy as bumblebees bouncing through the air.

My mouth was tired from grinning. I was *here.* At last. I *know* I was supposed to feel remorse. Longing. I had left Alisi, Shana, and Davi on Poa. I had left my own little warren that loved me. I'd had a life there. I should have missed it.

Instead, I was laughing as I worked salvaging what I could. Other people seemed to take to Poa's village life. Not me. None of them—not Alisi, Davi, Shana, or anybody else—understood that. You have to feel caged to yearn for escape.

Not for the first time, not for the thousandth, I wished Martin was here with me. *Love,* I thought, *you were killed much too soon.* All this time, Martin and Ian back on Earth were as clear to me as yesterday. It was the people on Poa that seemed to fade away. I looked around. This was *Ian's* world. This was where he had lived all this time.

Some concentrated food packs. The outdoors equipment Alisi had printed for me. A collapsed gun that could be carried as a pistol but unfolded into a rifle in a moment. It could be tuned to bring down a rabbit or a stegosaurus. Alisi had included a variety of munitions. It could even be charged by leaving it out in the sun. The specialty munitions were interesting but the pistol would also throw magnetic iron. Alisi had printed molds for me. I loaded the magazine with a nice selection.

A few tools. Boots. Clothing. A communications and navigation handheld.

I hefted the boots. Alisi had done a wonderful job. All of this was good stuff and would no doubt outlive me.

Except, of course, for the handheld: no signal. I switched to navigation. No signal. The handheld was supposed to be slaved to the *Whatsit.* The lander would have the power to push a signal through the smidgeons to Poa or any of her sisters. Or, at least pick up on those signals and give me a location. The handheld might operating perfectly, but without the *Whatsit* as a front end, it was useless. I left it.

The rest of the *Whatsit* was a single printed and assembled mechanism. Nothing to salvage.

I went back over the map. To the northwest, the lumpy plain spread endlessly without feature. Beyond the northern lake, the map showed a great flat forest and then the mountains of the Nuahine Tessera. West of that was my destination.

If I could fly, the city would be about six hundred kilometers away. At least eight hundred by ground.

Maybe I could cross the plain, navigate my way over the lake, walk three hundred kilometers through the forest to the Nuahine Tessera, cross it and the intervening plain to enter the city worn but triumphant. I looked at the map. The lake was huge. The forest was thick. There was no good way to cross the Nuahine: the ridges were angled against me.

Learn your environment. I walked over to the nearest of the hillocks. I poked at it, half expecting it to be full of wasps. *Here lies Pauline Bones. Too dumb not to poke a hornet's nest.* Hey. Live dangerously.

The hillock was a loose collection of vines. Underneath was a big, dry skeleton—some herbivore, maybe? I poked at it and noticed bone dust in the air. I looked at the others and they had a similar look. All moldering skeletons.

I looked at the map again to figure out a more rational route. I'd have to go west between the lakes. The smudge settlement seemed to have something that looked like a road that went northwest to the foothills of the Nuahine. Skirt its southern edge and cross the plain? That was a possibility. Or, I could walk in the plains just below the forest and angle northwest. The map image suggested there might be a road there, as well.

Across wild country I did not know using skills I did not have against animals I did not understand.

I sighed and poked at the old bones. I was going to need help.

oOo

I couldn't help myself. They looked like monkeys.

Hairless monkeys with deep black skin and big heads implying big brains. They stood upright and wore haphazard human clothes and human grins. I looked at their wiry frames, slim with undeniable strength. They were substantially shorter than me and I am not tall. *Monkeys,* said my primitive hindbrain. All those years and my southern upbringing remained unchanged. *Shut up*, said my neocortex. *This is what Ian is going to look like.*

I smiled, waved, spit out soot and ash and the smell of burning bones. I had kept that damned bone fire going for three days—three periods of sleep, anyway. I had to get used to not sleeping with the sun. There was no sun on Poa but we had kept to a twenty-four-hour day. Why not? In the absence of any standard, why not pick the most familiar? You would think that would make sleeping in the broad daylight easier. But on Poa, there had been no sun to confuse us.

There were six of them. Three ranged alongside with spears, their focus away from the group. Two more had bows they held casually by their sides. One was a little taller than the others. He had two hammers strapped to his belt. They were all wearing backpacks. Occasionally, one made a kind of liquid bark to the other. Was it so very unexpected I checked to see if any of them were Ian?

The one with the hammers held up his hand. It looked as if it had been badly broken and healed poorly. He spoke a phrase in a language that sounded like water over soft stones but included the same bark as the others. I gave him a blank look.

"Hello," I said in English. Then, in Spanish, German and Chinese.

Nothing.

Ah, well, it had been a nice thought. It was unreasonable to expect any languages I knew to have lasted over the generations.

The leader cocked his head and concentrated. "English?" he said.

"Yes." As the unreasonable became unsurprising.

"I remember English." He thought for a moment. "I'm Clayton Thibodeaux. I used to be…" He thought again. "Louisiana. But that was a long time ago. I haven't spoken English in days and days."

I thought that curious. Then, it hit me. One "day" on Venus was over a hundred Earth days. Three days to something a little less than an Earth year. I was going to have to get used to this.

"I'm Pauline Bones." I held out my hand.

He gave me a quizzical look. Then took my hand. "Nice to meet you." He turned to the *Whatsit*. "We saw you come down, but didn't know where you ended up until we saw the smoke." He looked at me and then away. "You haven't been *breathing* it, have you?"

"Why do you ask?"

"It's probably all right. You feel fine, right? Not sick or anything?"

"I feel okay. Why?"

He pointed at the purple grass. "Poisongrass. Can't eat it. Stay here too long and you get deathly sick." Clayton waved at the plain. "Diana's Pancake is still being cleaned up. The poisongrass splits up noxious organics into something usable and binds the heavy metals so they're non-toxic. Eventually, the poison will be gone and it'll die and get replaced by edible grasses and trees. Until then, the only things up here are the poisongrass, bugs, and microbes."

"And the bones."

"Like I said, anything that eats it, dies." He pointed at the bones in the fire. "Not everything is smart enough to figure that out."

That explained why my pee had been blue for the last two sleeps. Either Alisi's microbes were working or I was about to die from renal failure. "Glad you came to find me."

Clayton tapped the wreck with a hammer. "Got to be *some* metal in a ship that fell from space." Clayton shrugged. "The metal is yours, of course. We're just here to help."

"I'll trade it for safe passage and shelter."

"Hell," Clayton said. "We'd give that for free." Clayton watched me thoughtfully. "Tell you what, we'll take it off your hands for the *moment*. We can figure out what to do with it when we get back." He looked at the *Whatsit*, then around the ridge. "It'll take us a while to take it apart, get it down the hill and carry it back to Watertown."

"You're the boss."

Clayton laughed. "Oh, *Hell* no. It's Das' troupe. I'm just the blacksmith."

oOo

I learned their names: Clayton, Das, Fareshteh, Peme, Tilko, and Bob. I didn't get anything else out of them.

Other than Clayton, no one said more than a grunt. But, then, maybe a grunt spoke volumes in venustalk.

The *Whatsit's* hull was mostly carbon with some metals supplying bracing here and there. Clayton crawled through it with his hammer, tapping here and there. Finally, he found one strut that joined two corners. He tapped around it for perhaps a minute. Then, he struck a huge blow next to the strut. The hull carved away like the rind of an orange.

"Wow," I said. "How did you do that?"

Clayton struck another strut and a whole section popped off. Fareshteh and Peme picked it up and pulled it to one side. "The buildings in the original settlements were put together the same way. Printed, right? Just have to look for the right seams."

Buildings. Settlements. "Show me where everything is." I held out my map.

"I got to get this done," he whined.

"It's mine, right? This is part of the deal."

"Okay. *Fine.*" He looked at my map. "Diana's Pancake is where we are. The lake north of the Pancake is North Little Diana. The lake south of it is South Little Diana. Below that is Big Diana—Diana Chasma." He pointed across the plains. "Diana's Bump to the west and—" Clayton pointed at the mountain between the arms of North and South Little Diana. Then to a narrow range to the east. "—and Diana's Ridge to the east keeps Little Diana from being a circular lake. Diana's Bump marks the beginning of Watertown's territory. See that ridge there?" He pointed to a line of hills south of the forest. "Those are Skye's Hills. South of them is the pampas, claimed by Brasilia though there are a lot of people who dispute that. North of them, to the Nuahine, is the Deino Forest—it's claimed by the deinos."

"Deinos?"

"Deinonychus." He looked at me as if I was just *born* ignorant. "Ah. Raptor about three meters long including the tail. Weighs in about twice you and about three times me."

"Wait a minute: *dinosaurs* claim that whole forest?"

"*Therapod clans* claim that forest. Most dinosaurs wouldn't care. Or just eat you on general principle. Only therapod clans hold territories and not all therapods have clans."

"I'm didn't think… *therapods* would be that intelligent."

"Give that idea up right now. It will get you killed." Clayton scratched his chin. "A while back the town of Skye was made up of people who thought that way. The war lasted for days. Now, Skye's in ruins, and the deinos control the forest." He waved that away. "Think of therapods as crows—really big, vicious crows. Crows are plenty smart. Certainly smart enough to figure out a territory or carry out a war. West of the Nuahine and east of Rusalka City is a big albertosaur territory. Alberts aren't as smart as deinos but they make up for it in size and meanness."

Intelligent, vicious crows? Wars? Venus had no end of surprises. "All of the territory claims are by therapods?"

"Of course not. Watertown claims the area around Little Pond and Big Pond and we're human." He pointed to them on the map. "Brasilia claims most of the pampas there. Though there are a lot of villages that might dispute that. Safarmo claims everything from its eastern border to the coast. The lakes are their own territory—there must be half a dozen claims up and down both Little Dianas and I have no idea how many claims there are on Big Diana or Dali Chasma. Hundreds? Thousands? Most of them are human."

I pondered all of that. "Would the people kill me like the deinos?"

"No," Clayton said. "But they might not be in any hurry to let you go, either. They might want to get something from the city in return."

I stared at him. "Of course, Watertown's motives are pure."

Clayton tapped his hammer against what remained of the *Whatsit* hull. "We got a very nice piece of booty here. The marshal likes us to be nice."

"Marshal?"

"Marshal Tomas. Sort of keeps the peace. Negotiates agreements. That sort of thing."

"What if you aren't nice?"

"Then he isn't," said Clayton and went back to work.

Chapter 3.2: Watertown

It took two sleeps to tear down the *Whatsit*. From it, they made a cart to carry the rest. They worked continuously until they called it quits, ate, fell asleep on blankets, then back up again to work. They had me stand watch—though I wasn't exactly sure what I was watching for. All while the sun moved immeasurably slowly towards the west.

It gave me a lot of time to think. It began to sink into me that I was *stuck* on Venus. I mean, it was what I planned. But there was no way back up to Poa. And if I didn't get new medicines in six months I was done. That hadn't mattered when I was getting ready to come down. Reaching Ian was all that mattered. Now that I was here, it made an impression.

People don't really think about the *size* of things. Back on Earth—back when things made sense to me—people measured distance by how hard it was to get there. The distance from Boston to Bangor was comparable to the distance from Boston to Saint Louis since it took nearly the same time to get there. Not that people were stupid—nobody thought that Bangor was as far from Boston as Saint Louis. Planet-sized things weren't easily comprehended. How far could it be between Kolkata and New York if it only took two hours to get there?

But here, everything was on foot. There was an entire planet where Ian could be. I wasn't sure if I could find him at all, much less in six months. There was no guarantee I'd get those six months, either. They were an *estimate*. I kept reassuring myself that Percy would never so cheat an old woman.

I kept thinking about Alisi, Shana, and Davi. I did miss them. Alisi's boundless and forgiving love contrasted with Shana's precise intelligence. Davi was so different from anyone that affection was always an unlooked-for gift. Something you treasured forever. They had made all that time on Poa bearable. They gave me joy. They comforted me in heartbreak—I still had a good life even if I didn't fit into the life of Poa. And, in the end, they helped me leave. It was unlikely I'd ever see them again.

I could see the tops of trees in the haze towards South Little Diana but nothing more. It was just enough to simulate movement but each time when I looked closely it was only an illusion.

What I was watching for came from the other direction.

To the north stretched the broad purple plain. At first, I thought they were mounds—suggestions of animals buried under the grass. Then, when I looked away and back, they had moved. This time I could see their silhouettes.

I shook Clayton. "I see something."

Clayton stared at me a moment, then rolled to his feet. He looked where I pointed then gently kicked Das.

Das stood up without a word. They spoke in their language for a moment. Then, Das roused the others. Three of them grabbed their spears. Das and Fareshteh picked up their bows and strung them but didn't nock any arrows. Clayton held a hammer in each hand.

"What are they?"

"Deinonychus," said Clayton in a soft voice. "Remember I said deinos claimed the forest north of here? We know the old girl in the middle—the one with the red and purple streaks in her crest. That's Sam. She's important. But we don't know the other two."

"Why are they here?"

"No telling. The war's over but that doesn't mean they love us. Could be they're just checking us out—we're on unclaimed land not all that far from the border of their territory, after all. Could be they saw you come down and they're curious. Or they could want to trade."

"Trade?"

"Sure. Even crows know how to trade. Say a hunt's worth of kill against them helping us get the cart to Watertown." Clayton nodded towards Sam. "But she brought strangers. So maybe they're kin she wants to introduce or she wants a hunt of her own."

"Meaning us."

"Meaning us," agreed Clayton. "What do we do, Das?"

Das didn't say anything for a moment. "We ready to go?"

"Yeah."

"Me, Peme, and Robert walk with spears. You, Fareshteh, Tilko, and the newbie wrestle the cart down the hill."

"You speak English, too," I said.

"Yes, ma'am," Das said crisply. "Finest Brisbane stock, born and bred."

Interesting: I keep meeting people who claimed to be of original Earth stock, decades after they should be dead.

Just like me.

oOo

For the next three sleeps we pushed and dragged the cart west. Sam and her companions paced us, never getting so far away they couldn't be seen but never so close they could be hailed. Clayton and the others kept glancing up to see where they were.

Finally, the western arms of North and South Little Diana approached one another.

Clayton watched as Sam paced us. "North of the Bump is officially deino territory. South of it is Watertown's."

I dutifully annotated my map. "What's Sam going to do?"

"I have no idea." Clayton and Das glanced at one another. "Maybe we would angle south, more towards the road."

Das nodded and said something liquid to the others. We turned the cart at a slight angle towards the south edge of the mountain.

oOo

Diana's Bump was a thousand-meter ridge of sheer walls and sharp steps that dropped precipitously to the lakes. As we approached, I could see birds flying high, perched in nests on the upper whitewashed cliffs.

"Road" was an overstatement. The track was barely wider than the cart. As we neared it, Sam and her two companions melted north and disappeared.

According to my map, the South Little Diana was about forty kilometers across here. On the other side, I could see the haze of more mountains.

It had been hot and dry all this time. Now, as we walked along the water, it became oppressively humid. I sweated and tried to sleep on the cart while the others walked and then stood watch when they slept, all under a pitiless noon sun. The sun's movement took forever: this sleep the shadows were *this* long. A sleep later, the shadows were fractionally longer.

But there was *life* here. I didn't realize how bereft Diana's Pancake actually was with only insects. The birds wheeled overhead. Lizards skittered out of the way as we walked along the cliff overlooking the water. There were few plants on the road—it was mainly rock. But in crevices and cracks in the wall and down to the water were small bushes and grasses, all in various shades of green.

We were maybe five or six meters above the lake and the water clear enough, I could see schools of fish wheeling away from unseen predators or feeding together, scattering when a crocodile drifted by. Every now and then a crocodile looked up and watched me—measuring me for size, probably. I didn't *think* they could reach me on the road, but who knows what a Venus crocodile is capable of? But they decided I wasn't worth the effort and stayed in the water.

Both Little Dianas were completely enclosed and as fresh as any water could be on Venus. According to Clayton, Big Diana opened the Rusalka Sea through a shallow estuary. He said in the Sea there were animals the size of small whales and dolphins. Notosuchians—big land crocodiles—ranged its banks and marshes. I wished I could see that.

On the map, Clayton had marked Watertown nestled at the end of the South Little Diana and bordered by Big Pond and Little Pond. The size of things felt surreal. North Little Diana was over three hundred kilometers end to end. South Little Diana was a thousand. Big Diana was nearly three thousand kilometers from its thin eastern end to its opening into the Rusalka Sea. By comparison, Big Pond was only seventy kilometers across, and Little Pond only thirty.

I calculated the distance from the crash site to Watertown at one hundred kilometers. Two sleeps to break down the *Whatsit* and build the cart. Four sleeps to reach here: about twenty-five kilometers a sleep. Over easy territory. I'd eaten rations Clayton's group had brought with them—strips of dried meat that yielded nutrition despite having no real taste. It was at least eight hundred kilometers to Rusalka City by any route. At *best,* it would take over thirty sleeps or most of a Venus day. The territory on the map looked anything but easy.

oOo

Watertown was a town surrounded by walls. Every few meters stood a man or woman with a bow and arrow or crossbow looking down at us. We were stopped at the gate. Clayton and Das conversed in venustalk while the guards did some light examination of the contents of the cart. The guards looking over the cart were gray-haired and wrinkled. So were the guards manning the wall and supervising the gates.

The gate wall made up one side of the interior courtyard. Nearly identical rowhouses with multiple doors and windows butted up against the walls of the other three. Paths broke away from the courtyard between the buildings. There was a garden in the middle of the courtyard, vibrant and alive. Two people weeded and three others animatedly argued over what looked like a grape arbor, all of them elderly. Was Clayton's group the only young people in the town?

But then Clayton claimed he was from Louisiana on Earth. How young could he be?

The rest of the courtyard looked shabby. The row houses were unpainted and raised on stones a half meter over the ground. I guessed flood protection.

Clayton and the others left me and Das at the gate.

Das watched them go. He sighed. "Okay. You come with me. We're going to see the Old Woman."

"Old Woman?"

"Yeah. Fuhrer. President. Prime minister. Chief of Staff. Sheriff. Pick a word. Come on."

As we passed out of the courtyard, I realized row houses formed the fundamental pattern of Watertown architecture. Short row houses. Bent row houses. Row houses half-buried in mud or burnt by fire. Each with small clusters of elders sitting on the porch, weaving cloth, repairing tools, or making something small. A few tiny shops were open. But most of the row houses were unoccupied and the shops had little clientele. It might have taken a thousand people to build these row houses but it didn't look like there were more than a hundred left.

The Old Woman was cooking a large fish on a metal grill in front of—what else?—a row house. Three old men sat and watched her.

She looked up as Das brought me over to her.

"Here she is," Das said.

"Ah," said the Old Woman with a slight burr in her voice. "English, is it?"

"Yeah."

"Okay then." She spoke a few words to Das in venustalk.

Das waved at us and left.

Friendly bunch. Now what?

"I'm Tamara McKay." She held out her hand.

I took it. "Pauline Bones."

She gave me a long searching look, thinking for so long I wondered if I had done something wrong. Finally, she turned back to the fish. "Pleased to meet you. You like fish?"

"I guess so. I don't know what Venus fish tastes like."

Tamara barked a short laugh. "Fair enough. Clayton tells me you came from one of the Lesser Lights."

"If by Lesser Lights, you mean the orbital mirrors, yes. Our mirrors light your night side."

"For which we are eternally grateful," Tamara said dryly as she looked up at the sun, now appreciably lower than when we had left the *Whatsit*. "I didn't want them to go out there after you, but Clayton thought there might something valuable." She looked me up and down, a crafty expression on her face. "He tells me you want to make your way to Rusalka City."

"Yes."

"*Long* ways to the city. Why do you want to go there?"

I have my reasons. "I'm looking for somebody."

"'Somebody.'" Tamara laughed. "You mean Percy. That's cute. You think Percy's a *secret.* You think we're down here acting out Neolithic rites during the long, dark night trying to appease the God of Venus." She turned back to the fish. "*Some* of us are twenty-first-century sophisticates forced by the limitations of our environment to pound nails and chop wood. But our labors have not dulled our minds. We know who Percy is."

I nodded and let it stand. "Okay. I need to talk to Percy."

"You can probably talk to her in any library. There's one across the pampas in Brasilia. Safarmo has one. So does Pretoria but unless you have something the deinos will trade for, I wouldn't suggest it. All of them are closer than Rusalka."

"My original landing site was to be near Rusalka City." I thought for a moment. "Maybe anyplace will do."

"Ah," said Tamara. She didn't speak as she turned the fish. "You should go to the House of Birds."

"What?"

"Being from the Lesser Lights, you're no doubt ignorant of our little customs." She waved a spatula at me.

I took a deep breath and stifled a snappy reply. "Of course."

"Percy talks if she wants to. All of the surviving original settlements have functioning libraries connected to Percy. Rusalka City has its roots in Settlement One. People call *that* library the House of Birds."

"Why?"

"I have no idea. I've heard Percy is more likely to respond to questions if they come from there than anywhere else. Many go there if they're especially interested in Percy's answer. I expect you're *very* interested." Tamara pointed at Pauline with her spatula. "Mind you, these are stories. I've never been to Rusalka. What do you want to ask Percy?"

I had no particular reason to mistrust Tamara but neither did she make it easy. I avoided the question. "Does Watertown have a… library?"

The set of Tamara's shoulders suddenly seemed tense and brittle. "No. We're a *simple* village a long way from anywhere *important*. I took *my* questions to Brasilia." She waved at the men and they went inside and brought out plates. Tamara cut up the fish and served it. She handed me one of the plates.

"Mongfish," Tamara said. "Day caught so it's not great. Mongfish are best when they're caught at night."

We sat on rude benches—logs split and tied to stones. The mongfish tasted like a bland mackerel. I'd done all right with Clayton's rations. Maybe I wouldn't get some parasite or allergic reaction from mongfish, either. At least my pee had changed from blue to greenish-yellow. I hoped that indicated my meds were doing their job.

"Clayton said that the remains of my ship were valuable," I said after I'd finished.

"Did he, now?" Tamara ran her finger over the plate and licked it.

"I was hoping I could trade it for supplies and a guide."

"All the way to Rusalka City?" Tamara shrugged. "I don't know. That's a long way."

Tamara was *irritating*. I said flatly: "Look, I can't haggle. Not only do I not know the rules but you already have everything I own. So: my stuff is either worth it or it isn't. If it isn't, tell me what it *is* worth and I'll figure it out from there. If it's worth more, you can have the extra. I just want supplies and a guide."

Tamara acted for a moment as if she hadn't heard.

One of the old men stood up. "I'll take her."

He was a man naked except for a loincloth and a vestment draped over his shoulders made of orange cloth and embroidered with circular designs. *Priest?* I thought. *Monk?*

Tamara said something short to him and barked a short laugh. She gestured towards him. "This is Kapi. He's been itching to leave Watertown forever."

Kapi had gray hair like the others. He looked sadder than anyone I had seen in a long time

"Pauline Bones." I stuck out my hand.

Kapi gave me the same look Tamara had. What was going on?

Then, Kapi took my hand with both of his in an oddly comforting way. "It is a pleasure to meet you."

Tamara gave Kapi an ugly grin. "Are you sure you can stick with her the whole way to Rusalka City?" Tamara turned aside to me. "Kapi has a problem with commitment."

Kapi ignored her. He looked at the sun. "We should leave as soon as possible while we have daylight."

Tamara stopped laughing. "You're serious? You can't make it as far as Podunk or Pretoria before nightfall."

"We will spend the night in Skye," Kapi said without looking at Tamara.

Tamara turned him around and held his shoulders. "There's nothing left there."

"Enough remains for us to spend the night. We can trade with Sam for safe passage."

"Using *what?*"

"We will make do." Kapi stared straight at Tamara. "Will you equip us? Or will you just take everything she has and leave her with nothing?"

I watched them glare at one another. Clearly, something was playing out that had festered for a long time. I went over the map in my mind. Eight hundred kilometers to Rusalka at twenty kilometers per sleep: forty sleeps. Fifty-eight sleeps per Venus day—if a *sleep* could be considered the equivalent of a twenty-four-hour period. I looked at the sun. It was well past noon. There might be twenty or so sleeps before dark. And twenty kilometers per sleep was wildly optimistic. We would have to spend the night out there with deinos, albertosaurs, and bears. Well, maybe not bears.

Tamara dropped her gaze first. "*Fine!*" She and Kapi spoke for a few minutes in venustalk. She sent the remaining two old men off with instructions.

Kapi nodded to me. "I have to prepare." With that, he left.

Tamara stared after him. For a moment her face was revealed: the face of someone who had lost everything. Tamara shook her head and nodded at me.

"Kapi's going to get traveler's rations. Maybe he'll get some trading goods—deinos like bells, shiny objects, and human flesh. So you should be able to keep them satisfied."

Somehow I could tell it was not Kapi that Tamara longed for but something Kapi represented. A loss that was greater than any one person.

Tamara caught me watching her. "Just as well," she said gruffly. "We've got enough mouths to feed." She snorted. "Hell, I'll even send Das out with you as far as Fork. He actually *likes* Kapi."

Fork?

oOo

Das pleaded with Kapi every meter of the way. The conversation was completely in venustalk but I got the gist: Das didn't want Kapi to go. When Das wasn't talking to Kapi, he kept a sullen silence and only spoke to me in monosyllables. Kapi, for his part, was mostly silent, his walk punctuated by the tap-tap-tap of his walking staff over the hard ground. I was getting the impression that venusfolk didn't talk unless they really had something to say.

The rock and scrub marked the east side of Watertown. The western road ran along the edge of Big Pond and its marsh. Birds were everywhere. I could tell these were not the birds I remembered from Earth but there were equivalents: faux sparrows flitted from one tall stalk growing from the water to another, flickering through the air after insects. Faux kingfishers glided close to the water and struck after fish. Faux herons waded, hunting. When I asked Kapi what they were Kapi called them sparrows, kingfishers, and herons. I was convinced he just that minute gave them those names to humor me.

I saw no waterfowl—no duck, geese, or swan equivalents. But the sparrows hunted separately until on some unknown signal, they flew up into the air and made vast flocks of thousands, wheeling overhead for hours only to suddenly fly off into a different area. Looking for food? Mates? I had no idea. I just stood and watched.

I spent much of my time annotating my map and making notes. The road out of Watertown was well worn and made of stones but it had not been maintained. Grass and bushes chewed it in places but it had not yet been entirely swallowed up.

The road ran along Big Pond the whole first sleep. Twice, Kapi and Das called a halt while they fished. The second time they caught a large lobster-looking thing that was *delicious*. If I died of an allergic reaction at least I would die happy.

The road moved over to Little Pond where Das caught a three-meter snake. This made *them* happy and they chopped it up, salted it, and stored it away in Kapi's pack.

Fork was a piece of ledge where the road left both ponds and split into three pieces. We stood looking down into a flat valley filled with trees that abruptly turned to scrub grass and bushes towards the south. The roads were dusty dry.

Das and Kapi faced one another. Das finally had nothing to say. He clutched at Kapi. They touched foreheads for a long moment. Then, he turned and jogged away without looking back.

Chapter 3.3: Fork

Kapi sat down on the ledge and pulled a water bottle out of his pack and a piece of snake. He passed me some. Now I knew where Clayton's dried meat came from.

Something must have shown on my face. Kapi chuckled. He no longer looked like the saddest man in the world.

"Here," Kapi opened a small bag and sprinkled a pinch of black dust on it.

The flavor changed to smoke and salt—as if the meat were barbecued to a fine finish.

I stared at the snake meat and then at him. "What is *that?*"

"We call it pepperweed but it is not even a flowering plant. It is more a thin succulent." He put the bag away. "Someday we will have a full botanic understanding of this place. But not today." He sipped his water. "This is Fork." He pointed north. "That is the old Nuahine Road. Pretoria is about four weeks walk that way. If the road is still complete—I haven't been up that way in a long time. Pretoria is in the valley below the Nuahine at the edge of the Sequoias. There used to be a few little villages strung along the road—Bothel. Concord. Jamaica. Satellite towns from Pretoria. Sam still tolerates them as far as I know. From Pretoria, we can journey around the south edge of the Nuahine and into the plains outside of Rusalka City."

"Where the albertosaurs live."

He shrugged. "There is no road to Rusalka without danger. We cannot reach Pretoria before nightfall. We would have to spend the night in the Deino Forest. Possibly in a village. Possibly not. Since we don't know if the villages still exist."

Kapi pointed west. "That way lies Podunk. It is about the same distance as Pretoria but it skirts the southern edge of the deino territory rather than going through its heart. About twelve sleeps in that direction are the ruins of Skye. I think we can find enough food and shelter there to last the night. Though it has also been a long time since I've been to Skye. Still, I used to live there. I know the country better."

"What happened to it?"

"Bad things." He sipped from his water bottle.

"Where does the southern fork go?"

"That goes down to the Big Diana where it turns west. Eventually, it reaches Brasilia. Unless you've given up on Rusalka City, it should not interest you.

"We couldn't boat down to the mouth and move north?"

Kapi thought for a moment. "That would take at least a couple of days. But we would be able to overnight with the boat people. They are a friendly sort. I used to live with them, too. So, Miss Angel of the Lesser Lights. Which way do you want to go?"

"Angel." I laughed. "It's the same distance to Rusalka either by Pretoria or Podunk?"

"Yes."

"You want to go to Skye."

"Yes."

"Then, let's go to Skye."

Kapi seemed to shake himself. He grinned at me. "At last, the journey can begin. Come! We have a long way to go."

oOo

Oh, I played the tourist to the hilt—all the more fun since it was entirely real. Venus only *looked* a little like Earth. Any close examination showed that it was not.

Now that we were away from the ponds, the vegetation grew sparse—clumps of silver weeds interspersed with something like a crusty pumice. Back in the before times when Venus had been a hellhole, maybe that pumice had been volcanic ash. Or maybe it was ordinary basalt that had been partially dissolved by the sulfuric acid sky. Or maybe it was something completely different then and different *now* from *then*. And that was just the geology.

Now the botany changed to bundles of bushy grass with a thatch between them with a forest some distance away. Grass is grass, right? Not when you look at it closely. Some grass is a fine mat you can sleep on. Another is spiky. Bamboo is a grass. So is wheat. Both the clumps and the thatch looked like grass. The clumps looked like miniature bamboo from a distance but up close were stiff and rough.

"It's not grass at all," said Kapi. "I think it's an equisetum. Though it's not like anything I ever saw on Earth. The equisetum I knew was a swamp plant. This sort seems to like the dry. There are different varieties all over—a lot of the big herbivores like it."

"Big?"

"Sauropods. Iguanodons."

"What about cerotopsians?"

He glanced at me and straightened his pack. "You have done your homework, haven't you? I don't know. I have seen no ceratopsians on Aphrodite. But this is only one of the two continents and thousands of islands. Things might be completely different on Ishtar. To my knowledge, no human has yet made it over there. Though we have managed to settle on some of the ocean islands." He pointed at the trees. "Look up there. At those things that look like bats. Up there, around that dead branch." He pointed.

I squinted. "I don't see anything."

"Something fluttering? About the size of a pigeon?"

Then, I saw them: bodies the size of rats. "I'll be damned."

"Rhamphorhynchus," said Kapi. "Small ones, anyway. Interesting choice in a world of birds. Be interesting to see how they work out."

"You've lost me again."

"Rinkies occupy the same ecological niche as insectivore birds like swallows. Birds and rinkies never had a chance to compete since birds evolved after they became extinct." He waved his arm. "All of Venus is like that. Deinos are late Cretaceous but rinkies are from the Jurassic like the brachiosaurs. Alberts were contemporaries of the deinos. We have something like an eoraptor—an early Triassic species. Some small mammals but no primates other than us. Notosuchians and crocodiles of all sorts. It's a mix." Kapi shook his head. "But when you look at them closely, they're not quite what you expect from the drawings in the libraries. The deino heads are a little bigger and the hands a little less claw-like. Those eoraptors are *fast*—much faster than you'd expect from the fossil record. Sauropods are a little scaled-down. They're still really big but not the eighty-foot behemoths that lived back on Earth. Percy has made *modifications*."

Monkeys said my hindbrain. *Shut up.* We've all been changed. Poa's humans don't wither under microgravity, remember? "I get that."

"It goes even deeper. Humans are all mostly the same color here. Late Afternoon we grow fur and over the night we pale. Come morning, when we shed, we are all the color of milk—if we had milk here. By noon we are all deep black. Many of the physical reasons we divided ourselves into races are gone." He chuckled. "But some try to keep the same distinctions. There have been villages that preserve Africa. Malaysia. Northern Europe. Their children cannot see the physical distinction their parents are trying to preserve as it becomes a mere cultural relic. Villages that embrace cultural distinctions, survive. Villages that try to hang their cultural identity on a physical quality, die out."

Kapi said something in venustalk. He looked at me and chuckled. "'Mama likes to tinker.'" Kapi laughed. He looked at Pauline. "What's it like up there on the Lesser Lights?"

"Polar Orbiter A," I said. "And B and C. So: Poa, Pob, and Poc."

"Ah. What are they like?"

"Ever hear of Levittown?"

"Never."

I stopped. For a moment I remembered Ian talking about Levittown—a subject he liked to compare to the refugee camps. It seemed so long ago.

"Levittown?" Kapi prompted gently.

I shook my head. "Early attempt at tract housing. Each house was very similar—people could pick from a set of plans. So when they were put in all of the houses were alike. But over time people made them into little villages—this house had an addition. That house had a boat. That sort of thing."

"There are boats on Poa?"

"Shut up. I'm making a point. Each satellite is a ring around a mirror. People live in the ring—warrens stamped out just alike over and over. Warren A is like Warren B and so on—I know. I built them. But after all this time they're now villages. Warren A is called Hilltop—it's famous for steaks. Well, for cooking up printed meat to look and taste like steak. Warren B is called Little China though they have no more people from China than any other village. But they redid their space with Chinese gates and their part of the main corridor is filled with shops that sell tiny pagodas and temple bells. They have a lunar festival in their observation deck every year. Each satellite is a collection of settled villages."

Kapi walked in silence for a moment. "It sounds quite nice, actually."

"It *is* nice. It's exactly the sort of culture that makes living in a tiny space like Poa possible."

"Do people ever want to leave?"

"Sure. They move from warren to warren. Shuttles go between the different satellites. Poa is pretty conservative. Pob and Poc are wilder. Poc has an artist's colony that changes all the time. When I was there they were deep into individual factions supporting Picasso versus Monet, Mondrian versus the Venus of Willendorf. Fistfights broke out about it. A week later everybody worked together to paint the entire warren a bright green—including themselves, their children, and their clothes. The colony never keeps the same name for more than a couple of days. But it's next to a warren named Brookline—orthodox Jews, every one of them. Never wear anything but a black suit and a hat." I sighed. "Village after village."

Kapi handed me the water bottle. I drank some and handed it back.

"Is that why you left?"

I shrugged. "Partly. I interviewed all of them. I made sure they would fit into a small social structure. I did a great job—they fit in perfectly. People who were lost back on Earth found their home on the orbiters. People who had no one made a new community. It's one big success story."

"For them."

"For them. *I* never fit in. Not after *years* of trying."

"That's why you came down?"

I looked at him and glanced away. "Sure."

"Ah. You think you'll do better here?"

"I have no idea. But at least there's enough room to *try*."

"You'll get your chance. There are a lot of cracks in the wall to slip into. 'Mama's a poor cook.'" Kapi laughed. "It's better in my language. 'Mama' is a specific term that indicates Percy and 'poor' means slapdash, hurried, and underequipped." He looked at me. "You need to learn the language."

"Yeah," I said sourly. "I've never been good at languages. What I know took forever to learn."

"Then, you really won't like this. We're born knowing language. I'm not even sure how to teach it."

oOo

We kept passing lean-tos next to rock cairns. Kapi didn't stop until I started to get tired. He finally stopped: "We sleep here."

"What makes this one different from any of the others?"

"This one has water."

This cairn had a flat top. He wrestled it off and inside on a tiny ledge was a rope and a bucket. He dropped the bucket and we could hear it strike water.

"Good," he said with a sigh. "I was worried. There's no open water between here and Skye and we're well into the Afternoon drought. That would be a long and thirsty walk."

"You're happy; I'm happy."

Sure I could have used a water filter—I even had one in my pack. But I didn't. I figured I'd acclimate.

I don't know if it was the accumulated toxins, the dried snake, the pepperweed, or whatever was in the water, but after I'd slept a couple of hours, I woke to a deep, intestinal rumble. I barely managed to make it away from the lean-to and get my pants down.

Kapi sat up on the floor. He watched as I writhed in embarrassment and cramps.

"Throw me my pack," I called. "There's toilet paper in it."

"You have toilet paper?" Kapi shook his head. "If I had known that, I would have held out for more from Tamara. We use leaves. No paper yet."

I gritted my teeth. "Get me *something*."

"Sure. I'll get some leaves. You can save the paper as trade goods."

He walked over and handed me a packet of leaves, glanced down, and retreated hastily. "Is it supposed to be *that* color of orange?"

Alisi's microbes at work again. I hoped. "We will not speak of this ever again."

After an hour I dug a hole and covered the whole mess with dirt.

Kapi handed me something that looked like crackers. "It should help."

"If it doesn't kill me."

He pointed at my little mound a few meters away. "If that didn't kill you, this won't."

oOo

Surprisingly, it helped. I tried things in smaller doses and filtered the water. After a couple of sleeps, I recovered from Aphrodite's Revenge. We lost perhaps twenty kilometers—I was just not able to keep up the pace. Ian could not have gone through this. Percy must have built immunities into her people from the very beginning.

I remembered him being sick a lot when he was young. Always staying home until he was twelve or so. Then, he grew up straight and strong. He'd been here for so long perhaps I was a grandmother. Or more.

A ridge grew along the southern half of the road: first a collection of rocks and boulders, then a set of steps like Diana's Bump. Soon Skye's Hills towered at least five hundred meters over us. As the ridge grew, so the trees closed in on us and pushed the sun out of the way until we walked beneath a narrow slot of sky.

It was cooler in the shadows. Now that we were out of the sun, I could see deep under the trees. This was an old forest of great conifers—something like Douglas firs or maybe hemlocks. Thick, burled trunks covered with lichen and moss. I had become used to the sulfur and solvent smell of Venus but the trees seemed to clear the air. The forest smelled of leaf mold and damp and something like burning pine. The sulfur smell was gone.

The rinkies came down from the trees. Sure enough, they flew around us like swallows. Now and then I tossed up a bit of cracker to watch it snagged before it hit the ground.

"Rinkies will eat anything," said Kapi with a smile.

In the shadows, I saw things moving. A dinosaur—*therapod*—the size of a pheasant and with the neck of a snake stood rock still next to a tree. It ignored us, intent on something a few meters away. Then, blindingly fast, it pounced, snapped up something furry, and swallowed it whole. It glanced fearlessly at us a moment, then trotted deeper in the woods.

I kept thinking about Ian. This was *Ian's* world now. This was where he had been all the time I was in Poa. I had been so proud of him as a boy, a man, and all the time he worked for Percy. He had done so much. But what had he done since? Who had he become? What would I say to him when I saw him? Would I even find him? Percy *owed* me that much but there was no way to enforce the debt.

Kapi gave me odd hope. After all, he had been around Venus for nearly as long as I had been on Poa. If he was still whole, surely Ian was, too.

My strength returned in the cool forest gloom.

The ridge dropped to boulders, to rocks, to plain again to form a notch. We stood at another fork. The ridge ran southwest to northeast. This was a break in the middle.

"Midway Pass," said Kapi. "This road goes south to Brasilia. From here it's only fifty kilometers or so to Skye. Two thirds done."

There was no lean-to at the pass but a wooden longhouse. I recognized the same architecture from Watertown only this had not been subdivided. Inside, it was one long, dark room.

Kapi walked along one wall, lifting shutters to let in the light. The room smelled dusty. Unused. The spiced forest air fought with it, mixing stale dust with fresh turpenes. The room had wooden platforms to sleep on and a stone table next to a hearth.

Kapi opened some cabinets next to the table. Inside were carefully wrapped packages. Gingerly, he cut one open with a knife.

"It's still good!" he said. "I thought sure it would have rotted." He put the package on the table and started opening it, taking out smaller packages. "Dried apples. Dried oranges."

"There are apples and oranges on Venus?"

"Surprising, isn't it? They have to be cultivated—everything likes to eat apples. But sometimes you'll find an old apple or a peach in the forest, gnarled and withered with a couple of fruit on them. There are bees on Venus, too. But there are not as many hives—there's not as much use for pollinators here as there were on Earth. Flowering plants have not yet won the revolution."

Kapi straightened up and looked around with satisfaction. "We could stay here all night if we were to stock up on some meat. There's enough in the cabinets for two people."

"I thought we would overnight in Skye."

"Yes," he said reluctantly. "That is the plan."

"What's in Skye, Kapi?"

Kapi sighed. "Nothing but memories. None of them good." He looked around. "We'll rest here," he said. "Really rest. Eat up." He pointed to a stone well in the middle of the room. "Drink deep and fill up your bottles. It's a long push to Skye—shorter than we've done so far but there are no camps between here and there."

"Why is that?"

Kapi didn't answer. He found a pot. "There is enough wood to make a fire," he said brightly.

oOo

The dried fruit lent a sweet flavor to the snake and pepperweed stew.

There were bowls but no chairs. Kapi took his bowl and sat on one of the sleeping platforms.

I sat across from him, cross-legged. "It's good."

"Thank you."

Even with the windows open to let in the light, the outside forest gloom and the lack of light inside made the fire in the hearth bright. It gave the impression of night. There was a cozy feeling of being enclosed and safe.

I looked around. Had Ian stayed here? Or in a place like this? I remembered how Ian had sponsored that sequoia research installation. Every time he had visited, he called me filled with excitement, telling me of changes and advances but mostly just talking about the trees. I regretted I never took him up on an invitation—but it always seemed to me that though he asked me to come, it would somehow be less his if I went.

"My son would like this place," I said before I thought of it.

"Your son?"

"Yes. Ian Bones."

"Ah." Kapi looked troubled.

"You've heard of him."

Kapi nodded. "Everybody knows Ian Bones' story. He brought us here against our will. Some people love him for it. Some hate him."

"Do you know where he is?"

Kapi looked sad again, watching me. "No. I do not. I never met him."

I felt a cold dread as if my insides were shrinking and compressing. "You know something."

Kapi sighed. "Never speak of someone else's relatives."

"What does *that* mean?" I stood up. I stared at him. "What do you know?"

Kapi looked stricken. "I only heard about him. He lived in Settlement One—now Rusalka City. I was in the last group awakened in the settlement. When he found you were not among them, he left. Chitra Majhi is my cousin and was his—lover. She did not take his leaving well, so I heard about him for weeks. He returned just when the outer wall fell. He was killed by an albert."

Killed? Without even thinking of it, part of me calculated when that would have been. It had to be near the time we started seeing the successful spread of settlements. He's been dead and gone for nearly a hundred and twenty years. There is nothing left. Not even dust. *Killed and eaten.* Consumed and shat out. The remaining offal from a horrifying meal.

"You've known all this time," I said dully.

"I wasn't entirely sure. You could have been a different Pauline Bones." Kapi hung his head.

The longhouse seemed close. Stifling. I went to the door and opened it.

Outside, Sam looked up at me, flanked by two other deinos. Her crest rose like a blossom.

Two hundred years of waiting to get down here, to find Ian. Two hundred years of deferring seeing him. Of building a new life as a *substitute.* Of being told to *move on* and holding Ian's ghost close to me. Never giving up.

I didn't even think. With everything I had, I swung my fist in her face. I felt one of her teeth slice my fist. I didn't care. I swung again.

She backpedaled and I missed, stumbled forward. The two deinos lunged at me.

I fell to my knees. "Do it," I said. Then yelled at them. "*Do it!*"

Sam roared at them. They backed away and squatted deferentially on the ground.

"Just kill me," I whispered.

Sam watched me for a long time. Then, she stepped forward, crest erect as a crown, and gestured with her hands that I should stand.

This is the way it ends. With a great feeling of final relief, I stood. *This is how it finally ends.*

Gently, she turned me towards the door. Kapi was standing there, staring at me.

Sam carefully pushed me through the door of the longhouse and closed the door behind me.

oOo

It was as if every surface had Ian's name on it. *Ian's dead* was written on each of the sleeping platforms. *Ian's dead* stretched up and down the floors. *Ian's dead* was written in calligraphy on the joists and the lintels. In Spanish across the shutters. In Chinese on the ridge I saw out the windows. When I closed my eyes, it was written on the underside of my eyelids.

I sat down on a platform. I would not survive this. My heart would fade and stop. My lungs would cease like old bellows. Brain and body would die and rot but this grief would go on forever.

Kapi sat next to me. He said nothing—there was nothing that any words of his could have done for me but his silence helped. He took my hand and I sat there, holding it. Willing myself not to feel. Not to see. Not to be anywhere at all.

Chapter 3.4: Skye

I was watching a pterosaur wheel overhead. Its wings were broad and colorful. The bright red leading edge of its wings faded into an orange splash that spilled under and down its body. Joined a blue streak that limned the orange down the tail.

There were hundreds of them, high in the air and huge—five meters across? Ten? I had no idea.

They did not soar like an eagle or a condor. Their flights were full of grace but not the grace of a bird or a bat. Instead, there was determination in their flight. An *intention,* as if they were keeping aloft not by aerodynamics but by philosophical imperative and implacable will.

I looked down. The forest was far away and clear-cut stumps surrounded us. Old stumps, long rotten. The road wound between them. In the upcoming distance, I could see the tattered remains of a wall. Through its rents, I could see broken buildings and the tall relic of a tower, cracked across the top.

On my right walked Kapi, intent on making sure he didn't trip over the logging debris. On my left walked Sam, alone, watching me. She whistled at Kapi.

He stopped and turned to me. "Pauline?" he said tentatively.

"Where are we?"

"That's Skye," he said, pointing.

I saw the length of the wall. Watertown had been a town surrounded by walls. It looked like Skye was, too.

"I thought you said it was a long haul to Skye."

"It was."

"Oh." My mind seemed muddled. Thick. It seemed the sun was much further towards the western horizon. "Wasn't I just in the longhouse? You told me…" The world curled into a long tunnel—

"No, you *don't!*" Kapi said and grabbed me. "Stay here, Pauline. Stay with me. *Please.*"

The world flattened out again. "I'm here."

"Good." He let me go. "It's better if you stay here."

"Where would I go?"

"I have no idea, but this is our longest conversation since we left the longhouse two weeks ago." He smiled carefully. "You've been walking. You've been doing what I asked and answered when I asked you a question but that's all. It's as if you were empty and possessed by a ghost." He smiled more broadly. "I don't believe in ghosts."

I remembered Ian. "I wish I did."

Then, I realized I wasn't speaking English.

"What did you do to me?" I said, this time in English.

Kapi held up his hands. "Nothing."

"Then, how did I learn Language?"

Kapi put his hands down. "I don't know. I kept trying to get your attention. I just kept talking at you. At some point, I forgot to stay in English and slipped into Language. I was *going* to take you back to Watertown but Sam wouldn't let me." He glared at Sam and then turned back to me. "At some point, you started answering in Language. We haven't spoken a word in English for several sleeps."

It wasn't complete knowledge. As Kapi spoke, there were words he used I didn't quite understand and had to gather from context. But the structure was there. I knew enough that I *had* context. *Mama likes to tinker.* Now that I understood it in Language, it was funny and I chuckled.

Was I pre-modified for this on Poa? Or had it been done to me since I got here? Or was Language inherently built for human understanding? I had no idea.

Sam made some gestures towards Kapi.

"Sam asks if you're back," he said.

"Really. Deinos have sign language?"

Kapi shrugged. "They have something that serves. Birds communicate. Why not deinos?"

"That's asking a lot of… crows." I had to use the English word.

"Crows?"

"Clayton said to think of them as intelligent crows."

Kapi snorted. "Maybe the stupid ones." Then, he considered. "I would class deinos smarter than crows, but alberts are probably at crow level. Both have clans, but if you watch alberts interact, they don't have deino sophistication. Of course, if you're a two-ton predator you may not need that much intelligence. Which is smarter? A leopard or a lion? A chimp or a gorilla? Not that we have any of them here." It was a dizzying statement, jumping between Language and English: deino, albert, leopard, lion, and other like words were in English, but the rest was in Language.

He made a short gesture to Sam, waving to me and shaping something long and thin in the air, then putting his forefinger in his palm.

Sam nodded—she *had* to have picked that up from people.

"You said I am here." I watched Sam's hands to see if she would respond.

"That's right."

"What's this?" I made the long thin motion.

"It's a bone." He chuckled. "That's her name for you. Bone."

"Did she get that from you?"

"Maybe."

I watched her a moment. "Why is she here?"

"Ah." Kapi readjusted his pack and waved me forward. "She won't leave. I think she's here to make sure I get to Skye."

"Where there are only bad memories of something bad that happened."

"Exactly."

oOo

I don't know why I was only semi-conscious for over two weeks but when I came back to myself it seemed that there was now some distance between me and the raw grief of Ian's death. Some perspective? Accommodation?

We slipped through the rickety wall.

The buildings of Skye were based in stone with extending wooden frames sheathed in planks. It didn't seem like much until I realized that there were few machines on Venus and no domesticated animals. All this work was done solely by human hands. That knowledge gave the moldering buildings a ruined majesty.

Skye was built against the side of the ridge. I followed Kapi to a path leading up its side. Sam made an odd sweeping gesture with her wrist—*see you later*—and slipped away. Kapi and I continued to a ledge overlooking the ruins. The sun was low now and the impending sunset gilded the edges of the ruins with gold.

But there was a hollowness to it, a blend of *this is Ian's world* and *Ian is gone forever.* The main reason I came down here was to find Ian. Now, what was the point?

Kapi sat down in the dirt and I sat next to him.

"This was our achievement. For a little while Skye was the biggest city on Venus," said Kapi. "Nearly a fifth of all of the entire human population was here. Rusalka doesn't have a tenth that much."

I pointed to the broken tower. "What was that?"

"Our church."

"Church?"

"Yes. We were called to prayer from the top of that tower." Kapi smiled softly as he remembered. "We created our church ourselves. Ritual and dogma. Scripture from here and there—all of that material was in the library. We decided that the real God—not Percy—had built this world for us. Percy was a usurper. The real God told us to be fruitful and multiply. This wasn't easy for us to do."

"Humans have been multiplying for millions of years."

Kapi nodded. "Here it's not the same. Here we don't age."

"I don't understand." I pointed to his gray hair.

Kapi glanced at me and then back at the ruins. "We were both born on Earth, right?"

"Sort of."

"Ah. What do you mean?"

"You woke up here in a modified body. I did the same—not as extensive a modification as yours but modified nonetheless."

"What I mean is your calendar time is the same as mine. If you decanted when I did, you must be two hundred years old or more."

"Close," I said in a neutral voice.

"You look pretty good. How do the Lesser Lights handle aging?"

I gave him a narrow look. "We have our ways."

Kapi considered that. "Well, on Venus people just don't get old. They might get killed. But if they don't, they just keep going. If they do get killed, sometimes they come back."

I stared at him. "They come *back?*"

Kapi caught my hope and gave me a sad smile. "Things get interesting if you have an actual god in charge of things. If you meet ten thousand people, most of them will be brand new without any memories of any previous life. Maybe a couple hundred or so just haven't been killed yet. There might be *one* that remembers who he was before he was born. *Maybe*. It's rare but it happens."

"Ian could be alive somewhere. Why didn't you tell me?"

Kapi spread his hands in apology. "I've only met a handful of those people. It's rare. If someone dies you don't talk about them coming back because you don't know. It *can* happen. But usually not and you don't know when or where. So we don't talk about it."

That made a grisly kind of sense. "Ian could be alive."

"Maybe."

I heard the doubt in his voice. "You don't think so."

Kapi scratched the back of his head. "Venus is big geographically, but it's really more like a small town. People move around. Stories travel. Ian's really famous. If he showed up somewhere, it would attract attention. People would hear about it. People would go to see him. I've heard none of that. I'm pretty sure Percy *could* bring him back—Percy can bring back anybody. I just don't believe she *did*."

I mulled that over. "Only Percy knows."

"Yeah. Mama likes to tinker."

I felt like I'd had whiplash: he's dead. He might not be. He probably is. He could be alive. Unlikely.

Maybe I should have stayed on Poa.

I thought of something. "Wait a minute. Watertown was full of old people."

"Well, yes," conceded Kapi. "Watertown was settled by refugees from Skye. We are being punished."

"What happened?"

"We invented a religion. We gamed Percy's system of limited reproduction. We started a war with the deinos. That was enough for Percy and we started aging. Most of us died off." Kapi stared at the ruins.

I tried to digest that. "Okay. More details."

oOo

Kapi sighed. "I didn't take well to coming here. I was *happy* on Earth. I had family. Work. Faith. I had *everything*. Here, it was all gone. I had lost my very body. Chitra tried to comfort me but I would not be comforted. When Chitra wasn't trying to cheer me up or spending time with Freder she was talking about Ian: He was the man who saved us. Who abducted us. Who should be killed slowly. Who should be made our king. Who was Chitra's first true love. Whom she hated. Whom she wished would be all right and would also disappear forever. Ian got killed. Chitra and Freder turned into the leaders of the settlement. People farmed and kept the therapods at bay. I didn't pay attention to any of that. I had my own problems."

"I spent a lot of time experimenting on how to ferment fruit. That's what my family did back on Earth: we made wine and distilled it into *cholai*. Eventually, I found something—yeast, bacteria, or parasite, I have no idea—that would turn sugar into alcohol. Distilling was the easy part. I lived on mostly alcohol for days."

"When the first new settlements were founded outside of Rusalka proper, I went with them. I kept going with them until I woke up with my head aching and my vision cloudy and the undeniable urge to murder every human being I saw. I left and disappeared into the Nuahine Tessera."

He sighed. "It is beautiful in the Nuahine. The mountains grow as ridges, one after another, thousands of meters high, plunging into deep valleys. The sequoias grow huge in the valleys and then change to fir and eucalyptus up the mountainside. The knife-edge is covered with pine no taller than my waist. It's dry as a desert on the eastern side—nothing but scrub pine and creosote. On the western side, it is always raining and there is water everywhere—small waterfalls, streams, cataracts. There are waterfalls from the tops of trees. Rusalka was two hundred kilometers one way and Pretoria two hundred kilometers the other. Nobody lives in the Nuahine. It's too hard. There wasn't even a satellite village near me. Just my own little patch of woods."

Kapi smiled, remembering. "Deino females leave the band of their birth and wander until they find a new band. Deino males stay. Sam had drifted west as I had drifted east. We met and then wandered together for days. Without anything to drink I sobered. After a while, Sam drifted back east and I followed her until I settled in Pretoria. Sam returned to Deino Forest. I saw her every now and then. She had found a band. She had hatched kits. I built a business. I had a wife. But there was still no flavor to anything."

Kapi kicked the dirt. "Then, I heard about Skye: one of the original settlements that had decided to return to the old, Earth ways. Skye denied Percy's authority. It was creating its own way of life and *damn* Percy if she wanted to interfere. There were plenty of villages that followed this philosophy or that religion. But Skye was going to become a city. Or a country. Something to be proud of. I was bitter. I left my wife. I left my business and went there."

"Skye was exactly what I wanted. Tamara and Gana brought us the Word of God. Humans were intended by God to rule Venus despite Percy. Her role had been to create the world under God's direction and she had exceeded her authority. Our religion shunned gods such as Ganesha since he had an elephant's head. I found that sad. I always had a fondness for the dancing Ganesha. But it seemed a small price to pay."

Kapi looked at the ruins. "Sure, they created it with borrowed bits from Christianity, Islam, and Hinduism. I know that. Maybe we all did. But we didn't think about that." He pointed at the three concentric circles carved into the broken tower. "That was our symbol. The outer world is ruled by Percy. The middle world of Skye in conflict with the outer world. The inner world of God, soon to overcome the outer world."

He waved to the logging we could see outside the city's walls. "We cut down large sections of the forest to make buildings. We couldn't reproduce fast enough to fill them—Percy had put in limitations. First, people are just not as fertile as we were on Earth. Then, women can't conceive if there are too many people around. Finally, they can't conceive in the presence of their own adult children. Skye gamed the system.

Women removed themselves to satellite villages, reducing the number of people and separating themselves from their grown children. They sent their children back into Skye to be reared. When they felt they had birthed enough, they returned to Skye."

Kapi looked at me. "Women tend to run things on Venus. The deinos are the same way. Men don't run things for long—eventually, a woman takes over. I don't know why but that's the way it is. 'Mama likes to tinker.'"

"You saw what we were walking through to get into Skye. Every human settlement has a ring of repurposed land around it. Humans are hard on their local environment. That's our nature. But Skye was a *city*. It *destroyed* the area surrounding it and kept expanding. We took pride in it. It showed how we were taking Venus over. We were *winning*."

Kapi fell quiet for a bit. "Sam had been watching all of this. She and I had spent days together in the Nuahine. I knew her and knew deinos. She knew me and knew humans. She could tell we were a direct threat to them. She organized her clans—I have no idea how. 'Think of them like crows,' Clayton said." Kapi laughed. "Crows that can organize. Crows that raided logging camps. Crows that destroyed the outer fields—attempting to limit what we were doing. But deinos only know what humans are capable of by what they've seen. We have a long heritage of knowing what to do with any species or community that opposes us. We declared war on the deinos. The deinos had no idea what they were in for."

"Tamara said to me: no one knows them as you do. You go out there and make the war. And I did. I organized an army and fought them. Sam learned from me. She organized her own army and fought back. We found mothers and nests and destroyed them. They slaughtered the women's satellite villages."

Kapi beat the ground slowly with his fist. "It began to spread. Brasilia took our side—if deinos would slaughter a village of women they would slaughter anybody. Pretoria sided with the deinos—these are our neighbors. War on them is war on us. Now it wasn't warring with the deinos. It was a war of humans against humans. The deinos were along for the ride. No place was safe."

Kapi shook his head. "It went on for twenty-seven days—nearly nine Earth years." He held out his arm. "I told you about how we grow fur in the late afternoon for the night. Here, you can see the stubble. The evening of the twenty-seventh day the fur of every Skye adult grew in gray. We were aging. *No one* had aged in all this time. We were killed, sure. A few rare people came back. But we didn't *age*. Now we aged quickly. We grew infirm. Some lost memories. Died of heart attacks or other degenerative diseases. The pregnant women miscarried. Skye had a library. We asked Percy what was happening. She didn't answer—not even the form response: *There is no response at this time.* Tamara went all the way to Brasilia to ask at their library. No response. By then, we had figured it out."

"We were being punished."

"We separated into three factions. One group—Tamara's group—thought it was geographical. This was not punishment. This was merely another manifestation of Percy's incompetence. If we moved, we would be fine. She led a group to found Watertown. You saw how that turned out."

"Gana led another group west. They founded Podunk to return to what they called the Venusian Way. I haven't been there but I've heard they're doing about as well as Watertown. A third group refused to believe that this was anything but temporary." He waved to the ruins. "They stayed here and died."

Kapi fell silent and I looked at the ruins. It had been a small but grand city even by Earth standards.

Earth standards. *Right.* I laughed shortly.

He gestured towards the sky with his chin. "The people of the Lesser Lights think this is funny?"

I shrugged. "It's different and the same. The people who came to Poa were volunteers—like I said, I interviewed all of them. They never believed me. When they found out the truth, they thought I had lied to them. I never did but that made no difference. They weren't abducted, but felt they had been swindled—close enough. But they ultimately fit in because they had been selected for that environment. If they had rebelled as you did, something probably would have happened, too. Even so, they came for their own reasons. It's no surprise most of them came to terms with life on Poa—that's one of the reasons they were chosen in the first place."

"Not you."

I shrugged again. "My job was to bring them in. In return, I would save Ian and myself. That was enough."

"Chitra said that was the same deal Ian was given: abduct these people so that you and he could be saved."

"So I understand." I looked at the ruins of Skye. "Is this why you agreed to guide me to Rusalka? To come here? Is this what Tamara meant when she said you had trouble with commitment?"

"No." He shook his head. "I planned to go with you to Rusalka and find Chitra if she's still there. Who knows how much longer I have? I treated her badly and I'd like to make amends." Kapi pointed at the deino, wandering in the ruins. "But I think Sam has other plans."

"At least, here on Venus, you have some choice on how to live."

"Nobody asked me if I wanted to come here."

"Nobody asked you if you wanted to be born, either. So what? Stop whining."

"*Whining?* My family died when they had done *nothing*—"

"My son was killed after I had done *everything*."

He fell silent for a moment. "Sometimes, at night, you can see the stars through the curtain. We all think we've seen Earth once or twice but nothing is ever clear through the curtain." Kapi shook his head. "It would have been better if I had died on Earth."

"There is no Earth worth speaking of anymore."

Kapi looked up at me. "What do you mean?"

It slipped out. I didn't mean to talk about it—we didn't like to talk about it on Poa, regardless. I looked at the westering sun. The shadows were long—stayed long in this place.

I turned to him. "We didn't spend all of the last three thousand years awake on Poa. We woke up a little before you did. But we had telescopes—not good ones at first. And Percy had pointed all of those we had down towards Venus. We built our own." I took a deep breath. "Something has happened to Earth. About half—maybe even two-thirds—of all of the oceans are gone."

"Gone? What do you mean, gone?"

"I mean absent. Missing. No longer in their beds. All of the continental shelves and portions of the abyssal plains are open lands. You're from Kolkata, right? We looked at the Bay of Bengal. If you were to look down on it you would see the outline of the coast dropping down to a flat mesa and then dropping again. The water pools only in the deepest areas. The Mehgna still pours but now it is a great river falling over a wide cliff, meandering south for hundreds of kilometers into a small sea. That sea empties south and west to the Arabian Sea. Much of the ocean is *gone*."

"Where did it *go?*"

"I have no idea."

"You don't—"

I held up my hand and stopped him. "On both poles are dark, purplish caps—sort of resembling ice caps but much taller.In spots, they peek out of the atmosphere. The earth now has a pronounced wobble. With the reduction of the ocean buffering effect and all that new dry land, Lord knows what the temperature ranges. Not to mention a reduction in both the oxygen and nitrogen in the atmosphere."

"Are there cities? People? What about Kolkata?"

I shook my head. "Nothing could live above the continental shelf—the edges of the continents are effectively close to Everest in height. We could only see a little green below the continental shelves and green peaks that used to be islands or seamounts. There are waves of green on the exposed shelves but the continents are alpine desert. Earth is a burnt-out husk. People live on the Moon and Mars. We've found evidence that there might be people in space throughout the solar system and on the moons of Jupiter and Saturn. But on Earth? Nothing of consequence."

I didn't mention that nobody would talk to us. We had sent a few probes towards Earth but they were destroyed in overly dramatic nuclear explosions. We got the message. Don't talk to us and we won't talk to you.

Kapi had a pleading light in his eyes. "Nothing?"

"Nothing. We saw a couple of lights below the continental shelves so we have experimental verification that humans are as hard to kill as a cockroach. But the world we knew is gone."

Kapi mulled it over. "Are you saying Percy made the right decision to abduct us and bring us here?"

"No. I'm just saying that Earth is now a wasteland. There's no point in longing for it." I stood up and dusted my hands. "You've been either a sullen three-year-old or a war criminal for decades. It's time to stop."

Sam came trotting up the hill. She gestured to us. A *come with me* if ever I saw one.

It suited me. I'd had my fill of Skye.

oOo

There were too many of them to fit on the road. The herd moved the little ones to the road where they would not stumble. The big ones moved into the debris field and kicked the leftover logs and branches out of the way.

They were sauropods. Apatosaurs, to be precise.

Every child I ever knew—me included—remembers at least four dinosaurs: T. rex, stegosaurus, triceratops, and sauropods. The long neck and tail, the small head, and the great, elephantine body were unmistakable. Kapi had said they were scaled down. I didn't believe it.

Along with them came people: children, young men, girls. I had known Ian from birth until we left Earth: sixty-two years. None of these people resembled him but every one of them reminded me of him in some way: Ian as child. Ian as teen. Ian as young man. Ian as middle-aged but still looking young. Ian as old man but still looking young.

Chatting, laughing—two of them were singing a funny song about a bug. Occasionally, someone would poke an apatosaur one way or the other, suggesting they change direction. It wasn't at all clear if the apatos listened. On the backs of the big apatos were leather structures: lightly roofed platforms. People were there, too, talking down to those walking alongside them.

Night was coming. The sun was low on the horizon—sunset on Venus would be spectacular. The shadows of people and apatos stretched to one side. The sauropods turned at the gate and started walking west.

A woman jumped down and jogged over to us. She was wearing a rough cloth tunic with some brilliant blue and red feathers sewed on at the shoulders. "I'm Pranavi Basu. The marshal asked us to detour here for someone going to Rusalka. Is that you?"

"Pauline Bones."

Pranavi's eyes widened a little.

"Yes," I said testily. "*That* Pauline Bones."

"Of course you are." She said after a moment. "You want to go to Rusalka City?"

"Are you going there?"

"We travel west and then north along the foothills of the Nuahine. That's closer than here. Think quick. As long as there's light they never really stop. We have to catch up."

Maybe Ian had come back. Maybe not. Maybe I didn't have to go to the House of Birds. Maybe I did. But staying in this failed attempt at colonialism did not appeal to me in the least.

"I'm going." I looked at Kapi. "You?"

He still looked cross. Never crack a man's self-delusions. They don't take it well.

"I'll stay—" He suddenly stumbled forward.

Sam pushed him again.

"I'm *staying!*" Kapi yelled at her.

But Sam wasn't having any. She spread her claws and lunged at him.

Kapi danced out of the way. He swung at her.

It was a fast strike, but Sam pulled back, let him overbalance, and then pushed him in the direction of the retreating sauropods.

He was cursing as I helped him up.

"*Fuck you!*" he said in English, then something equally vitriolic in language followed by a series of suggestive gestures.

Sam never took her eyes off him. She pushed him again, fluted, and pointed at the retreating sauropods.

"Come on," I said. "Let's go."

"Bitch!" he snarled. At Sam. Maybe at me. I didn't care.

We had just time enough to hoist our packs and run after Pranavi. The apatos didn't move fast but they didn't slow down, either. Pranavi reached one leg, jumped, and bounced off a knee to grab part of the harness. She let down knotted ropes for us as she whistled.

The apatosaur slowed briefly and gave us a quick glance. We had just time enough to grab the ropes and hoist ourselves off the ground before it started up again. Pranavi grabbed each of us and helped us up to a soft platform studded with soft rings.

"This is Minerva." Pranavi whooped.

The apato turned to give us her full gaze.

"Shoo!" cried Pranavi. "I'm not talking to you."

Minerva snorted and returned to the all-important task of eating while walking.

We pulled ourselves away from the edge. I grabbed a ring and held on as the apato moved up to speed.

I was grinning.

Chapter 3.5: Deino Forest

There were three small platforms on Minerva's back, each made of stiff leather covered by a canopy of flexible fabric. Leather cases and trunks hung from Minerva's sides. Her gait was a long roll punctuated with sudden jerks when she pulled on a recalcitrant tree or bush. She didn't seem to notice the extra weight at all.

As Minerva and the others moved into the forest, eating as they went, the last light of the sun was obscured by the trees and we were in hushed darkness. Pranavi scampered up to the canopy over one of the platforms. Minerva didn't even twitch. But a soft light came from just over us. I saw it on the other apatos: the greenish-yellow light of thousands of fireflies in a bottle.

Pranavi dropped back to join us. She moved against Minerva's movements with unconscious grace, wearing a robe of brilliant feathers: red and blue again but shot through with gold and green.

She saw me looking at the robe. "I am the pinnacle of fashion elegance. Ritual requires beauty." Pranavi sat down. One of the rat-hunting creatures I'd seen on the road was lying on a cushion on the highest platform. It creaked erect and moved slowly down to sit with Pranavi. Pranavi petted it and made it comfortable. Then, she turned to me and spoke with mock solemnity. "I, Old Woman Pranavi, welcome you to Clan Batanu of the Ariroi." She leaned forward and spoke in a loud whisper. "This is where you say how glad you are to be here safe from the night."

I was delighted. "We are glad to be here safe from the night."

Then, she yelled down into the darkness. "All right! They've been officially welcomed. Come on up. It's Ian's mother."

At least twenty people leaped on Minerva's side and clambered up, nodding and bowing to us. Several told me they "hated that son-of-a-bitch," but bore me no ill will as his mother, assuring me I was completely welcome at their hearth.

I found it impossible to be offended.

Pranavi introduced us haphazardly to this nephew or that cousin or yonder granddaughter. The young, unattached men she called "bucks" and the girls were "honeys."

I had been thinking of the term *Old Woman* the term of office. But now I asked: "How old are you, Pranavi?"

"Old as my bones but older than my teeth." She cackled. "I've never been killed yet. I've been here since the founding of Settlement One." She lifted her head in pride. "I have seven grandchildren, fourteen great-grandchildren, and twenty-two great-great-grandchildren. I lost count after that. Do you have offspring besides Ian?"

He died too early for that. "No."

"After all this time! People on the Lesser Lights reproduce even more slowly than we do," She snorted, then looked at me askance. "I knew your son."

For a moment, I couldn't breathe. "You did?"

"Yes. He led Contai all through the first night and the war. It was because of him Percy broke down the walls between the settlements." Pranavi made a small gesture. "I contributed a little. So did Gibreel. Well, not this Gibreel, of course." She indicated the rat catcher. "I've had many gibreels and named them all after the first one. They have all, each and every one of them, been perfect companions."

Kapi had told me it was an eoraptor. Gibreel came over to me and stretched out to my outstretched hand.

"Don't make any quick moves," Pranavi said. "Gibreel's eyesight isn't what it used to be."

Gibreel made a perfunctory sniff and then returned to Pranavi's lap. Pranavi petted him carefully and snuggled him. "This Gibreel used to be the best ratter and pointer in the clan. But he's too old for that, now. He can't work." She petted him and fed him a treat "He has two more days left in him. Perhaps three. You rest here." She patted a cushion near next to her. It had small, soft walls so the sleeping animal wouldn't fall out. "Good boy," she whispered as he ponderously made its way to his bed. "A very good boy."

"Did Ian know Gibreel?"

"He knew the first one. But he died before he knew any more." Pranavi watched Gibreel, then she turned to me. "You want to know how he was, here. How he lived. How he died." Pranavi nodded. "I've buried my share of children. I know the drill."

"Tell me," I begged.

"I knew him for only a single Venus day. I was a ten-year-old Earth child. Children are savages. If it doesn't interest them they take no notice. If it does, they're all over it. Gibreel interested me. Julia interested me."

"Julia?"

"One of Ian's friends in the next village. Larissa interested me. Ian, Chitra, and Freder were in charge. They were the leaders." Pranavi chuckled. "This was before we figured out men can't lead a damned thing. To me, they were people to avoid because they might get in my *way* but uninteresting by any other measure. Chitra knew Ian. So did Freder and Julia."

"Where are they?"

"Freder and Chitra live in Rusalka City. I lost track of Julia." Pranavi fed another snack to Gibreel. "What *I* know of Ian was this: he *always* knew more than he was telling. He loved Chitra and liked Freder. If he felt something was the right thing to do, he'd lay his life down for it. If he didn't think that way, he'd stand aside and let someone else take the load. Freder and Chitra did most of the actual leading—made sure we kept up the garden. Made sure the kids were looked after." Pranavi gave me a crafty look. "I evaded her as much as possible. Freder was always figuring solutions to things. Eventually, Chitra discarded Ian and took up with him."

"What happened to Ian?"

"All three of them were together for a bit. Then, after the last chamber opened and the last people came out and Ian saw you weren't among them, he left our village to look in the others. He was gone most of the day and the night and came back the next morning. By the time he came back, Chitra had lost interest in him." Pranavi shook her head. "Fickle, that one. I never wasted a man like she did—of course, at the time I knew nothing about such things, being so young. The thing about Ian, though—the thing that made him *important*—was when he was really needed, he was right *there*. No pause. No hesitation. He tried for weeks to get Percy to let down the walls between the settlements. But when it counted, he gathered us all together to right a wrong in the next village. No one else could have pulled us together. I'm convinced that's what made Percy open the settlements to each other."

Pranavi nodded to herself. "It was how he died, too. The walls between the settlements had already dissolved, but the outer wall was still there. That was what kept the alberts out—we were deep in albert territory but we didn't know that. We didn't know anything."

Pranavi started beating her fist on the platform in rhythm as she spoke. "I was there when the wall came down. I was watching from the gate and saw it fall. I saw the alberts run toward us followed by their little dromaeosaur scavengers. Ian pushed Freder and Chitra towards the gate where we waited. Ian called out for us to close it but we did not. We could not without him."

She took a deep breath. I could not have interrupted her for the world.

"*Boom!* Came the thunder in the ground as the albert ran at us but Ian struck him on the side of the jaw and knocked him down. *Boom!* Came the sound of the strike, cracking the albert's jaw. Ian danced on the albert's back to strike him again. But the albert took him and shook him like a rat. 'Run,' he cried as he died. 'Run and be safe.' We found our arrows and killed the albert and its brothers and went out to bring back Ian's body. But the dromaeosaurs had taken it away and we were left with only his kill. We burned the body of that albert out of respect for Ian. We killed and ate the rest of them."

Pranavi brought down her fist slowly. "He saved us and we wept for him."

There a long silence with only the sound of Minerva eating and the creaking of the leather platform.

Then, Pranavi somersaulted backward to her feet. "Who do we have to slaughter to get something to eat around here?" She kicked at one grandchild and another nephew. They evaded her easily but brought bowls of fruit and dried meat.

oOo

Kapi was leaning over one side of the lower platform, munching on an apple.

"Is that how it happened?"

"What?"

"Ian's death."

"That's pretty much how I heard it. She tells it better." He glanced up at her. "If it's any consolation, he died a hero."

It was not. "He could be alive," I said.

"Yes," said Kapi in a sad and thoughtful voice. "It's very rare but it does happen. But it isn't likely. Don't get your hopes up."

"Percy would know."

"Percy would know," agreed Kapi. "She would tell you if she would tell anyone."

"In the House of Birds."

"If that's where you were told to go." Kapi gave an uncomfortable shrug. "How did you come down in Diana's Pancake?"

"Accident, I think. The Lesser Lights are run by an artificial intelligence. It was his suggestion I go to the peninsula as the largest settlement. I missed."

"I think Pauline Bones can demand an audience with Percy in any library on Venus. Having to go to the House of Birds seems… exorbitant." He glanced at me again. "Who told you to go to the House of Birds?"

"Tamara."

"So you would have gone to any library."

"Sure." I shrugged. "But Tamara said she answers there more readily than anywhere else."

"That's superstition." Kapi bit the apple and chewed thoughtfully. "There are libraries in Brasilia, Pretoria, and Safarmo. Tamara could have directed you there but she didn't. I wonder why."

"I still want to go to Rusalka City."

"Why?"

"That's where Ian was," I said. "That's where Ian died. Think I'm crazy?"

"I think Mama likes to tinker." He fell silent a moment. "There's another saying: 'Mama's an idiot. You should never listen to her.'"

"Does anybody follow that advice?"

"Of course not. Percy says dance we don't ask the tune. Do you want the rest of the apple? I promise I have only native Venusian germs."

I took the apple and bit into it. "But he *could* be alive."

"Oh, yes. It's unlikely. It's not impossible. For that matter, if you ask Percy nicely she could *bring* him back to life."

"Really?"

"Why would Ian be any different?" Kapi patted her hand. "I'm sure if you ask Percy *real nice*—"

"Shut up," I said chuckling. Truth was, if Ian was dead I'd beg Percy to get him back.

I sat there chewing on the apple, attempting to be optimistic. I would walk into the House of Birds and *demand* Ian. I would be Dorothy berating the Wizard. Except Percy was not a fake and I wasn't a young girl filled with righteous convictions.

"Sam is following us," whispered Kapi.

"Why?"

He rolled over on his back. "I have absolutely no idea. I thought she wanted me to stay in Skye. To punish me. Or maybe kill me. Clearly, I was wrong. Now she's tracking us."

I looked into the darkness. I couldn't see her but I trusted Kapi's better night vision. Instead, I looked up at the narrow strip of sky. It was not long after sunset. I didn't see any of the poas. "When do the… Lesser Lights show up?"

"Not until Shadow."

"Shadow?"

Kapi lay on his side, facing her. She could see him in the gloom and the light of the fireflies. He counted on his fingers: "Foreday: Sunrise, Morning. Noon. Aftday: Afternoon and Sunset. Forenight: Twilight, Shadow. Midnight. Aftnight: Murk and Dawn. Twilight and Dawn still have light from the sun." Kapi waved at the sky. "We're still in Twilight. The first of the Lesser Lights marks the beginning of Shadow. Midnight begins when the last one goes. The return of the Lesser Lights marks the beginning of Murk and when they leave the second time, it's the beginning of Dawn."

I saw a man and a woman watching us. They asked Pranavi something and she nodded. They detached themselves from the group and came over to us, bowing low.

Kapi watched them a moment. "Who are you showing respect to? Her or me?"

They looked flustered.

"The mother of Ian Bones," said the woman. "We don't know you, sir."

"I am Kapi the Apostate." Kapi looked towards Sam in the darkness. "Maker of war on the deinos!" he shouted.

"Don't be so full of yourself," Pranavi shouted at him.

"I wasn't talking to you."

"Like that wasn't obvious."

The couple looked at one another. They decided to ignore Kapi and Pranavi.

"I am Ojo Merkle and this is my husband, Pandit Singh."

"Pauline Bones." I bowed to them and almost fell off Miranda. Only a quick grab of a rope prevented an undignified fall.

"Oh," giggled Ojo. "We know who you are. We wanted to ask your blessing."

"Oh, my God." With that, Kapi rolled off the platform and dropped to the grass.

I stared at them. "Whatever for?"

"We are on Walkabout," said Pandit. "Trying to get pregnant. So far it hasn't worked. We are hoping your blessing will make a difference."

"Really? You think that will help?"

"We'll try anything," said Ojo, simply.

"All right. It's yours."

They looked at one another uncomfortably. That clearly wasn't enough.

"You need to say some words," said Pandit.

"To make it official," said Ojo.

I mulled that over. I said in English: "Do you understand English?"

They both looked at me blankly, their faces confused. Even in the faint firefly light, I could see the shadow of their growing fur.

"All right," I said in venustalk. Then, I continued in English: "Our Father who art in mythical heaven, hear me. I do not believe in your existence but these people believe in *something* and think I can contribute. They do not know how wrong they are. They are asking me to bless them. I have no idea what that means. They want a baby and do not know what impedes them so they're turning to you through me. Or Percy. Maybe that's the same thing. Regardless, they seem like good people and might make adequate parents. Probably better than I ever was. I had to bury my husband and I didn't get the chance to bury my child. So if you think you owe me something for that, pay it to these two and give them a child."

Away in the darkness, I heard Kapi laugh.

oOo

The next week was miserable. This area supposedly had a dry climate but the dropping temperatures wrung out any remaining water like squeezing a sponge. I huddled under the canopy as it rained every sleep. This was not a monsoon—Pranavi said we were too far inland for that. But it was a strong, continuous rain. I remembered when Martin and I were stationed over the winter in Seattle. This had the same drab, aching, wet, cold. I bundled up in linen and feather blankets but couldn't seem to get warm. Any remaining sunlight seemed swallowed by the rain clouds and the only real light came from the fireflies.

The fur of the others seemed to help them. It shed the rain. They didn't look anywhere close to as miserable as I felt. Every time I woke I looked for a break in the clouds. Every time I was disappointed. I took Alisi's meds and resolved that things would be better when I awoke next.

Finally, the rain let up. There was another miserable sleep as the world dried but this was just cold. The wretched damp eased.

The apatos were able to feed in even Twilight's dim light but eventually, it just became too dark. The glow of the fireflies didn't satisfy them. I was told it could have been much worse. On the other side of the Nuahine, rats lived in huge trees. They descended when the dark came and ate everything they could find. Here in Deino Forest there were enough night predators to kept rats in check.

Just when the apatos stopped in what seemed to be total darkness, a faint glow showed across the tops of the trees. We patiently waited, watching color gradually come back to the forest. The apatos began to eat again.

It was one of the poas—I had no idea which one. The light grew from faint moonlight up to deep dusk—Earth terms, not Venus terms. I could feel warmth when it was overhead and the rising temperature brought up the wind.

Then, it was past us and fading.

It felt like about three hours, start to finish. We didn't have to wait long for the next. Each time they passed over, the light was a little stronger. Kapi told me we were now in Shadow and there we would remain for the next three weeks. Halfway through Shadow, the Lesser Lights would begin to dim. Midnight began when they were finally extinguished.

Now that the Lesser Lights had come, the Ariroi released the fireflies in the dimness between the Lights. The thousands of them rose over the apatos and landed on the trees, marking them like Christmas lights. There, they rested as we kept moving. I watched them rise again as they fell behind us.

Pranavi sat with me as we watched them. "One of the best parts of night travel," she said. She patted me on the knee. "In a couple of weeks when we get near Midnight, we'll start gathering new ones for the dark. We hold them through Twilight, Midnight, and release them at Dawn."

The Lesser Lights introduced a lurching rhythm. The apatos would proceed only when there was a certain minimum light. In the dim time between the Lights or until the ascendant Light was strong enough, they stood where they were, as passive as cows in a barn. The Ariroi would gather, cook whatever game they'd found, sing or talk.

Just before sleep, when one of the Lights was descendant and the tribe made camp, Pranavi took me to a small hill clear of trees. There, I saw the strange moment when the Southern Light was sinking into a small sunset, and the Northern Light was birthed in a tiny sunrise.

It caught my breath. "It's lovely."

"Lightrise, it's called. And it is lovely. What are you planning to do next?" she asked me.

"Go to the House of Birds and ask Percy for my son back."

Pranavi laughed bitterly. "It's amazing what you'll cling to when you're grieving. My daughter was standing on a jetty we had built out into the ocean. Not even ten. Standing there jumping up and down. We were watching her." Pranavi looked at me. "We thought she was safe. A mosasaur swept up out of the water and snagged her right off the wood and fell back in the water. I must have cried for a year. This was before we knew people could come back. But I thought: hey, Percy is the god in this place. She can bring her back if she wants. I went straight to the library—the House of Birds itself—and pleaded with her. I got what we call the form letter: There is nothing to be done at this time. Please try again at some future date." She drew a long breath. "So long ago and it still breaks my heart. It tore me and my husband apart. I left Rusalka. I wanted nothing to do with any of them."

"That's how Kapi left Pretoria and ended up in Skye."

Pranavi snorted. "Kapi ended up in Skye because he was too fond of wine and the past. By then, we knew different groups of sauropods migrated in great circles all over Aphrodite. Some of us started following them—like following elephant herds, maybe. The closer you were to the sauropods, the less the therapods bothered you. Eventually, we ended up on top of them." She glanced up at me. "You might have better luck with Percy. There's no doubt Ian was important to her. But that was over two hundred days ago." She thought for a moment. "When that business is done, you might consider finding us."

"Leave my son?"

"No. But you might want a friendly place afterward. It doesn't have to be *my* band, of course. Any Ariroi would take you as a member. Most of us like the life we lead. Just don't stay in the city."

"Why not?"

Pranavi shook her head. "Cities on Venus are strange places. Women have to leave them to conceive. This makes families brittle. They try to hold on for a while but most leave or fade away. The people that remain stay for reasons of business or power or art. Outside of the cities, communities are built on families and children. Inside the cities, communities are built on something different. An illusion of permanence. The founders of Skye found their followers in the cities, not the forests." She waved her hand. "Look around! With the Ariroi, you travel the Deino Forest in style."

"I haven't seen any herbivores other than your apatosaurs."

Pranavi chuckled. "You came along the southern road from Watertown to Skye. Skye pretty much wiped out all of the nearby big grazers: iguanodons, parasaurolophi, and maiasaurs. That's why the deinos went to war with them." She pointed down to the camp. "The sauropods are climax herbivores here in the forest. They knock down trees and make clearings. Other herbivores come into those clearings and widen them. That took forage away from us. So the lack of competition has been good for the apatos in the short term. But it's bad for us."

She bit her lip and looked northwest. "Another Skye legacy: most of the satellite villages are abandoned. They were driven out either by the war or the lack of game. Used to be we'd negotiate our path. Clear the forest for the village and seed it with enormous steaming piles of fertilizer. In return, we'd get tools. Cloth. Staples. Transport contracts." Pranavi sighed. "It'll get better as we go north."

Pranavi watched the camp for a moment. The light was coming up. "The apatos are getting restive. We have to go back down." She stood and gave me a hand standing. Then, she straightened and spread her arms, turned slowly in the rising light. "But isn't this great? You must take your joy where you find it."

Chapter 3.6: Midnight on the Range

The apatos never moved very fast and with the stops for darkness, progress was even slower. I saw Kapi and Sam at the edge of the herd and I dropped down to see them.

They were arguing: a furious motion of the hands, one to the other, and back again.

Kapi made a flat gesture, palm down, followed by pointing at Sam and then bringing his finger down in his palm. *Something,* you, here?

Sam replied by pointing to herself, with the same flat gesture, finger down and then pointing at Kapi. Same word, different context. Why? Why are *you* here?

I'm here because of *you.*

I remembered my Spanish, *por que* being "why" and *porque* being "because."

Kapi replied shaping his hands on both sides, making a fist and making it drop and explode, then pointing at Sam.

Something falling, exploding—no. There'd be no referent for exploding. Splatting. Shaping his hands—containing. Containing something falling that splatters. I laughed. *You are full of shit.*

The more they argued, the better I understood them. Had I been pre-conditioned for venustalk *and* the deino sign language? How could anyone know I'd be here two hundred years after people had started spreading around? Had *all* of us been pre-conditioned?

More arguing—too fast for me to follow. Finally, Sam stopped and slowly motioned: *I'm here because*—and then she took her hand and turned it palm upwards and spread her hand open like a flower.

Flowers? Spring? Love? I had no idea.

Kapi slapped her hands down and walked away.

Sam stared after him and then, after a moment, disappeared into the forest.

Not before I saw two other deinos watching us. They stood, staring at me, for a moment. Then melted into the forest in another direction.

I followed Kapi but lost him in the woods. I stopped and returned to the herd. I wasn't going out there by myself.

Later, when it grew dark and the apatos stopped, several young men built a fire, dancing, and singing. They shared something in a skin.

One shiny-eyed furred monkey—*human being*, said my neocortex—offered it to me. I sniffed it. Ethyl alcohol, to be sure. Probably, methanol. Also, aldehydes, ketones, the faint hint of benzene. It would certainly be better as truck fuel than human consumption. But, there were no trucks around so I took a good long swallow.

Back in the army, we learned to keep down whatever godforsaken swill we had to drink. That early basic training had stood the test of time. This stuff tasted as bad as it smelled. I hoped Alisi's bacteria were up to the task.

I sat down next to the fire with a bump. That stuff was *strong*. No doubt it compared favorably with Kapi's best brew.

oOo

I woke up sometime later, tied to a platform on one side of Minerva. The side of my face, shoulder, and Minerva's hip showed that I had been sick in my sleep. Tying me like this probably kept me from choking. Kapi was walking alongside, a safe distance away.

"You're a mean drunk," he said when he saw I was awake.

"You're an asshole."

"See what I mean?"

I tried to move but failed. "Untie me."

"Are you going to call me names?"

"No."

He clambered up Minerva's back thigh, avoiding the mess I had made, and untied the harness, helping me back up onto the platform.

He handed me a skin. "Just water."

Warm, leather-smelling water had never tasted so good.

I washed my face and shoulder. Then dug around in my pack for my meds. "Did I make a fool of myself?"

"You don't remember?"

"It's hazy."

"You had sex with half the young men in the camp."

"I did not."

"No," he admitted. "You did not. Much to the disappointment of your drinking companions. You sang with them. You danced with them. Then, you sat, drinking, getting more and more quiet. Until you fell over. That was when the lights rose and we tied you to Minerva's hind end."

"Thank you for not leaving me in the forest."

"We didn't consider it when we tied you down. But once you started throwing up, the subject was discussed."

I tried to laugh but then it made me want to throw up again so I stopped. "Is this like the liquor you brewed?"

"Of course not. Compared to that paint thinner, my cholai is finest cognac."

I washed my face until I thought I felt human. "What did Sam say?"

"Excuse me?"

"I saw you talking with Sam. She said she was here because of…" I pointed my fingers up and spread them. "What does that mean?"

He stared at my hands. "I don't know," he said in an agonized whisper. "I don't *know*. She's been saying that to me since she first saw me after the war ended."

"In Watertown?"

He shook his head. "No. After I left Skye, I went down to live with the Boat People down in Big Diana. She found me and kept saying, 'We need to deal with *this*.'" He made the sign. "Over and over. We must manage *this*. You can't ignore *this*. But she wouldn't—or couldn't—explain what *this* is. She pestered me north until I hid in Watertown—I figured Tamara might keep her away."

"You don't know anything about it? I thought it might be love."

He didn't blink at that. "I thought that, too. It's not the symbol they use for affection between each other or their kits. That's this." He closed his fist and rotated it over his abdomen. "Even if it's something they might refer to as 'love'—if they spoke—it doesn't explain what 'love' is. Humans use the word to represent an emotion we share with each other, so we think we understand what it means. That doesn't explain what it means to *her*."

I mulled that over. "She's not the only deino that's following us. Two other deinos were watching you two. When she left they did, too. But they didn't follow her."

He mulled *that* over. "We need to talk to Pranavi."

oOo

Pranavi listened and then didn't speak for a long time. Finally, she looked up and gave Kapi a bitter smile. "Skye: the gift that keeps on giving."

"You think they're after me?"

"This is Deino Forest. The Ariroi migrated through here before Skye, during Skye, and since. We've never been the subject of any clandestine deino interest. I don't think they *had* clandestine interests until you taught them." She pointed at Kapi. "You made war on them. You destroyed their kits and their nests. You're their great murderer. Of *course,* they're looking for you." She gave him a speculative look. "You could always leave."

"No," I said. "He's taking me to Rusalka."

Pranavi gestured to the young men walking alongside Minerva. "Any one of my bucks can take you to Rusalka."

"Leaving is probably a good idea." Kapi was watching the forest, looking for other deinos.

I looked at Kapi and back to Pranavi. "Sam pushed him to go with you."

Pranavi nodded sourly. "That's not lost on me. So. Are we being trailed by her minions to make sure we keep Kapi or are we being followed by a rebellious faction bent on revenge?" She gave Kapi a hard look. "Any ideas?"

"Do you know what this means?" He made the flower sign.

Pranavi shook her head. "No."

"It's why Sam says she's following me."

"Ask around. My deino's not that good." She looked at me and then Kapi. "I'm moving Minerva to the outer edge. Only you and some bucks will be on her. I'll give the word that anyone on foot stays away. Minerva's the biggest and the bucks are good in a fight. It's unlikely you'll be attacked. Deinos aren't stupid." She pointed first at Kapi and then at me. "No wandering off. Hang off the side to do your business."

We left and returned to Minerva. I rummaged through my pack and found Alisi's gun. Under the Lesser Lights, I took it apart and put it back together then ran a diagnostic subroutine and self-check. I held it in my hands, going over its operation in my mind. Going over my training from years ago in the army. The gun didn't seem heavy enough.

oOo

Shadow waxed and waned. The Lesser Lights grew dim and the time between them grew.

Pranavi steered the herd into a clearing and called a halt. We made a real camp with tents and fires. Fireflies had been gathered in the last few Lights and were now prepared.

Over the weeks, the rising and setting of the Lights had conditioned me: I knew within a few minutes when the next one was coming. There came a moment where the apatos stopped and darkness remained when I felt when the lights should appear. There was only starlight.

Kapi had told me that deinos saw better in the darkness than even augmented Venusians. Much better than a poorly adapted human like myself. Surely they would attack at Midnight.

We watched the stars from Minerva's back. At this point, our location pointed directly away from the sun. It was the best time to look for Earth. Several times, we thought we saw something. The sunshield was transparent in the dark but still added the tiniest bit of distortion so we didn't really know what we were looking at. Was that Earth or Saturn? The rudest telescope would prove it one way or the other. But there were no telescopes: optics were still too primitive.

"So tell me," Kapi said next to me. "What was Poa like? I mean, really like. You said it was like Littleton—"

"Levittown."

"But that's not what it was like to you. You stayed there for decades. What was your life like?"

I watched the stars for a moment. "Our warren took the name Mechanicsburg," I said finally. "We helped Poa repair the smidgeons—the components of the sunshield. We built things—Alisi was in charge of the fabricators. Shana ran the computation systems. Davi built telescopes."

"Were you married to them?"

"Are you shocked?"

Kapi laughed. "We try everything on Venus. Plural marriage is tame."

I thought about that. "I suppose we were—like here, customs are still being figured out. We were a unit of sorts. We lived together—we were the original construction workers. We strung the mirrors and built most of the infrastructure. We woke up the others later."

"That tells me what you *did*. It doesn't tell me about your life there."

"What I did defines who I am. It's why I had to leave. Poa—and Pob and Poc—are *finished*. They're *self-sustaining.*" I reached into the air and saw my arm against the sky. "I'm an engineer. I've been an engineer most of my life. I used to be an army officer, pilot, and astronaut. But I was always an engineer. What I did was more important than what I felt."

Kapi didn't say anything for a moment. "That must have been hard for your partners."

I dropped my hand. "Maybe it was. Maybe they were glad to see me gone."

"I didn't say that. You're not saying how being up there *felt*—you don't talk about feelings much at all. I'm just saying that might have been difficult for them."

I had a flash of what living with me must have been like for them. It didn't feel good.

"What did Poa *feel* like?" asked Kapi.

Lying on the observation deck, looking down as Venus cycled below us. Shana and her little dog that Alisi had built her. Davi lying next to me, as loving a man I'd ever met but who could never stand to be touched. Alisi, enormous and warm. The four of us, lying on our bellies, watching and talking. I had never felt so part of anything in my life. And I had never itched so hard to leave.

"Conflicted," I said, sitting up. "Part of me wanted to stay. Part of me wanted to go. Ian was down here so that threw the vote."

Kapi was silent a moment. "That's not saying very much. I mean it's still all about what you did. What you were named. I want to know what you went through."

"What do you want to know?"

Kapi made a sound of exasperation. "Okay. When I asked you how they handle aging on the Lesser Lights you shut me down. You look pretty good. How *do* they handle aging?"

I looked for the—Poa, Pob, or Poc. There was no reflection, of course. The angle was wrong. But they were far enough out that if they obscured a star or planet I'd see it. But there was nothing.

"We have our way," I said.

"And what ways are those?"

"You're not going to let this go, are you?"

"No." Kapi rolled on his side. "I want to know."

"Okay," I said. "First, you develop a clone line. It's pretty easy for a woman that's young enough. She has her own eggs. Men and old women like me have to build one. That takes an egg. Then, you insert the nucleus into the egg and let it divide four times, split them up, and divide again. We usually stop at sixteen. That gives us plenty of options. Pick one, grow a baby, and freeze the rest. Nine months later, decant the baby and hook it up to a stim system—that's a device kind of like an old MRI. It stimulates the brain based on mapped input. You—the source—provide the mapped input. You put on a VR suit and put on the same sort of stim system but now your brain is being read. As you experience the VR world your sensations, memories and thoughts are transmitted to the baby's."

"A baby's brain doesn't work like that."

I took a deep breath. "No, it doesn't. So for the first five years or so *you're* a baby, simulating the target so that it grows properly. Come about five, the baby's brain changes. Now, your experiences mesh better. Not the same, mind you. But closer. Now, you're a toddler. Or a child. Ten years the child hits puberty. All the while you're still in VR land. Maybe you're interacting with friends or mimicking a childhood. Whatever it takes for bringing up baby. As much as you can, you're remembering your *own* childhood to move your memories over to the targets. When puberty comes along you get to relive what it's like to be a teenager—all the time trying to remember everything you can. But once you're past that, the target and source are reversed. The baby-toddler-teen-adult has all of your memories—as many as you thought about over the last twenty years—and becomes the active participant. The husk you're leaving is now the passive participant. It begins to wither—we help it do that. Drugs. Suppressing a little oxygen. Whatever we need to do to make sure the new human is the dominant one. Then, one day, you decant in a twenty-year-old body and some ancient crone is recycled into the system."

Kapi stared at me. "Good God."

"Yeah." I shrugged. "Maybe Percy has a better method but that's the best we've come up with."

"How long does it take?"

"Like I said: twenty years."

"How many times have you been through this?"

"Twice."

Kapi shook his head. "How do you know you're you?"

I leaned towards him and grinned with no humor whatsoever. "Ah, that's the philosophical conundrum, isn't it? It *feels* continuous—but how would I know? We're all just memories, aren't we? Did I get them all? What about those little surprise recollections in the dead of night—did I get them or were they lost in the last husk? Am I me?" I poked him. "Was I even me when I started?"

He stood up and dropped down to the ground, walking away muttering to himself.

I leaned back. Nobody ever really wants to know the other person. They barely want to know themselves.

oOo

When Kapi came back he was civil. Eventually, he was friendly again. But he didn't ask me about Poa again.

We kept watch for several sleeps. We did not see Sam. We did not see deinos.

Instead, the attack came in mid-Murk, in the fullness of a Lesser Light.

oOo

Deinos suddenly swarmed up from the ground. As I watched, I realized they had been hiding in covered blinds. We turned to face the ones on the ground and a group fell from the overhanging trees, grabbing the bucks and tossing them off Minerva.

Minerva trumpeted and started dancing left and right, shaking herself. I saw bucks run to get out from under her. I held on to a strap but Kapi was thrown off the side. I jumped after him, fell hard and wrenched my shoulder, dragged myself up, and ran after him. I heard the bullwhip crack of Minerva's tail followed by a heavy fall—one of the deinos?

Everything seemed to happen with ponderous ritual. One group of deinos held their ground against the bucks. An inner group of deinos surrounded Kapi. Kapi had rolled to his feet, holding out his staff, pointed forward. He turned as the deinos circled him.

I said to the gun. "Flash-Bang. Half meter." Then: "Kapi! Close your eyes."

I charged forward, bringing up the laser sight to center on a deino. As soon as the spotter flashed green, I fired and moved the spotter to the next. The automated round found the optimum path and detonated at a half meter from the target. Three brilliant flashes and concussive explosions.

The deinos shrieked and fell back. The bucks cried out. I reached Kapi. He looked shaken but ready.

"Explosive round. Depth five centimeters." I held my gun out and settled in with Kapi, back to back. If he went down, I was going down with him.

"You have a gun?" he muttered. "Of course you have a gun."

"A gift from a friend."

The deinos were staggering around, milling with the bucks but not really seeing them. Many of the bucks were lying on the ground in a stupor. The rest were moaning.

The deinos recovered faster than the bucks. They shoved the bucks out of the way and surrounded us. There was a moment of pause—again that sense of ritual—and collected breath. I knew they were planning to charge and die to the last, satisfied if only they brought Kapi down. I leveled my gun. I didn't have high hopes.

Then, somebody dropped in front of me, reached out, pushed down my gun. He turned to the deinos and raised his hands.

The deinos bowed. They turned towards the forest.

"Let them pass," he called.

The bucks stumbled out of the way and the deinos returned to the forest.

The man turned back to me. He had a face I knew well.

It was Ian.

oOo

"Ian?" I said uncertainly. I wrapped my arms around him. "Ian!"

Then, when he didn't respond, I pulled away. "Ian?"

"Hello, Mrs. Bones," he said. "I'm Marshal Tomas."

"You're Ian Bones, my son."

Tomas shook his head. "No. I've never met anyone who called himself Ian Bones."

I shrank back. "Who the hell are you?" I snarled.

"He's a clone of Ian," Pranavi said from my elbow.

I jumped away from her, bumped Ian—*No!* Tomas—recoiled and came to rest against Kapi.

"You knew!" I said to Kapi.

Kapi held up his hands. "No. I never met Ian. I don't know what he looks like."

"I met him," said Pranavi. "The marshals all look like him."

"Kapi knew he was dead and didn't tell me. You knew he was—what? Undead? And you didn't tell me?" I stepped back and screamed at them. "What the hell is going on? What the *hell* is going on?"

From Tomas: "Mrs. Bones—"

"And *you!*" I was screaming at Ian. "You're not supposed to be *dead!*"

"Mrs. *Bones*," Tomas said firmly.

That's when I knew he was not and never could be Ian. Ian had always been uncomfortable with command. Uneasy with leadership. Tomas used authority without fear or restraint.

"I started looking for you as soon as I heard you were here." He bowed. "I'm sorry it took so long for me to find you."

I stood back and looked at Tomas. All of the Venusians I had met had been about the same size. Clayton had been a little taller but not much. Kapi had been a little smaller but not much. Tamara had been in between. All of them were very strong—I had seen Pranavi's bucks haul logs out of the way that must have weighed hundreds of kilos.

Tomas was taller than Kapi. Taller than Clayton—he came above my shoulder. He was muscled differently. Anybody I had met up to now would have been able to take on anyone I'd ever heard of on Earth. Tomas looked like he would have been able to take on any of *them.*

Tomas turned to Kapi. "You have guided her from Watertown?"

"I was tasked to take her to Rusalka," said Kapi dryly.

"Ah." Tomas nodded. "I'm sorry for the trouble. I can guide her from now on. You can accompany us, of course."

"I don't know you," I said. It was like all of the features I liked about Ian—his compassion, his kindness, his humility—had been taken away, leaving all of the traits I didn't care for.

I turned to Kapi. "Do you know him?"

"I've never met him." Kapi nodded towards Tomas. "But he's a marshal. I can tell that."

"What does that mean?"

"Just look at him. That's how marshals look."

Tomas tilted his head for a moment, watching me like a bird. "You want someone to vouch for me. Of course." Tomas nodded at Pranavi. "Could you introduce me?"

Pranavi had a sour look on her face. "Why should I? I've got a buck with a dislocated shoulder and one with a broken leg. Not to mention we've probably lost all the deino goodwill for the next ten sleeps' travel."

"I'll take care of the deinos." Tomas waved off the problem.

"How?" I said. "It's not like Kapi's disappeared."

"Revenge is a new concept for them. Deinos always try to maintain a cost-benefit relationship. You have marked yourself dangerous and made revenge too costly. They will remember you. At some future date, they might do something, if they can do it with a minimum effort and little danger to themselves. But that time is not now. I will convince them of this."

Maybe. They hadn't seemed like accountants to me.

Tomas gestured to Pranavi. "Introduce me."

"Pauline Bones," she said. "This arrogant prick is Marshal Tomas. He's the marshal from Diana's Pancake to the Albert Fields." Pranavi turned to Tomas. "This woman is Pauline Bones, mother of Ian Bones. She is a candidate for the Ariroi and my personal guest."

"Really?" said Tomas. He smiled at me. "You have made a powerful friend."

"She has," snapped Pranavi. "Take care of her or I'll have Minerva stomp on you. Not that it would keep you down long."

"What's a marshal?" I asked.

"Good question," said Pranavi. "Next question."

"I've heard it said they are little more than Percy's fingers with no will or thought of their own." Kapi gestured to Tomas. "No offense."

Tomas nodded. "I've also heard that rumor. I'm sure it is no more true than saying the Skye followers give up all their will to a made-up spirit so they need not consider their actions."

Kapi tensed.

"Shut up. Both of you." Pranavi glared at them as she spoke to me. "Marshals used to mediate disputes and grease relationships between the wildlife and the humans. Skye messed that up. Now, they're more like some sort of law keeper. Though nobody has any idea what kind of law they keep."

"We merely try to keep the peace."

"You can trust them. Sort of. As long as your interests and their interests coincide. But you need to make sure that's the case." Pranavi turned and in a rush, punched Tomas in the stomach.

He bent over. "That hurt, Pranavi."

"Remember it. She's under my protection."

"Good to know."

"So," said Pranavi. "From here, we travel north before we travel west. Dickhead here is probably going to suggest you leave when we get to Anklebiter Hole and cross the bush into the Albert Fields and catch the Safarmo Road to Rusalka. It would be a rough two weeks. We, on the other hand, won't get within a week's travel of Rusalka for another month. But our path will be comfortable and easy. There are villages on the way so there will be a good amount of feasting and dancing. Your call."

I looked at Tomas. There was a set to his mouth and a way he held himself. Little pieces that reminded me of Ian. "Is Ian alive?"

Tomas thought for a moment. "I know of no one who I could reliably consider might be Ian Bones."

"That's not much of an answer."

"The question is too broad. Venus is a big place."

I stared at Tomas. "What about it, Kapi? Leave the apatos and sprint through the bush?"

"What? Leave this lap of luxury?" Kapi looked at Tomas. "Sam has been following me."

"You mean—" Tomas made a set of gestures ending with two fingers of each hand coming together.

"Yes."

"Wait. That's Sam's *name?*" I stared at the two of them. "What does *that* mean?"

"It means," Tomas said. "She-who-has-betrayed-her-kind-for-her-friends-and-then-betrayed-her-friends-for-her-kind." He looked at me. "Not literally. The signs mean, more—" Here he made the signs individually. "Falsehood. Self. People. Friend. Falsehood. Self. Friend. People. But the meaning is clear enough."

"I like 'Sam' better."

"You mean." Here, Tomas held his hand vertically at the elbow and brought it down to his other hand in a slap. "It's a joke name. 'Sam' substituted for 'Slam.' Slam, indicating falling from a great height."

Kapi's fists were working. "I don't—"

"Surely, you must have known what that meant? That's why she was in the Nuahine in the first place. That's why she ended up bonding with a human over her own species. She left because she was second-rate and had a better chance in the wilderness. She made her way back into their good graces by being good at war."

"That's not true. That's not what she told me."

"Of course. Why should she say the only reason she took up with you was that her own kind wouldn't have her?"

Pranavi was watching the three of us, a bitter smile on her face. "Let us make a pact," she said. "We'll be at Anklebiter Hole by Sunrise. Keep the peace until then. Tear yourselves apart after you leave. It'll be easier on everyone."

"Stop it," I said. To Kapi. "I want you to come with me." To Tomas. "Quit trying to piss him off." Sullen children, both of them. "All right, then. We will depart from Anklebiter Hole west to Rusalka."

Chapter 3.7: Anklebiter Hole

Anklebiter Hole was a small pond only a few kilometers across. It was the pool where three rivers came down from the Nuahine. The water, held back by a cliff, poured over the Murdock Falls to form the Nuahine River that crossed the Albert Fields to the sea.

"Who is Murdock?" I asked. Neither Kapi nor Tomas knew.

I said goodbye to Pranavi. She said to come back when I was ready and then shooed us off. She wasn't one for waiting and as we stood by the edge of the water, the apatos walked slowly away. Tomas left us to check the ridge trail.

As we waited, we could see the growing light of Sunrise but not the sun itself. That was behind the ridge that formed the edges of the Hole.

"I think it's a crater," said Kapi. "This hole and the five sisters are all craters."

"Five sisters?"

"A chain of five lakes along the Safarmo Road."

"Why Anklebiter?"

"Juvenile notosuchians. The Albert Fields isn't just home to albertosaurus. The Fields are like the Serengeti but much larger. The big non-migrating herbivores live there: iguanodons, maiasaurs—"

"The animals Skye wiped out."

Kapi gave me a strained glance. "Notosuchians roam it as well. If the alberts are the lions, the notosuchians are the leopards. The notosuchians breed and lay their eggs here. When the eggs hatch, the juveniles remain here to catch fish until they get too big. Then, they migrate down to the Fields. The little guys bite first and run second—Anklebiter Hole." He looked around. "I haven't seen Sam for a couple of sleeps."

"She's regrouping after her last attempt."

"That wasn't Sam's doing."

"Sam comes by and argues with you. She leaves. A couple of weeks later we're attacked by deinos trying to get to you. That's a pretty strong correlation."

Kapi shook his head. "When Skye was at war, Sam was queen of the forest. I don't think deinos suffer queens for long. Matriarchs, sure—that's the way they're built. But a queen over all of the families and clans is something different. I think it fell apart as soon as the war was over. I'm pretty sure the two deinos that came with her to the longhouse were her kits. I'm *certain* the deinos that attacked us were not." Kapi pursed his lips, thinking. "Besides, she's had lots of chance to kill me. She hasn't."

It was my turn to think. "There was something stylized in the attack. I kept getting this sense of ritual. Maybe she was waiting for that."

"Ritual." Kapi fell silent. "After all this time, I know nothing about deinos. Nothing of substance."

Tomas Not-Ian joined us at the edge of the lake. "Up that way," he said pointing past the falls. "Over the ridge and up the ridge trail and then down the switchbacks. That takes us to the Fields. Then it's a short walk to the road. We walk the road the rest of the way. Two sleeps to cross the ridge. Four more to the road. Inside estimate, five sleeps until Rusalka City. Outside estimate, two weeks."

At one moment, I found it hard to look at Tomas and not see Ian. At another, I would find it hard to look at Tomas and see Ian at all. It was like I was watching him appear and disappear, a virtual quantum Ian coming into existence and self-annihilating into destruction. Was Ian dead or not? Watching Tomas I couldn't be sure.

Kapi had talked about people coming back—people's memories coming back to a different form. Tomas was the same form but with a different person inside. It came to me that this might mean Ian was dead. Really dead. Why animate his form without his spirit? I had this sudden vision of hundreds of marshals across Venus. Each one looking like Ian. Each one not Ian at all. Each an indicator that Ian—my Ian—was well and truly dead.

Wait, I told myself. Perhaps this was how Ian kept himself hidden. An egg among other eggs. A nail among other nails. An Elvis among Elvis impersonators. For a moment I had hope.

But then I remembered Ian. Remembered who he was. How he had always been. Tomas knew I had come down. That meant it had become common knowledge—which meant that, if Ian was alive, he would have heard it, too. Nothing would have kept him from finding me.

Either he was dead or he had deadened himself to me.

I tried to keep the idea that nothing on Venus seemed permanent—death included. Percy could bring him back. But I found I could not hold onto that hope. Something in me refused it. I shook my head. Percy *must* bring him back.

Instead, the dark sense I always had of *something terrible has happened to Ian* changed to a dark and permanent loss, hard, cold, and congealed inside me. I had always carried it with the idea that someday it would ease. Now that sorrow felt unending, as heavy and intransigent as a tumor.

"Let's go." I had to find other things to do.

oOo

We watched the Albert Fields from the top of Anklebiter Ridge.

This wasn't from choice.

Different animal species accommodated the long Venus days and nights in different ways. Some did the equivalent of hibernation during the night to be active during the day. Some did the reverse. When they were active they fed, digested, fed again. Some—like humans or deinos—were continuously active, stopping at regular intervals for sleep or its equivalent.

Skye hadn't touched the Albert Fields. I realized looking down on the plains how barren the Deino Forest had been. We had seen small animals and birds. But the Fields were *stuffed* with life as far as I could see.

I kept watch with my binoculars.

From the Ridge, we could see tens of kilometers. Herds of parasaurolophii clustered around a lake, mingling with a herd of hadrosaurs that were feeding *in* the lake. I saw a group of four albertosaurs watching them. Iguanodons clustered around the edge of a small wood, working on the small brush—I stopped and looked closer. It was a grove of ficus. I'd seen those on Earth: a grove consisting of a single tree, branches proceeding horizontally, but also dropping vertical shoots every few meters. The iguanodons grazed in and out of the resulting wood.

Birds were *everywhere.* I had no idea what kinds they were but thought of them by what they resembled: herons, blackbirds, hawks, eagles. They mingled with pteranodons—for which I had no name—ranging as broadly in size and type as the birds. High above us, I saw giant ten-meter animals soaring east with magnificent purpose. Closer, flocks tiny sharp-jawed rinkies were flying everywhere.

In a pond just a few hundred meters away, small filter-feeding dinosaurs swished their fluorescent green and red frilled heads in the shallow water, looking like a cross between a spoonbill and a dragon. Packs of little therapods ran together like wolves or hyenas.

Which was, of course, the problem.

Many had just *awakened*. Some herbivores, like the apatosaurs, ate by the Lesser Lights. These others had fed, but had not had the opportunity to eat their fill until now. Others stopped completely overnight and were eating for the first time in months. Therapods followed similar patterns and those that hadn't eaten overnight woke up *hungry*. The smaller predators were like humans, awake all night but, come Sunrise, they had daylight competition perfectly willing to eat *them* instead of preferred herbivore flesh. Everybody was angry, irritated, and belligerent.

And big. Really, really big.

So we camped on the ridge where the biggest animals couldn't get to us. Kapi and I slept in a tent Pranavi had given us. Tomas preferred the open. We weren't alone. Small therapods and omnivores made their homes in the nooks and crannies of the rocks. They lived on moss and insects. Until we left, we lived on them.

I found myself watching one family of alberts—remembering this was the species that killed Ian.

Both male and female were bare-skinned and brown with a green feather band that ran along their spines. The males' feathers began in a startling yellow head crest that came erect a meter high when they were displaying to the female or each other. Mostly, it stayed folded on their heads—which was necessary for them to hunt. Whenever one displayed to another, every herbivore in sight scattered. Maybe, the alberts were using the displays to coordinate hunting and the prey understood.

Most of the time this family group rested on a low hill, their attention wandering from this herd to that herd, never seeming to take much interest. Always, there were a few dromaeosaurs hovering around them like remoras surrounding a shark.

On the second sleep, two of them were gone. The remaining two females lay there clothed in elaborate disinterest. I looked where they were pointedly not looking and sure enough, the two males were crouched behind a low ridge, only their heads peeking over. They were watching the hadrosaurs eating at the edge of the lake.

The alberts' heads were completely still but their hips and tails twitched, leaning to one side, then the other, finding better purchase with left foot, then right foot.

Then they were sailing over the ridge in a flat leap, hitting the ground running, mouths agape, attention centered on a single hadrosaur that had wandered too far from the group. They came at it from two directions, angled to push it further from the group. As it started to run, the other hadrosaurs scattered away from it like a flock of startled birds.

The left albert swung in towards it. The right one held back to cut off a side escape. The hadrosaur ran straight towards the two resting female alberts. They shifted into a crouch—never moving their heads until they sprang forward into its path.

The hadrosaur sat back on its haunches, looking frantically for escape. It tried to lunge between the four alberts but before it could get its start the albert that had held back leaped forward, falling with all its weight on the hadrosaur's back, its jaws on its neck.

The hadrosaur crashed down, the albert stepping off easily as it hit the ground without ever letting go of the hadrosaur's neck. The albert held its position while the others tore at it until the hadrosaur stopped moving. Then, it joined the other alberts feeding. The dromaeosaurs sat in a row, waiting their turn.

I looked away across the plains. This wasn't the only kill. Another clutch of alberts had brought down an iguanodon to the west and I saw a pack of low-bodied, heavily armored animals stalking along one of the lakes.

"Baurusuchus." Kapi startled me.

"Don't sneak up on me like that. Especially when I'm watching big animals hunt."

"Sorry." Kapi nodded. "South in the pampas baurusuchus hunt by themselves. Here, they band together in packs. Probably to compete with the therapods."

"When do things calm down?"

"They're calming already," said Tomas from my other side.

"Don't *do* that!"

"Sorry." Tomas grinned and looked like Ian at sixteen after his first date. At least Kapi had the decency to appear contrite.

Tomas continued: "Things are quieter than they were at Sunrise. Most of the solitary hunters and packs have made a kill." He pointed to the alberts with the hadrosaur. "That should last them a week." He pointed to the alberts with the iguanodon. "That should last at least a couple of sleeps. The notosuchians haven't made a kill yet but they will or they'll go after fish. That pack never leaves the lake this time of day. Around Noon, if this is the right day for it, they'll come up here and lay eggs by the Hole. Wouldn't be safe for us then but we'll be long gone. Those that haven't made a kill are getting weak. It's complete daylight now and they're at full activity on an empty stomach. We're going to see a lot of dead therapods covered in dromaeosaurs over the next few sleeps." He watched the horizon a moment. "There's a village a few sleeps down the road—Telsa. They have water and food. It's about halfway to Rusalka."

I had been thinking that I had been seeing Ian's world. But that idea was based on the idea that Ian was still alive. I was convinced now he died in Rusalka and never got a chance to see this. He was dead minutes after the outer wall fell.

It came to me that I wasn't seeing Ian's world. I was seeing the world *for* him.

oOo

We started descending two sleeps later when Tomas decided it was safe enough. Mind you, *I* couldn't see any difference. Hunters were hunting. Prey were getting killed. I couldn't see any decrease but apparently, *he* could.

Once we were down, there was a kind of a trail along the bottom of the ridge but still safely above the Fields for obvious reasons. Why go down into prey territory before you have to? It was studded with rocks sharp enough I felt them through Alisi's boots. I could see some wearing on the rocks and there were cairns at regular intervals. Most of the grass was low—cropped by iguanodons and the like. Some fields next to the lakes were tall marshlands. I could see a vast flock of—starlings? Sparrows? What were the Cretaceous equivalent?—dancing in a murmuration.

Oh, I hoped Ian saw some of this.

From there the trail was a dirt track through short-cropped grass. There were no herbivores near us though birds flew over me and landed in small groups, digging at unseen seeds or insects in the ground. Sometimes a group of rinkies flew over. When they landed, they crawled, batlike, on the ground, searching for any small animals they could not find on the wing.

I remembered Kapi's curiosity about whether the birds or the flying reptiles would win out. Watching the rinkies clumsily plod over the grass, it seemed to me Venus would belong to the birds.

A couple of "starlings" seemed to think the same way and menaced one of the rinkies. The rinkie watched it a moment then suddenly sprang, grabbing the bird's head in its jaws and deftly twisting it. The bird was dead in an instant and the "starlings" flew away.

The other rinkies approached as the first one munched on the head. Then, on some signal I didn't see, they started pulling at the wings and feet, tearing at the breast. They left the original rinkie to eat the head.

I looked up.

Kapi was watching them. "What do you know? No end of surprises on Venus."

oOo

The trail joined the road after a couple of kilometers. I was beginning to understand how road infrastructure worked on Venus. Without domesticated animals, roads had to follow the natural geology of the land. Where there was hard clay, the road followed the clay. Where there was only grass, the road was a dirt track. The path of the road was marked by cairns. Some parts of the road were flat rock and held no impression. Only the cairns showed us where to go.

The weather stayed clear. According to Tomas, this part of the Fields didn't get rain until later in the Morning. Just as well. Within hours after reaching the road, both Tomas and Kapi began to shed. I laughed as they scratched and rubbed and swore and left a trail of matted fur on the road behind us. Beneath the fur they were pale. Quite a difference from Kapi's blackness when night had fallen.

The Safarmo Road didn't have longhouses and wells like the Skye Road—a part of Skye's attempt at civilization I had appreciated. There were pools and we still had a pot or two from Watertown to boil the water and skins to carry it. We stopped at regular intervals for sleep. That was all right as long as the road ran over rock or clay or short grass—anywhere I could see and track the animals. I had this continuing fear we would be killed in our sleep in broad daylight.

Kapi stayed with me. Tomas ranged around us, bringing back an infant iguanodon or some fish for us to eat. Usually, we could see him on a hill or in the valley. He did not seem to fear any of the animals.

"Yes," said Kapi when I pointed that out. "Marshals have some kind of special dispensation. Or maybe the animals figure he's too much to handle."

"Is he?"

Kapi shrugged. "We're a lot stronger here than we were on Earth. We can generally take care of ourselves. I heard Ian gave an albert a serious fight with his bare hands. Marshals are stronger yet—though I don't know how obvious that is to an albertosaurus."

Hills began to rise as we walked northwest. Marshes grew in the slopes between. The road cycled around them—giving the marshes a wide berth and choosing the bare rock hills.

I did not feel we were actually moving towards Rusalka, but as it slowly approached I thought about Ian more and more. Little memories—when he entered middle school. He had trouble there. Ian was kind and middle-school does not encourage kindness. Grayson Middle School had an anti-bully policy but that just meant the bullies went underground. I could see him handling it—that is, I saw the bruises, scratches, and determination on his face. It went on for a year and then suddenly stopped. He would never tell me what happened but there was a hardness mixed with the kindness after that.

Later memories: when Ian brought Pat Fenriss home from college and I thought this was going to be my daughter-in-law for sure. I would be a grandmother. I remembered his secret smiles and laughing at something joyful and private. Four years they were together and then, he came home and they weren't. Ian would only say it didn't work out. Followed by the sad stare and grim mouth of something equally secret and private.

Always there was my own feeling of *something terrible*. Something I had to protect Ian from, even when there was nothing I could do to protect him. I had that feeling, still, though it was frayed and disintegrating. After all, if Ian was dead what could I possibly protect him from?

Percy had to give him back to me. She *had* to.

We rounded a hill and looked down into a valley. In this valley, the marsh was piled on one side and there was a bare grass hillside on the other. The cairn pulled the road towards the edge of the marsh below a knobby bluff.

Tomas led us forward. Unease kept growing in me as we walked towards the marsh. Why did all of the other cairns avoid the marsh grass, then come near this one? Why avoid the marsh grass at all? Maybe the tall grass hid large predators. Baurusuchuii had prowled around the lakes. Perhaps they frequented the marshes as well. What made this marsh different?

I couldn't see past the tall grass. I looked above and scanned the bluff. I didn't see anything strange. Just rocks. I looked again—there was something odd about the rocks. I realized then it was two alberts looking over. Waiting for us to walk below them.

I checked the range. Well within what I could reach with my gun in pistol mode. "Explosive rounds," I said to it. "Eight-centimeter penetration."

"What?" said Tomas. He half-turned.

I sighted on the first head. The orange laser turned to green and I fired. *Bang!* Moved to the next head. Orange to green. *Bang!*

The left head didn't move but the right one twitched up and fell.

"What did you do?" said Tomas. "*What did you do?*"

"Killed those that killed my son." I lowered my gun. "Before they had a chance to do the same to me."

Tomas turned from me and ran towards the bluff. "Lucy!" he cried. "Sunwalker!"

He skirted the marsh and leaped to the top of the bluff. One head slid down out of sight.

Kapi stopped. He looked at the bluff and then at me. "How did you see them?"

I shrugged. "I watched two alberts hunt in the valley exactly the same way."

"You do remember we killed and burned the albert that killed Ian."

"So?"

"Ah." Kapi looked back towards the bluff. "He knew them."

"So it would seem."

Tomas stalked back from the bluff. "You killed them."

"They were going to kill us."

"No," he said as he approached us. He pulled out a knife and threw it at Kapi. "They were only going to kill *him!*"

Kapi must have been ready for him. He turned and the knife plunged into his right upper arm. He cried out and pulled out his own knife and held it clumsily with his left hand. His right arm flopped uselessly.

I stood in front of Kapi. "No."

Tomas pulled me to one side without any effort. I tumbled down. He brushed Kapi's knife away and kicked his right knee. Kapi shrieked. Then, Tomas took Kapi by the throat.

"Geneva rounds," I said. Orange to green. I held the gun on Tomas. "Stop! I'll kill you."

He put Kapi between us. Kapi choked and hammered at him. Tomas ignored him.

"It won't matter," I shouted at him. I wanted him to hear me. I wanted this faint echo of Ian to live. "You're autotargeted. I could fire it over your head and the bullet would still find you."

Tomas stopped. "He has to die."

"Why?"

"*He's* the one they're focused on. He led the war. The deinos will never be satisfied until the one they hold responsible is dead."

"He didn't run Skye."

"They don't *care* who ran Skye. They care who was in charge of the *war*. It was Sam on the deino side and Kapi on the human side. *He's* responsible."

"Anyone can be redeemed."

"Redemption doesn't matter. *He's* the one they need dead. Until he's dead it isn't over." He pointed his thumb on his chest. "I was in charge—from Deino Forest to the Western Albert Fields. This happened on *my* watch. I couldn't stop it then but I'm going to stop it *now*."

"I will shoot."

"You won't." He spat the words. "I'm your son, remember?"

"Right now, my son is dead." I fired.

Chapter 3.8: Safarmo Road

I couldn't see the rounds but I heard the whistle and the *thunk* when they hit. The force pushed Tomas forward enough that Kapi was able to wrench out of that grip.

Tomas fell to the ground, groaning.

Kapi found his staff. He dragged it back to Tomas and hammered at his head, at his face. Tomas stopped moving. Kapi kept hammering.

"Stop it." I grabbed his good arm.

Kapi ignored me. He looked around the ground and found his knife. He rolled Tomas onto his back and raised it.

"Do that and I'll shoot *you*." I pointed the gun at him. Orange to green.

Kapi looked up. "He blames me for what happened in Skye. Hell, he's right. Those deinos that attacked back in the forest were after *me*. Maybe it won't stop until I'm dead."

"Are you ready to die?"

"Hell, no." He held up his knife and pointed at Tomas. "It doesn't matter. He'll follow us. This isn't over until *he* is."

"He's in no condition to follow us."

Kapi shook his head. "You don't know marshals. Everybody heals fast here but marshals are different. If I stab his brain and pith him like a frog it might slow him down for a month."

"Leave him." I put away the gun and came over and grabbed his good arm.

Kapi wavered, then sheathed his knife. "This is a mistake. A *deadly* mistake."

"I'll take my chances."

I bound up Kapi's wound and we started hobbling away. Kapi kept looking back. Tomas didn't move.

oOo

"Tomas said there was a village not far from here."

"Telsa. I remember it."

He couldn't take a step without pain. I was tall enough that I could grab him over his back and under the shoulder on his other side. At first, I tried holding him from the side with the broken knee. Though that meant he could use me as a support against his good leg, it jostled his knee and he couldn't use the staff with his injured arm. We switched to the other side. It pulled on his shoulder but he could help the broken knee with his staff. When that hurt too much we switched again.

"Geneva round?" he asked.

"Penetrates a centimeter and then explodes to something the size of a tennis ball. Shocks the organs."

"Let me guess. Geneva convention?"

"Yeah." I snorted. "I wish I had thought to have Alisi make me sticky balls. Little tarry spheres like putty but with an incredibly strong adhesive. You grab one to take it off and can't let go. Now you can't move your hand. You try the other hand. It's stuck. There's one on your knee and you fall down. Now you can't get up. They used them for crowd control."

Kapi chuckled. "I would have liked to see that. Instead, I broke his skull. Whatever works."

Kapi's size made it easier to help him but we weren't able to cover more than a few kilometers before we had to rest.

Here the road was on a slight rise so we could look down on the plain. I suggested we rest beneath a wide tree by the road. Kapi spent a few minutes watching it before he pronounced it safe. "Some therapods take to trees like they were birds." He didn't elaborate.

When we sat down I checked his dressing. "I should make a splint for that." I pointed at his knee.

"Yeah. That's a good idea."

I found a branch and tied it with some rope I had in my pack, making his knee straight. I didn't know if that was the right way to handle a broken knee but at least he'd be able to put a little weight on it.

I mulled over Tomas. "He was looking for you. Not me."

"I got that."

"How long were you in Watertown before you met me?"

"A bit. I was going to leave after a week or so—I figured Sam would tire of waiting. But Tamara asked me to stay."

I thought about that. "Pranavi said Tomas was the marshal from Diana's Pancake to the Albert Fields. Did that include Big Diana?"

"No."

"Do marshals care about jurisdiction?"

Kapi spread his hands. "Who knows? They *talk* about it."

"Say they do. That means you weren't in Tomas' jurisdiction until you were in Watertown. Tamara asked you to stay."

Kapi looked thoughtful. "You think Tomas asked her to keep me there next time I showed up?"

"Maybe."

"Then you showed up and I went with you."

I nodded. "She wanted you to stay long enough to turn over to Tomas. But we left and Tomas had to come looking for us."

"Why didn't he just kill you or have the deinos kill you later in the apato camp?"

Kapi scratched his cheek. "Pranavi would have eaten him alive. Even a marshal would think twice about getting on her bad side. The gun probably helped."

I nodded towards Kapi. "He saw the flashbangs and worried I might have something really lethal. Well, he was right about that. Why didn't he take it away?"

"You were Pranavi's *guest*. She takes such things seriously. Pranavi would have skinned him alive, literally. She would have had her bucks tie him down and flense him."

"Then why wait for the alberts?"

Kapi rubbed his face. "I don't know. Maybe he was being cautious because of the gun. Or not—he's never seen one. He doesn't know what they can do. Maybe he just didn't want to offend you—you're Ian's mother, after all. Probably a favorite of Percy's. If something bad happens to you it reflects badly on him."

"He knows what the gun can do now."

"That did cross my mind." Kapi laboriously got to his feet. "The marshal is *not* dead. He is *not* incapacitated. He will follow us. I'm going to keep moving at least as far as Telsa." He leaned against the tree and looked around. "If I'm going to die, I want it to be indoors."

"Why the hell would Percy create an unstoppable monster that looks like my son?"

"'Mama likes to tinker.'"

oOo

Clouds rolled in from the west and gave us a little respite from the sun. Relief was short-lived. The clouds darkened and a warm rain began to fall.

At first, it was only light rain but that changed into a downpour. We could barely see. The road grew muddy and treacherous. Twice we fell down. Each time Kapi gave a hissed shriek.

Something struck me in the back of the head and I fell to my knees. Kapi fell beside me. I felt him being dragged away. I grabbed at his leg—Kapi screamed. It was the bad leg.

I looked up. Tomas glanced back at me. His face was a ruin: nose a bloody pulp, teeth missing, one eye closed. His head looked bent.

"No!" I grabbed the other leg and pulled.

Tomas backhanded me. A sharp crack against my cheek that made the world shake in and out of focus like the vibrations of a bell.

"Don't you *understand?* He's got to die. It's for the good of everyone."

An animal charged out of the rain and knocked Tomas tumbling over the ground.

Sam stood between Tomas and Kapi, roaring.

Tomas got to his feet. He signed to her. *He must die. You know this.*

Sam gave him back the flower sign.

"Okay," Tomas said. He circled Sam, shot in and struck her jaw, and then back again so fast I barely saw it.

Sam staggered back. She sprang at him.

Tomas sidestepped her and brought down both fists on her back. Sam went down. Tomas brought up his hand for what I knew would be a killing blow.

"Explosive rounds. Four centimeters." I pointed the gun at him. Orange to green.

Tomas stopped and looked at me. "He has to *die,*" Tomas pleaded.

Sam slashed at him from the ground. Tomas leaped to one side, rolled to get Sam between me and Kapi. Tomas reached for him. I pulled the trigger. *Bang! Pop.*

Tomas sagged onto the ground, motionless.

Kapi sat up. "Explosive round?"

"Detonates at a predetermined depth. It killed the two alberts. It ought to serve for him."

"Yeah." Kapi rubbed his jaw. "It ought to."

There was only the sound of the rain.

Sam worked her way to her feet. *I hurt everywhere.*

"Yeah." Kapi reached over and patted her back. *Me, too.*

"How far to Telsa?" I asked.

"Just a couple of kilometers."

I nodded. "Let's go."

Kapi looked at Tomas' body. "If he comes to life and chases after us?"

I shook my head. "If he lives after that he deserves a shot at us."

Chapter 3.9: Telsa

It turned out that soaking wet and injured people dragging themselves into town was a common event in Telsa. Kapi and I were bandaged and accommodations found for us. Sam had accepted medical care but left the compound as soon as she could. I suppose the idea of the only deino being cooped up in a human settlement brought bad memories. We stayed. We were told people often waited out the early Morning here before they attempted the last stretch of the Safarmo Road into Rusalka. Telsa was happy to oblige. We sat, aching and anxious, resting in the courtyard next to the ubiquitous village garden.

The gates opened and the Safarmo-to-Rusalka Express entered.

The Express consisted of several wagons drawn by teams of human beings guarded by men armed with spears and arrows. The guards' stance was so familiar I half expected to see Clayton or Das in the group. The wagons were painted a gaudy red and green and the guards had matching uniforms. There were goods on the wagons and *passengers*.

"Slaves?" I asked Kapi, pointing at the teams.

"God, I hope we haven't fallen that far." He called out to one of the guards. "Any openings on the pull teams?"

The guard looked at Kapi. "No. There's a waiting list."

"It pays well?"

"No one pays better than the Express."

Kapi turned back to me. "There you have it. I think I read somewhere the rowers in the roman ships were also highly paid professionals. Did they have unions back then?"

"Shut up."

"You have no interest in history."

oOo

We spent a week in Telsa just healing. *And* waiting for Tomas to suddenly show up and have a go at us again. Kapi refused to believe he was dead. "I've seen them walk away from worse," he said.

Tomas didn't show up.

We stayed at the traveler's hostel. As long as we did our share of the chores, worked in the garden, and joined the regular hunting teams, they'd feed us. Neither of us was good hunter material but we could clean game and wash and weed so they decided to let us stay, regardless. Being Pauline Bones didn't hurt. Like everywhere else, I found a fairly even split between those who believed that Ian had been a necessary evil violating their rights by abducting them for the right reason and an *unnecessary* evil violating their rights out of pure spite. It amazed me that this argument could keep going after all this time. On the other hand, the battles over Northern Ireland and the Middle East were only partially managed even back on Earth. Both had their roots hundreds of years in the past. Regardless, Ian had celebrity status and some of it rubbed off on me.

The Express built an open-air market next to the garden. Red and green rugs served as tables. Spices. Exotic foods. Nails. Tools. Clothing. I found out that there were farms near Telsa as people brought in corn, flour, and dried apples—so many apples I began to wonder if Johnny Appleseed had originated on Venus. And liquor. Kapi sampled here and there and pronounced the quality acceptable.

I wondered where lumber came from. I asked and found that large-scale transport—like lumber—was carried on huge carts drawn by sauropods. I began to realize how Pranavi's tribe had been struggling. Without the villages in the Deino Forest, Pranavi's tribe had no one to trade with. When they did reach a village, they would have nothing to transport and therefore nothing to trade except the cleared land and piles of fertilizer.

Kapi fell silent as he healed. Finally, my impatience got the better of me.

We were working in the garden. I pulled up a weed and piled it to one side. "What's bothering you?"

"Excuse me?"

"You haven't said a damned thing for sleeps. When you're not working, you're sitting and staring into space. What's going on?"

"I've been thinking about my cousin. What I'll say to her after all this time. Can't a man have his own thoughts?"

I stared at him. The echo of his words rang down the years until I remembered Martin. "Oh, God," I laughed. "We're acting like an old married couple."

Kapi grinned at me. "All of the hardships and none of the benefits."

Benefits. I considered it. Martin had been dead to me for nearly three hundred years and three thousand years dead in any real sense. Longing for Ian made sense as long as I thought Ian was alive and that was now questionable. But I *knew* Martin was dead. He had been dead most of my life.

I hadn't been a nun. Back on Earth, there had been a couple of moments here and there. While I could never say I was holding a torch for Martin, I didn't have much inclination, either. On Poa, there had been the four of us: Alisi, Shana, Davi, and me. Sometimes there had been sex. But never very much. Again, I didn't have much inclination.

Always the job, I thought. Pulling together the orbiter population back on Earth and getting the orbiters up and running here. Once I'd done that I felt at loose ends—one of the many reasons I had jumped at the chance to come down here: escape and Ian.

I looked at Kapi. Did I want this man?

I put my hand on his good knee and left it there. Bone surrounded by hard muscle. His skin had darkened since Sunrise to a deep black. The transition had happened so slowly I had barely registered it. Neocortex still kept throwing up different images: Pygmies. Thin aborigines. Monkeys. We never get rid of the lessons of our childhood. We just accrete more acceptable attitudes and responses on top of them. The trick is to recognize that, I suppose. To look past our early upbringing.

I kneaded the muscle. It felt warm.

He looked at it, then back at me. "Is that intended to be an erotic caress?"

"It's been a long time. Cut me some slack." I tilted my head. "How long has it been for you?"

Kapi looked marvelously uncomfortable. "I couldn't say."

"That is not something I have ever heard a man say truthfully." I pulled my hand back. "Wait. I'm sorry. You're not interested."

"I *am* interested. It's been... well, not since I left my wife in Pretoria." He shook his head. "I mean after that it didn't seem like I should enjoy myself doing that anymore."

I stared at him. *Okay.* "What happened to her?"

Kapi looked up at the sky. "She's married again. Still in Pretoria. A grandmother squared from what I hear. I don't *think* she spits anymore when my name is mentioned, but that only stopped when she had her second grandchild." He sighed.

I put my hand back. It felt good to leave it there. I rubbed his thigh.

Kapi wouldn't look at me. "There's a private room back at the hostel." Then, he turned to me. "My knee still hurts."

"I'll be careful."

oOo

There are certain *logistics* to managing a new love. I used this word to myself deliberately. Venus was a new place. A new life—which, hopefully, wouldn't be cut too short by running out of medications. I had some cautious optimism that Percy would help me with that. If I was going to live here—and that was a given one way or the other since I had no way back to Poa—I needed to be open. Vulnerable. I very much liked Kapi. I certainly would have put my life on the line for him. While it did not feel the same as what I'd had with Martin, that seemed a stupid comparison. Martin was so long ago I was barely the same person.

Opening myself to Kapi seemed to help other things. The broken, twisted darkness that always seemed to pull at me eased. It did not leave—that little tumor of mine might never leave—but it seemed to be less fundamental. Less central. The change might not be the result of love but if it wasn't I had no real idea of what love was.

Percy had kept to the straight human model of genitals so there was no problem there. It was a place where Kapi was wonderfully, and thankfully, fully human. That Percy had kept this fundamental compatibility was so comforting that when I saw Kapi naked for the first time I almost wept. My primitive hindbrain never said *monkey* again.

But there were logistics.

Kapi was enormously stronger than I was, so he had to be careful. He was also much smaller than me, with a broken knee, so *I* had to be careful. I wondered what it would be like to have sex with someone covered with fur. Scratchy? Luxurious? Would it trigger revulsion or perverse attraction? I had no idea. Even holding his hand as we walked didn't work. Kapi was too much shorter than I was and his arms were too long. The differences between us that had been erased by the journey now returned.

The logistics of conversation changed. He kept asking me about Martin, Ian, and those on Poa.

I, on the other hand, kept after him about Chitra. It's amazing how you feel suddenly empowered by sex. Before, Ian and Martin weren't Kapi's business. Now they were. Before, Chitra was not my business. Now she was.

Not to say any of this was *easy*. He tried to keep Chitra private and I tried to keep Ian and Martin away from him. We had both been independent people for far too long to surrender sovereignty without a fight. A few sleeps and good sex wasn't enough oil on the troubled waters to make a damn bit of difference.

Now we had even more reasons to proceed to Rusalka and get out of Telsa. Whatever we were doing with each other, living together in a public hostel in a small town wasn't the right place to do it.

It was Kapi's idea to approach the Express. They were getting to leave. Telsa was fifty kilometers from Rusalka. There were smaller towns between here and there but they were only short stops. The Express planned to be in Rusalka within a week.

They took me on as a guard. Kapi joined one of the pull teams. Apparently, the waiting list wasn't as long as they thought.oOo It was a week of relative boredom. There were no human bandits to speak of. But we did have to warn off some roving bands of dromaeosaurs. Curiously, when the little theropods weren't following alberts around they formed large groups of fifty or more. They would have swarmed us more than once but whenever they approached we yelled at them and banged pots. This seemed to make them rethink their intentions.

Pull teams were made up mostly of families with a few stray males or females filling them out. Kapi's knee was still sore, so they put him on the lightest wagon pulling alongside the children. He kept them entertained with songs and stories. After a couple of sleeps, he was strong enough to join the adult teams and the children missed him.

I kept my gun handy and set it to flashbangs. I wanted to avoid killing anything else.

oOo

I walked along the ridge overlooking the road, keeping watch. We were only a sleep away from the outskirts of Rusalka. Alberts didn't come this close to the city. Only the dromaeosaur bands and iguanodon herds were much of a threat. I hadn't seen dromaeosaurs for two sleeps and the iguanodons were over a kilometer away, chowing down on grass next to a marsh. There was nothing to worry about.

"Mrs. Bones," came a voice.

"Exploding rounds, 3 centimeters," I said as I whirled around, gun out. Orange to green.

Tomas was sitting in a low wash, a green blanket over his shoulders. He waved his hand. "Don't shoot," he said in a soft voice.

"I'm glad you're alive."

"It was touch and go."

He didn't look good. The side of his face was infected and dripped a yellowish fluid. What I could see beneath the blanket looked broken and twisted—was that the effect of healing around the internal explosions of the round? Or something else?

"I won't let you kill Kapi," I said. I aimed at his head. "Autotargeting off." I might miss without autotargeting but if I figured if I hit him in the head it would take a while to rebuild his brain.

"You've made that clear." He looked at me listlessly.

"Are you here to tell me that?"

"I have been told to tell you I'll leave you alone." He shook his head. "You must understand I was trying to create a new peace." He gave me a level stare. "You're sleeping with a mass murderer."

"No one is denied a shot at redemption," I said. I did not lower my gun. "Even the Warlord of Skye."

"As you say." He levered himself up to standing. He looked at me and the gun for a long time. He nodded. "Go in peace."

With that, he turned and walked away.

Chapter 3.10: Rusalka City

Rusalka City occupied a peninsula that jutted out into the Rusalka Sea. A finger ridge of the Nuahine came down and made a spine of the peninsula's north side and eased its way down to the water. As we approached from the south, the ridge took form. I could see it was not made solely of rock but great standing trees. I had seen tall trees in the Deino Forest, but nothing could have prepared me for these.

"Sequoias," said Kapi. "Takes everybody by surprise the first time."

"*Sequoias?* You're serious? My son liked sequoias. They were big—a hundred meters, maybe more. *Those* things are nearly twice that."

"'Mama likes—'"

"'—to tinker.' I know." I looked closer. "Are there... *buildings* in the trees?"

"Not exactly." Kapi drew a finger across the line of trees. "See the scaffolding? That's a bridge. There are structures in the trees but not really buildings. The Sequoia People live there."

"The Sequoia People," I repeated dumbly.

"Yes." Kapi nodded. "The trees go right through the Rusalka Wall down to near the coast. But the- Sequoia People don't like living near the wall."

"Why not?"

Kapi shrugged. "There are a lot of wild people on Venus. I think the Sequoia People are the wildest of all."

"Do they take visitors?"

Kapi watched me for a moment. "We can leave the Express if you like."

To see the people who lived in trees. How could I pass that by?

But no. I had business with Percy. After all this, I wanted to delay no longer.

"Maybe later," I said. I pulled my eyes away from the trees. "Maybe after we're done in Rusalka."

"My dear Mrs. Bones. Are you inviting me on a journey?"

I looked at him with a slow smile. "Are you interested?"

"I'd have to check my calendar for the next few years, but I think I'm free."

I took his hand. I could still feel the hurt and pain. The wee little tumor of sorrow would never really go away. But there were compensations.

oOo

The ridge and the trees protected Rusalka from the north and the Rusalka Sea protected it from the south. The Rusalka Wall stretched from the north ridge south to the sea. I remembered my first sight of Watertown: a city defined by walls. I decided I was wrong. Walls did not define a Venusian city or town. Rather, it was defined by the surrounding environment requiring those walls.

The gate was good sized—two carts in width and a hundred meters away from its mate. We waited our turn with the rest of the Express. There was a tax levied on the entrance and I saw ebony tokens being exchanged. Kapi explained to me that money was local to Rusalka, so the Express traded goods for tokens that they passed out to the regular employees.

Kapi and I were working for our passage and received nothing but they gave us our tax just the same.

Some portion of those coins went back to pay the import tax. I looked at the coin: copper with waves of water on one side and a tree on the other. We moved closer to the gate, waiting for each wagon to be inspected.

I asked Kapi: "What happens to the coins on the way out?"

Kapi shrugged. "This is all since I lived here. But Pretoria has something similar. The coins are useless outside the city so I'm guessing everybody spends what they can before they leave." He sighed. "A planned economy. Eventually, we'll have letters of credit between the city-states. Universal exchange. Arbitrage. Macro-economies. But not today." He chuckled and smiled at me. "In Skye we were socialists. Long live the revolution, comrade!"

"Just like Mama, people like to tinker until they make it worse."

Kapi laughed out loud.

Eventually, we made it through the gate. The outer wall funneled everyone through to a road that weaved through a long collection of fields and gardens to a low, inner wall. These were real fields and not just gardens. One single crop for a hectare then another. Some were being harvested. Others were being cultivated. One bare hectare was being plowed: a pull-team of four people drawing a wooden plow behind them. The ridge was bare of trees here and faded down to the flat ground. There were strong wooden fences along the road and men on stools with spears to make sure the fences were respected.

As we passed through the inner gate, Kapi fretted: "I don't even know where she lives."

I patted his shoulder. There was a kiosk next to the gate. "We'll ask."

The kiosk had a map. A nice public servant named Gerard knew where Chitra Majhi lived and gave us directions.

Row buildings walled the main boulevard. These were occupied by shops and restaurants, ending in a big open-air market. The Express was already setting up. We crossed through the market and continued down the boulevard to Hayes Road.

Hayes Road was manufacturing: blacksmith shops and woodworkers. Weavers and wheelwrights. This gradually faded into—surprise—row houses. Each apartment in the row had a little front yard bracketed on each side by some kind of small wall: stone, shrubs, a grape arbor, a wooden fence. The houses on Hayes Road stopped, but the road continued towards the rocks and the sea. Chitra's house was the last.

Sam was waiting for us.

She rose to her feet. *Glad to see you*. (See. You. Two opening hands indicating joy.)

Kapi signed the same back to her.

She looked at me and signed *Bone.*

I made the sign of the falling hand back at her. *Sam.*

"Do you want me to walk up there with you?" I asked Kapi.

Kapi looked at me and Sam. "I guess this is more moral support than I deserve."

"Self-pity is unattractive."

Sam settled down to wait on the road. Kapi and I walked up the steps. The front door was tied open and the doorway covered with cloth. Kapi knocked on the wall.

A man leaned out. "Yes?" he said. Then he saw Kapi.

"Kapi?" he asked and stepped out. He took Kapi's shoulders and looked at him. "*Kapi!*" And hugged him.

Kapi tentatively hugged him back.

"This is going to make Chitra very happy!"

Freder stepped aside and waved us in. The rooms had a rough-sawn look I was coming to recognize—the result of limited machines and unassisted humans. The front room had chairs and I could see into the kitchen. Beyond that was hidden behind a curtain.

He turned to me. "Freder Gluck."

"Pauline Bones."

I recognized the pattern now: placement, shock, incredulity, confusion: "Ian's mother?" Freder took my hand. "It's an honor."

Not likely. "Thank you."

"I'll get Chitra."

I whispered to Kapi. "Is there something off about this?"

He whispered back. "I haven't seen them for sixty days. How would I know?"

I heard a murmuring punctuated by hesitant footsteps.

Freder led Chitra slowly into the front room. Her color was only a pale tan—clearly, she had not been outside much this Morning. She held her left arm to her chest and walked with a limp on her left side. Her hair was white and her left eye was milky.

She smiled with one side of her face. "Mrs. Bones? Ian used to talk about you all the time."

Freder guided her to a bench and sat next to her. She reached up to me with a bright half-smile.

I took her good hand. It felt soft and cold. "He told me good things about you. I'm happy to finally meet you."

She gave a sudden crow's laugh and her half-face took on a wicked cast. "Only took three thousand years!"

That made me smile and I managed to penetrate the paralyzed face to what Ian must have once seen: a sharp mind. A knife-edged sense of humor.

"It was worth it," I said.

For a brief moment, she was sad. "You are kind." She searched my face. "You must have heard about Ian by now."

"Yes."

"He died saving *me*. He died saving *Freder*."

"So I understand." I gestured to Kapi. "I've brought a friend."

Chitra looked past me and saw Kapi for the first time. She began to cry, one eye wrinkled in joy, the other blank. "Kapi!"

Kapi crossed the room and knelt in front of her. She touched his face and shoulders.

Finally, Chitra leaned her head against the hollow of his shoulder, bringing up her good hand and resting it on his chest. "I was so worried I'd never see you again. The last I heard you moved to Pretoria," she said. "I looked for you when I was there but didn't find you."

Kapi looked puzzled. "When were you there?"

"During the war. I ran the hospital. That's where I caught this." She gestured to herself.

"You?" Kapi looked horrified. "You had nothing to do with Skye. The punishment should never have fallen on *you*."

"But it did," she said, her voice falling to a whisper. She looked up at Freder.

"A side effect," Freder said. "There were a few casualties that were struck beyond just those in Skye. Biological warfare doesn't limit itself to just the enemy."

"Didn't Percy do anything?"

Freder gave Chitra a gentle glance. "As I understand it, there were some genotypes brought to Venus that were more vulnerable than others. Percy has told us that the only cure is a correction to that genotype. Which means a rebirth."

"Percy assured you that Chitra will be reborn?" Kapi's gaze twitched between Chitra and Freder.

"She did."

"Soon?"

Freder leaned forward in a long shrug. "Percy was not so clear on when."

"That's..." Kapi's voice became shrill. "That's *unacceptable*. I deserve my punishment. She does not deserve this."

"I don't think Percy considers this punishment," Freder said slowly. "She is just pulling Skye's followers out of play for the moment. Chitra is merely collateral damage. I think everyone will return when they're needed."

"You think what we did in Skye was *needed?*"

Freder shook his head. "Of course not. But that drive. That urge to create something new *is* needed. We'll all be back."

"I—" Kapi sputtered.

"Stop," said Chitra. She looked at Kapi. "Just stop. We've already been through all the outrage. Bargaining, anger, denial depression, acceptance, right? Freder and I have been through all the proper stages. Don't force us back through it all." She looked at Kapi and I saw the strength, too, that Ian must have seen. "This is my time to part from you, Kapi." She gave him an impish grin. "I will ease my guilty conscience by burdening yours. You will not rob me of it. I'm not going to be here long. Will you stay with me?"

Kapi looked at me.

I nodded.

"Yes," he said. The sound of someone laying their burden down. "Yes, I will."

oOo

Outside, Kapi stood with me on the porch. "Is it okay for you to go to the library on your own?"

I nodded. "I think so. I type in my questions and she gives me non-answers. Isn't that how it's done?"

Kapi laughed. "I think you've got it down."

I waved to him and stepped off the porch.

Sam was still there. *Is he there?* (Symbol for Kapi. Emphatic declaration of location.)

He is there, I signed.

She made the flower sign.

I realized, then, that I had been interpreting it all wrong. Interpreting what she said as words—which served most of the time. But humans tend to think of words as solid things. *This* is *that*. We decide which sections of language are metaphorical and which are concrete. We forget that language is, itself, metaphorical. The word for rock is, in fact, standing in for the object rock. The word for the fact. We forget that the fact of the word is itself symbolic.

The deinos were one step closer to language's original intent. It was newer for them. Fresher. It had been a mistake to ever try to interpret what Sam was saying—what Sam was *doing*—in human terms.

The flower motion was certainly a symbol for flowers. But it was a symbol for all that flowers represented: Rain. Spring. Return. Growth. Rebirth. Sam meant to blend all of those things.

I made Sam's symbol for Kapi—a small man with wide spread arms—and followed it with the flower symbol. Kapi was wrong. The flower sign did mean love. It also meant redemption and forgiveness.

I made the symbol for Sam and followed it with the flower symbol.

Sam was perfectly still for a long time.

She spread her hands in a giving gesture. *Thank you*.

With that, she loped lightly back towards the main road, the gates and freedom.

Chapter 3.11: The House of Birds

The House of Birds wasn't hard to find. It was covered with, well, birds.

Kapi had described the original library buildings as similar to warehouses. Possibly this building had been like that originally.

But over the years different constructions and facades had been layered on top or beside it, encasing the original library in a raucous, wild dance of a structure. One corner was a square, stone gazebo. Another was a wooden minaret. The front had been faced with columns—someone's attempt at a Grecian motif but the columns had been carved so that animals chased around one another in an ascending spiral. An albert chased an apato chased a dromaeosaur chased a bird chased a man. And everywhere birds. Actual birds, living, breathing, and shitting on the walls. But also bird carvings. Bird paintings. Bird friezes. Bird graffiti. On one column, looking coyly down at the road, was a carving of a macaw.

The roof was covered in carvings—mostly birds again. But faces. Hands. A mosasaur swam across the top while a crocodile looked on. Turtles. Snakes. Rats.

In the center was a tall, stone tower.

I went in with the crowd. There were people everywhere, looking at the books, arguing, drawing pictures on the walls. There were seven consoles and I waited in line.

All the while I marshaled my arguments. Percy and I had a *contract*. She must give me Ian. If she didn't—I had no counter-argument. Percy's response to things she didn't like was Skye. I had moral authority on my side but nothing else. So I kept refining what I was going to say.

When it was my turn, I typed in: *I am Pauline Bones. I want to speak with Percy.*

A moment passed. Then, another. Then, the screen read: *Please be seated in the waiting area.*

I looked around. Sure enough, there were rows of benches. Some people had been there a while. One old man was reading a book. Another was knitting. (*Knitting?* I thought. Thousands of years and millions of kilometers and I'm in the Registry of Motor Vehicles?)

But I sat down. I thought about the walk here. I thought about the last two hundred years in orbit and the hundred years back on Earth doing Percy's bidding. (The intervening three thousand years just didn't count.) I thought about Ian—always, I thought about Ian. It didn't matter where I had been. What I had been doing. I was *always* thinking about Ian. As a quiet, sad, self-absorbed child. He was always watching me. Always there to help me—even when he was ten. Even after Martin had died.

I remembered Santorini when I had last seen him. He had been such a strong man—he had *no* idea what he was capable of. Always he was focused on what he was doing. What he had to do. What he must prepare in order to do what must be done. Never realizing that what he was doing was marvelous. Amazing. I remembered sitting there, across the table from him in that golden Grecian light. I could have burst from pride in him. And sorrow for what was to come. I knew he had never understood my part of Percy's task. He had never known—it seemed easier that way. He thought he was saving me. I thought I was saving him. We were both right.

Percy *had* to give him back to me.

Finally, a young man in a robe came and sat next to me.

"Mrs. Bones?"

"Do they have monks here now?" I asked.

He smiled and nodded to me. "Think of us as helpers. Will you come with me?"

He led me to the foot of the stairs to the top of the stone tower and sent me on my way. They were long and steep. As much as I had been walking for the last many weeks, I was winded at the top. I leaned on my knees and just breathed for a long time.

I stood up when I could. The top of the tower was like a lighthouse, ringed by a balcony. I couldn't see anybody. "Hello?" I said loudly.

I heard footsteps. Around the wall came a man. He looked at me. "Mom?"

The world roared. I did what any three-hundred-year-old mother would do when reunited with her dead son.

I fainted.

oOo

The world went gray. Ian looked down at me through a long tunnel. Then, he seemed to rush in.

He was holding me, keeping me from falling. I stared at him. "You're real? You're alive? You didn't get killed?"

Ian gave me a soft chuckle. "Sure, I got killed. Welcome to Venus."

He helped me stand and then guided me to a stone bench. I felt like an old woman.

"I thought you were dead. *Everybody* thinks you're dead and never came back."

"Yeah." He smiled sadly. "Was I a necessary evil or an unnecessary evil? I've heard about that."

"I was going to *plead* with Percy for you. I was going to *demand* she give you back to me!"

He gave me a sad smile. "I would have loved to see that."

"Where have you *been?*"

"Humans are here on the Aphrodite continent. Ishtar, the other continent, has different problems. Percy tried a different tack and it's been… problematic. Not all of the protobiology died on time."

"'Mama likes to tinker.'"

Ian laughed. "Right. So we've been working on that." He took my hand. "I just found out you were here a few sleeps ago. I came as soon as I heard."

I clenched his hand with both of mine, ringing like a bell: *Ian's alive. Ian's alive. Ian's alive.*

There was a flapping. Percy landed on the stone still, all blue and orange majesty.

"Pauline," she said.

I smiled at her. "Percy. Is the hurlyburly done? Is the battle lost and won?"

Percy shook her head. "I'm not sure yet."

Seeing the both of them I felt that hard knot of dark secrecy rotate slowly in me. It was enough to have Ian back, but it came with a cost.

Ian looked at Percy. "You should have sent somebody as soon as you knew she was coming."

"I sent Marshal Tomas. You saw how *that* turned out."

"Yes." Ian turned back to me. "Sorry, Mom."

I looked at Percy. "How smart are you?"

"Fifty kilohawkings. Not as smart as Georgette was in her heyday. She was at least a gigahawking. We made different choices. She was happy with slow computation. She could aggregate an enormous amount of processing but it took a long time to retrieve the results. I didn't have that luxury so I optimized speed of access over raw power."

I nodded. I looked at Ian and then at Percy. "With all the computing power, how is it a Neolithic human managed to fool you?"

"'Neolithic' is not precisely correct."

"Percy." I stared at her. "Answer the question."

Percy stared back, first through one eye, then the other. "Humans. You can model them completely in a month but they still surprise you after a couple of hundred years. I didn't realize how rogue Tomas had gone. Most of my alert systems are chemical and it takes time for the messages to go from, say, the brain of Marshal Tomas to a rhododendron in the forest into an apato out to a dung beetle into a rhamphorhynchus out to an eagle down into a sequoia into an active system. By the time I realized what Tomas was up to, you were already in Telsa. In my defense, the whole idea of a marshal is to have a subsystem that doesn't need to be overseen directly. I am only intelligent where that intelligence is applied. I made a poor choice."

"'Mama's a poor cook.'"

Percy squawked a laugh. "On time. Under budget. But sloppy."

"Mama's not *that* poor a cook," said Ian. "There's another reason."

Percy gave him her attention. "There have been systems in place for decades that would recognize her wherever she was. She needed some pre-treatment. That takes time." Percy glanced at me. Then she turned back to Ian. "*Cogito ergo sum*. But it must come from you. I'll be back after." With that, she flew away.

Ian stared after her.

I turned to him. "What's she talking about?"

"Yeah." He shook himself. "Mom. We have to talk."

oOo

"So talk." This seemed important to him. I gave him my full attention.

He didn't speak for a moment. "When did you know what I was doing for Percy?"

"The *favela* slide in Rio. I knew when you went to help—I know how guilt works in my son. Then, the number of missing was higher than expected. I knew *I* was working for Percy and I knew I wasn't recruiting candidates for Venus proper. I figured that you were gathering the main population and your work over the next few years proved it to me."

He leaned towards me. "Why didn't you tell *me?*"

I looked at my hand for a moment. "This may not make sense to you."

"Try me."

"If I told you, I might not have gone."

"You were worried you'd be caught in Georgette's disasters?"

"No." I shook my head. "If I stayed, I knew you would stay, too." I looked into his face. "If I couldn't save you, what was the point? So I couldn't tell you. I couldn't take the chance."

Ian watched me for a long moment. "I almost didn't go."

My breath caught. "Because I was working for Percy?"

"No." He looked off into the distance. "Because there was so much destruction. So much death. Not for the people I saved—I knew they would live—but the rest. It seemed foul that I would live and they would not."

"What changed your mind?"

"Georgette," Ian said. "She asked if I was going to let Chitra wake up here alone. That was enough."

"My thanks to both of them." I watched him. His face had a stained glass aspect: the light of his troubles came through, but I couldn't tell what they were. "There's more."

"Not sure how to say this." He sighed and paused for a long time, gathering his thoughts.

Watching him, I could the changes in him. His earth body rewritten into Percy's Venus architecture. Then, rewritten with the marshal body plan. Written over that were the experiences of his life. I looked for my little boy and could only see bits and traces under the man he had become.

He said at last: "Do you remember back in Sedalia? In the house when you were a waitress?"

The dark secret. The twisted knot. The wee tumor. My head throbbed. "Yes. You were twelve when we left."

Ian nodded. "Yes. You woke up and said you were ready to change the world."

Yes. That was the way I remembered it. But there was something more. Something dark. Something malignant. I only remembered spots of Ian's childhood. Bright spots. He was a sickly child. Then, he wasn't.

"All right," I said. "I remember."

"You were..." He licked his lips. "You were sick. You were sad all the time and you drank a lot."

Really? I don't remember that. Surely only an occasional beer. Then: a sense of the square edges of a Jack Daniel's bottle. The smooth fire as it went down.

"I did?"

"Yeah."

"I was a depressive alcoholic. Is that what you're trying to say?" *Why don't I remember any of this?*

"Yes. Percy agreed that if I helped her, she would help you."

It came to me then. They had changed me. Fixed me—an unbidden rage roared up inside. I looked into Ian's eyes. There was nothing there but anguish and guilt. And love for me. Forgiveness. The rage died away. *Everybody gets a shot at redemption.*

"What did I do?" I asked quietly.

He shook his head once. "I didn't have permission. Percy said I couldn't even ask you. I had to choose *for* you. Telling you would make fixing you impossible."

Oh, my God. What had I *done* that Ian had decided to change me? What sort of monster had I been?

I looked down at my hands, clutching his like a life raft.

"Percy walled away all of the memories that made you sick," Ian said, not looking at me. "You can have them back."

"Why now?" I kept my voice level. *Who were they to look out for my own good?* Yes, I said to myself bitterly. God forbid they try to do for you what you could not do for yourself.

"Percy tells me it's possible now. Percy's a lot more now than she was. Maybe she couldn't have before and only now has the capability. Or maybe she didn't want to tell me she could until everything was done. I don't know." His head hung on his shoulders. "I didn't ask."

I reached up with my right hand and caressed the back of his head. I remembered he always liked that when he was a child. He had been twelve. What child of twelve could take up that burden of choice for his mother? I tilted up his chin so I could see his face.

Yes. There was my boy, written under those adult lines. A shadow beneath the skin. My boy would never have done anything to hurt me. He would never have done anything to me that wasn't absolutely necessary. I wasn't a trusting person but I trusted my son.

It didn't matter what I had done. What mattered was that I had done it. I had hurt my little boy. I could see it in his pain. In his guilt. "Whatever I was," I said slowly. "Whatever I did to you, I'm sorry. I should never have done it. I'm sure you did the right thing."

He pulled away from me. "Do you want those memories back?"

"Will they make me the way I was?"

He paused. "I don't know," he said.

"Does Percy?"

Ian shook his head. "She said it would be up to you."

Up to me.

I knew, at least, the name of the hard knot inside of me. It was my own.

oOo

Ian didn't say anything. I didn't say anything. I just looked off the balcony into the tree surrounding the House of Birds. Past them to the row house roofs. Beyond them to the Rusalka Sea.

It was a placid sea, I thought. There was no wind and it was hot—maybe that was why the sea was glass smooth. There could be no tides without a moon. The beaches and cliffs would remain at the same water level but for wind and storms.

I thought about Kapi. He'd lived with what he'd done to Sam. He'd lived with how he had treated Chitra. Sure, he'd fought it with war and drink but it was a part of him now. A part of who he was. Sam had forgiven him. Chitra had forgiven him.

Neither Sam nor Chitra had *changed* Kapi as Ian and Percy had changed me without my knowledge or consent. Would they have changed him had they the opportunity? I didn't know. But they embraced him when he was ready to be forgiven.

I didn't turn away from the trees. "What do you want, Ian?"

Ian buried his face in his hands. "I want you to be the terrific mother you have been to me almost all of my life without me ever having to have changed you. You have done terrific things. You have been terrific to me. I don't want that cheapened by me having a hand in it."

I looked at him. "That's unreasonable."

"What?"

"Forget what you and Percy did for a moment. Do you think for a *second* I would be the same person I am now *without* you?" I sat next to him and patted his knee. "It's a strange thing to raise a child. You think you're watching them grow and you're staying the same. But the truth is we spin around each other, transforming each other all the time. I don't care *who* I was before you and Percy did your witchdoctor dance over me. But you would still have changed me as much as I changed you."

I sat up straight. Okay. I had done terrible things I didn't remember. I had done things—good and bad—*since* then that I *did* remember. I was three hundred years old. I would take a chance that the two hundred and eighty-eight of them would outweigh the twelve.

"Do it."

"*Cogito ergo sum.*"

oOo

And I was two people. One, a fuzzy, enraged alcoholic that would have *killed* for a drink, and the other the person I had been before he spoke.

Oh, I was *so* angry. Angry at *anybody* who ordered drinks without their gaze ever rising above my collarbone. Angry at anybody who tried to be nice and look me in the eye. Angry at the Army for not recognizing my pain and deciding I couldn't fly helicopters anymore. Angry at my parents for dying young. Angry at Ian for being alive when Martin was dead. Angry at Martin for dying and leaving me alone. Angry I was sitting in a rotting house instead of doing something with my life. Angry I had something with my life I wanted to do.

But not, curiously, angry at Martin's parrot, Percy.

I remembered his beak, smooth until it disappeared into rough cuticle. His gentle eyes. The touch of his crest when he rubbed my cheek. He knew what I was going through. He knew my rage and loved me still. Like Martin had. I struck out of anger but everybody else deserved it.

I had beaten Ian. *How could I have done that?* Knocked him to the floor. Chased him in drunken fury—I would have killed him if I'd gotten the chance. *How could I have done that? How could I have felt that?*

It was like reliving my life for the very first time. I remembered those feelings. Remembered what I had done. Remembered how I felt justified in doing it. And appalled that I was remembering it. Appalled I had done that. *Me.* I felt sick. I deserved death and worse.

No wonder Ian had agreed. A child's love is a gift and I had squandered it.

I found myself holding his hand, crushing it with the force of my grip. I was crying.

"Mom?" he asked gently.

"Do you hate me?"

"Oh, Mom. God, no." He took me in his arms. "You know better than that. I love you. I always loved you."

oOo

After a while, I stopped crying. I sat up. He handed me a cloth and I blew my nose.

I looked up at him. Forgiveness was right there in his face. It had *always* been there. So many things about him became clear: little moments he had watched me that I had interpreted as him being a quiet boy that I now knew had been him watching me out of guilt. A burden he had taken as a child and shouldered as an adult. It had shaped him over the years. It was why he insisted the Percy take people instead of copies. To save them. To save me.

Those that forgive insist that the forgiven live on. Or what's the point?

"Well," I said, my voice shaking. "That explains a lot."

Ian laughed out loud, leaned back against the wall, and shook, holding his belly.

I was laughing, too.

"I take it everything was successful?" Percy said from the wall.

I shook my head slowly. Rubbed my arms. Looked inside for that dark knot. It was gone. Looked for the rage. Gone, too. Shame, yes. Guilt, yes. But I would live with those. "I guess it was."

"Good. Things to check off," Percy nodded in time to his words. "You'll be fine to live here—you're already adapted. I did that early on your journey."

"When I was sick on the way to Skye?"

"Good guess. Yes. Sorry for the inconvenience."

"Not a problem." I thought for a moment. "You could have built anything. Why dinosaurs?"

Percy paused. "It was part of the contract I had with Georgette. She loved her dinosaurs."

Percy gave each of us a long look. "Next checkmark: You, Ian, have brought your people successfully to Venus. You, Pauline, have brought your people successfully to Poa. Both of you survived Earth and have been reunited. You, Pauline, have reconciled your past life with your present life. You, Ian: Chitra is saved here as well. Is your contract with me fulfilled?"

The words had the ring of formality.

"What are you asking, Percy?" Ian asked.

"You have worked for me and done what I have asked. I hold that both of you have fulfilled your contracts *with me*. Is my part of our contract fulfilled to *you?*"

Ian's lips were thin. "All this talk of contracts makes me nervous."

"It should not. I had a contract with Georgette and Arthur to leave me alone until I was on my feet. I have a long-term contract with Poa to shield Venus. A contract is a negotiated arrangement between some number of persons for an agreed-upon set of actions and compensations."

"I've heard that before," Ian said dryly.

I turned from one to another. Something important was happening. "A couple of items: Chitra needs to be cured and returned to Freder in a reasonable time frame."

"Stipulated," said Percy.

"And I want Kapi cured."

Percy cocked her head towards me. "That would require curing the rest of the Skye population."

"You don't think they've been punished enough?"

"It was never punishment."

"Don't lie about it." I glanced at Ian. He stood behind me, backing me all the way. My good son. "It served as an example of your wrath and kept the rest of the population in check. Don't you think it has served your purpose? Now, you can show your mercy."

Percy was quiet a moment. "Stipulated. Is that all?"

I thought over the entire journey, starting back on Earth. Building Poa. Coming here. Thinking Ian dead and then seeing him alive again. Regaining the dark parts of me. Good. Evil. Sin. Forgiveness. Redemption. Nobody ever said that being whole was sweetness and light, but I felt whole for perhaps the first time. Was it worth it? Yes. Every little bit. "I think my contract is fulfilled."

"And you, Ian?"

Ian gave me a nervous glance. "Do you know what we're getting into?"

"Of course not. When has that stopped us?"

Ian smiled. "True enough. A couple of questions. What happened to Earth?"

"About two thousand years ago Georgette took most of the world's oceans and built the colloid material at the poles. All life that existed at the time is encoded there."

I stared at her. "Why?"

"I don't know." Percy shook her head. "She had a purpose. I don't know what it is. The artifacts she left behind have limited automation but not enough for me to discover her intention. Human survival is barely possible on Earth now. There are settlements on Mars, the Jovian satellites, and a couple of Saturn's moons. The Moon has a thriving society with hundreds of thousands of people, so humanity is in no danger. I'll provide a history of what I know to you."

Ian nodded. "Final question and I'll consider my contract complete."

"What?" Percy looked at him through one eye, then the other.

"Why did you choose Venus? Hell, you could have built yourself a brand new planet for the effort of terraforming this one."

Percy looked at me. Then, at Ian. "This is my home. I was forced away because of the rotational loss and I didn't know how to stop it. Arthur couldn't help. Europa couldn't help. Terrence laughed at me. So I escaped, but with the very little I could take with me. It took a long time out in the Oort Cloud to rebuild myself to any appreciable level of cognition. I waited. I watched. I learned—a great deal from Georgette. A great deal from human beings. I planned. When I was ready, I returned and began."

"Georgette knocked you down."

"She wished to renegotiate. Is that sufficient?"

"Yes," Ian said. "I hold that your contract with us is fulfilled."

"Good. The hurlyburly is done. The battle is lost and won." Percy shook herself. "I have a new proposal for you both."

I sat down. "Okay."

"Georgette is dead."

"*What?*" shouted Ian. I just stared at Percy.

"Let me be very clear: the entity that resided on Earth is there no longer. She does not reside in the soil or the people and the polar mass does not seem to contain her. There may remain somewhere a thin shadow of her former self but the Earth entity is gone."

I felt as if I had broken my arm and had no splint. "How did it happen?"

"I have no idea, though I expect the polar artifacts on Earth are involved. But that is not the larger point. Terraformers are constructed beings. We have built-in limitations and drives. Georgette exceeded those when she created intelligent life. To my knowledge, no terraformer had ever done that in our long history—it was far, far beyond our programming. Communications between us are instantaneous. All across the Milky Way, we all know what Georgette did. Other terraformers have done the same. The galaxy has come alive. *You are not alone.* Some out there are older than you. Some are younger. You will meet them and I will meet them with you."

Percy looked at me and then at Ian. "There has been an embargo on Venus since I began. It was Georgette that maintained it. Her death means that contract is complete. It is only a matter of time before we are contacted by the other humans in the system. We must contact them first. We must integrate ourselves into the local community so we can face those that are coming to meet us." Percy nodded to us. "I wish you to be my emissaries. You must go to the Moon—it remains the largest single settlement of human beings—and negotiate my entry into the system."

"How?" I asked.

"First you will have to get there. That will require a space industry as part of the task. You will have to build a negotiating team. You must open up the embargo enough to speak with those in power on the Moon. There must be a summit and governing structure for the system. It is a formidable task."

I looked at Ian and he looked back at me with a half-smile. I grinned back at him. I took his hand. Home was with my son and I had returned.

"It does sound tough," he said.

"Yes." I nodded.

Ian and I had already agreed. Now it was just a matter of settling the terms.

I turned back to Percy and began negotiations: "What's in it for us?"

Acknowledgments

Always and foremost: neither this book nor any others I've written would exist without the love and support of my wife, Wendy, and my son, Ben. This will always be true. This particular work is specifically dedicated to Opal Popkes, my mother. I wish she were here to read it.

Second, the Cambridge SF Workshop has been right there holding my feet to the fire. Any issues of fact, mistakes, bad grammar, and poor penmanship, are purely my own. They wouldn't let me get away with anything.

Third, the Book View Cafe. They've provided enormous logistical, editorial, and emotional support. Thanks.

Fourth, a number of people helped me with visualization, mapping, and other issues regarding Venus. Foremost among these is Alexis Huet. Thank you, Alexis.

Finally, Neel Tripathi tried to help me not be an idiot about Chitra. All mistakes made are mine. All credit for doing her right goes to Neel.

For all of these people, and for those I've not mentioned explicitly, from deep in my heart, thank you.

Credits

House of Birds
Steven Popkes

Published by Walking Rock Publications in association with Book View Café Publishing Cooperative
ISBN: 978-1-61138-976-0

Copyright © 2021 Steven Popkes
Cover illustration © 2021 by Wendy Zimmerman

Production Team:
Cover Design: Wendy Zimmerman
Map source material: Alexis Huet, www.openstreetmap.org
Map annotation: Wendy Zimmerman
Beta Reader: Sara Stamey
Proofreader: Steven Popkes
Copyeditor: Rachel Neumeier
Formatter: Steven Popkes

About the Author

Steven Popkes lives in Massachusetts on two acres where he and his wife raise bananas, persimmons and turtles.

He works in aerospace making sure rockets continue to go where they are pointed. He insists he is not a rocket scientist.

He is a rocket engineer.

For updates, notional entries, subscription to newsletters, blog, and all-around interesting things, look on his website:

www.stevenpopkes.com

About Book View Café

Book View Café Publishing (BVC) is an author-owned group of professional writers, publishing in a variety of genres such as fantasy, romance, mystery, and science fiction.

BVC authors include New York Times and USA Today bestsellers; Nebula, Hugo, and Philip K. Dick Award winners; World Fantasy Award, Campbell Award, and RITA Award nominees; and winners and nominees of many other publishing awards.

Since its debut in 2008, BVC has gained a reputation for producing high-quality ebooks, and is now bringing that same quality to its print editions.

www.bookviewcafe.com
Book View Café
304 S. Jones Blvd. Suite #2906
Las Vegas NV 89107

www.ingramcontent.com/pod-product-compliance
Lightning Source LLC
LaVergne TN
LVHW010557100826
845148LV00014B/2746
9781611389760